CHARLEY SUNDAY'S TEXAS OUTFIT

CHARLEY SUNDAY'S TEXAS OUTFIT

STEPHEN LODGE

PINNACLE BOOKS
Kensington Publishing Corp.
www.kensingtonbooks.com

PINNACLE BOOKS are published by

Kensington Publishing Corp.
119 West 40th Street
New York, NY 10018

All Kensington titles, imprints, and distributed lines are available at special quantity discounts for bulk purchases for sales promotions, premiums, fund-raising, educational, or institutional use. Special book excerpts or customized printings can also be created to fit specific needs. For details, write or phone the office of the Kensington special sales manager: Kensington Publishing Corp., 119 West 40th Street, New York, NY 10018, attn: Special Sales Department; phone 1-800-221-2647.

PUBLISHER'S NOTE
This book is a work of fiction. Names, characters, businesses, organizations, places, events, and incidents either are the product of the author's imagination or are used fictitiously. Any resemblance to actual persons, living or dead, events, or locales is entirely coincidental.

PINNACLE BOOKS and the Pinnacle logo are Reg. U.S. Pat. & TM Off.

ISBN-13: 978-0-7860-3389-8
ISBN-10: 0-7860-3389-4

First printing: December 2014

10 9 8 7 6 5 4 3 2 1

Printed in the United States of America

First electronic edition: December 2014

ISBN-13: 978-0-7860-3390-4
ISBN-10: 0-7860-3390-8

PROLOGUE

1960

A cold rain had been falling for most of the afternoon. The sky was so heavily overcast it could have been midnight. Nearly every family living in the 1950s post–WWII housing tract had turned on their interior lights. There was only one dwelling not glowing with illumination like the others. A faint flickering of gray-and-white light slipped smoothly through the half-closed slats of hanging venetian blinds, barely making it through to the glass of a sizable picture window facing the street. Plus, there were muffled sounds coming from inside the residence—the roar of a thousand hoofbeats and exploding gunshots echoed over a thrilling background musical score.

Lightning flashed—followed by a loud clap of thunder.

In the living room, a nineteen-inch, black-and-white Philco television set was showing an old 1940s western—Howard Hawks's *Red River*. At that moment, John Wayne, playing Texas rancher Tom Dunson, was galloping on horseback, leading his outfit as they attempted to turn a runaway cattle stampede.

"Hooray!" "Yeaaaa!" "Whoopee!" yelled the Pritchard children who were enjoying the movie. Noel, who was eight, Caleb, two years older at ten, and Josh, about to turn fourteen, were devouring popcorn by the gallon from a large red bowl on the floor in front of them.

An older gray-haired man sat behind in a rocking chair. He cheered on the movie cowboys right along with the children.

Suddenly the TV picture was replaced by a gray screen with little, jumping black-and-white specks all over. The sound turned into static. Immediately there were "boos" from everyone in the room.

"Who in tarnation did that?" said the old man.

A pleasant-looking woman wearing a yellow print apron over a light blue housedress stepped through the door leading from the kitchen. "It does that sometimes, Grampa," she said, "especially during a storm like we're having now. Besides, your great-grandchildren are going to ruin their eyesight if you keep letting them watch television in the dark like that."

"No, they won't, Evie," said the old man. "My grampa Charley let me read by campfire light when I was growing up and it never bothered my eyes one bit."

He turned to the ten-year-old. "Caleb?" he asked, "why don't you turn off the television."

Caleb sauntered over to the TV. Instead of turning the TV off, he changed the channel. The picture came on again. A preview for the television series *Bonanza* flashed onto the screen. This advertisement, like the TV, was also in black-and-white.

"Man," said Josh, "it's an ad for *Bonanza* this coming Sunday night." He shook his head. "I sure wish we had a color TV. Since it began last year all my friends say *Bonanza* looks really great in color."

"Your grampa says we'll buy a color set when they're more affordable," said his mother. "Color television is still pretty new, you know. They'll get cheaper as time passes . . . besides, aren't you really watching the same story, whether it's in black-and-white or color?" She turned to the older boy, adding, "Isn't that true, Josh?"

"I like the stories Grampa Hank tells us," said Noel, climbing into her great-grandfather's lap. "When he tells us a story, I can imagine everything happening in my mind . . . in black-and-white, *and* color."

"Yeah, Grampa Hank," said Josh, moving closer. "Why don't you tell us one of your western stories?"

The old man smiled—he leaned forward in the rocker, kissing his great-granddaughter on the nose. "All right then," he said. "Why don't the rest of you gather 'round and make yourselves comfortable."

He turned to his granddaughter.

"Evie . . . Do you still have that old box of newspaper clippings your mother kept for me over all these years?"

"I know they're around here someplace, Grampa Hank," she answered.

"Good," said Hank. "Then these kids'll have some sort of reference when I'm telling my story."

"I think I remember where they are," said Evie. "I'll be back in two shakes of a lamb's tail."

Hank shook his head.

"I remember when uncle Roscoe used to say that."

Caleb turned the TV off completely. He and Josh moved over and seated themselves on the carpet in front of the old man's rocking chair. Their mother joined them, carrying a cardboard box filled to the brim with yellowing newspaper clippings.

When they were all settled, Hank began introducing his tale. "This one's all about *my* grampa . . . his name was Charley Sunday . . . you all know that of course . . . and this story's about how he brought the longhorns back to Texas."

"I didn't know the longhorns ever left Texas," said Josh, chuckling. The other kids laughed.

Evie hushed them with a finger to her lips. "Don't interrupt your great-grandfather," she said. Turning to Caleb, she added, "I certainly wish you'd act more like your older brother."

The old man smiled. "That's all right, Evie. I was just about Caleb's age myself when this story took place . . . In fact I was probably more naïve than Caleb is, too." He drew in a deep breath. "Now, where was I?" he said. "Oh, yeah . . . It all started in my grampa's hometown, Juanita, Texas. Over the years since, some of the old-timers involved filled me in on a bunch of the things that went on when I wasn't around, including some things that happened before I even arrived. And now that your mom just found the box of newspaper stories all about the event, when I put all those accounts together, along with my personal recollections . . . what you'll hear should more'n likely be pretty close to how it all went down.

"Now, like I was saying, the story begins on a Sunday morning way back at the end of the last century . . . 1899, to be exact. Church bells were ringing, and the choir had just begun to sing . . ."

CHAPTER ONE

1899

> *Yes, we shall ga-ther at the ri-ver*
> *The beau-ti-ful beau-ti-ful ri-ver*
> *Ga-ther with the saints at the ri-ver*
> *That flows by the throne o-of God*

Listening contentedly as church bells pealed in perfect confidence behind the escalating voices of the Juanita, Texas, Cavalry Missionary Baptist Junior Choir, Charles Abner Sunday just knew this particular Sabbath Day was going to bring something special.

The silver-haired Charley, riding along comfortably with his friend and cohort of many years, Roscoe Baskin—who also lived and worked on Charley's ranch—were on their way into town for weekly, Sunday-morning services.

They were in Charley's old double-seat buckboard—a rickety old bucket of bolts Charley had won in a pool game many years earlier—calmly bouncing along, with Charley driving the two-horse team.

Charley was dressed in his best three-piece pin-striper, topped off with the same "John B" Stetson hat he'd worn for more than a few years—the highlight of his customary Sunday-go-to-meeting garb.

Charley's experienced, raw-boned visage, etched from countless years of exposure to the Texas elements—and on a normal morning adorned with three or four days' growth of pure white stubble—was on this day sparkly and clean shaven.

Charles Abner Sunday was a tall and lanky man, sinewy and able bodied. He was built like many other older men who had worked daylight to dusk on the open range all their lives. Now in his early seventies, Charley had become sensible and sober minded over the years, having put his hard-living ways behind him when he met and married his wife, Willadean, those oh so many years earlier. The couple had lived a good and moral life together. They had four sons, all of them stillborn, and one daughter, who had lived. And even though Willadean had passed on some years ago, Charley still kept his memories of her as close to his heart as if she were still right there beside him.

Roscoe Baskin, Charley's salty, beer-bellied ranch foreman, a cowboy somewhere close to Sunday's age, was snoozing peacefully as they rolled along. He'd thrown on an old, threadbare dress coat and a frayed string tie for the special occasion. But that was as dressy as he'd let himself get—he refused to give up his old, worn, and faded work hat.

As they rode slowly up the main street of Juanita toward the glimmering, white façade of the local house of worship, Charley made his usual mental note: they were passing through a town that dripped heavily with a unique nineteenth-century mode of living—even though it was a way of life that was changing rapidly.

The local barbershop, closed on Sundays. The corner drugstore, also shuttered—except for the fountain where people were allowed to gather for a cup of coffee and a bite to eat on the Lord's Day after services. The Juanita hotel, closed completely ever since a newer caravansary had been constructed several streets over. Even the livery stable, weathered and beaten. It now boasted a single glass-top gasoline pump where a once fine, hand-carved hitching post stood sentry. The fuel was for local farm machinery or the infrequent horseless carriage that might pass through Juanita, plus, there was a large sign nearby advertising a brand-new automobile dealership that would be opening soon in Del Rio, some thirty miles to the west. Even so, every one of these deep-rooted establishments appeared to be falling apart in one way or another.

As they climbed a slight incline, nearing the church on that particular day of rest, they passed yellowing lawns going to weed that were desperately trying to grow alongside once white and now just as gray, paint-peeled houses.

Some other things that caught Charley Sunday's eye were the few ancient wagons and rusting farm equipment that dotted more than several of the withering homesteads.

Charley nudged his friend.

"Better wake up, Roscoe," he said softly. "We're almost there."

The sleepy old wrangler's eyes opened with a blink. Roscoe straightened up. He adjusted his wire-rimmed eyeglasses, pulled at his handlebar mustache, straightened his hat, then stretched.

"Well by golly," he said, yawning and extending his arms. "I see we finally made it. How late are we?" he added.

The buckboard was approaching the church, with its hitching posts almost full to capacity. Charley swung the team into a small space between several tied-off buggies. He pushed the brake with his boot and reined in the horses.

Once stopped, he dropped a tethered lead weight to the ground before he climbed down to tie off the horses.

While he was doing so, one of his team took a real good nip out of the strange horse that was tied next to Charley.

The surprised animal let out a very loud squeal. Then it swung its head around to return the bite.

Caught in the midst of it all, Charley got knocked off balance and had to grab on to a handful of harness to keep from falling down.

"Damn son-of-a-bitch!" he said to the horse.

Inside the house of worship, the good reverend, Caleb Pirtle III, stood silently, clearing his throat, mouthing the words to his upcoming sermon—rehearsing.

Upon hearing Charley's muted profanity through the several open windows, he tried his best to ignore the curse words his congregation had all heard before. Most of the members knew only too well that muffled vulgarities coming from outside always announced Charley Sunday's arrival.

As the junior choir continued on with their singing, several more loud horse whinnies echoed from outside, causing the congregation to again turn their attention away from the celestial chorale.

The good reverend's face flushed once again. It was apparent this had happened many times before.

Outside, once the buckboard and team were resting, Roscoe climbed down and put on the horses' feed bags, adjusting the head straps. When he finally walked over to Charley, both men shrugged at the still bickering animals.

"We're not that late, Roscoe," Charley told his friend. "They're still at the singing part of the service. Soul saving always comes later on."

One of the horses shook in its harness. That made a loud jangling sound that echoed in the early summer air. Charley patted the horse's rear end while at the same time noticing Roscoe was looking rather uneasy.

"Somethin' wrong, Roscoe?" he said.

"I don't know, C.A.," replied the senior cowhand. "I reckon I just wasn't raised on prunes 'n' proverbs like you was. I really don't think bein' a regular churchgoer is truly in my nature."

Charley patted Roscoe on the shoulder, similar to the pat he had given the horse. He smiled softly.

"I expect a lot of folks have second thoughts," he said. "I'm sure the Good Lord will understand if you miss one more Sunday meeting."

Roscoe nodded, looking quite relieved.

Charley threw him a wink. He had been through Roscoe's hemming and hawing about his personal religiosity on more than one Sabbath in the past.

Roscoe grinned.

"Thanks-a-plenty, C.A.," he said humbly, expressing his gratitude. He was even more than relieved—he figured he'd actually been saved.

"Why don't you run on down to the fountain at the café and get yourself a cup of Jamoka," suggested Charley. "Catch up on the town gossip. Read the newspaper. Pick me up in about an hour, all right?"

Roscoe began removing the feed bags and untying the horses while Charley chuckled to himself.

Roscoe continued to smile gratefully as he moved on around to the driver's side and climbed in.

"Hey, C.A.?" he called back as he reeled in the lead weight, "say a little prayer for me, will ya?"

"Always do, Roscoe." Charley smiled. "Always do."

Charley watched as his friend of many years backed the team expertly, reined them around, then drove off. Charley turned and started walking toward the church.

As he passed a nearby planter, he extracted his ever-present wad of chewing tobacco, depositing the smelly brown lump on the edge of the wooden box that held some drooping shrubbery trying to grow there.

Charley took off his hat and entered the church vestibule as quietly as he could, almost tiptoeing into the sanctuary. From there he moved unhurriedly down the side aisle, his hat in hand. *Good thing I remembered to take off the old "John B," he thought. Old Caleb always pitches such a conniption fit if I don't.*

By the time the good reverend stepped up to the pulpit, Charley had stopped for a moment, still searching for a seat. As usual, there were none left unoccupied in the rear.

"Mr. Sunday," Pastor Caleb Pirtle snapped from the pulpit, "why don't you try pew number three right up here in front of me? I'm sure Mrs. Livers will scoot over an inch or two for you . . . to let you settle in proper-like. Then I can begin my sermon."

Charley nodded awkwardly before he proceeded down to the front, aware that all eyes were on him. He reached the third row and smiled to the older lady who had moved over to make room for him. He sat down, nodding to the pastor.

"You can go ahead now, Caleb," he told the man of the cloth. "And thanks for the nice seat. I couldn't have bought a better one if you were chargin' money. Plus, I plumb forgot to bring my hearin' horn.

The congregation chuckled.

The minister cleared his throat.

"Thank you, too, Charley." He nodded. "Now I'll try and get along with what I have to say . . . if *you* don't mind."

Charley shook his head, smiling. "No sir, Caleb," he replied humbly. "You just go right ahead. That's exactly what I come all this way to hear."

There was a laugh-covering cough from someone in the crowd, then the good reverend began to speak.

Twenty minutes later the buckboard team was tied off in front of the Juanita Pharmacy fountain entrance—the horses' feed bags were in place once again. A sign in the front window stated that although the drugstore was closed for the Sabbath, the fountain was open for business—because, it said, *God's children must be able to nourish themselves regardless of the day.*

The door to the small fountain area was slightly ajar, and muted voices could be heard coming from within. Other than that, it was a peaceful scene indeed.

While wide-open windows cooled what they could of the inside of the small eating establishment, the fountain's owner stacked some glasses behind the counter beside the register.

With that done, he picked up a newspaper section and continued with his reading. He leaned his nose closer to the comics section that fronted the tabloid, chuckling—then he looked up.

"Hey, Roscoe," he said. "Did you see what them *Katzenjammer Kids* done today yet?"

Roscoe, sitting several stools down the counter reading his own portion of the paper, looked up.

"Katzenjam . . . ?" He stared blankly. "Oh, sure," he said, and smiled. "That captain's a hoot, ain't he?"

"Sorry about it being so warm in here, Roscoe," said the owner, apologizing. "I seen one of them newfangled electric ceiling fans advertised just the other day. I'll probably order one as soon as we get wired up for electricity in this part of town," he added, fanning himself with a menu.

"Summer's just around the corner, Jed," said Roscoe, sipping his coffee. "Some folks say it's gonna be a sizzler."

The proprietor was observing something out the front window.

"Wonder who that could be?" he questioned to himself out loud.

Roscoe looked up again. "Who's that?"

"Oh, no one," answered the owner. "Just some horsemen out for a Sunday ride, I suspect. They didn't look familiar to me . . . Nobody local, that's for sure."

"Yup," said Roscoe, going back to his newspaper. "Probably just some travelers got lost off the main road. More'n likely they're lookin' to ask someone fer directions . . . or a public toilet."

"Then you should ask yourselves this question," the good Reverend Caleb Pirtle droned on. "Have I achieved in this life *all* the material possessions I want? Or just the necessities I *need*?"

Some members of the congregation nodded, while others shook their heads.

"Most of you, I suspect, would answer *No*," he continued. "Well, let me go further and ask you this: Are material possessions what you think our Good Lord put you here on earth to acquire in the first place? Or—"

KA-BOOOOOOOOOM!!!

A very loud explosion echoed through the town of

Juanita, Texas, sending shards of glass hurtling out onto dry, dusty Main Street.

In less than moments, a giant swirl of black smoke bellowed from a business establishment directly across the way from the pharmacy where Charley's buckboard was tied. The horses jumped at the sound, though they were not able to pull away from the hitching rail.

Roscoe, followed by the proprietor of the fountain, immediately stepped out onto the boardwalk, eyes gawking, as the smoke began to clear.

"Heavens ta Betsy," said the slack-jawed proprietor. "What in the Sam Hill is going on?"

Both men stood in awe as three masked horsemen galloped out of a side alley, turning onto Main Street.

"Son-of-a-buck," moaned Roscoe. "Someone's done blown the Juanita National Bank."

At the church, which stood on slightly higher ground than the Juanita Pharmacy fountain, the startled congregation was trying to press through the narrow double doors so they might witness what had caused the thunderous blast that had interrupted their peaceful service.

Charley Sunday, normally a very polite individual, put aside his good manners for the moment and managed to wedge his way through the unsettled multitude so he could be first out onto the porch.

He immediately heard galloping horses' hooves moving fast on the road leading out of town. From his vantage looking down on Juanita, he could see three masked riders moving rapidly toward the house of worship.

Several blocks behind the horsemen, Sunday also observed a large, dissipating cloud of black smoke with several small puffs still rolling upward from the center of town.

A number of parishioners, gathering behind Charley, appeared outwardly distressed at the sight of the menacing trio galloping wildly up the road, heading directly for the intersection where they stood gaping from the church portico.

"You're all way too nosy," Charley cautioned. "Better get your *be-hinds* back inside."

The worshippers, who knew Charles Abner Sunday to be more than straightforward when it came to matters such as the one at hand, ducked back into the vestibule.

Charley continued to keep a narrow eye on the approaching riders. He moved casually to the planter where he found his chaw of tobacco. He blew on it, then tucked it between teeth and cheek. All the while, the sound of the racing horses grew closer and closer.

Slowly and deliberately, Charley Sunday bent down. He raised the cuff of his trousers to reveal a smoothly polished, freshly oiled, .44-caliber, antique Colt revolver—it was a Whitneyville Walker. Also known as the 1847 Army Model—and it was Charley Sunday's gun of choice. He'd been required to use one by the Texas Rangers way back when he became a member of that prestigious law enforcement agency.

He removed the ancient six-shooter from his boot top, checking the cylinder before pulling back the hammer.

When the bank robbers were almost to the junction, one of the outlaws drew his weapon and fired several slugs of burning lead in the direction of the gentleman wearing the gray hat who stood on the church steps. The bullets went way wide of their intended target.

Charley didn't flinch. He unceremoniously spat

some tobacco juice, raised the Walker with both hands, sighted in on the approaching bandits, and took aim with the eyes of Argus.

As the riders careened their animals into a slip-sliding turn, speeding past Sunday's position, the old rancher squeezed off several shots.

Two of the riders were hit. Both fell from their saddles in a tangle. The third man's horse stumbled and went down, throwing him into a small ditch.

The two wounded outlaws slid viciously across the sunbaked dirt and into a cement curbside where they glanced off, then hit, several buggy wheels. The momentum shoved the rigs forward, bumping one another and frightening horses until both men were stopped abruptly by a sturdy, cast-iron fireplug.

The terrified horses bucked and jumped, pulling at their yokes. There was the briefest of moments, and then a massive plume of water gushed high into the air. Several more buggy teams whinnied loudly, adding to the chaos, rearing high in their harnesses.

Charley calmly walked on down the church steps, crossing the street to where the first two bandits had been halted.

Ignoring the cascading water, he made his way to the first bleary-eyed robber and dragged him away through the mud. He brought the heavy barrel of his Colt Walker down on the outlaw's head before moving back to the fire hydrant, where he dragged the second robber away from the spewing water. As he had done with the first, he thumped the second outlaw with the gun's barrel before casually turning toward the third bank robber who had remounted his horse and was now watching dumbfounded as Charley finished his business.

Gun still in hand, Charley started toward him.

"I'll be danged," he said, recognizing the man; then he shouted, "Throw down your gun, John Bob Cason. I'm making a citizen's arrest."

The bank robber, Cason, drew his pistol and wheeled his horse, but Charley fired the Walker three more times into a tree branch that hung precariously close to the outlaw's head.

The heavy limb dropped with a thud, nearly knocking Cason from his saddle but completely dislodging the pistol from his grip. Without his weapon John Bob Cason could only eye Charley with a squint and a snarl.

"I'll get you for this, Charley Sunday," he shouted, "and I still intend to kill you for gunning down my partner."

Then he spurred his mount up the road in a cloud of boiling dust.

Charley emptied his Walker Colt, firing wildly at the escaping outlaw.

With the other two robbers collared, Charley lugged them over to where several members of the congregation had gathered.

One of the men, Willingham Dubbs, was busy pinning a gold sheriff's star to his lapel. He appeared to be boiling mad as Charley reached the small group of church elders, dropping his two charges at the fuming law officer's feet.

"Damnit, C.A.!" huffed Willingham Dubbs. "If I told you once, I told you a hunnert times what I'd do if I ever caught you carryin' that old hog leg of yours into Juanita again."

Sunday eyed the sheriff sternly. He spit some more tobacco juice, narrowing his eyes.

"A man's gotta do what a man's gotta do, Willingham. So get off your high horse," he warned. "All I done was to put a spoke in their wheels before you did . . . And that's a fact.

"Go on now," he continued. "Lock 'em up. Then we can get back to our Sunday meetin' with our Lord."

Charley continued to stare down the sheriff. After spitting another smooth, slick stream of tobacco juice, he turned abruptly and moved back toward the church where he again deposited his tobacco wad in the planter.

As he passed through the remainder of the flock, the ones who had stayed around to witness his confrontation with the sheriff, Charley began to whistle.

As the soft strains of "The Yellow Rose of Texas" began to drift from the old cowman's puckered lips, Charles Abner Sunday found it somewhat difficult not to smile.

Charley's old two-seat buckboard squeaked along at an unpretentious pace. This was a very familiar route for Charley and Roscoe—the only road between Charley's ranch and Juanita.

Situated here and there beside this peaceful roadway were several newly constructed advertising signs. A few of them offered those who happened to pass by "new and modern conveniences for house and home."

One in particular shouted out the advantages of steam tractors over horse-drawn machinery, along with the San Antonio location of the company that sold them.

Roscoe's face played a symphony of smiles and Charley grinned broadly as his friend offered him a brand-new cigar.

Roscoe dipped his head as Charley selected his stogie. Then he took one for himself, striking a Blue

Diamond match and lighting the two cheroots. "That's my little gift to ya, C.A.," said Roscoe, chuckling and puffing . . . "fer gettin' the one up on Sheriff Dubbs." He coughed, puffed again. "I sure wish I'd bin there ta see the ol' buzzard's face. I bet he could've give birth ta twin calves, by golly!"

Charley sucked on his cigar, smacking his lips. He glanced over as the buckboard passed yet another sign—a foreclosure sign.

"Hey," he said to his seatmate. "Didn't that used to be the Shahan place?"

Roscoe, who had to turn almost completely around in his seat to catch a glimpse of the property, turned back, nodding.

"Sure was," he answered. "I heard tell that Happy done sold all his cattle . . . what was left of 'em . . . and he still couldn't meet his mortgage payment. They kicked him and the missus off the property last month. He's bin tellin' everyone he's always wanted to retire early anyways . . . Besides, they always wanted ta live in a smaller house when the children were grown."

Charley's eyebrows rose slowly. "Yep, most likely the *Poor House.*" He let out a trickle of cigar smoke. "Sure ain't like the old days, is it?" he reminisced.

Roscoe shook his head. "No-sir-ee. Times are a-changin', C.A."

"Now ain't that a fact," said Charley. "A man used to be able to graze cattle for a hundred miles in damn near any direction around here."

He took another long draw on his smoke, looking out at the dilapidated fencing that enclosed a once fine cattle ranch. He pointed. "That's where Barlow had his lower forty, wasn't it?" he said.

Roscoe answered, "You and me spent many a cold night out in them pastures, pardner." He shivered at the thought, smiling to himself. "Them were the days, weren't they, amigo?" he added.

"Yep," answered Charley nostalgically. "A damn good way of life. It's just too bad. It was a good way. Even the bad days beat the hell out of what I'm seein' now."

Roscoe chuckled out loud.

"Reckon we should've known it was all comin' to an end when they started brandin' cattle," he said.

Charley threw his friend an awkward glance.

"Stick to the truth, Roscoe," he cautioned. "We may be getting old, but we ain't ready for the antique store just yet."

They turned off onto a long, dusty road nestled between rotting wooden fencing that held back absolutely nothing.

If reflected in human terms, Charley Sunday's ramshackle spread, at least what was left of it, was located less than a few miles from Juanita. At first glance the place appeared to be snoozing. The empty corrals and vacant ranch yard had been silent and inactive for some time.

Charley pulled the old buckboard into a dirt enclosure, rolling right on through a very insignificant flock of squawking chickens, and on past a worn-out wagon that was minus three wheels. He stopped between the dilapidated barn and the two-story ranch house, which, at one time, must have been quite something to look at.

Charley nudged Roscoe, who had been sleeping again.

"Hey, ol' pard," he said. "You might want to wake up. We're home."

Roscoe opened his eyes, blinking. He looked around at the familiar, lackluster setting.

"Ya know," he told his friend, "it'd sure be nice if we had somethin' ta do 'round this ol' place again."

Charley bit off a chaw of tobacco.

"Well," he pondered. "Maybe you can start by rustlin' us both up some midday vittles. Remember, we still gotta go back to town later on this afternoon to pick up Betty Jean, Kent, and Henry Ellis at the stage depot."

Chapter Two

As the Uvalde to Del Rio short-line stage made its way to the next small town along its route, Charley's ten-year-old grandson, Henry Ellis Pritchard, glanced out a dusty isinglass window, while at the same time playing with a wooden stick and ball game his father had brought back for him from Mexico. He tossed the tethered sphere into the air, then tried to catch it in the hand-carved cup that had been glued to the top of the handle.

Once again the boy took a quick glance out the window to his right. His animated eyes held an edge of expectancy that rode delicately, almost stubbornly, on a building anticipation of something long awaited.

Broken-down farm after farm, ranch after ranch made their appearance as the four-up stagecoach rolled past at a good pace.

Henry Ellis's mother, Betty Jean Pritchard, sat in the opposite seat beside the boy's father, Kent. Both were facing the youngster. The boy's parents, though native to the Lone Star State, were of the newer generation. And their dress—typical Austin city dude—appeared to be just a smidgen out of place in this flannel and denim section of Texas.

The parents appeared to be talking to, but not looking directly at, their son, who continued playing with his wooden toy.

"I do wish you were goin' to San Francisco with us, Henry Ellis," his mother was saying. "But we didn't think you'd mind too much if we left you with your grampa one more summer. This may be the very last time any of us'll be seeing"—she stopped abruptly, then changed what she was about to say—"any of us'll be seeing the old place ever again, you know."

The two adults traded glances.

The boy didn't respond. He appeared to be much too absorbed with the stick and ball game and the passing scenery.

Henry Ellis's father turned to his wife.

"Is Charley finally going to sell?" he asked in a low whisper.

"I don't think so, sweetheart," Betty Jean replied. "I don't think he has that choice. He wrote me in his last letter that the bank's gonna foreclose on the place unless he can somehow start to make it pay for itself again."

Kent shook his head.

"Then he's going to lose it." He shrugged with a sigh. "There isn't any way in the world your father could turn a profit on that old ranch anymore, darlin'. Civilization is squeezing him out, anyway."

She touched his arm. "But he's still my daddy," said Betty Jean. "And I just know if he loses his ranch, it'll break his heart. Maybe we should loan him some more money . . . just to get him through these hard times."

"Awww, Betty Jean," said Kent. "You know we've lent him a whole lot more than we can afford . . . and

Charley's hard times never seem to end, do they? I'm afraid being a cattle rancher is out of the question for your father anymore."

"We're there," shouted Henry Ellis, pressing his nose against the window again.

Charley and Roscoe stood by with the two-seat buckboard as the stage trundled into town. There wasn't the usual hoopla for the coach's arrival like there had been in the past—(one) because it was still the Sabbath and most folks were at home getting ready for evening services or an early supper, and (two) the short-line coaches were becoming fewer and fewer with every passing year, plus the locals now preferred to go out to the train depot and watch the better-dressed Pullman-car passengers instead.

Charley and Roscoe watched as the stage driver reined in the four-horse team and the coach came to a standstill.

"Since the stage don't stop at the train depot," said Charley, "I wrote to Betty Jean explaining that we'd pick 'em up here in town and they could ride out to the ranch with us, drop Henry Ellis, and share some refreshments. We'll drive 'em on out to the depot to meet their California train connection later on this afternoon."

Most people provided their own transportation to the newly built train station located several miles up the road on the north side of town. The Juanita citizenry had tried its best to have the depot constructed closer to town, but the railroad had given in to the big ranchers in the area and built their tracks and the whistle stop station closer to the cattlemen's combined holding pens instead.

Charley and Roscoe watched as the stage driver jumped down and moved around to open a door for his passengers. Another man began off-loading their luggage onto a six-seat passenger wagon that would take his daughter and son-in-law's baggage to the train station.

Charley turned to Roscoe. "They only have a few hours before their train'll be here, so we best be getting them into the buckboard and out to the ranch so they got time to see the old place and help get Henry Ellis settled in."

The boy was the first one off the coach and when he saw his grandfather he made a beeline for Charley's open arms.

"Grampa, Grampa," said Henry Ellis as he ran into Charley's waiting grasp.

Charley kissed the boy's forehead, then tousled his hair before giving him a loving squeeze. "It's good to see you, son," he said softly, holding back a tear. "My, you sure have growed some since the last time you were here."

In a minute they were joined by Betty Jean and Kent, who carried the boy's suitcase.

Charley nodded to the front seat of the buckboard and Henry Ellis climbed up. Then he put his arms around his daughter and kissed her. He winked at her, then called over to his grandson, "You can ride up front there with Roscoe and me, Henry Ellis. That way your mother and father can have the whole backseat to themselves."

Betty Jean and Kent appeared to blush. Charley continued, "If I remember correctly, you two always did want the whole backseat for yourselves, anyway."

* * *

Henry Ellis spotted the one-wheeled hay wagon in the ranch yard, which made him beam. But when he saw the empty corrals, the smile faded quickly.

Betty Jean was oblivious to the deserted enclosures. All she could see was the paint-peeled house and barn—plus the messy screened-in back porch where Charley and Roscoe lived during the long, hot West Texas summers.

"The old place sure has gone to the dogs," she whispered to her husband, shaking her head. "Sure isn't like I remember it growing up. Matter a' fact, it don't even look as good as it did when we were here two years ago."

Charley pulled the buckboard to a stop beside the built-by-hand stone creek house that had once spanned a bubbling brook that had dried up long ago.

Henry Ellis was out of the buckboard before the dust had time to settle.

"Henry Ellis?" yelled his mother. "Where in tarnation are you runnin' off to, young man?"

Sprinting as fast as he could to a particular corral, Henry Ellis slid to an abrupt stop when a soft breeze caused the unlatched gate to swing wide open, revealing the enclosure to be quite empty.

The gentle swaying of the unlatched gate seemed to finalize something deep within the boy. A hint of a tear began to well up behind his unblinking eyes as he continued to search the unoccupied pen.

Behind him, his parents were climbing down from the buckboard, both having sensed their son's blighted hope.

As they stood watching the boy, Charley and Roscoe jumped down and joined them.

Trotting slowly from around the barn came a pretty old-looking dog—a large dog—a retriever/collie mix.

A shaggy animal, whose collie coloring—with a once pure-white breast, muzzle, underside, legs, and neck to contrast his rusty ginger back and rear end—had almost gone to solid gray.

His name was Buster, and he stopped for a long drink of water at the trough before continuing on slowly toward the new arrivals.

Charley moved in beside his daughter, kissing her warmly on the cheek. His eyes followed her look to where Henry Ellis stood—depressed and forlorn—by the vacant corral.

"Would you like me to handle this?" he asked softly.

Betty Jean nodded.

Charley cleared his throat gently before he moved off toward his bewildered grandson.

In moments, his grandfather's reassuring hand fell softly on Henry Ellis's trembling shoulder, causing the boy to jerk slightly.

As he recognized the familiar touch—his grampa's touch—Henry Ellis turned with tear-streaked cheeks, throwing the old man a questioning look.

Charley took the boy's quivering shoulders in his strong hands. He turned the youngster so they would be facing each other.

The two just stared at one another for a long moment, then Charley reached out and wiped away a small trickle still coming from the youngster's eye.

"I didn't sell your pony, boy, if that's what yer thinking," said Charley, speaking softly. "I might have had to sell all the rest of 'em off, but not Pinto Tom. And that's a fact."

Henry Ellis sniffed back another tear, his eyes never wavering from Charley's.

"Then where is he, Grampa?" the boy wanted to know. "Where's Pinto Tom?"

There was something special between Sunday and the boy that was obvious by the direct, yet sincere, way in which they could communicate.

"When you had that storm last winter up where you live in Austin," Charley explained, "well, we had some pretty cold and wet weather down here, too. Pinto Tom wasn't a young horse, son. You know that. He was getting along in years . . . he used to belong to your mother before you were born, remember?"

Henry Ellis knew this to be the truth, so he nodded, agreeing.

Charley continued, "Well, Pinto Tom finally caught his death, Henry Ellis. Me and Roscoe and ol' Doc Evans did everything we could for that animal, but it was all too much for ol' Pinto Tom.

"He fought to live as hard as a horse could fight, son," Charley went on. "But like I said, he was an old horse . . . and when God's creatures start getting on, He kind of wants 'em back up in heaven with Him, I reckon. It's all part of living here on earth, boy . . . everything has to die."

Henry Ellis's eyes were wide, he didn't quite understand.

"B-but you're old, too, Grampa," he stuttered. "Does that mean that you're going to die, too?"

Charley chuckled. "I ain't that old, Henry Ellis, and you know it," he said. "I suspect I still got a couple of good rides left in me."

Another tear spilled gently from one of the boy's eyes, starting a slow zigzag down a rosy cheek.

Underlying fear crinkled Henry Ellis's nose. He backed away from his grandfather, moving slowly toward his parents.

"I want to go home," he blurted out in a trembling tone. "I don't want to be here anymore."

Just the thought of his grandfather's mortality terrified the boy. This was a fact he had never before given any thought to—even though it had always been there, somewhere deep inside.

He turned and ran past his astonished parents, flying into the backseat of the buckboard.

Charley threw Roscoe a solemn look—then he moved to Kent and Betty Jean without hesitation before they had time to rescue their son.

He held up his hand, speaking with great concern.

"Leave him be, all right?" he said. "He'll be back to normal after a while, I suspect. A boy his age just ain't up to accepting certain things as fast as we grown-ups are."

Embarrassed by her son's actions, Betty Jean showed more than a little irritation.

"If he's going to throw one of his tantrums, Kent," she barked, "just maybe you ought ta set him straight again. Paddle his little butt."

The father's own sensitive discomfort kept him from carrying out his wife's directive. Kent stood his ground.

"I don't think that'll solve anything, darlin'," he told his wife.

Charley stepped in, putting his arms around his daughter in a warm embrace—an attempt to calm her down.

"Hey, now," he said. "You two kids run off to your vacation and don't be worrying none about Henry Ellis. Me and Roscoe can handle the boy. He just needs some time with his own self, that's all."

"Maybe me an' Charley can take 'im out an' show 'im where we buried the pony," suggested Roscoe.

Sunday frowned at his friend, then he made direct eye contact with his daughter. "When the time is right," he said, nodding, "we might just do that. Now you two go on over to him . . . tell him me and Roscoe will always be here for him. And tell him Buster missed him a whole lot more than a bunch, too," he added, indicating the sleeping dog at his feet.

He kissed her on the forehead, then turned to Kent.

"You two have a grand time in San Francisco, all right?" he told them both. "You deserve it. And don't worry none . . . I'll get you to your train on time."

The two men shook hands, then Betty Jean threw a huge hug around her father.

"Dad," she begged. "Please don't spoil him. Try not to, damnit."

Charley nodded, smiling softly.

Betty Jean turned her attention toward her son sulking in the buckboard, then she let go with a holler that could have peeled the skin off a barbecued hog.

"Henry Ellis!" she shrieked. "Get your shameful ass outta there right now and bring your suitcase! *On the double!*"

CHAPTER THREE

Shortly after supper, Charles Abner Sunday and his grandson retired to separate chairs inside the long, screened-in back porch where Charley and Roscoe lived during the summer months. Henry Ellis had flopped himself across an overstuffed easy chair and was playing with his Mexican stick and ball game. Charley sat in his old rocker a few feet away, puffing on his pipe while he read the Sunday newspaper. Buster snoozed at the base of the chair occupied by Henry Ellis. Roscoe could be heard cleaning up in the kitchen. This peaceful scene lasted no longer than a few moments.

Charley's eyes widened and he sat up. "Hey, Roscoe," he called out, "bring me my magnifier, will you?"

In less than a minute Roscoe entered from the kitchen and handed Charley a thick wood-handled magnifying glass.

Charley thanked him; then he leaned in closer to the newspaper. "Listen to this, will you?" he said to the others. "Colorado Cattle Auction, it says. Three hundred authentic Texas longhorn cattle will be sold at auction on Saturday, June twenty-fifth, at the Denver, Colorado, fairgrounds.

"The longhorns belonged to the late F.Q. Dobbs, an eccentric Colorado silver miner and ranch owner who had once raised longhorn cattle in his native state of Texas long before he moved to Colorado and struck it rich in the silver-mining industry . . ."

He looked up at Roscoe, raised his eyebrows, then said, "Some say he hit a real mother lode."

His eyes shifted back to the newsprint. Again he continued reading out loud. "Homesick for Texas and missing his longhorns, the late Mr. Dobbs purchased sixty-two head of longhorn cattle a few years before the War Between the States began and had them driven to Colorado with a larger herd. Over the years Mr. Dobbs's herd grew . . . presently numbering close to three hundred head, give or take a few, before Dobbs succumbed to old age just last month. Now his family's wishes are to sell the entire herd, lock, stock, and barrel. So, come one and all . . . get your own trophy set of Texas longhorn horns while they last."

"It says that right here," said Charley before he continued on reading:

"Use the hides for your leather furniture coverings and outdoor clothing. The tails make good dust brooms. Plus the hoofs make superior ashtrays. This will be the auction of the century."

Both Henry Ellis and Roscoe moved in closer.

"Do you think they're talking about honest-to-goodness, *real* Texas longhorns, Grampa?" said Henry Ellis.

"Heck, even if they was real longhorns," Roscoe said, chuckling, "longhorn's ain't nothin' but useless relics these days. No one raises longhorns anymore what with all the newfangled cross-breedin' that's going on. Why do you think they're auctioning them off? No one wants 'em, that's why."

Charley looked up at his old friend. "Now hold on, Roscoe," he said, "just maybe someone *is* interested in raising longhorns these days. Or maybe I should say *interested in saving* longhorns."

It took Roscoe a second or so to figure out exactly what Charley was hinting at.

"You?" he said with a surprised look on his face. "You want them longhorns? I reckon you're forgettin' how old you're gettin' to be, too."

"I want one," yelped Henry Ellis, now showing his excitement beside the overstuffed chair.

"You wouldn't want one of them big ol' smelly things," said Charley, grinning to himself. "It'd stink up your bedroom to high heaven back home. Besides, your mama would disown me as her daddy if I ever brought one of them critters up to Austin for you."

The boy stopped showing his excitement but continued to grin, drawing in a deep breath, letting it out slowly, complacent beside his grandfather.

Charley settled back, speaking wistfully—yearning out loud—sighing.

"I sure would like to have *me* a few of them big ol' smelly things myself," he mumbled.

Roscoe glanced over.

Henry Ellis looked up.

"Why's that, Grampa?" asked the boy.

Charley smiled reflectively, edging himself out of the chair where he stood silently, shaking the kinks out of his tired old body. Then he sauntered over to the screen door. He pulled back the corner of the shade before looking out toward his empty corrals. He continued to stare out at the ranch yard, voiceless, for several more moments.

Roscoe and Henry Ellis watched him with interest.

Finally, without turning back to face the others, Charley spoke.

"Oh," he said with a sigh, "I don't know, really. It was just a thought that came to me."

Charley continued to ponder on something for another moment or two, then he turned and went outside, his mind still in deep thought. Buster followed him. The screen door banged shut behind them both.

Henry Ellis turned to Roscoe, puzzled over his grandfather's actions.

"What did he mean by that, Uncle Roscoe?" the boy asked, "about wishing he had some of those longhorns?"

Now it was Roscoe who reached over to rumple the boy's locks, his eyes never leaving Charley, who he could see through the screen standing silently and still thinking out in the ranch yard.

Roscoe finally answered, "Oh, I 'spect he's thinkin' that if he had him some a' them Colorado longhorns . . . we just might be able ta get somethin' goin' around this ol' place again."

CHAPTER FOUR

"Hey, Geronimo!" yelled the whiny-voiced Sidney Pike to his brand-new employee—a twenty-six-year-old Indian by the name of Rod Lightfoot. Rod was working feverishly at a desk in a back room at the Pike Meat-packing Company—a Denver slaughterhouse—owned and operated by none other than Sidney Pike himself.

"Get your blanket bottom out of your tepee and into my office before you give me apoplexy, you stupid, lazy-assed redskin."

Sidney Pike was a dissolute weasel, a rascal, a rogue, and a scoundrel. A manipulator, equal parts charm and bullshit, a coyote in a shall-collar suit, double-breasted waistcoat, and square-toed shoes with spats. Ruthless venality was not beneath him. He could be elusive and smooth talking, as well as a shifty dog in the manger. But Sidney Pike did not see himself as some-one who was corrupt. Sid thought of himself, simply, as a very smart cookie.

Rod was standing at attention in front of Pike in less than a minute, waiting nervously for his new employer's instructions. He brushed a stray lock of his long black hair away from his forehead and waited for his boss to speak.

"I firmed the deal, kid," Pike told the young Indian. "I just talked to the auctioneer who'll be handling the bidding the weekend after next. He says those Texas longhorns are as good as mine already. All you have to do is be there that Saturday, enter my bid officially, and sign some papers as my representative." He laughed. "Then those cows will belong to me legally—horns, hooves, and tails. And there'll be nothing anyone can do about it."

Rod nodded. "But Mr. Pike," he started to say before Pike cut him off.

"I don't want to hear anything more from you, Lightfoot. You're only acting as my unlicensed legal representative, not my lawyer."

CHAPTER FIVE

That evening, as happened every now and then, Charley Sunday's old paint horse, Dice, was secured to a fancy hitching post beneath a dazzling red, white, and blue sign that shouted:

FLORA MAE'S PALACE HOTEL
Saloon & Billiard Parlor

Across from where Charley had tied his horse was a very stunning white carriage—a specialty number—with all the bells and whistles. The vehicle's two horses were also pure white, a matched team. They were in harness and standing with the vehicle, which was anchored in the owner's private space.

The inside of the hotel's bar and poolroom was elegant, yet homespun at the same time—due, more than likely, to the tastes of the establishment's proprietor.

The room was nearly empty at that early hour on a Sunday evening, with only three people in attendance: the bartender, Charley Sunday—who was shooting a game of pool with a pleasantly dressed lady. The lady being a well-kept woman, just a few years Charley's junior—a very attractive, *older* woman who could still show her ample bosom without appearing ridiculous.

She was Flora Mae Huckabee, a properly coiffed redhead who was also the hotel's owner. Wealthy in her own right through her late father's investments in the state's cotton industry, Flora Mae did her best to appear prosperous and informed, even though her dirt-poor, dirt-floor upbringing could slip out every now and then. Her self-taught manners had been acquired before the old man struck it rich in a crooked poker game that backfired, leading the Huckabee family toward its accumulation of great wealth.

Flora Mae stood back watching as Charley prepared himself for a bank shot. Her eyes were zeroed in on his backside as she smiled to herself.

"You still got a real cute rear end," she said in a low, sensual voice. "Do you know that, Charles Abner Sunday? Why, I'll bet you could still pound a hell of a nail if you had the mind to."

Charley angled his stick to the ball, shooting and making the predicted pocket.

With eyebrows twitching, he moved around the table to line up on the next ball.

"Don't go interrupting me with your sex talk while I'm preparing my shot," he said in a cautionary tone.

Charley realigned his cue, aiming carefully.

Flora Mae, realizing she was directly in his line of sight, shook her shoulders, causing her breasts to sway. They bounced voluptuously.

Charley shot for the pocket—and he missed.

"Dang your hide, Flora Mae Huckabee," he growled. "Don't be doing them kinda things in front of me when I'm trying to think."

Flora Mae pursed her lips, throwing him several baby kisses.

"Oooooo," she teased. "Mama's sooo sorry. Was the big, rough cowboy-man attemptin' to use his 'wittoe' brain?" She grinned broadly. "Hell, I'm a butt man myself. I wouldn't know what to do with a man's brain if I ever found one. Which I ain't," she added. She chuckled out loud at her own crude joke.

Charley stepped around the pool table, moving to the bar. He found his glass of lemonade and took the last gulp.

The bartender came over with a pitcher, refilling his glass.

Charley half rested his rump on the pool table, tipping back his hat. When he eventually spoke, his words flowed slow and even.

"This is serious business, Flora Mae, darlin'. . . Dead serious," he told her.

Flora Mae immediately sensed the somber tone in Charley's voice. She moved in next to him.

"Do you wanna talk to me about it?" she asked, showing concern. "You know, like we used to, when we were younger?"

Charley's face wrinkled in apprehension.

"Ah, hell," he spat. "What would a woman know about longhorns, anyway?"

"Before Daddy's life-changin' poker game, I knew a lot about cattle," she said. "For a while, back then, I was even known as an expert cattlewoman."

"Cattle *thief* is more like it," said Charley. "You Huckabees sure had that reputation."

Flora Mae let that one slip by. Instead of counter attacking, her face continued to sparkle with expectation. She was still waiting for Charley to tell her what was on his mind.

Finally, Charley drew in a deep breath. He appeared to be somewhat embarrassed.

"All right," he began. "I read a story in the newspaper earlier today that's kind of had me going for the past few hours."

Flora Mae leaned in closer. "Is that what's got your goat, Charles Abner Sunday?" she asked him. "Was you readin' about that old cattle-ranchin' silver miner who just croaked up there in Colorado? The one who left his herd of longhorns behind? The ones his family'll be auctioning off in a couple of weeks?"

Charley nodded. "Yep," he answered. "And the notion come to me that if I was only able to get my hands on just a few of them longhorns, maybe I could keep what's left of my ranch."

This time it was Flora Mae who drew in the deep breath.

"That sounds like an awful slim notion to me, C.A." She sighed, shaking her head.

"I know," said Charley, nodding. "Roscoe says I don't even have two nickels to rub together to make a dime."

Flora Mae thought for a moment, then a glint began to glow in her eyes.

"Of course," she said modestly as a small smile curled her lips. "If you was able to find yourself a silent partner . . ."

She let her words hang for another long moment as Charley thought on what she had just said. Then it hit him that Flora Mae was suggesting that *she* be included.

He stood up abruptly, backing off several steps.

"Oh, no," he sputtered. "Not *you*, Flora Mae."

He looked around anxiously for a place to discharge some tobacco juice. He saw a cuspidor on the floor beside the bar and spat.

"You and me, pardners?" he added. "Nooo, ma'am."

"Don't be a-backin' off like some scaredy-cat farmer's daughter, Charley Sunday," she warned with narrowed eyes. "It ain't yer trousers I'm tryin' to get into this time. Can't you just stop thinkin' of me as a love-starved ol' woman for a change, and try to see me for the good friend I really am? For just once in your miserable life?"

She raised an eyebrow, smiling gently. "What I'm sayin' is that I'd be willin' to back you," she proposed, "if you'd be willin' to let me."

Charley narrowed his eyes, taking a very long look at her.

"I don't want your money, Flora Mae," he told her. "Then I'd be obligated to you."

"Jeeeezus H. Keeee-rist!" she howled. "Over all these years, you still can't see it, can you? *I LOVE YOU*, Charles Abner Sunday, and I'd be willing ta do just about anything for you."

She sniffed back a tear.

"Since my daddy passed," she continued, "a woman of my circumstances needs a man in her life. A steady man," she added.

Charley scoffed.

"Now it sounds like you're talking that *marriage stuff* again," he informed her.

"*Companionship*, Charley, not marriage," said Flora Mae, correcting him. "A woman of my means would be downright dumb or just plain stupid to get married nowadays. All I'm sayin' is that I'll always be here if you ever change your mind, and that I'd be willin' to give you a tryout, if you'd just let me."

Charley took a slow sip of his lemonade.

"Well, right now," he replied, "I got longhorn cattle on my mind. *Not* companionship."

"So don't be so damn stubborn, you old fool," said Flora Mae. "I seen that newspaper story, too. And you don't got the exclusive rights, you know. I was already figgerin' on the profit I could make once I got some of them cattle down here to Texas where folks appreciate things like longhorns."

"You sure have become greedy in yer old age," mumbled Charley. He threw her a look of disgust. "*I* had the idea in the first place and now *you* want to cash in on it."

Flora Mae bubbled with frustration.

"Charley," she implored. "Just hear me out for once in your life, will you?"

Charley backed away some, holding up a hand, nodding.

"All right, all right," he said, partially giving in. "I'm listening."

Flora Mae went on. "All I'm doin' is makin' you an offer you can't refuse," she said. "Can't you see that? But you're so selfish and set in your dumb ol' ways that ya can't even tell sugar from scum."

She stood up as her fury reached its peak.

"I *only* want you to be my *agent*, damnit!" she added, pointing an angry finger at him.

"Your what?" said Charley.

"My bidding agent," she affirmed, "for them longhorns up in Colorado."

She sat back down slowly—a small tear was beginning to form.

"It's just that I got so little experience when it comes to cattle auctions," she sniffed. "Besides, I gotta stay here and run Huckabee Enterprises. You know that."

"I don't want your charity, Flora Mae," Charley said again, spitting more tobacco juice toward the spittoon.

"This ain't got nothin' to do with charity, you old poop," bellowed Flora Mae. "I'm offerin' you a business opportunity, mister. You get me as many of them longhorns as you can," she raised an eyebrow, "an' I'll let you have ten percent of 'em."

Charley did some simple arithmetic in his head, mulling over what Flora Mae had just said.

"Ten percent?" he pondered. "And you're saying you'd be willing to pay me that ten percent in long-horns?"

"Any way you want it, Charles Abner Sunday," replied Flora Mae . . . "On the hoof or in the hand . . . ten percent in dollars—or ten percent of however many of them critters you can get me at that Colorado cattle auction."

Charley narrowed his eyes once more.

"You ain't joking, are you?" he said softly.

Flora Mae shook her head. She wiped away the small tear.

"No, Charley, I *ain't* jokin'," she said in all serious-ness. "I've already discussed the matter with my board of directors, an' they've agreed that it sounds like a worthwhile venture. They've allotted me fifty thousand dollars, Charley. So I'll be countin' on your expertise with cattle, *and* your good mind for management, to make this thing work out for the both of us."

A long, slow smile began building on Charley's lips. As the smile widened into a grin, he took her hand and the two new partners shook vigorously.

"You've got yourself a cattle agent, Flora Mae Huck-abee," he told her. "You've got yourself a deal! Hell, I'll even take you dancing if this thing works out like you say."

He stopped, turned, and held up a finger.

"But my taking you dancing won't have nothin' to do with 'companionship,'" he said flatly. "And that's a fact!"

CHAPTER SIX

Henry Ellis was sure it was his grampa Charley's strong arms that were lifting him gently from the chair on the screened-in porch, where he'd fallen asleep reading.

"C'mon, kid," he heard a high, gravelly voice say softly. "It's gettin' late . . . time for you to get some real shut-eye in yer own bed."

The boy opened his sleepy eyes and looked up into what he thought would be his grampa Charley's amiable face. But it wasn't Charley—it was Roscoe instead. Henry Ellis immediately felt a hollowness claw at the inside of his stomach, a touch of fear.

"W-where's G-Grampa?" he wanted to know.

"It's all right, Henry Ellis," said Roscoe in a reassuring tone. "Yer granddad's still out yonder doing some serious thinkin'. He'll be home by and by."

"But it's late, Uncle Roscoe," said the boy, glancing through the screen into the blackness of the night outside. "After my grampa left, you told me he'd be back before I went to bed."

Roscoe guided the boy over to his already made up

bunk on the porch and began helping him pull off his shoes while the boy unbuttoned his own shirt.

"When your grampa has something on his mind, Henry Ellis, something as important as he's been thinking on tonight, it ain't likely we'll be hearin' him creep in 'til the wee hours, I suspect."

Henry Ellis raised an arm so Roscoe could help him into his nightshirt.

"I just hope he's all right," said the boy, who had by then begun to slip out of his trousers.

"Oh, your grampa Charley's all right," said the old wrangler. "Now, you just climb in there an' close your eyes. Try to get back to sleep. And just you remember," he said, winking, "your grampa ain't one to go back on his word. Why, I'll bet he'll be right here waking you up so he can give you that good night hug before you know it."

CHAPTER SEVEN

Around midnight, four ragtag cowhands entered Flora Mae's establishment, moving to the bar—laughing, pushing, and shoving one another to see who would be first to the suds.

The largest of the group, a heavily muscled man they called Bull, sported a disheveled bandanna over a worn collar-band shirt, a rough leather vest, and shotgun chaps. He reached out and easily pulled the other three back so he'd be first to the beer.

He pounded on the bar top for service.

"Hey, barkeep," he shouted, "four big ones . . . NOW!"

"Sorry, gentlemen," said the bartender, "we can only serve lemonade and water on the Sabbath."

Bull nodded to the clock on the wall behind the bar. "Well, that clock up there says it's Monday already . . . so how 'bout those beers?"

The bartender shrugged. "You are correct, mister," he said. "Even though it still feels like it's the Sabbath."

All the men laughed boisterously as the bartender moved as quick as he could to fill the order.

He set the foaming mugs on the counter before them. The four cowboys chugalugged.

The bartender was ready with their refill. With those second foaming mugs in front of them, ready to be consumed, the men finally took a moment to look around the room.

Charley had gone on to play another solitary game of pool, paying no attention to the loudmouths at the bar.

"Hey, Slim," roared Bull to the skinny one wearing the red neck scarf beside him. "Why don't you play us some sweet music? This joint is deader'n a preacher's pecker."

He tossed Slim a nickel and the thin man with the greasy hair moved over to the player piano and inserted the coin.

After a moment, the piano roll began spinning and shortly after, twangy, musical notes blared forth from the automatic musical instrument.

Slim moved back to the bar, dancing with himself along the way—twirling—just having one hell of a good time.

All four downed their mugs, slamming the empty containers in front of the anxious bartender once again.

Bull told the man to "Keep 'em comin'!"

The bartender, like Charley, an older man himself, hurried to fill the order.

Bull left his mug and moved over to the pool table where Charley was dropping balls, one after the other, into the pool table's pockets.

As Bull scrutinized the silver-haired cowboy with the bushy eyebrows, Charley kept on shooting, not really paying much attention to the newcomer's presence.

The muscled cowhand leaned on the pool table

across from Charley, watching, as the old man set, then shot, the last ball into a far pocket.

"Not bad for an old fart," smirked Bull, cocking an eyebrow that looked as if it had recently been rubbed in a cactus patch.

Charley glanced up with a hard look. He was still deep in thought. He turned his attention back to the pool table and began racking the balls.

"I'll play you four bits a ball," announced Bull. "Wha'd'ya say, old man?"

"I'd say you're in my way," answered Charley, leaning toward the bar and spitting more tobacco juice into the spittoon. "*Young* fart," he added quietly.

He finished racking the balls, then moved to the other end of the table to prepare for the break.

Bending and aiming, he sent the balls flying in all directions. No less than four of them found pockets.

Bull scratched his head.

"On second thought," he mused, "let's make that two bits a ball."

Charley circled the table, looking for his shot. "Not tonight, sonny boy."

Bull started to make a move toward the older man, then thought better of it. He smiled and turned away, walking back to the other men at the bar as Charley ran the table.

Charley straightened up, smiling to himself.

The bartender moved over and began topping off the four cowboys' mugs.

"Never seen you boys around Juanita before," he said, making conversation.

"We're just passin' through, amigo," said Slim, taking another sip. "We're joinin' up with a new outfit over near Hondo startin' tomorrow. This is our last night ta howl."

He laughed.

"Well, Juanita's a quiet little town," the bartender told him. "God-fearing folks live here."

Slim replied sourly, rolling his eyes. "Yeah, we noticed." The men chuckled, then continued drinking their beer.

A small, timeworn, bantam rooster–size cowboy walked in from the outside. He was dressed in rough cowboy clothing, right down to the battered, high-crowned felt hat he wore pulled down so tight it bent both of his ears forward.

He had on a pair of well-worn leather batwing chaps, and his large-rowel Mexican-style spurs jangled, almost musically, along behind him.

He stopped just inside the swinging doors, looking around. After a thorough study of the room and its occupants, Feather Martin smiled. Then he approached the bar.

"Why, evenin', Feather," acknowledged the bartender. "Pour you a beer?"

Feather nodded, licking his lips, smiling even wider.

"Uh, you got money this time?" the bartender added. "Flora Mae gave me orders about you."

Feather beamed. "I won first place," he boasted. "Calf-ropin' . . . down at Eagle Pass. Paid fifteen paper-dollar bills in prize money." He laid a brand-new one-dollar bill in front of the man.

The barkeep took the money; then he went to the register and made some change, putting the coins down in front of Feather. He *didn't* bring the man his beer.

"What's that all about?" asked Feather, frowning.

"That was for the last few beers you had in here," said the bartender. "If you want to drink in the Palace anymore, Flora Mae said you was to pay up your tab from before."

Feather shoved two more bills toward the man. "Just gimme a beer, dangit! That's what I come in here fer."

The bartender moved to the tap, pulling a mug. He slid it down the bar to Feather.

The old cowboy took the container carefully in two shaky hands, blowing off the remaining foam. Then he slurped down what remained in several quick gulps.

The trail hands watched the little man having trouble holding his mug. They chuckled to themselves.

"Easy now, half-pint," warned Bull. "You don't wanna go downin' all them suds in one swaller."

The men laughed louder, thinking they had found a new plaything. Feather finally knocked back the dregs and set his empty mug on the bar.

"Hit me again," he told the bartender as he slid a nickel across the bar. Feather was already beginning to feel better.

The man wearing the apron took Feather's mug and refilled it.

At the pool table behind the others, Charley continued to shoot balls. Every so often he looked up from his game, focusing on the wrinkled and bewhiskered undersized cowboy. Sunday smiled to himself, remembering something from the past.

Feather elbowed up on his second beer.

Bull and Slim slid in on opposite sides of the little fellow, crowding in next to him.

Bull started it off: "Did we hear you right?" he asked. "That you won at a ropin' event or somethin' like that?"

Feather nodded.

Then Slim asked him, "What's yer main event, runt, cricket hoppin'?"

The four cowhands roared at that one.

The old codger tried to ignore the men, but they kept crowding in closer. He held out his mug; the bartender took it, filled it, and handed it back.

"Ya know," Bull said to Slim, "that ol' player piano over there seems ta be jumpin' pretty good. Maybe if we set this little feller up on it, we might just see ourselves a championship ride! *If* he gets lucky."

They all laughed again.

Feather sipped slowly, paying them no mind.

Slim started to take the old man by the arm.

"C'mon, shrimp," he urged, "inta the chutes."

Before Slim could move one more inch, his eyes bulged out and the veins in his neck ballooned, ready to explode.

Feather had buried one of his Mexican spur rowels about three-quarters of an inch into Slim's right calf.

Feather yanked it free.

"Ju-das Priest!" howled Slim as blood spurted.

Bull turned in astonishment, just in time to get the full force of Feather's beer mug flat on his nose.

The mug's thick glass did not shatter, but the distinct sound of crunching cartilage resonated throughout the room.

Both Slim and Bull dropped to the floor. Bull, out cold for the moment, and Slim, holding his leg in an attempt to ease the pain.

Feather shrugged, turned again to the bartender.

"I reckon I spilt some of my *cerveza*," he said nonchalantly. "Better fill 'er up again."

The other two trail hands who had been watching left their places at the bar and approached Feather.

Before they could reach him, they were stopped cold with "Better hold it right there, gents. I wouldn't want this ol' hog leg to go off accidentally."

It was Charley Sunday. He had replaced the pool cue with his Walker Colt. It was out of his boot top and in his right hand, aimed directly at the two remaining cowboys.

Charley, now in a very somber mood, moved in slowly with the outsized gun cocked and ready. He motioned for the injured men to get up. They did, with some help from their buddies.

Feather slid in beside Charley, facing the foursome. Charley waved the gun's barrel in the direction of the door.

"Now suppose you boys get back on whatever you rode in here on, then get your butts off to wherever you're going to," he said.

The others helped Slim and Bull find their footing. Disgruntled, the four men moved toward the swinging doors and out into the early summer evening.

As they mounted, then rode off into the darkness, Slim was heard to say, "God-fearin' folks, my ass."

Charley and Feather stood silent, side by side, waiting until the sound of the trail hands' departing hoofbeats faded.

Only then did Charley put the pistol back in his boot.

Flora Mae had been watching Charley handle the entire situation from her office door. Now she moved in with three shot glasses and a bottle, setting them all on a small table nearby.

"I'd say that calls for some of my private stock, boys," she said, smiling. "C'mon over an' join me."

She began pouring three healthy ones—a double for Feather. She motioned for the men to sit. When the glasses had been filled, she sat down with them.

Charley and Feather knocked their drinks back.

"How would you like to go to Colorado with me, Feather Martin?" Charley asked the little cowboy.

"If they got beer an' whiskey there, I might consider it," said Feather, belching. "'Scuse me, ma'am," he added, wiping his mouth with a dirty, long underwear sleeve. "I believe I might have offended you."

He was already showing signs of having had just a little too much to drink.

Flora Mae threw Charley a cautious look.

He hesitated.

Then Flora Mae shook her head. "Yer the boss, C.A., you take whoever you want."

Charley looked Feather directly in the eye. He spoke to him in a very sober tone.

"We're goin' up to Colorado, Feather, to get us a few longhorns. If you want to join up, you'd be welcome. I just might be able to use some of your, uh, livestock *expertise.*"

Feather tossed back his second shot of Flora Mae's special whiskey, then looked Charley right back in the eye.

"I'm used ta four-star accommodations," he stated bluntly, "just as long as you know that in advance."

Sidney Pike rocked back and forth in his plush swivel chair, munching on a hard-boiled egg. His male secretary, Mr. Quigley, showed Rod Lightfoot in. "What have you got for me, kid?" Pike asked without looking up.

"Uh, I've been doing some research, Mr. Pike, and I, uh, thought . . ."

Pike cut him off. "Research?" said the meat packer. "What research? I didn't hire you to do research, Lightfoot. I hired you to follow my orders."

"But Mr. Pike," said Rod. "What you're planning on doing to obtain those cattle may be illegal."

"Illegal, shmegal," said Pike. "Just do as I say and we'll have every one of those longhorn cows in my company's pens by the end of the week."

CHAPTER EIGHT

Henry Ellis was helping Roscoe pin some wet laundry to the clothesline in the ranch yard when he spotted his grandfather returning on his paint horse. A motionless body was draped over the saddle of a black horse Charley was leading behind him.

Buster was snoozing nearby at the bottom of the porch steps. He looked up, saw that it was his master, then he put his chin back between his paws and promptly went back to sleep.

"Hey, Uncle Roscoe," Henry Ellis shouted, "Grampa's home. He's got someone with him."

Roscoe, with his mouth full of clothespins, glanced toward the road. He saw Charley and the extra horse coming their way. He spat out the clothespins angrily. He muttered some Western obscenity under his breath while he slipped off the worn laundry apron he was wearing.

Roscoe moved to meet Charley as he reined Dice into the yard, pulling up beside an old watering trough.

"Just where in the devil have you bin all night, C.A.?" Roscoe asked sternly while the rumpled Charley stepped down from the saddle. "Henry Ellis an' me got ourselves up an' had a full-course Texas-size breakfast on the table. But when I went ta roust you, yer dang bed hadn't bin slept in all night. We both bin worried sick about ya, C.A."

Henry Ellis nodded in agreement. "That's right, Grampa," the boy added. "I was really scared."

Charley held up his hands, stopping them both from speaking. He pulled out a bulky legal-size envelope and began fanning himself with it.

When they finally showed some interest, Charley smiled a peculiar smile.

"That's better," he told them. "One thing I never took too kindly to was a whole bunch of yelling when my head was about to explode."

Roscoe pulled on his earlobe.

"What'd you do last night?" he asked. "Looks ta me like you tied one on pretty good."

"That's right," said Charley. "What about it? I had me a lot of serious thinking to do."

"'Bout what?" asked Roscoe.

"Oh," Charley hedged, "about our future, I suspect."

He stopped fanning himself and began to open the envelope.

"*Our* future?" Roscoe echoed. "Just wha'd'ya mean by *our future*?"

Charley pulled a thick sheaf of bills from the envelope, causing Roscoe's eyes to bug out.

"Now what'd you do," he asked brusquely, "rob the Juanita Bank . . : all by yourself?"

"Oh, I reckon you could say that." Charley chuckled. "Only this was purely a legal transaction. Flora Mae Huckabee give it to me."

"What in the dickens for?" Roscoe wanted to know.

"We might not be makin' much of a profit on this ol' ranch, but the bills is all paid. Ain't they?"

Charley leaned in close.

"Flora Mae is backing us," he explained. "We're all going to Colorado to bid on them longhorns we read about."

"Yipee!" yelped Henry Ellis, clapping his hands.

That got Buster to barking.

Both boy and dog began to run in circles, carrying on like it was somebody's birthday.

Charley laughed out loud. It made him feel good to see his grandson letting off some steam.

"Unload Feather off his horse, will you, Roscoe?" said Charley. "I have some important things to do inside. C'mon, Henry Ellis."

Charley turned and started for the house with the boy following right behind.

Roscoe called after him crossly, "Important things ta do? *You* got things ta do? *I* got important things ta do, too."

"Just unload Feather," Charley told him.

Still confused, Roscoe turned to the other horse with Feather slung over the saddle.

When he took hold of an arm, a half-empty bottle of whiskey could be seen in Feather's hand.

"Oh, Lordy," moaned Roscoe. "If the world could only see the famous Kinney County Championship Calf Roper like he really is."

Henry Ellis could see Feather open his eyes a crack. He blinked a couple of times in the bright noonday sun. Finally, the old cowboy was able to make out the double images of Roscoe Baskin and the boy standing in front of him.

"Howdy, ya ol' turd-bird," he muttered in Roscoe's direction. He held up the bottle.

"Care ta join me fer a nip fer old-time's sake?"

Roscoe's eyes narrowed. He could only stare at the crumpled excuse for a cowboy he'd seen in the same condition so many times before.

"No, by golly," he told the little man. "Ain't you noticed the boy is here? But *I* can give *you* somethin' else fer *old-time's sake,* if that's what you want."

He grabbed him by the nape of the neck, lifting Feather out of the saddle.

He got a better hold on the squawking old coot by grabbing on to the seat of his tattered trousers with his other hand.

Roscoe picked the little man up and carried him over to the watering trough, dumping him into the moss-covered reservoir.

Feather came up sputtering, the bottle still grasped securely in his hand—its spout expertly covered by a practiced thumb.

He stood up shakily, knocking some water off his hat.

"Now, what'd ya want ta go an' do that fer?" he asked.

"Because I don't know what's goin' on around here," answered Roscoe, "an' I want ya sober so maybe I can find out."

A half hour later, Feather was snoring away again—this time he chose Henry Ellis's bunk. Across the room, moving upward, on a map of the southwestern United States, Charley's pencil landed on Denver, Colorado, and there it stopped.

Charley, Roscoe, and Henry Ellis sat around a small table set up hastily in the center of the room. The group munched on sandwiches and peanuts as Charley went over the chart, showing them the entire route he planned for them to travel.

Lucky old Buster, under the table—beneath everyone's feet—was surreptitiously accepting tidbits whenever one was offered.

"I figger if we leave on the morning train," Charley was telling them, "we ought ta be able to get to Denver in a few days."

"It's still a crazy idea, C.A.," muttered Roscoe. "Wantin' ta bid on them longhorns."

"Well," Charley said with a sigh, "I figure if I'm lucky, and the good Lord's bidding on them longhorns along with me, I'll come out with ten or fifteen of 'em. Maybe I'll even find me a bull in that bunch. Who knows?"

Roscoe shrugged.

"What makes you so sure you'll find a bull?" he said. "Let alone any cows . . . in a herd a' steers?" he asked politely.

"That herd didn't grow to three hundred head over the years by magic," said Charley. "Plus, that's a chance me and Flora Mae decided we'd have to take. Now finish up yer san'wich," he added.

"What about Feather?" asked Roscoe.

"Better we keep him drunk until we get there," said Charley. "If he sobers up and finds out what he's got himself into, I'm sure there'll be a lot more than just hell to pay."

Chapter Nine

Charley led the small caravan riding his paint horse, Dice, out front. Following behind were Henry Ellis and Buster in the buckboard driven by Roscoe. Feather's horse trailed behind, tied to the tailgate—a small, pie-faced black he called Chigger. For the moment, Feather was still out cold on the buckboard's backseat behind the boy and the dog.

The procession crossed a railroad siding before turning and continued on, finally aligning itself beside a stretch of side-by-side wooden corrals. A sign nailed to a post said they were THE KINNEY COUNTY CATTLEMEN'S STOCK ASSOCIATION LOADING PENS—most of them were packed full of bawling cattle.

Henry Ellis could see to the far end of the loading pens where there was a yellow building with a green roof. A crowing-rooster weathervane topped a four-foot cupola rising from its peak. Several sidings held puffing engines with their strings of cattle cars. Cowboys urged the livestock into narrow chutes that led the animals up wooden ramps and into the waiting cars.

"There's the depot," said Roscoe, nodding toward the building.

"And there's our train," said Charley, pointing to a swirl of black smoke approaching from the east.

"How do ya know that one's ours?" said Roscoe.

No cattle cars . . . it's the only weekly passenger run north they've got."

As the group pulled up to the railroad depot Henry Ellis could see a fine-looking white carriage, with its matched team of pure white horses and uniformed driver waiting by the loading platform. When Roscoe jumped down to anchor and tie off the buckboard and team, the boy watched as his grandfather nudged Dice, then trotted over to where he dismounted beside the carriage. Charley used the iron step to raise himself up so he could put his head inside. Then he proceeded to have a conversation with the vehicle's passenger.

Henry Ellis continued to watch until he heard his grampa's laugh, followed by a female's high-pitched giggle. He looked away quick. A feeling of embarrassment had come over him as if he'd been caught spying on someone and heard something he had no right to know about. He put his arm around Buster and gave the dog a loving squeeze. "That sure sounded to me like Grampa has a lady friend," whispered the boy, "didn't it, Buster?" The dog whined, then licked his face. "Kisses from you are all right, Buster," he said, "but not from no women."

Charley pulled his head out of the carriage window. He looked over toward his grandson, smiled, and called out, "C'mon over here, Henry Ellis. There's someone I'd like you to meet."

Henry Ellis jumped down from the buckboard, making sure he helped Buster, who followed after him. Both boy and dog made their way over to where Charley stood by his horse. Charley ruffled the boy's hair—then he took Henry Ellis by the arm and both of them walked over closer to the carriage.

Henry Ellis hadn't taken his eyes off the open window since he had jumped down from the buckboard. Even now, as Charley stopped beside the carriage, placing his grandson beside him, Henry Ellis could still see nothing but darkness inside the window.

The golden handle of the carriage door began to turn slowly. Within moments the door started to open and a lady's foot—encased in a black velvet slipper—appeared, finding its way to the footstep. Charley let go of the boy's shoulder and reached out for the gloved feminine hand that was being extended from the inside.

The boy watched in awe as his grampa Charley assisted the well-dressed woman to the ground. When they were all facing one another, Charley made the introductions.

"Flora Mae Huckabee," he said, "I'd like to introduce you to my grandson, Henry Ellis Pritchard . . . Henry Ellis, this is Miss Flora Mae Huckabee."

Henry Ellis removed his hat. "Uh . . . nice to meet you, ma'am," he said, dipping his head.

Flora Mae countered with a sweeping bow. "My pleasure, Henry Ellis. Your grandfather has told me all about you."

As she came out of the bow, standing to her full height again, one of the longer peacock feathers on her hat nearly swatted the youngster across the face.

Henry Ellis ducked back, swatting back at the feather's intrusion.

Flora Mae made an awkward attempt to put her arms around him, but Henry Ellis kept ducking away from her advance.

"I'm not trying to hurt you, boy . . . I just wanted to give you a little peck on the cheek."

That's what I thought you were trying to do, thought Henry Ellis, looking over to his grandfather for help.

Charley made a choking sound as he stepped between the two. "What Henry Ellis means, Flora Mae, darlin' . . . I mean, what he's being so shy about is, uh, well, he ain't never been that close to a woman of class before . . . with the exception of his own mother." He turned to the boy. "Ain't that right, Henry Ellis?"

Henry Ellis held steady eye contact with his grandfather as he spoke. "I'm sorry, Grampa," he said, "I thought she was going to kiss me." He made a face while turning to Flora Mae. "I don't like no kissing, ma'am," he added, "unless it's from my ma or Buster here."

Charley and Flora Mae broke out laughing. The boy just stared at them, dumbfounded. He didn't have a clue about what they found so amusing.

Charley stepped in between them, taking each by the arm. "C'mon, you two . . . let's go help Roscoe get the buckboard and the horses loaded up for our trip."

With a little help from some freight workers, Roscoe had already loaded the buckboard and tied it down securely on the end of a splintery flatcar. Now he was leading the unhitched team up a heavy ramp and into a boxcar linked to the front of the flatcar.

Flora Mae, the boy, and Buster followed along as Charley, leading Dice, walked them over to the livestock car. He looped the horse's reins around a piece of iron that was part of the livestock car itself, tying the old horse right beside Feather's mount, Chigger. He looked around, concerned, calling over to Roscoe, "Where'd the little fella go? Where's Feather?" said Charley.

Roscoe motioned to a door on the shady side of the depot. Above that side entrance was a small, hand-lettered sign that read ICED BEER.

Charley grinned. "Keep him in there 'til we leave," he said. "And make sure Dice, Chigger, and the team get enough water." He moved on up to the passenger car, where a uniformed conductor stood examining his watch.

Flora Mae rummaged through her purse, pulling out their train tickets. She handed them to Charley. "Here're your tickets, Charley," she said. "The claim stubs for your baggage, the buckboard, and the horses are right there with 'em."

"Thanks, Flora Mae," said Charley as he handed the tickets over to the conductor.

"You don't have to do that just now," said the conductor. "I'll be collecting them officially after we get underway." He handed the tickets back to Charley.

"You might as well keep this one," he said, handing one of the tickets back to the conductor. "A certain member of our outfit is still inside the depot . . ."

"Uh," said the conductor, "I met the little feller you're talking about earlier. I'm afraid he stunk so bad I told him he'd have to ride in the mail car."

"What about Buster?" interrupted Henry Ellis. "Doesn't Buster need a ticket?"

"Who's Buster?" asked the conductor.

"Buster's my dog," said Charley. He turned to Henry Ellis. "Go tell Roscoe I got his ticket and that we're boarding pretty soon. And tell him not to forget Feather. Then you come on back here and help Buster up these steps. I'll go ahead and board now, find us some seats so we can sit together."

Henry Ellis turned and moved off toward the live-stock car with the dog following.

The conductor watched the boy walk away. When

Henry Ellis was out of hearing range, he turned to Charley. "I'm afraid there ain't no animals allowed in the passenger car, mister. All dogs, and such, have to ride in the mail car, too."

Charley growled, "The hell you say. Buster's always rode in the passenger car with me before."

The conductor shook his head firmly. "Not anymore he don't."

"But I'm telling you . . . he's always rode with me."

"How long's it been since you took a train trip, mister?"

Charley sighed. "I don't know . . . maybe two years ago, three . . . Why?" he asked.

"Well, things have changed . . . the rules," said the conductor. "Maybe your dog was allowed to ride along with you in the passenger car in the old days, but we're about to turn a big page into a new century this year, mister, and, well, the new regulations say dogs ride in the mail car. No exceptions," he added.

"What's going on, Grampa?"

Everyone glanced over to the boy who had returned from talking to Roscoe. He had a confused look on his face while he knelt and stroked Buster's coat. "Did I just hear him say Buster can't ride with us?"

Before the conductor could explain, Charley hushed him with a wave of his hand. "Mind if I handle this?" he said.

The conductor closed his mouth, looked away.

Flora Mae's eyes focused on the boy.

Charley moved in closer to his grandson, patting him gently on the shoulder. He reached down and patted Buster, too.

"I'm afraid that's so, Henry Ellis," he said. "New rule says Buster's got to ride in the mail car."

To everyone's surprise Henry Ellis wasn't the least

bit discouraged. "That's fine with me, Grampa," said the boy. "I'll just ride in the mail car with Buster."

Charley and Flora Mae traded looks.

"I mean," Henry Ellis continued, "someone's gotta stay with Buster . . . he's not a young pup anymore, you know."

Flora Mae knelt down beside the boy who was still on his knees petting the dog. She stroked Buster's nose. "That's a mighty fine gesture, Henry Ellis," she said. "But y'all have a ticket to ride in the passenger coach with yer grandpa and Roscoe . . . where it's warm . . . and they got cocoa and hot food in there, too."

"Naw," said the boy. "I can sleep next to Buster. We can keep each other warm."

"Well, if that's the way you want it, son," said Charley. "I might as well ride back there with you and Buster, too. I'll leave it up to Roscoe and Feather to figure out what they want to do."

"That other fellow over there," said the conductor, "Roscoe, I think I heard you call him."

Charley nodded.

"Well, I don't care what he wants to do," said the conductor. "He can ride up with the engineer, if that suits him. It's the little smelly one I don't want mixing with the other passengers. I sure am pleased that he'll be riding in the mail car with the rest of you." He turned and started to go—then he turned back. "Oh, yeah," he said. "There'll be a couple of U.S. Marshals checking on the mail car every now and then. We're pickin' up the Decker Mine payroll in Del Rio before we head north. They tell me it's a pretty large sum this trip."

Chapter Ten

By the time the sun was setting for the day the train had traveled quite a few miles north of Del Rio. Inside the mail car Charley struck a Lucifer match, which sputtered and sparked until an orange and blue flame appeared. He lifted a dusty lantern to eye level before touching flame to wick. As he lowered the glass on the lantern, that section of the car slowly grew brighter.

Henry Ellis and Buster had been napping next to the snoring Feather for about an hour. Charley set the lantern on the shipping crate he and the others were using as a card table; then he picked up his hand and rejoined Roscoe and Wally, the payroll guard who had boarded the mail car when the mine's iron money box had been loaded on board at Del Rio. They resumed playing.

Buster opened his eyes, raised his head, and sniffed the air. In a moment there was a knock at the door, which brought the dog to his feet. Henry Ellis woke up just as his grandfather said, "Come in." The door opened wide and the conductor entered carrying several plates covered by red-and-white-checkered linen napkins. Two other men followed, both carrying more covered dishes.

"Thought we'd better bring you folks some supper," said the conductor as he set the plates down on another wooden box beside the card game. The other men set their plates down, too. "These gentlemen are U.S. Marshals," said the conductor, "Bill Smith and Bob Wilson."

"Nice to meet you," said Charley, not looking up from his cards.

"Howdy," said Roscoe, involved very much in his own hand, too.

Both men held out their shakin' hands without making eye contact, and the two marshals shook with them. "I see you already made acquaintance with our mine payroll escort, Wally Jones."

All of the men nodded, making no comment; then they continued on with their game.

"If you got Wally here guarding the payroll, what do you need the marshals for?" Charley asked the conductor. He still didn't look up.

The conductor pulled up another shipping box and sat down next to Charley. "That's the other thing we come in here for . . . besides our bringing you folks some nourishment. I just got word by telegraph from Del Rio that the Cropper Brothers' Gang might try to waylay this train before it gets to Colorado. If that fool gossip turns out to be truthful, we're all mighty lucky these federal lawmen decided to ride this train."

"I hope you and your friends are well heeled," said one of the marshals.

Quicker than a wink, Charley had his Walker Colt out of his boot and in his hand. He spun the heavy weapon not once, but twice. "Does a hungry mule eat hay?" he answered. "We're all retired Rangers, mister, if that'll help," said Charley. "We've handled our share of trouble over the years."

"That's nice to know," said the marshal, throwing a glance to the other law officer.

"Well, anyhow, now you got three more guns," said Charley, "me, Roscoe, and Feather over there." He pointed to the little old codger who was still snoring away beside the boy and the dog.

"Are you sure about him?" asked the marshal.

The conductor said, "He was dead drunk when we carried him aboard. He don't look like he'd be of much help to anyone."

"Oh, Feather's right fine in a tight fix," said Charley. "As drunk as he looks on the outside, his inside Ranger instincts are as sober as you are."

Charley slapped down his cards with a big grin. "This hand is mine, gentlemen."

Roscoe and the guard sighed and threw in their cards. Roscoe gathered them up and began to shuffle.

"Hey," said the conductor, "why don't you gentlemen go on and eat your supper while it's at least warm. We'll get outta here and let you dine in peace."

He stood, moving over to the marshals. "That grub was kinda hot when we brung it in here for you. Hope it ain't cooled off too much since."

As the conductor and the two marshals turned to leave, Henry Ellis went over to the covered plates. He removed the napkins from the food and began serving the others.

CHAPTER ELEVEN

From a low, sandy hill near Painter's Tanks—a natural water-catch where he and his gang were camped—Sam Cropper watched through a pair of rusted Army binoculars as the single beam of a locomotive's head-lamp showed the way for an engineer who was completely unaware his train was headed for its possible destruction.

Sam Cropper, with a slick, snake-like, black mustache centered between nose and upper lip, had dismounted. He was stretched out on his belly with his elbows dug in at his sides to help steady the field glasses. He was at the top of a small sand dune, which gave him the needed height to follow the train's progression. He brushed back a lock of greasy black hair, then reset his hat, bringing the glasses to his eyes once again to continue his surveillance.

"How far is it now?" asked his brother Dale—an un-kempt man with long gray hair and a shaggy beard. Dale was standing close by holding their horses.

"Not much closer than it was a minute ago when you asked me the same thing, Brother Dale," said Sam

Cropper, lowering the binoculars and getting to his feet.

He handed the field glasses to his sibling, who tucked them away in his saddlebags.

"If the men are ready to ride as soon as we get back to the tanks," said Sam, "we could beat that train to Pipes Canyon with time to spare."

He swung into his saddle, dug in his spurs, and rode away.

His brother followed right behind.

Inside the mail car suppertime was over. Henry Ellis was moving around gathering the dishes while Charley and Roscoe watched Wally deal three new hands of poker. When the boy approached Feather he found that the old cowboy had fallen asleep again, this time with his nose in the beans. Buster had also noticed the untouched fare and was sitting almost nose to nose with Feather waiting to see if he was ever going to wake up and eat. The boy giggled to himself at the sight. He turned and whispered to the others:

"Hey . . . you gotta see this, Grampa . . . look at Feather and Buster."

Charley glanced over along with the other two. "Go ahead and give that grub to Buster, Henry Ellis. All Feather's doing is dribbling snot onto his potatoes."

Everyone laughed as the boy slid the plate out from under Feather's nose, then set it on the floor where Buster gobbled it up in no time—snot and all.

Right about then the train began to slow down slightly, causing Charley and Roscoe to exchange glances.

There was a knock on the door again and the conductor stuck his head in. "I didn't want you boys to be worrying none about the change in speed. We're starting the climb into Pipes Canyon. It's kinda steep at first but it levels off once we're over the hump."

"Seems like a good place for a train robbery if you ask me," said Roscoe.

"Oh, no," said the conductor. "Those two marshals are positive the Cropper Brothers'll hit us somewhere near Adobe Wells, if they hit us at all. And that's four miles on the other side of the canyon."

"All right," said Charley. "Just let us know if those marshals change their minds."

The Cropper Brothers, along with the rest of their bunch, waited on horseback in the natural shadows of the opening to the gorge. The train chugged toward their position, on its way up the grade leading into Pipes Canyon. Sam Cropper watched as the train's headlamp reflected off the mica embedded in the walls of the chasm. He pointed to Dale and three others. "All right, men," he said, "you know what to do." He pulled his neck scarf up over his nose. The others did the same.

A moment passed, then he nodded to the rest of the gang. "As soon as we get the mine's shipment, I'll stop the train and you other men can come on ahead."

The locomotive reached their position and rolled on by. Sam and Dale Cropper spurred out alongside the rest of the train with the three chosen men following. The remaining gang watched after them as they disappeared into the darkness.

In the mail car Charley and Roscoe were trying to wake up Feather. Henry Ellis, Wally, and Buster looked on as the old cowboy shook off their advances. He pulled away from them and turned over. "Le' me alone," he mumbled, "I'm sleepin'." As hard as they tried, Feather would not open an eye for them.

"All right," said Charley, "just leave him be if that's the way he wants it."

Charley turned back to the others. "You got a gun, Wally?" he asked the payroll escort.

"I sure do, Mr. Sunday," he said. "If I didn't I wouldn't be much of a payroll guard, now would I?"

He pulled a .38-caliber Smith & Wesson double action from his coat pocket and showed it to Charley.

"Henry Ellis?" said Charley. "You go on back there and hide amongst them other parcels. Take Buster with you."

He turned back to the others. "Roscoe, you and Wally go on over there to the right side of the door and find yourselves some cover. I'll just stay right here and duck down some."

"But the conductor said the marshals figure the robbers won't hit us for another five miles or so," said Wally.

"You just do what I tell you to do. You don't see no marshals in here giving orders now, do you?"

"Do you think those two lawmen are in on it, C.A.?" said Roscoe.

Charley shrugged. "Better to think they are than not, don't you think?"

CHAPTER TWELVE

Galloping hooves with iron horseshoes kicked up a lot of sparks and gravel as the Cropper brothers, Sam and Dale, along with the three other gang members, spurred their horses into Pipes Canyon following the steaming train.

The last car in the short procession was the flatcar containing Charley's two-seat buckboard tied down and secured at the far end.

As the riders moved up beside the flatcar, the three outlaws transferred from their saddles to the moving conveyance.

Sam and Dale Cropper raced on ahead before transferring from their foaming mounts to the livestock car next in line. As Dale made his leap he almost missed the metal step he was aiming for, but Sam was there with an outstretched hand for his brother and he was able to pull him to safety at the very last moment.

By then, the other three gang members had traversed the length of the flatcar and jumped across to the livestock car, joining the Croppers. Sam gave them all a nod for their know-how—then he turned and started climbing up a ladder that led to the livestock car's roof. Dale and the others followed behind him one by one.

Inside the mail car everyone had slipped into their hiding places. Charley reached over and turned down the lantern's flame until there was very little light at all.

About then, there was another knock on the door and the conductor shoved his face into the darkness. He held up his own lantern, then smiled. "I think they're all asleep," he said to one of the two marshals who were right behind him. As he turned to go back, the steel barrel of a Colt .45 crashed into the side of his head. He was immediately pulled back by the second marshal and laid out on the small platform between the cars. The door closed behind him.

"Did ya see that?" whispered Roscoe.

"Sure did," said Charley in a low voice. "Ya'll just stay put now and wait." After a long moment he added, "Looks like I was right about them two marshals."

The five members of the Cropper Brothers Gang advance party made their way across the roof of the livestock car, alerting the horses below to their presence. The animals reacted with stomps, whinnies, nickers, and snorts.

Sam made his jump from the livestock car roof to the top of the passenger car in a single leap. His brother Dale began his attempt and barely made it— slipping, and nearly falling, as his sibling kept him from an early death one more time.

The other three robbers decided they weren't going to kill themselves before the robbery had even taken place, so they slithered down ladders and poles, climbing up again on the passenger car, eventually joining Sam and Dale topside before they moved on.

Inside the passenger car one of the marshals was explaining to a female passenger how the loud noises coming from the roof were nothing more than small rocks and gravel falling from the steep sides of the narrow canyon. The woman's gaze drifted up to the ceiling.

Up top, the outlaws had reached the other end of the passenger car and now began climbing down the iron ladder to the foot platform below. When they had all descended, they exchanged looks—then Sam and Dale drew their guns and stepped across to the mail car platform. The others produced their own pistols, crossing over after the brothers.

Inside the darkened mail car nothing moved except Buster's hind leg. The dog had begun scratching himself behind his left ear.

"Can't you hush him up?" whispered Charley.

Henry Ellis took hold of Buster's rear paw and the scratching stopped.

The boy's eyes widened considerably as the rear door opened slowly.

Sam Cropper, followed by his brother Dale and the other three outlaws, stepped quietly into the darkened mail car.

Their only source of light was the orange glow of the tiny flame inside the lantern's globe on the box that had been used as a card table. Nothing moved—no sound was heard—until a loud snore cut the air.

Five revolvers were cocked in unison. "What was that?" said Dale.

Another snore was heard—all eyes turned in the direction of the obtrusive reverberation.

And there he was in all his glorious splendor— Feather Martin. He was still passed out cold, only now he lay faceup on a pile of empty mail pouches. And right there on the other side of Feather was the iron strongbox containing the mine payroll.

"There it is," said Sam Cropper.

"So far this has been like slicing butter . . . real smooth," said Brother Dale.

"Well, don't just stand there waitin' for it to come to you," said Sam. "Go on over there an' get it, Brother Dale."

"Obliged," said Dale, motioning for the three henchmen to follow.

As they all decided at once to step over Feather instead of going around him, Feather passed some gas and turned over so he was facedown. One of the bandits stopped in his tracks directly over Feather where he got a good whiff of Feather's recently expelled vapors.

"Oh, hell," he said, gagging. "That's enough to strangle a maggot."

"Don't be wasting time," said Dale. "Get your butt on over here."

Since Feather's spurs were now positioned "rowels up," it didn't take that much for them to hook on to the outlaw's own spur rowels. When the bandit reached out to regain his balance, he grabbed hold of a large piece of Dale's shirtsleeve. Dale reached out for something to grab and latched on to the other two bandits' shirt collars, causing all four of them to fall on top of Feather in a mangled pile.

"Geeezus God!" yelled Feather, and a shot rang out.

A few more bullets were expelled with their black powder flashes lighting up the mail car with each shot.

From where he'd hidden himself at the other end of the car, Henry Ellis could barely make out what was happening those few yards in front of him. The one thing he could feel was the long hair of Buster's coat, reminding him that the dog was still at his side.

"Go get 'em, Buster," he urged. "Go help Grampa and Uncle Roscoe."

Buster let out a nasty growl. He began barking as loud as he could.

Eventually the confusion and tumult of the sightless fight came to an end.

Someone found the lantern and turned the wick up. As the flame grew larger and the interior grew brighter, it was apparent Roscoe, Feather, Wally, and Buster had everything under control.

At first Henry Ellis grinned in relief, but when the door behind the others swung open to reveal the two marshals with their weapons cocked and ready, his smile faded completely.

"Everyone hold it right there," the first marshal shouted.

"You're all covered," said marshal number two.

Buster hadn't moved an inch. He remained standing in the same place and continued barking.

Relief was now showing on Sam and Dale Cropper's faces as well as their three henchmen.

Roscoe, Feather, and Wally raised their hands as soon as they figured out whose side the marshals were really on.

Sam moved over to the near wall and pulled on the emergency brake cord.

The engine's wheels locked and the train screeched to a steaming stop.

Sam turned to his brother. "Dale . . . you and those other three open the side sliding door so we can shove that payroll box off the train when it's time."

Dale and the men nodded. Dale took care of the door while the others went to the locked iron box and began their struggle to slide the heavy load across the floor planks. It wasn't an easy job.

One of the marshals turned to Sam. "Don't you think you better have someone go back and tell the rest of the gang what's happened?" he said.

Sam nodded. "I'll have them send the wagon up here for the strongbox. Dale," he called over to his brother, "jump off a' this train right now. Wait for the others, then we'll use the wagon to haul this strongbox."

Dale nodded. He turned to the open door and jumped.

There was a moment—then:

"Ahh shit." It was Dale's voice. "I think I broke my toe . . . Sam!"

Buster's barking was incessant. The dog wouldn't stop.

"I'm going to shut that dog up once and for all." Sam raised his revolver and pulled back the hammer, aiming it at the defiant canine. Buster stood his ground with Henry Ellis's arms wrapped tightly around him.

"Get out of the way, kid," said Cropper, motioning with his gun's barrel.

Like Buster, Henry Ellis wouldn't budge.

"I said get away," repeated the gunman. "I'm going to shoot that dog and I don't want to hurt no kid while I'm doing it."

"That'll be the day."

It was Charley's voice coming from behind a shipping crate where he'd been concealed. He slowly stood up with the Walker Colt aimed directly at Sam Cropper.

The outlaw realized it was all over. He immediately cocked his gun.

BLAM! BLAM!

Charley's Colt had blazed only once—yet two shots had been fired.

Everyone turned in complete surprise.

Finally Charley spoke up. "I didn't gun Sam Cropper," he said. "I was aiming to. But that marshal over there on the floor beside Sam shot him by mistake trying to draw against me. My shot hit the marshal when he stepped in front of Sam."

All heads turned again. The first marshal, with smoking gun still in hand, lay crumpled on the floor. Marshal number two, along with the other three train robbers, already had hands raised high.

"Sam," echoed Dale Cropper's voice from outside the sliding door, "Sam . . . Can ya gimme a hand? . . . Sam!"

Chapter Thirteen

The mail car door slid open to reveal a small New Mexico railroad siding. It was the middle of the night. Several local lawmen escorted the handcuffed and bandaged Cropper Gang from the mail car to several waiting police wagons. Charley, Roscoe, Feather, Henry Ellis, and Buster watched from the sliding door as the wagons pulled away.

The bandaged conductor moved in beside Charley.

"After all that," he began, "I'd reckon you folks might like a nice, comfortable bed to sleep on in the Pullman car." Before Charley could speak the conductor continued, "That'll include your dog, mister," he said, smiling . . . "plus the smelly little guy, too, I reckon."

Every one of them slept halfway through the next day.

It took them until Friday to get to Colorado. Henry Ellis had the time of his life riding in the passenger car, sitting between his grandfather and his uncle Roscoe, laughing and joking with the older men and listening to their tales about the Texas Rangers and the good old days.

Feather had opted to continue his ride in the mail car along with Wally the guard and Buster the dog. Feather had asked the conductor politely if the train could stop in one of the small towns they passed through so he could pick up some more "refreshment" for himself.

After he'd been allowed to do that, the pint-size cowboy was able to slug down his favorite whiskey all the way to the Rocky Mountain State. Though, more often than not, the crusty little cowpoke was passed out cold.

CHAPTER FOURTEEN

When Charley, Henry Ellis, and the others stepped off the train it was early Sunday morning, barely two weeks since Charley and Flora Mae had seen the longhorn story in the local Juanita paper.

It wasn't long after they'd unloaded the horses and buckboard that they found someone who showed them the way to the cattle pens where the auction was going to be held.

The three hundred Texas longhorns had been crowded into at least a quarter of the corrals that made up Denver's stockyards.

Charley led the way on Dice. He was followed by Feather on Chigger. Roscoe, Henry Ellis, and Buster, riding in the buckboard, tagged along behind.

While Charley and Feather dismounted, Roscoe and Henry Ellis climbed down from the buckboard and moved to the nearest fence where Roscoe lifted the boy up, placing him on the top rail so he could have a better view of the longhorns.

Feather stumbled over, joining them. Buster followed. The dog was enjoying the cooler climate; he found a nearby fence post where he raised a leg and then relieved himself.

For a long time, the small group stared in awe at the enormous—to them—herd of cattle.

"Will ya just look at 'em," declared Feather, interrupting the silence. "Real, honest-ta-goodness Texas longhorns. Hot damn!" he yelped. "It's sure bin one hell of a long time since I seen one a' them critters."

"See any bulls?" asked Charley.

Feather squinted. "I see some cows," he answered. "Mostly steers."

"Well," said Charley, pointing across the arena, "I reckon I better go on over there and sign up."

"Hey, *there's* a bull!" shouted Feather, pointing to another corral.

"C'mon," said Roscoe. "They're packed into them corrals so tight together, how can you tell it's a bull?"

Feather smirked, strutting his stuff. "By the contented look in his eyes," he confirmed.

Charley smiled and moved away.

Henry Ellis jumped down from the fence and ran after him. So did Buster.

Roscoe stepped in beside Feather, leaning on a rail.

"You wanna know somethin', Feather Martin?" he asked with a straight face. "The only thing you know about bulls is how many shovels it takes to fill *you* up."

A little later on, a few eager observers were sitting here and there in the rodeo bleachers behind the auctioneer's podium. Others strolled casually toward the auction area.

Red, white, and blue pennants fluttered in a light breeze from every corral fence.

Charley, Roscoe, Feather, and the boy were now seated on a closer fence rail, watching as the people arrived for the event.

Buster, of course, was curled up on the ground below the humans, licking his fur and paying no attention at all.

The auctioneer, a potbellied man with gray hair under a slick tan Stetson, appeared to be involved in some last-minute paperwork, while a couple of his associates were putting the final touches on the podium.

Roscoe checked his pocket watch while Feather took a small bottle from his rear pocket, turned away from the others, and took a long swallow.

"You go gettin' yerself roostered again," Charley told the peewee cowboy, "and I'll personally nail your hide to a barn wall."

"Just cuttin' a frog outta my throat, boss," coughed Feather. "Little hair of the horse."

Charley and Roscoe exchanged glances.

Charley nodded toward Henry Ellis who appeared to be caught up in all the color of the occasion.

Roscoe winked at Charley as the auctioneer, across the arena, checked his pocket watch one more time, noting that the bleachers were still pretty empty.

He raised a megaphone to his mouth. "Ladies and gentlemen," he said. "May I please have your attention?"

All eyes turned to the podium.

The announcer went on: "Can I see the hands of all those registered as official bidders?"

Charley raised his hand.

After a moment, he looked around, realizing that he was the only one in acknowledgment.

The auctioneer saw this as a potential problem, so

he bent down and whispered something to one of his associates.

The associate whispered something back and the auctioneer raised his megaphone again. "Is there a representative from the Pike Meatpacking Company in attendance?" he asked.

There was absolutely no response to his question, only a slight murmur from the sparse crowd.

The auctioneer again bent down and whispered something to his associate. The man nodded, then disappeared into a nearby building.

The auctioneer turned back to the meager crowd.

"The Pike Meatpacking Company has made a pre-auction offer for the entire herd of three hundred head," he revealed. "The State of Colorado's Livestock Auction Official Rules say that we must allow fifteen additional minutes for a Pike representative to make their presence known before we can proceed."

Charley was taking it all in, thinking deeply, when Roscoe turned to him.

"What about us?" he said.

Charley peered across the way to the auctioneer. He raised his hand.

The auctioneer looked up, squinting. "Yes, sir?" he inquired through the megaphone.

Charley yelled back to him, "I seem to be the only other bidder, mister."

The auctioneer smiled gently. "By Denver, Colorado's, Livestock Auction official rule number one sixty-seven," he explained, his words echoing across the empty arena, "the herd must be sold as an entire lot . . . *if* a pre-auction bid has been submitted to that effect. The Pike Meatpacking Company *has*, in fact, made a pre-auction bid of fifty thousand dollars. This *is* an entire lot bid, sir."

He referred to some legal papers on the podium in front of him. "I have my instructions right here if you'd like to read them." He went on, holding up some documents for Charley to see.

"But that ain't what it said in the Juanita *Centennial* newspaper," shouted Charley.

The auctioneer shook his head, continuing to hold up the papers. "I have my instructions," he repeated, "right here in my hand. It's an *all or nothin'* auction, sir. I have to abide by the rules."

Charley settled back on the fence, appearing more than a little upset.

"Sounds like a fix ta me," mumbled Feather.

"They do pre-arrange these things sometimes, I've heard," added Roscoe.

Suddenly, Charley jumped down from the fence. He looked back to the others with a determined expression.

"Anybody seen a telephone around here?" he said. "I need to talk to my pardner."

Henry Ellis climbed down beside his grandfather. "I saw a telephone on the wall at the place where we signed up, Grampa," he said. "You just tell me the number you want to call, and I'll have the operator get it for you."

A ripple of anticipation ran through the small crowd as they waited. Roscoe and Feather were still sitting on the fence. The smaller cowboy took another sip on his bottle. He handed the container to Roscoe, who downed a swallow himself.

Suddenly Feather pointed toward the auction podium, where Charley—with Henry Ellis and Buster at his side—could be seen talking with the auctioneer.

After several moments of intense dialogue between both parties, the auctioneer nodded. Charley, his grandson, and the dog moved to a small building nearby and went inside. The auctioneer went to the podium and began to go through some more of his papers.

It wasn't long before Charley, Henry Ellis, and Buster returned to the corral fence; Charley and the boy climbed up beside the others.

Questioning looks from Feather and Roscoe got no response from the stoic Charley—or the boy.

The auctioneer once again picked up his megaphone. "There's still no sign of a Pike representative," he told the audience. "*And*, by the rules, I must begin this auction on time. High bid is fifty thousand dollars from the Pike Meatpacking Company for this entire herd of three hundred magnificent, longhorn cattle."

Before he could go on, Charley raised a finger. All eyes went to the old rancher.

"Fifty thousand . . . *and ONE*," he bid with a determined shout.

More murmurs ran through the undersized crowd.

Roscoe's and Feather's looks snapped around to Charley.

"I have a bid of fifty thousand and ONE dollars," said the auctioneer. "Do I hear another bid?"

All were silent. Only the breeze whipping lightly at the patriotic pennants made any noise at all.

The auctioneer looked around apprehensively for any other bidders, knowing that there were none, stalling for more time.

The associate poked his head out of the tent flap,

got the auctioneer's attention, shrugged, and shook his head.

The auctioneer again raised the megaphone.

"Fifty thousand and one going once," he said, his eyes still searching the crowd. "Fifty thousand and one going twice . . ."

The crowd's eagerness swelled as the marvel of what was happening before their eyes began to sink in.

"Going three times," the announcer said with a sigh.

Then: "*SOLD* to the cowboy in the white shirt, sitting on the fence beside the good-looking young man . . . with the sleeping dog at their feet." He slammed down his gavel to finalize the deal.

Some light applause rippled from the spectators, along with several "*Whoopees*" from Roscoe and Feather.

They both jumped down from the railing, converging on Charley and Henry Ellis who had beaten them to the ground.

Of course, the sounds of excitement woke Buster, and the old dog began to bark, even though he didn't know what he was barking about.

Charley picked up his grandson and swung him around in a circle. Charley was grinning from ear to ear.

"Did I do all right?" he asked his grandson.

Henry Ellis, also grinning, said, "You betcha, Grampa! Now you're a *real* cowboy again."

Roscoe moved to Charley's side. "What've you done now, C.A.?" he asked. "Gone crazy? That fifty thousand was 'sposed ta include the transportation money ta get them sons-a'-bucks back home ta Texas."

Charley started to show some irritation with his pal.

"Hold your horses, Roscoe Baskin," he began. "Just a few minutes ago, I talked to Flora Mae on one of those telephone contraptions and she told me to 'Go for it' . . . so I did. She's calling a special Huckabee Enterprises board meeting right now this very minute to try and get us some transportation money. So don't go getting your long john butt flap tangled in your spurs before you got all the facts straight, all right?

"In the meantime," he added, "why don't you start giving some credit where credit's due: to *ME* . . . for just becoming the proud owner of ten percent of that beautiful Texas longhorn herd."

He turned to Henry Ellis, clasping the boy on the shoulder, pulling him closer. "*And* to my grandson, here," he said with pride. "It was *him* that loaned me the dollar."

Feather let out an ear-shattering rebel yell as they all threw their arms around one another.

Buster continued to bark.

Across the arena, a perspiring Rod Lightfoot, dressed in a disheveled secondhand business suit, and wiping his soiled hands on a greasy rag, was arguing about something with the auctioneer and his two associates.

With a final shake of the head, the auctioneer pointed off in Charley's direction before turning away.

Rod stared across the dirt arena to where Charley and the others continued their early celebration.

Rod appeared to be rather embarrassed about his personal appearance at that particular moment. Still aggressive in his actions, he made up his mind. He straightened his rumpled suit, ran his fingers through his hair. Then he made his way toward the small group on the other side of the arena.

Charley and the others were laughing at the auction's outcome when Lightfoot approached them.

"Excuse me," he said. "I'm looking for a Mr. Charles Abner Sunday?"

"You found him, son," said Charley, grinning. "What is it I can do for you?"

Rod stood to his full height, holding out his hand.

The two men shook.

"My name's Rod Lightfoot," he said. "I represent the Pike Meatpacking Company. I was supposed to bid on these longhorns today, but I'm afraid my buggy didn't know just how important it was that I be here. It broke down on the way and I had to fix it myself. I understand that you bought the cattle, Mr. Sunday. Now I'm prepared to buy them back from you."

Charley smiled softly as the two stopped shaking hands.

"Sorry, son," he apologized. "The longhorns ain't for sale to nobody. They're going back to where they belong . . . Texas . . . every last one of 'em, so help me God, just as soon as I can arrange for a way to ship 'em. And that's a fact!"

"I'm prepared to meet any price," declared Rod, "*over and above* what you paid for the cattle."

Sunday shook his head once again.

"Money ain't gonna solve anything, son," he replied. "Ten percent of that herd belongs to me now, and I'm obligated to someone else for the rest of 'em. I'm truly sorry if you're in a fix, but there ain't nothin' I can do about it now. So help me God."

A look of utter desperation crept onto Rod's face.

"Mister Sunday," he began. "I'm working my butt off trying to get into law school . . . I've read all the law books I could get my hands on. Not too many Indians around here have ever tried anything like this before. In spite of my inability to obtain a law degree, the Pike Meatpacking Company is the first real job I've had where I can utilize what I've learned and still study the books in my time off.

Now I'll probably lose that job when my boss finds out I screwed up on this cattle deal."

It was apparent that Charley felt compassion for the younger man, and Charley even felt obliged to give him another firm shake of the head.

"Like I said, son, I'm sorry that you're in a fix. But I just got out of one myself . . . possibly a worse one than you're in. Right now," he continued, "my first and only priority is getting these animals properly delivered to the person that put up the money for 'em back in Texas."

Rod stood silent, totally exasperated. There appeared to be nothing more he could either say or do. So he just shrugged and turned away, moving off toward the other side of the arena.

Roscoe looked at Charley, realizing that his old partner felt bad about the young man's situation. But all he could do was shrug.

Feather and Henry Ellis both harbored deep sentiments about the position Rod had found himself in, but those feelings were soon laid aside as the celebration continued.

CHAPTER FIFTEEN

A black, box-shaped, covered buggy pulled up under a tree nearby and a very attractive woman stepped down. She was dressed in a plain blouse, short jacket, and long skirt, and she carried a small notepad in one hand. The man who had been driving the horse-drawn photographic darkroom got out after she did. When he had secured the one horse, he began to unload several boxes from a covered rear opening in the body of the rig. Those boxes contained camera equipment, which he began setting up on the grass that surrounded them all.

"Hello . . . My name's Kelly King," the woman told Charley. "I represent the National News Syndicate. You must be Mr. Charles Abner Sunday."

Rod stood beside a wall crank telephone inside the auction's main headquarters building holding the earpiece to his ear. He was listening as someone talked on the other end.

Rod had removed his coat, vest, and tie, revealing a shiny, brass US Army buckle.

Rod's eyes were looking out a window where he could see the horse-drawn darkroom across the arena. He watched as Charley and the others stood by silently as they were photographed one by one.

"That's right, Mr. Pike," Rod said into the mouthpiece. "The old cowboy plans on shipping the entire herd to Texas. By the way, the National News Syndicate people just now showed up . . . No"—he shook his head—"I don't know how they got wind of it so soon."

"For Chrissake, kid," said Sidney Pike into his primitive table telephone as he sat at his lavish office desk in his downtown Denver headquarters talking to Rod Lightfoot. "If they even think about talking to you, keep *my* name out of it."

"Yes, sir," said Rod, nodding his head. "I'd never do that, sir."

Pike squirmed in his plush leather chair as he carried on his conversation with Rod.

"Between *you* and that stupid auctioneer," he continued, "I'm surrounded with incompetence. You have to get those cows back, Indian . . . My ass is on the line."

"Uh, sir," said Rod carefully. "I *do* realize that this is a serious matter—"

"You bet this is serious," screamed Pike, cutting him off. "I've already received full payment for that meat, plus my Chicago distributor has already sunk I don't know how much into their sales campaign. That's a lot of money, Lightfoot."

Rod was beginning to perspire. "I really *am* sorry, Mr. Pike, I—"

"Face it, Indian," Pike told him bluntly, "you screwed up."

He struck a match, lighting a large cigar. Then he reached over and poured a stiff drink from the carafe on his desk.

Rod attempted a remedy.

"Maybe if you returned the money," he suggested.

"Are you out of your mind?" Pike howled. "I already *spent* the money, you indigenous idiot. Do you think I'm some kind of a schmuck? I'll go ahead and call the railroad and the trucking companies and put the kibosh on any chance that old Texan might think he has of getting those longhorns out of this state.

"And *YOU*, Flapping Eagle," he added, "*YOU* work on getting those cows back for me . . . *Any way you can.*"

"Y-yes, sir, Mr. Pike," said Rod. "I'll do whatever I can."

"You do *EVERYTHING* you can!" shouted the meat packer, slamming the earpiece back where it belonged.

After a long moment, he lifted the earpiece again and waited for the operator's voice.

Minutes later Pike waited for the table phone to connect. When it did, his expression changed abruptly to one of saccharine verity. He smiled a nauseatingly sweet smile to himself and spoke into the mouthpiece.

"Hello, Interstate Livestock Transportation?" he began. "This is Sidney Pike of the Pike Meatpacking Company. You remember me, don't you? Five hundred big greenies every month . . . *on the hoof?*"

Later on, inside the auction's headquarters building, Kelly King was talking on the same wall crank telephone Rod had used. "Just take this down word for word, boss. I'll have a lot more to fill you in on tonight after I check into a hotel." She cleared her throat: "This is Kelly King for the National News Syndicate," she began, "reporting from Denver, Colorado. Headline: An Old-Time, Texas Cowboy Has Just Purchased a Herd of Three Hundred Longhorn Cattle . . . Saving Them from the Butcher's Cleaver."

CHAPTER SIXTEEN

Rod, looking more depressed than ever, sauntered along beside the corral fence thinking to himself. Finally he stopped where Feather and Roscoe were helping several Colorado cowboys haze some of the longhorns from one of the holding pens into another.

Henry Ellis sat nearby stroking Buster's coat, watching from an old three-legged stool someone had left there.

Rod moved up beside the boy and leaned against the fence, his mind swirling with absolutely no solution to his problem.

After a moment, Henry Ellis took notice of the unhappy man's presence.

"Hello," he said simply, throwing the stranger an easy wave.

Rod glanced over to the boy, acknowledging with his own "Hello."

"Did you get some bad news?" asked Henry Ellis.

Rod shrugged. He wasn't that interested in casual conversation right then, especially with a ten-year-old.

The boy took Rod's silence for what it was and picked up the dialogue himself.

"That's my grampa," he said. "The cowboy who bought the longhorn herd."

He pointed across the arena to where Charley stood, concluding an interview with Kelly King.

The photographer held his flash powder high, and when he activated the camera's lens control the powder exploded, illuminating them both.

"That's him over there being interviewed for the newspaper," Henry Ellis continued. "My grampa's famous, you know."

Rod glanced over in Charley's direction, his interest drawn immediately to Kelly King.

"Uh-hum," he mumbled. "What's he famous for?"

Henry Ellis abandoned the dog and stood up. He took a step forward, leaning on the rail beside Rod.

"Oh, a lot of things . . . in Texas," he boasted. "My grampa was a Texas Ranger in the olden days."

He pointed over to Roscoe and Feather.

"Them too," he added. "The three of them rounded up a whole lot of outlaws way back before I was born."

Rod was only half listening. He was still staring at Kelly across the way.

"That's nice," he muttered, then he caught himself. "*About* your grandfather and his friends, I mean."

Another flash went off as the photographer took another photograph.

Suddenly there was a loud commotion near the transfer pens. Some "whoops" from the cowboys and the frenzied braying from a frightened steer—followed by the sound of splintering wood.

Rod and Henry Ellis turned quickly, just in time to see that one of the longhorns had crashed through a gate and had run into the arena.

Almost without thinking, Rod broke for a horse that

was tethered nearby. He stepped professionally into a stirrup, swung into the saddle, and kicked out after the runaway.

The longhorn steer appeared to be running in a direct path across the arena; more than likely he was heading for the area where he'd seen the flash.

Rod, astride the galloping horse, pursued relentlessly.

Charley and Kelly King were still in deep conversation when Charley looked up and blinked—he saw the approaching threat and shook the newswoman's shoulder.

"Better stop it right now, miss," he warned. "Here comes trouble!"

The photographer heard Charley's alarm and scrambled.

Charley grabbed Kelly, pulling her aside, just as Rod dove from the moving horse's back onto the stampeding steer. Rod grabbed it by the horns, bulldogging the animal, twisting its head, and dropping it to the ground within inches of Charley and the startled lady.

Rod held the longhorn down until some other cowboys could get a rope on it. Only then did he release the horns so the cowboys could lead the animal away.

By then, Henry Ellis, Feather, and Roscoe had run over, followed by Buster.

Rod picked himself up as Kelly twirled a finger and called to her photographer, "All right, Gerald, wrap it up; I'm sure we've got plenty of photos."

Charley stepped over to Rod, offering his hand. The two men shook.

"That was some real fine horsemanship, son," he told the younger man. "Where in tarnation did a citified man like you ever learn to ride like that?"

Rod appeared to be somewhat embarrassed, but he

still answered: "I learned to ride on the reservation, sir. One of the ways I'm raising money for my law school tuition is by entering small town riding and roping exhibitions."

Charley caught a glimpse of Rod's US Army buckle, and he nodded his approval.

"My friend Roscoe over there," he began with a subdued chuckle, "he used to wear a special buckle kind of like yours. But he got so tired of lifting up his belly every time someone wanted to see what it looked like. So he got the same thing tattooed on his left arm, instead. That made showing it off a lot easier."

Roscoe turned a bit crimson.

"That ain't true, C.A. Sunday, and you know it."

The others all chuckled at Charley's humor.

"Were you involved in our recent conflict with Spain?" asked Charley.

"Yes, sir," said Rod. "I fought my way up San Juan Hill with Teddy Roosevelt."

"So you were a Rough Rider."

"It was Roosevelt who personally signed me up in the Menger Hotel Bar, across from the Alamo in downtown San Antonio. I don't think I knew what I was getting myself into except it was the first time in my life where being an Indian was considered a good thing and not something bad."

Charley shook his hand proudly, then turned back to Kelly King.

"Miss Kelly," he began. "This here's Mr. Rod Lightfoot . . . that lawyer fella I've been telling you all about. And might I add, he's one heck of a cowboy, too . . . As you just witnessed."

Kelly held out her hand. Rod shook it. Both of them locked eyes on the other for a very long moment—something was definitely clicking.

"Kelly King," said Kelly with a blush, "National News Syndicate."

Rod smiled. "I know," he answered awkwardly. "I've read some of your stories before."

Charley sensed the mutual attraction right away. He nodded to Roscoe, who reached into his shirt pocket and pulled out some bills, handing them to Charley.

"Say, youngsters," Charley began, "while I contact the railroad and set up a shipping time, why don't you two see if you can find us all some vittles. There must be somewhere around here to buy some food."

Neither Kelly nor Rod seemed to hear what Charley was saying; they were much too distracted by one another's presence. So Charley just stuffed the money into Rod's shirt pocket anyway. Then he moved away.

Henry Ellis, Feather, and Roscoe were left standing beside the enamored couple.

"Gee, Rod," said the boy, "that was really great!"

Roscoe added, "That sure was some nice cowboyin', son."

All Feather could think of to say was, "Couldn'ta done it better myself."

Buster just barked.

Before an hour had passed, Roscoe had fashioned a canvas covering for a canopy beside the buckboard. Feather was nurturing a small campfire nearby.

Rod, and the photographer Gerald, had eventually gone out in search of some food. Charley and Henry Ellis were nowhere to be seen. Kelly sat talking to Feather, while Buster slept under the buckboard.

It wasn't long before Rod and Gerald drove up in the horse-drawn darkroom. They climbed down before entering the small campsite carrying several neatly tied boxes of Chinese food.

Buster followed along, sniffing at the boxes, hoping, of course, that there would be something inside with his name on it.

Everyone helped themselves to the boxes before finding a place to sit.

A tired looking Charley entered the camp, holding his grandson's hand.

Roscoe jumped up to greet the two, stuffing some noodles into his mouth with a pair of wooden chopsticks.

The others looked on with interest.

"When do we load 'em out?" mumbled the excited Roscoe, still chewing.

Charley threw him a look of sheer exhaustion before moving to one of the Chinese boxes and opening it. He sniffed and made an awful face.

"Are we gonna get a-goin' in the mornin'?" questioned Feather. "Before sunup? Is that when we're gonna start transferrin' these butt heads into the railroad loadin' pens, boss?"

Charley could only shake his head slowly as he moved on past the group and climbed up into the buckboard, where he sat.

Henry Ellis slid in beside his grandfather.

Charley's head hung low—so did the boy's.

"There's not going to be any shipping," he informed them.

There were surprised looks from everyone.

"No one will do it," Charley added, shaking his head.

Roscoe slowly slid his hat back on his head, then he moved over, standing below his old friend.

"You mean ta say there ain't no trains in this town?" he questioned. "No cattle cars? No nothin'?"

Charley shook his head again, drew in a long, deep breath, and let it out.

"Oh," he began, "there's transportation all right. I just didn't get any cooperation."

"What's that supposed ta mean?" asked Feather.

Charley answered, "Just that there's someone with a little more grease than I have hereabouts who doesn't like the idea of us coming into possession of that long-horn herd."

He turned to Rod.

"I don't suppose that could be your boss, could it?" he added.

Rod shrugged. "Pike's got the means . . . *and* the power," he answered politely.

Charley sat up straight. He cleared his throat to get everyone's attention.

"It don't really matter who done what," he told them all. "There ain't going to be any shipping of those cattle. At least not around these parts, there ain't. And that's a fact.

"Now," he continued, "I've just been talking on the telephone to my financial partner, Miss Flora Mae Huckabee, back in Juanita. And me and her decided we'd *drive* these horns all the way to Texas if we have to. And now it looks like we have to, don't it?" he said, and sighed.

Roscoe did a double take.

"*Drive 'em?*" he said.

Henry Ellis, like the others, had been standing mouth agape at the idea. Now his lips widened into an excited grin.

"Y-you mean like you did in the 'olden days,' Grampa?"

he stammered. "A real, honest-to-goodness 'cross-country cattle drive'?"

Charley nodded slowly. "Longhorn cattle drive," he said.

He smiled and ruffled the boy's hair. "Like you said: Just like we done it in the olden days, son."

Charley looked to the others for their reactions.

Roscoe and Feather appeared to be hemming and hawing.

"So what's the matter with you two?" he asked. "You both did it all the time when you were young men. Are you afraid that you're too old now to give it one more try?"

Roscoe and Feather were still showing some hesitation.

Kelly whispered something to Gerald—then he turned and disappeared around a corral.

Kelly stepped in closer to the group.

"Of course you should drive them," she concurred. "It's mostly open country between here and Texas."

Rod stepped in closer.

"The law's on your side, too, Mr. Sunday," he told Charley. "Most counties in these parts still have livestock right-a'-ways on their books."

"What are livestock right-a'-ways?" asked Kelly.

"Those are legal directives that give livestock precedence over anything else on a public thoroughfare," he answered.

Charley gritted his teeth.

"Me an' Flora Mae know that, son," he said.

He turned to Feather and Roscoe. "And so should these two mule-faced jackasses . . . Now I said we was gonna drive them brush snakes to Texas, and that sure as hell is what we're gonna do."

He sighed again.

"It's a dirty job," he reminded them, "but someone's gotta do it. And we're all we have right now."

"B-but," Roscoe faltered, "we ain't got enough hands, C.A."

Charley turned to Rod.

"What about you, Indian?" he asked. "I just saw what other talents you have. Are you willing to gamble on an old Texas cowman?"

Kelly stepped in before Rod could answer.

"I'd be willing to come along," she said. "I can ride, rope, and I can cook, too. I'd just like to have Gerald, my photographer, allowed to follow along with us, if it'd be all right with you. This should make one heck of a great human interest story, believe me."

"You're more than welcome, Miss Kelly," said Charley, "as long as the both of you can pull your own weight."

He turned back to Rod.

"Son?" he prodded.

Rod hesitated, then: "Sure, sure," he told Charley, "I'll come along with you . . . Why not?"

Charley turned back to Roscoe and Feather.

"These two youngsters ain't afraid," he told the pair. "And I know I don't have to ask Henry Ellis. I know the both of you'll have to do the work of three, and that's a fact, but—"

Roscoe cut in. "At my age, my butt and a saddle don't stick to one another like they used to, but we've bin ridin' river fer too long together fer me ta unsaddle just yet, C.A. Sunday," he told Charley. "I'll go."

Charley threw a wink to Roscoe, nodded, then turned to the smaller cowboy.

"Feather Martin," he asked. "What about you?"

Feather continued to vacillate, then realized he was the only one left.

"Well," he grumbled, "I still say yer barkin' at a knot."

Nevertheless, Feather didn't seem to be that amused. He took the final swig from his pocket pint of whiskey and nodded to Charley in agreement. "Hell," he said, "I reckon I'll come along with ya . . . even if it's only ta see the elephant."

Gerald, the photographer, who had left earlier, walked back into camp and sat down beside Kelly. He whispered something in her ear.

The newswoman smiled; she stepped forward.

"My powers that be in New York City just gave me permission to cover your cattle drive as a continuing feature story, Mr. Sunday." She beamed. "That means what I observe and write about every single day will appear in every single newspaper my company contracts with. So, you men better make this a good one."

Charley threw her a wink before he turned to the entire group.

"All right, you men, let's get going," he commanded. "We'll trade, tack, and grub up this afternoon. We still got some time before dark. And tomorrow we'll brand them critters. We'll move 'em out the following day.

"Oh, and we still got some serious alterations ta make to the buckboard," Charley added.

"Why's that?" questioned Roscoe.

"It's gonna be our chuckwagon," said Charley. "We need to pull out the backseat, build some sides on it to make it a wagon, change out the axles and wheels, and build a cook's cupboard in the back for our grub and other supplies."

"And I suppose I'm gonna be the cook," grumbled Roscoe.

"Do you want to eat *my* cooking?" asked Charley. "Or Henry Ellis's? Or maybe Feather's?"

"All right then," Roscoe eventually confirmed. "I'll do the cookin'."

"I figured you'd understand." Charley chuckled as he took a large bite of the Chinese food. He chewed a while, then said, "Rod? Feather? I'll be needin' both of your professional know-how if we're gonna do some savvy horse tradin'. So, let's get our butts in the saddle; I want to be back here before suppertime. And that's a fact!"

CHARLEY SUNDAY

by Kelly King

He was born in Northern Mexico in 1829—that same massive area of Northern Mexico that would one day become the Republic of Texas after Sam Houston defeated the Mexican army at San Jacinto.

"My parents migrated to this new land in 1820," says Charley Sunday, "when Stephen F. Austin convinced the Mexican government to allow three hundred American families to settle in the territory. Three years later, in 1823, Austin decided these pioneers needed some kind of armed force to protect them from hostile Indians and other dangerous elements.

"The Mexican government," Charley went on, "allowed Austin to form a group consisting of not more than ten volunteers who would be allowed to range over the vast territory, keeping an eye out for the bands of renegade Indians that could only bring trouble to the settlers.

"In 1846, when General Zachary Taylor needed men to follow him across the Rio Grande into Mexico to once again wage war with America's southern neighbor," Charley told me, "I was inducted into the Texas Ranger organization at seventeen years of age and was immediately sent off to Mexico with the Rangers as a part of

Taylor's army. We fought and defeated the Mexicans in due course.

"Over the next forty years, or so," he says, "during the War Between the States and in its aftermath . . . the reconstruction period . . . when Texas was governed by the Northern Army of the United States, I kept up my relationship with the Rangers, riding with them when we legally could, and standing by with them when the Yankee lawmakers would shut us down.

"In 1876, when the agency was called back to duty full time, to again serve as protectors of the citizens of Texas from the daily hazards involved just by living on Texas soil," he says, "I went back to work with the Rangers on a regular basis . . . until I retired, three years after my wife Willadean died."

During that early period of ups and downs for the Rangers, Charley had met and married the woman whom he'd hoped would become his lifetime companion. Her name was Willadean Clarke, soon to be Sunday. Willadean became the mother of their only living child, a girl, Betty Jean (born 1862). Until Willadean's death from pneumonia in 1887, the couple was inseparable—that is, when Charley wasn't away with the Rangers or out of town on cattle business.

"Just before the War Between the States broke out," continues Charley, "I bought myself a spread of my own . . . five hundred acres of grazing land on the outskirts of Juanita, Texas, where me and my Willadean raised our daughter and tried to breed longhorn cattle."

From 1862 through the duration, Charley fought bravely for the Confederacy. He returned to Juanita in July of 1866. "It was a long walk back from Virginia, where I found myself at war's end," says Charley. "Plus, I had to work my way home if I wanted something to eat. That took some time."

During the years he had been away at war, Charley's

ranch had fallen apart, he told me. And the U.S. government had confiscated every longhorn he owned when the
Yankees moved in to preside over Juanita and her citizenry.

"My wife and daughter had survived the war years and
were still living at our ranch when I finally got home," he
says. "They had been feeding themselves from our fruit
orchard and a small vegetable garden Willadean had
maintained since I rode off to war in 1862 . . . and they
had somehow gotten possession of a milk cow that was
still producing."

On several occasions while Charley was away
Willadean had to use his Walker Colt to defend herself
and their child from marauders that seemed to run wild
while the menfolk were off to war, plus she even used
the weapon to challenge the Yankee-appointed local
sheriff when he was sent to remove them from their own
property—something Charley took care of only days
after his homecoming.

"I hunted that blue-coat local ex-lawman down and
shot the yellow-belly with my old Ranger Colt," he says
with subdued anger as well as a lump in his throat. "I
reckon I shouldn't have done it," he goes on. "But I was
angry that someone local was messing with my family,
and my property, while I was off fighting for the Confederacy.

"For the last twelve years I kind of let everything continue to fall apart, including me," he says. "Plus, I lost the
cattle I'd been able to start over with in the great drought
of 1893. Since then me and Roscoe, my foreman, get by
on a small income I get from leasing some of my acreage.
My only living kin is my daughter, Betty Jean, and she has
lived up in Austin since she got married after her mother
died. But Betty Jean's given me a grandson, with the
name of Henry Ellis. And when I get to see the boy, which
is usually every other summer, I do whatever I can to

teach him a little more about my life and the history of Texas . . . the way it was.

"I never had a son that lived past birth, you know," Charley tells me with tear-rimmed eyes. "And Henry Ellis is probably as close to being my son as a real son would have ever been. Like I said before, I'd do anything I can for that boy . . . Anything."

Charley told me that this Colorado to Texas cattle drive more than likely wouldn't have happened if it weren't for Henry Ellis. "When we were up there in Denver and everyone thought we were at our rope's end, I decided that we'd drive the longhorns home to Texas . . . just so the boy could see how we done it in the olden days."

CHAPTER SEVENTEEN

"Hell, I'm only gonna be using 'em for a month or so," Charley was telling Ned Baylor, the owner-operator of Baylor's Barn, one of fourteen livery stables where horses were traded and sold in Denver, Colorado.

Twelve of Baylor's best geldings stood tied to several hitching posts beside the two men.

Roscoe, Feather, and Rod stood nearby, listening, waiting to assist if Charley needed them.

Henry Ellis and Buster observed from the buckboard, while Kelly sat beside the boy and watched as Gerald photographed the course of events from a position near his photography buggy.

"Makes no mind ta me," answered Baylor, a sloppily dressed horse wrangler wearing an untucked, long-sleeve, dirty and patched cotton shirt, and a worn-out felt derby to shade his weather-wrinkled face. "I still ain't gonna rent 'em to ya. So there. If ya wanna buy 'em, *then* we can deal."

He saw Gerald's camera out of the corner of his eye. He smiled and nodded to the lens.

"Oh, all right," said Charley, knowing he hadn't time

to bicker. "How much for these twelve we've been talking about?"

Baylor scratched his chin. "Well," he pondered. "Them's twelve a' my better stock."

"The hell you say," countered Charley. "I've seen healthier horsemeat inside a bowl of dog food."

"They ain't no prize winners," Baylor apologized, "that's for sure. But I guarantee ya they are good cow ponies. Some a' the best in my barn."

"So, how much do you want for them cow ponies?" Charley asked again. "And please give me a *fair* price . . . one that'll allow me to do some dickering."

Baylor toed the dirt with his boot.

"Oh," he said, hesitating. "I might just sell 'em to ya at a good price, mindin' ya sell 'em back ta me when yer through."

"That's the same as renting," bristled Charley. "That's what I wanted to do in the first place."

"I don't rent," recapped the stubborn Baylor. "I sell."

Frustrated, Sunday spat some tobacco juice.

"Oh, hell's bells," he muttered, wiping his mouth. "Just what do you think a good price might be then?"

"One hunnert a head," said Baylor casually.

Charley reared back, puffed his cheeks, and blew out a whistle.

"That's highway robbery," he howled. "The last horse I seen advertised for that kinda money won the blue ribbon cup at the Ken-tuck-y Derby."

"Now yer pullin' my leg," said Baylor. "Let's trade."

Charley thought a minute.

"Fifty," he offered.

Baylor couldn't help grinning.

"Seventy-five a head," he countered. "And that's final."

Charley glanced over to where his friends stood watching.

Feather shook his head.

Rod did the same thing.

Roscoe just shrugged.

"Uh," said Charley to the barn owner. "Will you excuse me for a minute? I need to discuss this matter with my business partners over there."

"You feel free ta do whatever ya have ta, mister," Baylor told him, "I'll still be here."

Charley sauntered over to the group and they huddled for a few moments.

It was Feather who finally turned and walked back to where Baylor waited.

The man of small stature took a long minute to look Baylor up and down, sizing him up.

"We ever met before?" he asked the larger man.

"Don't think so," answered the horse trader.

"Yep," said Feather. "We did . . . a long time ago."

"Really?" said Baylor. "And when would that have been, shorty?"

"Back when us kids all called you a snake on stilts, or a fat ol' tub a' lard. Is that what they call ya now? . . . a fat ol' tub a' lard? Or is it still straw man?" he taunted. "Gawd, you used ta be twig-thin, ya ugly ol' buffalo."

Baylor's eyes narrowed. He took a closer look at the miniature cowpoke—then his eyes lit up.

"Why, yer Melwood Gene Martin, ain't ya?" he said. "We went to the same schoolhouse together back in Spofford, Texas. It was you that used ta beat me up every day after school. Sure, I remember you."

Feather stood on his tiptoes to make eye contact with the larger man. He leaned in real close.

He said, "It's 'Feather' Martin these days, high pockets. Now, how 'bout you an' me doin' some *real* horse tradin'? *Before* I get ticked off. And let's start things off right by you throwin' in all the saddles and tack we'll be needin' . . . fer nothin'."

"Excuse me," interrupted a woman's voice from behind.

It was Kelly.

The two men stepped back from each other, doffing their hats to the woman, smiling.

"What can we do for ya, ma'am?" asked Feather.

"Well, uh." She blushed, showing some embarrassment. "I was standing quite a distance away and couldn't really hear what you two were saying." She raised her pad and pencil, ready to write. "Do you think you could repeat your last conversation over again for me . . . and after that, pose for a newspaper photograph?"

That evening, while Feather, Roscoe, Henry Ellis, and Charley unloaded, sheltered, and fed the twelve new horses, Rod found his way over to the auction headquarters building, a short distance from the campsite, where he made another call to Sidney Pike.

He waited anxiously as the operator went about putting the call through, and with the longhorn cattle braying all around him, he was sure no one could hear what he was about to say.

There was a click, indicating the phone had been answered.

"Hello?" It was Pike's voice on the other end.

"I've been trying all evening to reach you, Mr. Pike," Rod explained. "I thought you'd like to know that the old cowboy intends to *drive* those cattle all the way to Texas."

"What?" roared the meat packer. "He's got to be out of his mind . . . He can't do that, can he? Legally?"

"I'm afraid he can," Rod affirmed. "And he is . . .

starting the day after tomorrow. We'll be moving out before sunup."

"*We'll be* moving out?" questioned Pike with the slight rise of one eyebrow. "'We'll' sounds like the whole *fuc-kow-ee* tribe. Does that mean *you're* going along with them, too, Cochise?"

"That is correct, Mr. Pike," said Rod. "Mr. Sunday asked me to join them, so I said yes. I assumed you'd want me to stick close to the longhorns," he added as an afterthought.

"You bet your red ass I want you to," encouraged Pike. "All right," he went on, changing the tone of the conversation. "You just keep your eyes peeled and your ears flapped open for me until I can figure something out. Understand?"

"Yes, sir, Mr. Pike," replied Rod. "Oh, by the way, the National News Syndicate is sending a reporter along with the cattle drive. You can always find out just where we are by checking the latest edition of any newspaper."

"Geeze," howled Pike. "Then you better keep a low profile . . . no interviews. Just keep a close watch on those old geezers for me. I'll come up with something."

Early the next morning, after the herd had been watered and fed, the branding began. Charley had decided on a *CAS* brand instead of one that used Flora Mae's initials, because the *CAS* brand was much easier—and faster—to make with a running iron.

Even though Feather had reminded him there were laws against using running irons in Texas, Charley had thought: *What the hell, we're in Colorado now, so who cares?*

They used the running iron.

Kelly had wanted Gerald to be down in the dirt with his camera and the cowboys, but Charley nixed her request. He told her Gerald and his camera were all right, but from a distance.

"Too dangerous," he had said. "That camera contraption might just spook the cattle."

"Grampa!" yelled Henry Ellis as Charley burned in the *CAS* initials on the first steer's rear end. "You're hurting him!"

Charley looked up.

"That's not so," he told the boy. "And even if it did, it's only for a second or two."

Roscoe cut in with his own advice.

"Us Texans have bin brandin' longhorns like this fer as long as there's bin cattle ta brand, son," he added. "Don't ya think some busybody would a' made a fuss and then the government would a' made it against the law ta do it by now if it really hurt the critters?"

"But I saw the smoke," the boy cried. "I could smell his hair burning. Plus the longhorn squealed."

"That's all a part a' brandin', kid," said Feather. "An' brandin' is all a part a' bein' a cowboy. Don't you wanna be a cowboy?"

Henry Ellis nodded timidly. "Uh-huh," he answered.

Rod stepped in, bending down beside the youth.

"I felt like you do, Henry Ellis, the first time I ever saw a branding," he told him gently.

He put a hand on the boy's shoulder.

"But it's got to be done," Rod leveled with him. "Otherwise, if some of the longhorns got loose, or lost, or even stolen, while we were driving them to Texas, we wouldn't be able to identify them . . . and someone else might just claim them for their own."

"You don't want that ta happen, now do ya, kid?" added a solemn Feather.

"N-no," answered Henry Ellis, shaking his head.

"So ta be a real cowboy . . . a *good* cowboy . . . like yer grandfather an' Feather Martin," said Roscoe, "you just have ta learn to put up with some things ya don't particularly like."

"That's true," said Rod. "I had to learn. These guys did. Now you can learn, too."

Charley, who had been watching the exchange all the while, now held the running iron out in front of his grandson.

"Here," he said to the boy. "Why don't you give it a try? A real cowboy has to start sometime."

Henry Ellis hesitated. He started to move forward—then he paused again.

"I'm scared, Grampa," he told Charley.

"Everyone's frightened the first time," Charley said. "Why, your uncle Roscoe over there was downright petrified. Feather, too."

"And me," chimed in Rod. "I was so terrified I couldn't even do it the first time . . . my father had to take me by the arm and guide me through it."

Henry Ellis's face began to brighten.

"Really?" he asked them all.

Everyone nodded.

"Your grampa, too," said Charley himself. "I was probably the scaredest of 'em all."

He held out the iron once again.

"Now come on over here," he coaxed. "And I'll personally guide your hand on your very first try at branding a Texas longhorn."

Henry Ellis's mouth broke into a wide grin. He nodded to Rod as he started toward his grandfather.

When the boy was ready, Charley's experienced hands directed the boy's own shaking hands—which held the cool end of the red-hot running iron— moving them, ever so carefully, toward their target.

And when the tip of the iron was barely a fraction of an inch from the maverick's behind . . .

Buster, dreaming over by the buckboard, let out a piercing yelp!

Changing the two-seat buckboard into a usable chuckwagon took longer than Charley had planned. In fact, it turned out to be much more difficult than branding three hundred head of Texas longhorns.

They were able to find all the scrap wood they needed for the sides and a cook's cupboard. The problem was finding larger wheels and axles.

Feather finally located a set behind a gunsmith's shop in town and got them for a good price. The only problem was that both the axles and the four wheels hadn't turned in years and the wood used to make them was dried out and cracking.

Charley told them to throw on as much grease as it would take to get everything moving properly and if something went wrong out on the trail they would worry about it then.

CHAPTER EIGHTEEN

1960

The rain continued to fall outside.

"I don't think I'd be able to brand a cow even if I was getting money for it," said Noel. "It'd probably hurt me more than it would hurt the cow, anyway."

"Don't you be acting like a sissy, Noel," said the girl's great-grandfather, Hank. "Henry Ellis felt the same way until everyone told him about their own experiences with branding the first time, or haven't you been listening?"

"I could do it," piped in Caleb.

"Me too," said Josh. "It wouldn't be that hard if you knew it had to be done."

"I branded a steer once," said their mother, Evie. "Grampa Hank taught me how."

"That's right," said Josh, "when Grampa Hank's grampa passed on . . . Grampa Hank inherited the Longhorn Ranch."

"Not exactly," said Hank. "My grampa Charley left my mother the ranch in his will . . . then she left it to me when she passed on. I had taken a course in college called Ranch Management and thought that between what I learned in school and what I got handed down to me from my grampa made me an expert when it came to running a ranch. But I never got to find out."

"Why was that?" asked Noel.

"Because, back then I thought making money the quick and easy way would help me with fixing up the place a lot faster than if I waited for the longhorn herd that was on the ranch to grow large enough so I could sell some of 'em off."

"Then it was you who bet the ranch away in a poker game?" said Josh. "I remember hearing something about that when I was a little boy."

"I had a good hand," said Hank. "Only it wasn't as good as the one the guy I was playing with had. Four deuces," he added.

"You had four twos in your hand," said Josh, "and you didn't win?"

"No," answered Hank. "*He* had the four deuces. I had three aces."

"But before he lost the ranch he taught me how to brand a steer," said Evie.

"And you were darn good at it, too," said Hank. "No whining or complaining."

"Anyone ready for more popcorn?" asked Evie.

Four hands went up, including Hank's.

Evie grabbed the red bowl and got to her feet.

"It won't take me long," she said.

As she walked away Caleb raised his hand.

Hank pointed to him.

"Why did they turn the old buckboard into a chuck-wagon when they could have just as easily bought or rented a real chuckwagon, Grampa Hank?"

"Well," Hank began, "Roscoe didn't own a saddle horse of his own. He always used the two-seat buckboard if he needed to go anywhere. That's why they took it along on the train in the first place."

"In case he needed to go somewhere," said Noel.

"The outfit was grateful they had brought the two-seat buckboard along," said Hank. "The cost of a new chuckwagon back then was nothing to sneeze at. Re-modeling the buckboard saved Charley a whole bunch of money in the long run."

"But he spent a lot of money on those extra horses, too," said Caleb. "Why did he do that if he was trying to save money?"

"All cattle drives need extra horses," said Hank. "You need them if something happens to a horse on the first string, or if a horse gets tired out . . ."

"Kind of like a football team," said Josh.

Hank nodded. "That's a way of looking at it, Josh. The extra horses are there as insurance . . . And it usually takes at least one cowboy to watch over them, all the time. Charley couldn't spare the extra man, so he let the horses run with the cattle."

"I don't know how they slept on the ground every night," said Noel. "They must have had a lot of aches and pains."

"Henry Ellis got to sleep in the chuckwagon with Buster the dog," said Caleb.

"Sometimes even Miss Kelly slept on the ground," said Hank.

"I feel sorry for her just thinking about it," said Noel. "I love my bed."

"I'm sure you do, little one," said Hank. "I hope you'll never have to sleep on the cold, hard ground."

Evie came back into the room carrying the red bowl filled with freshly popped popcorn.

"Here you go," she announced, "a fresh, new batch of Jiffy Pop for everyone."

She sat again on the floor placing the bowl where everyone could reach it.

"I don't know about the rest of you," she continued, "but I'm ready for Grampa Hank to go on with his story."

"Me too," said Noel.

"Me too," echoed Caleb.

"I'm ready," said Josh.

"All right then," said Hank. "Now where was I?"

CHAPTER NINETEEN

1899

The following day, it took more than a few hours before dawn to move the three hundred longhorns out of their corrals and shepherd them into a large bunch on a sizable, grassy, flat area near the Denver stockyards.

As the early morning sun was barely beginning to throw its halo on the rim of the horizon, a small group of horsemen waited quietly in the center of the milling cattle—Feather, Rod, and the three Colorado cowboys Sunday had hired: Neil, Sleepy, and Lucky, who appeared to be almost as old and grizzled as Charley and his pals.

Roscoe was sitting in the driver's seat of the well-stocked chuckwagon-buckboard nearby. Like the others, he was looking off toward the sound of approaching hoofbeats.

Henry Ellis sat beside Roscoe on the chuckwagon's seat, with Buster secure in the bed behind them.

The object of their interest was a lone horseman, silhouetted in the dawn's early light. He spurred out, traveling the distance from the barn, to and through the stockyard gates, then on up to where the longhorns and his men awaited him.

All remained calm, for the moment, as the rider reined up beside the cowboys.

It was Charley Sunday.

After a long look at his unique band of drovers, Charley's determined eyes moved from one man to another, finally stopping at Rod.

"You ready, son?" he asked calmly.

Rod nodded.

Charley took a good look at the herd in anticipation of the drive ahead.

The cattle, surrounding them all, made low gentle sounds, braying peacefully.

Roscoe and Henry Ellis looked on excitedly from the chuckwagon-buckboard's front seat.

Kelly was observing while Gerald photographed the scene from where he had set up his camera at the top of a loading chute near the rear of the horse-drawn darkroom.

Feather was ready, as were Lucky, Neil, and Sleepy.

Charley took one final look at his oddball outfit, rubbed his nose, spit a stream of tobacco juice, and looked around at the herd. Then he turned back to the others.

With great pride in his voice, he told them, "Take 'em to Texas, gentlemen."

Feather flicked a toothpick from his teeth, stood in his stirrups, and raised his hand for all to see.

"Yeeeee-haaa!" he yelled.

The others began to swirl their hats and lassos in the air, their spurs finding horseflesh.

Rod was next with a "Yaaaaaaa-heeeee!"

Roscoe couldn't resist.

"Ahhhhhh-haaaaa!" he bellowed from behind the reins of the chuckwagon.

Followed by Henry Ellis beside him, with a "Yaaaa-hooooo!"

"Eeeeeeee-haaaaa!" shouted Charley.

Rod urged them on with "Get going, you little doggies!"

And Neil, Lucky, and Sleepy added their "Yaaaaa-haa!" "Shoooooo-Eeeee!" and "Yippy-yip-yip!"

Even though Gerald was taking photos with the camera, Kelly couldn't help herself—she had to add to her own excitement with a rip-roaring "Yaaaa-hooooo!"

Then she stood up, turned to Gerald, and said, "See you down the road a piece."

Gerald acknowledged and continued taking pictures as Kelly ran over to the chuckwagon, gave Buster a quick pat, then climbed in beside Henry Ellis. A smiling Roscoe popped the reins on the horses' rumps and the old, rickety wheel replacements began to turn.

At first, everything went pretty smooth. The cattle appeared to move effortlessly across the Colorado countryside with the cowboys hazing them along—prodding the slow ones—and, every so often, riding out to bring in a pesky maverick.

Roscoe, Henry Ellis, Kelly, and Buster bounced along in the chuckwagon, making their way through the dust and the slow-moving longhorns.

Charley rode Dice at the head of the drive, directing the entire campaign.

By the looks of him, Charles Abner Sunday was a satisfied man.

CHAPTER TWENTY

The newspaper photo showed the longhorns and the cowboys in progress. Kelly King's written words below added the expected commentary:

"An old-fashioned cattle drive began today," she wrote for her reading audience, "just outside Denver, Colorado. Three hundred Texas longhorn cattle on their way home at last.

"This modern-day cattle drive is being made possible by a group of crusty old cowboys from the Lone Star State of Texas, who are reliving the days of yore.

"I will be traveling with these brave men as they make this amazing cattle drive back to Texas, courageously fighting their way across today's contemporary obstacles, taking these longhorns back to where they historically belong.

"An event such as this has not been undertaken with longhorn cattle in quite some time. A thousand-mile cattle drive: living with the elements, cooking every meal from scratch, eating from tin plates, outdoors twenty-four hours a day, sleeping under the stars every night for however long it may take."

The newspaper was crumpled by two well-manicured hands.

Sidney Pike had been reading Kelly's report at his office desk and was very upset by what he had just seen.

He stood, grabbed a handful of cigars from a wooden humidor on his desk, then yelled into the next room.

"I'll be out of the office for a while, Quigley," he snarled. "Take messages."

Later on that same day, Kelly was on the ground with Gerald, her photographer, taking some low-angle shots of the oncoming herd.

From his lead position, Charley saw the two of them on the grassy knoll and he noticed that the cattle were headed directly for the two of them. *They're close . . . dangerously close to possible injury*, he thought.

He spurred out fast, riding on up ahead.

Charley reined Dice in beside the twosome, motioning for Kelly to stand. When she did, Charley tipped his hat back and told her, "You best be riding with Roscoe and Henry Ellis in the chuckwagon, young lady. This ain't safe at all, you bein' out here afoot."

Kelly nodded.

Gerald turned the camera toward Charley as he rode back to the herd and began shooing the longhorns away from the newspeople. But it was too late to get a good photograph.

Feather rode up to Kelly and Gerald.

Gerald immediately swung the camera around, training it on the pint-size cowboy.

Seeing the lens aimed in his direction, Feather doffed his hat, posed, and smiled real pretty. The camera snapped. He winked at Kelly. "The boys back in

Juanita will never believe this . . . my picture bein' in the newspaper."

Later, Charley was dismounted, holding his horse by the reins. He chewed hard on his tobacco cud, contemplating something nearby.

The entire herd surrounded him, having come to a standstill, held up by a four-strand, barbed wire fence.

Feather rode up, reining to a stop.

"What's the holdup, boss?" he asked.

Charley pointed to the fence.

"You're lookin' at it, Feather."

Feather squinted down Charley's finger.

"You talkin' 'bout them li'l ol' rusty pieces a' barbwar?" he inquired.

Charley nodded.

Feather dismounted in a jump, fished through his saddlebags, and brought out a pair of rusty old wire cutters.

He clicked them a couple of times for Charley to see.

"Little barbwar never stopped us back in the old days, now did it?" he said with a twinkle.

"Nope," answered Charley. "Because there weren't no barbwire back then."

Feather moved in to do his snipping.

It only took a few moments before the wire was cut between two posts.

Feather went on to make another few cuts and the fencing dropped to the ground, leaving a space large enough for the cattle to pass.

"Will ya lookit that," beamed the knee-high night herder. "The ol' fence just up an' fell apart."

They both remounted.

"We don't want to go starting any range wars,"

Charley said with a chuckle. "After they're all through the hole," he told the little cowboy, "get Sleepy and Lucky to help you restring that wire. Savvy?"

Feather tapped the brim of his hat, wheeled Chigger around, and galloped through the herd to help the other cowboys haze the longhorns toward the small opening he had just created.

Rod was working alone beside a farm to market road, keeping any strays from crossing the narrow dirt strip.

A large horse-drawn carriage pulled up behind him; the driver nudged the team over to the side of the road next to the young Indian.

Pike leaned out of the window.

"Well, Lightfoot," he said sarcastically, "I wasn't sure whether you'd still be here. I haven't read about you in the newspaper."

It was obvious that Rod didn't feel comfortable being seen in the company of Pike. He reined his mount around and, with rope in hand, hazed a wandering maverick back in the direction of the herd.

His horse jumped and reared as he turned its head back toward the carriage, a hoof coming dangerously close to Pike's cigar.

The meat packer ducked back.

"Geezes," he yelped. "What are you doing? Trying to kill me?"

"Oh, no sir, Mr. Pike," the youthful Native American answered blandly. "But I still want you to know I'm a part of them, just like I told you I was. But I—"

"Good going, kid," said Pike, cutting him off.

Rod had been ready to call off his association with

the meat peddler, but he was unable to get the right words out.

"Just keep doing whatever you're doing, Sitting Bull," Pike continued. "I'm in the process of calling in an old favor I'm owed . . . *a political favor.*"

Pike couldn't help laughing to himself. "By this time next week," he went on, "that herd will be one hundred percent, grade A beefsteaks and on its way to becoming authentic, mouth-watering, Eastern restaurant specials."

Before Rod could reply, the meat packer nodded to his driver and the carriage jerked away in a cloud of dust. The clatter of the horses' hooves plus the rumble of the carriage wheels overrode the peal of Pike's contemptuous laughter.

Rod watched after the departing vehicle, feeling quite miserable about his covert involvement in Charley Sunday's longhorn cattle drive.

After a few moments, Feather rode up, reining in a few yards down the road.

"Hey, kid," he called out to Rod. "Better get on through the hole in the fence; we're about ta close 'er up."

Melwood G. "Feather" Martin

by Kelly King

"If I hadn't been so dang small when I was born I suppose I wouldn't a' got the name Feather stuck ta me right off like I done," says Feather Martin, a cowboy on the Colorado to Texas drive. "'This'n here's a real featherweight,' the midwife that helped birth me was supposed ta have said when she picked me up fer the first time. Thank God they didn't call me Tiny . . . though there's bin times when some ranahan or another has called me that. 'And a loud one, too,' the midwife added. Because I came into this world cryin' like a bullet-shot coyote.

"I was born in what eventually became Spofford, Texas," says Feather, "down the road from Juanita. Back then it was just a gatherin' place fer poor pioneers that settled there 'cause they had run out a' money all at the same time. They had nowhere else ta go. But I lived in Juanita nearly all my adult life . . . 'ceptin' the years I was off ta war fightin' them damn Yankee S.O.B.'s. We still had ta do battle with them danged yellow-bellies again after the war was over when we came home. Once the great General Robert E. Lee signed them surrender papers the danged carpetbaggers swarmed inta Texas like the locusts done ta Egypt. Only thing that kept me out a' one of their makeshift jails back then was on account

a' my association with the Rangers. First thing those
lousy Lincoln-lovers done was ta close down the Rangers
and start a state police force of their own. My daddy died
fightin' 'em. I lost a couple a' brothers who got inta the
mix, too.

"I sure was glad when us Rangers was called back ta
full duty. That allowed me ta work again with my friends
Charley and Roscoe fer a spell. The three of us busted up
some pretty well-organized criminal outfits over the
years. I'm told there's a cell block in the Texas State Penitentiary at Huntsville dedicated to the three of us . . .
Naw, I'm just jokin' about that . . . but if they ever was
gonna build some add-on sections at Huntsville, namin'
one of 'em after the three of us would be all right by me.
We sure did send a heck of a lot a' bad actors down ta
Huntsville Penitentiary over the years."

After a brief pause, Feather continues, "Before I joined
the Rangers and met up with Charley an' Roscoe, I
worked my granddaddy's farm outside a' Spofford for
him. My granddaddy had been wounded severely in a
battle with Comanche raiders back in the early part a' this
century when Texas was still a part a' Old Mexico. They
shot him up badly, they did . . . with arrows. So bad a
friend a' his had ta cut off his left arm and leg. He worked
that land fer a long time on his one crutch 'til there
wasn't much left of him to be a farmer anymore. So his
son . . . my daddy . . . took it upon hisself to volunteer me
for the job. I worked on granddaddy's farm from the time
I was seven 'til I turned seventeen—even though granddaddy had passed on when I was twelve, I believe.

"At age seventeen . . . that was when I seen the notice
nailed to the local general store's bulletin board askin' fer
volunteers fer the Texas Rangers. I had a fella write ta
my daddy fer me tellin' him the farm had bin left to him
in his daddy's will. Then I signed those rangerin' papers
and never looked back."

Feather says he spent some time in San Antonio. "Then

they moved me up ta Amarillo for a spell. That's where
I run inta Charley Sunday fer the first time. Some of the
local Indians that'd bin sent off inta Oklahoma Territory
as punishment for burnin' down a pastor's privy thought
they'd jump the reservation and ride back to their old
huntin' grounds to see if there was still any buffalo left
below the Canadian River. That's when me an' Charley
was assigned ta move them Indians back north inta Oklahoma Territory. Durin' that little escapade was when we
met Roscoe Baskin fer the first time. Roscoe'd been del-
egated to move them Indians, too . . . only by a different
Ranger district. Anyhow, the two of us joined up with ol'
Roscoe and betwixt the three of us we rounded up them
renegades an' took 'em all back to their reservation
where they belonged.

"I'll bet by lookin' at me you'd never guess that I had
me a wife once . . . not no white woman, mind ya, but a
Indian squaw. I loved that woman, I did, but her older
brother found out about us and instead of dyin' like a hero
fightin' fer her honor, I just give her back to her family
when the brother and five other family members showed
up one mornin' to revenge my marryin' her without her
pappy's permission. We never had any papooses . . . that
I'm aware of. She was a mite chubby so when her brother
came fer her, I wouldn't've bin able to tell if she was with
child or not."

This cowboy's story continues. "I bin workin' on and
off as a cowhand fer over half a' my life, it seems. It was
never steady work . . . but whenever I could catch a herd
headed north that wasn't in conflict with my rangerin'
duties or the other important things that come up in a
man's lifetime every now and then, I'd take to the saddle
an' follow cattle instead of outlaws for a spell.

"The danged likker caught up to me a few years back
and fer a while there I thought I might become the town
drunk of Juanita, Texas. That never happened though, because Juanita already has a town drunk. And when a little

town like Juanita finds out it's got more'n one town drunk in their midst, havin' a town drunk stops being fun to 'em and wakes 'em up to the fact a' how easy it could be fer any one of 'em to be the town drunk. Honest to God, Kelly," he tells me as an afterthought . . . "I ain't even had the thought of whiskey in my head ever since we started this drive. I must be blessed, or somethin' similar. I bin thinkin' I might even go to a church service with Charley and Roscoe when we get back ta Juanita. On second thought, maybe that'd be too much fer them ta handle all at one time."

CHAPTER TWENTY-ONE

A couple of days went by without too much difficulty as the longhorns moved passively through the picturesque Colorado countryside.

Kelly and Gerald sent their daily reports back to New York by telegraph, telephone, and the good old U.S. Mail, while the drovers continually wore themselves to a frazzle pushing the three-hundred-head longhorn herd relentlessly—and with an understaffed crew.

By nightfall, all anyone could do was chow down as quick as they could, set out their bedrolls, and fall asleep. Morning—which was usually four a.m.—came before a person could blink.

The average American Joseph and Josephina, whether they were local- or national-news followers, were getting to know "Charley Sunday's Texas Outfit" pretty well. There were at least two Extra editions per week in most syndicated newspapers on the longhorns' progress, with Kelly having written the details. And a fairly good amount of the readers were beginning to buy every edition with astute regularity.

Charles Abner Sunday sat near the campfire, cleaning his old Whitneyville Walker Colt.

Roscoe was finishing up the supper dishes nearby, while Buster caught forty winks on a horse blanket beside Charley's feet.

One of the Colorado cowboys, Sleepy, played a pleasant tune on his harmonica, while the other two snoozed.

The news syndicate wagon was gone. Rod, Kelly, Henry Ellis, and Gerald were nowhere to be seen.

After a moment, Feather rode into camp, dismounted, and slowly walked Chigger over to where Charley was sitting. He appeared to be just a wee bit agitated.

Charley glanced up. "Feather?" he said out loud, just a little startled to see the undersized cowboy back in camp. "Who's minding the store? Aren't you supposed to be riding first shift nighthawk?"

"That Injun saddle-slicker was 'sposed to relieve me, boss," Feather whined.

Charley took out his pocket watch, then checked the time.

"Not until ten o'clock, he ain't," said Charley, spitting a stream of juice into the fire where it sizzled and steamed. "Besides, I let Rod and Kelly take Henry Ellis back into that town we passed by today so they could take in a minstrel show. Gerald, the photographer, took 'em all in his traveling photography darkroom. He had some developed photographs he needed to mail back to New York."

Charley spun the gun's cylinder, then began to reload each of the .44-caliber's six chambers with the required fifty grains of black powder, followed by the conical lead bullets he had made himself.

"They'll be back soon, Feather," he said. "Don't you be worrying your suspenders off over it if they are just a little bit late. If they are, I'll send one of the Colorado boys out to spell you."

He winked at his old friend. "A man gets along in years like you, Feather Martin, he's entitled to a warm corner when it starts getting chilly."

Before Feather could remount, a gruff voice boomed out of the darkness: "Hold it right there! *And* drop the gun, Tex!"

All heads turned as two badge-wearing county sheriff's deputies stepped into the campfire's light, their weapons trained on the old cowpunchers.

Buster's ears perked: he let out a seasoned growl.

The head deputy nodded to Sunday.

"Call off the dog and drop the gun, cowboy," he commanded. "I said, *drop it!*"

Charley nodded to Buster and the dog backed away, then he looked down at the old Colt.

"This here thumb buster?" he asked politely. "Would you mind at all if I just set her down gently? She's a family heirloom . . . an antique that's been with me for a lot of years."

The deputy nodded.

Charley carefully put the Walker aside.

The deputy stepped in closer, pulling an official-looking document from his shirt pocket.

"I have a warrant for your arrest," he said. "*All* of your arrests."

Not that much later, Charley, Roscoe, Feather, and Buster sat side by side on a lower jail cell bunk, all looking very depressed.

"Ain't that eatin' the drag dust," mumbled Feather, "a couple a' Colorado badges gettin' the bulge on three Texas peso packers like us."

"That's *ex*–peso packers," said Charley, correcting him. "We're all retired, remember? None of us has worn a Ranger star in ages."

"Must be somethin' personal, too," said Roscoe. "They let them Colorado rawhiders ya hired off the hook. Neil said they'd stay at the camp an' let Rod an' Kelly know where we were when they got back.

"Oh, an' by the way," he added, "one a' them deputies that arrested us told me that whoever got the judge ta sign that warrant was only interested in *us three*."

Buster's ears perked again—he let out a warning bark.

"That's right," said a voice from behind them. "Just *you three*!"

It was Sidney Pike.

He stood outside the holding cell with a deputy sheriff at his side.

The three Texans stood up slowly, turning around.

Charley pointed for Buster to stay on the cot—the dog lay down, putting his chin on his forepaws.

The men moved over to the bars. Charley squinted at the slick little city dude standing beside the law officer.

"Who in the hell are you?" asked Charley.

"Sidney Pike, of Pike's Meatpacking Company," the dubious businessman answered with more than a little self-importance. "*I* asked Judge Procter to issue that arrest warrant myself."

Charley eyed the man up and down, then he turned his look to the deputy.

"You're a lawman," he said. "It can't be legal. It doesn't matter who signed it."

Pike cut in.

"Oh, it's legal, all right. Judge Procter just happens to be a very old and dear personal friend of mine, Mr. Sunday," he boasted. "It just so happens that you're right in the middle of Procter's judicial district at this very moment, so, it's all official. Believe me, it's legal," he snickered.

Charley still directed his question to the deputy.

"What in the devil are we being charged with, then?" he asked.

The deputy shrugged, turned away.

Pike took out a cigar, bit off the tip, and made his point with his usual saccharine smile.

"It doesn't really matter, cowboy," he said. "Not in Judge Procter's county. You see, right now, my dear old friend, *His Honor*, just happens to be drawing up an injunction that will temporarily quarantine those longhorns . . . *and* hold you three right where you are until he can come up with something, shall we say, more permanent."

"*And,*" mimicked the now steaming Charley, "what're we s'posed to do until then, sit here makin' horse-hair bridles? What's gonna' happen to my longhorns 'tween now an' then?" he added.

Pike edged in close and whispered, "Judge Procter will order the cattle moved back to *my* pens in Denver, right beside *my* slaughterhouse." He winked at Sunday, then smiled wickedly. "Just in case," he added.

On that note, Pike turned abruptly, walking away. The deputy followed right behind.

Charley gripped the steel bars, calling after the departing meat packer.

"Those are *my* longhorns you little pip-squeak, and you know it!" he shouted. "You touch one hair on those

hides an' . . . *Pike?!!* You're a goddamn thief, damnit!
A goddamn cowardly, little thief!"

The outer door clanged shut and the cell block was
quiet once again.

Roscoe turned to Charley.

"Don't let it get to ya, C.A.," he told him. "Little slick
sum'bitch like that could put anyone on the peck."

Sunday began to pace.

Roscoe and Feather followed suit, step for step.

Buster, still lying on the cot—chin on paws—began
following his master's movements with his eyes.

Finally, Charley stopped. He turned to Roscoe and
Feather with irritation in his voice.

"Will you two quit tailing me like two mule-footed
horses to a sway-back mare?" he asked. "I got me some
serious thinking to do. And that's a fact!"

An hour later, the chuckwagon, which used to be
Charley's old buckboard, was tied off in front of the
county sheriff's office.

After a moment, the front door opened and Charley,
Kelly, Rod, Henry Ellis, Roscoe, and Feather moved
down the steps—followed by Buster.

Feather walked his horse over and tied him to the
rear of the chuckwagon. Then he climbed into the bed
behind the driver's seat, the dog bounding in after him.

Henry Ellis hesitated, then he turned to his grandfather who was tightening Dice's cinch. "Can I ride in
the chuckwagon with Uncle Feather and Buster?" he
begged.

Charley winked at his grandson.

"Go ahead." He smiled. "Just sit down and keep your
feet and arms inside, all right? Roscoe's going to ride

in the back there with you," he added. "Rod and Kelly will be up front. Rod'll do the driving."

Roscoe helped the boy up, handing him off to Rod on the seat of the wagon—then he climbed in himself.

Charley helped Kelly climb up to the passenger's side of the seat.

"Excuse me, Miss Kelly," said Charley, "but how did you do it? . . . Get us out of there, I mean."

Kelly smiled coyly. "Pike was still here when Rod and I arrived," she explained. "He was very polite and made it clear just what was going on . . . *and* that the judge was his 'personal' friend. So, I just told him that *I* had a personal friend, too . . . and that *my friend* was Joseph D. Sayers, governor of the great state of Texas."

Kelly handed some of her notes through a window to a telegrapher in a small town somewhere near the southeastern corner of the state of Colorado. The man moved over to a table and sat. Then he began tapping out her message in Morse code.

The telegraph wires hummed with Kelly's electronic words.

At the headquarters for the National News Syndicate in New York City a man listened to Kelly's written phrases in Morse code, writing them down on a piece of paper as fast as they came over the wire.

A company typist transcribed Kelly's story from the piece of paper to a typed page. Then more telegraphers sent the words on to the syndicate's nationwide city desks.

Finally a large number of printing presses rolled out finished newspapers for the multitude of fascinated readers who waited anxiously for the next episode of Kelly's cattle drive story to brighten their day.

* * *

Between innings at a big-city baseball field situated in a downtown area—and only moments after the excited crowd had finished singing several songs of the day—the announcer's voice rang out through a large stationary megaphone.

"Ladies and gentlemen," he began. "I have the latest update on Charley Sunday's Texas Outfit from the National News Syndicate's Kelly King." He flipped through a stack of papers in front of him, then cleared his throat. He read: "The longhorn cattle are in the Oklahoma panhandle today, just miles from their home turf in Texas. They should be crossing the Texas state line before week's end."

The numerous baseball fans jumped to their feet, cheering. Within moments, enthusiastic applause began to build throughout the pulsating throng.

CHAPTER TWENTY-TWO

Before dawn in a light mist, Feather Martin was rein-whipping his horse, Chigger, hell bent for leather toward camp.

Since it was just before sunrise, there were only a few of the outfit's drovers up and dressed for work, getting a head start on the lineup that waited for Roscoe to finish cooking breakfast.

Heads turned as Chigger's galloping hooves and Feather's yelling grew closer and closer.

Charley was in the process of securing his bedroll while Henry Ellis and Buster were doing their business on opposite sides of a clump of bushes a few yards downwind from the chuckwagon.

Feather slid Chigger into the center of the campsite, skidding on the horse's rear end across a thin layer of mud. The words he had been shouting during his hurried ride back from the herd's location were finally understandable.

"Blue Bell!" he was shouting. "Blue Bell is missing!"

He dismounted in one spectacular leap, then kept on running and shouting until he ran smack dab into Charley who was on his way to greet him.

"Blue Bell! Oh, my," Feather kept repeating. "Blue Bell is gone, boss. He was there one minute . . . then he wasn't."

Charley grabbed the little cowhand by both shoulders and held on tight.

"What do you mean, 'Blue Bell's gone'?" Charley asked, "Who's Blue Bell?"

Feather was grasping for words.

"Your bull, bossman," said Feather. "Your bull is Blue Bell."

Charley finally had to take a real good grip on him. He physically turned Feather around so they could talk face to face.

"Hush, Feather . . . slow down, will you?" said Charley. "Now what's all this about my bull?"

Feather was still huffing and puffing, so it took time for him to relay the story.

"I'd just sung 'em all ta sleep," he said, "and I was nearly finished countin' 'em. That was when I noticed that Blue Bell wasn't there. He's gone, boss . . . and it happened on my nighthawk shift. It's all my fault!" he bellowed.

"Blue Bell?" said Charley. "Where'd that name come from?"

Feather dropped his eyes. "Uh," he began. "That's the name I gave him."

"You named my bull Blue Bell?" said Charley.

"I give 'em all names, Boss. It gets kinda lonely out there in the dark. I like ta have someone I know personally ta talk to. Ain't nothin' wrong with that is there?" he growled.

"Just you simmer down now, Feather Martin," said Charley . . . "Hush. I don't want you dropping dead on me. I got enough worries."

Charley turned to the others who had gathered

around the two of them. "After we chow down, I want everyone to saddle up and be ready to ride."

"We ain't gonna find him, boss," wailed Feather. "I already looked everywhere for him and couldn't find nothin' . . . hide ner hair. He's vanished, just like that little pea in a shell game."

"Go on, get yourself a cup of hot coffee, Feather," said Charley. "The rest of you do the same. And as soon as it gets light enough to see something we'll head out to search for the bull." He paused . . . "For Blue Bell. Henry Ellis," he called out. "Kelly . . . Gerald . . ."

Coming from entirely different directions, the three scrambled until they were standing in front of their leader. Charley went on:

"I want you three to stay here at the camp. Watch over our things until we get back. Everything I've been dreaming about and planning for won't work out at all without that bull."

Charley also had two of the Colorado cowboys stay back with the herd while the rest went off searching for the bull's hoofprints.

Rod was the one who found them.

"Over here," he shouted.

The others galloped over and circled the area on the ground Rod was shielding. Because of the light drizzle, the bull's prints were easy to identify.

"Those prints have to belong to the bull," said Charley. "There wasn't another set headed away from the herd except for Feather's horse's when he was galloping back toward camp. And those hooves were shod hooves."

"We all know the difference 'tween horses' hoof-prints and cattle hoofprints," said Roscoe.

"I know that," said Charley, "but maybe there's someone here that don't."

Lightning flashed, illuminating the area. Crashing thunder boomed shortly after.

"Well, what are we waitin' 'round here fer?" said Feather. "Let's get ta follerin' them tracks before the rain starts ta really come down or the lightnin' kills one of us."

The tracks led them into a narrow canyon. On the other end it opened up into a beautiful green valley.

As Charley and his men cleared the canyon's outlet, they could see smoke curling from the chimney of a small wooden shack.

Charley spoke to his men in a lowered voice. "It appears to me that our bull didn't run off by itself after all," he said.

"An' after seein' the likes of that ol' shack over there, I'd bet my bankroll that it was rustlers that run off with Blue Bell," said Feather.

"All right," said Charley. "Here's what we're going to do."

They followed Charley's orders precisely, dismounting and moving toward the shack on foot. Within minutes they had the small cabin completely surrounded. Everyone made sure their weapons were loaded and at the ready.

When Charley was sure they were all in position, he stepped into the open, facing the door. He called out: "Everyone inside the cabin step out with your hands up. We've got you surrounded."

The tinkling of a piece of silverware dropping to the

floor could be heard coming from inside. That was followed by a very long, silent pause.

Outside, Colt hammers were pulled to full cock while Winchester lever actions put the brass where it belonged.

The long moment continued—finally the door opened just a crack. A white flag—a soiled dinner napkin on a stick—was extended and waved. A man's voice called out from inside.

"If y'all think we done somethin' wrong," said the voice, "something illegal, against the law . . . well, yer wrong. I'll open this door wider if ya promise not ta shoot us."

"Go ahead, open up. We won't harm you," said Charley.

The door began to open wider until the figure of the man could be seen. As he stepped through the open portal with his hands up, his teeth held between them a large piece of dangling meat . . . cooked rare, with blood still dripping.

Behind him, sitting at a table with forks and knives in their hands, were a woman and three children chewing on pieces of recently cooked meat that had been sliced from a smoking carcass that was on a spit in the fireplace.

"I'll be danged, C.A." said Roscoe. "They're eatin' Blue Bell."

Henry Ellis, Kelly, and Gerald watched from near the chuckwagon as Charley and the others rode back into camp. With forlorn looks on their faces, the men dismounted and went about tying off the horses.

Charley saw his grandson beside the newspeople.

He immediately led his horse over to where they were standing.

"We didn't have any luck," he said. "No Blue Bell. Uh, that's the name Feather gave the bull. Anything happen here while we were gone?"

Kelly and Gerald exchanged looks.

Henry Ellis couldn't keep a straight face.

"Something sure did happen while you were gone, Grampa," he said. "Just take a look over there by the creek."

Charley took a few steps so he could see around the chuckwagon . . .

. . . and there stood Blue Bell tied to a tree, his tail wagging peacefully.

"I'll be danged," said Charley, scratching his ear. "Where in tarnation did you find him?"

"We were here in camp watching over our things like you asked us to," said Kelly, "and a little eight-year-old girl from that farmhouse down the road led the bull into camp and asked us if he belonged here.

"You boys were sure gone a long time looking for something that wasn't there," she said. "So what took you so long?"

"Oh," said Charley. "You might say we were invited to share some barbecue. Barbecued pork, that is. We ran across a family that'd just hunted down a wild boar that was tearing up the wife's garden and they invited the whole bunch of us to join them for a meal."

CHAPTER TWENTY-THREE

The drovers moved the longhorn herd across the open Oklahoma countryside—through some low hills, across a flat valley or two, and through several small creeks and flowing streams.

It was apparent by the growth of whiskers on the drovers' faces that they had not taken the time for a shave. They were trail worn, shorthanded, and very tired as they struggled to keep the longhorns moving.

The old and battered chuckwagon-buckboard stood silently at the side of the trail, its impatient horses' hooves pawing dirt. Roscoe, on his back in the dust, worked on the rear axle, while Kelly and Henry Ellis sat patiently on the seat.

Buster watched from the rear of the bed, peeking through an empty space under the seat. He was still tied securely near his ever-present water bowl.

Charley rode up, waving to Kelly and his grandson. Then he looked down at his grease-stained partner.

"Can you fix it?" he asked, tipping back his hat.

Roscoe glanced up, shielding his eyes with his hand.

"Sure I can, C.A.," he answered stubbornly. "Buck-boards weren't built to be as tough as chuckwagons . . . even with these replacement wheels and axles. All I need is enough spit, glue, an' balin' wire, an' I can repair anything. You know that, pard. I just wish we'd had the time to strengthen these axles better before we started out."

"So do I, Roscoe," said Charley. "But seeing how we didn't have the time, just get it moving any way you can, all right?" He reined his horse around. "We can't go without grub. Oh," he added, "try and catch up as soon as you can."

He spurred away, riding back toward the herd.

Charley joined Rod Lightfoot, who was hazing the cattle along on the left flank.

"You holding up all right?" he called out.

Rod stood in the stirrups and rubbed his rear end.

"First my blisters turned to calluses, now my calluses have blisters," he joked.

"Not much like lawyering, is it, son?" said Charley.

Rod answered with a painful chuckle, "No, sir, it sure isn't."

Charley laughed. "Now you know what you've been missing sitting at that comfortable desk job of yours."

Rod paused. Something seemed to be bothering him.

"I don't want to go back to doing what I've been doing, Mr. Sunday," he told the older man.

"Oh?" answered Charley, turning in his saddle.

"No," Rod went on. "I guess I don't know *what* I want to do, but—"

"I thought you were doing everything you could to become a lawyer," Charley reminded him.

"Uh, that's true," answered Rod, too embarrassed to make eye contact. "I guess I just don't want to ever get involved with someone like Sidney Pike again. I just don't like being around the man."

"Have you told Pike how you feel?" Charley asked.

Rod lowered his eyes; he shook his head.

"Not yet," he answered softly.

"Well, there are some things a man just can't run away from, son," said Charley. "Things a man has to face up to."

"Yes," said Rod, "I know."

"Used to be in Texas a man settled his own problems," said Charley. "But that was when due process was a bullet."

"Hey," Rod cut in. "I don't want to kill anyone."

Charley chuckled. "Oh, I know that, Lightfoot." He sighed. "Just reminiscing, I reckon . . . Just reminiscing."

The cattle drive moved across the Oklahoma Panhandle gaining ten to twelve miles each day.

With every night's campfire Kelly typed the next episode of her continuing story taken from her daily notes. Every other day, or so, Gerald drove the horse-drawn darkroom into the nearest town and telegraphed Kelly's words—then he mailed his developed photographs to the New York City National News Syndicate office.

Every night, Henry Ellis climbed into his makeshift bed in the chuckwagon, exhausted. Once there, he fell asleep and dreamed, and dreamed, and dreamed. Usually those dreams consisted of what went on that day with the cattle drive. But on other nights he would dream of his heroes—Wyatt Earp, Wild Bill Hickok, and . . . Doc Holliday.

CHAPTER TWENTY-FOUR

The mysterious rider was lean and mean.

He was dressed entirely in black.

A flat-brimmed hat shaded his wrinkled brow from the blistering sun.

The skirts of his long frock coat were pulled back, revealing twin, pearl-handled, nickel-plated Colt .45s, sheathed in matching, silver-studded holsters.

He looked as though he had just stepped from the pages of a Ned Buntline dime novel. He stared straight ahead with narrowed eyes as he rode persistently after the longhorn herd.

Feather saw him first. The man was following the drovers and the herd in the swirling dust kicked up by the cattle's plodding hooves.

The half-pint cowboy turned in the saddle and called to Charley.

"Hey, boss . . . over here," he yelled.

Charley intercepted Feather's shout and rode back in the little cowboy's direction, reining in beside the anxious little man.

Feather was pointing back toward the lone rider.

"That there fella's bin doggin' us real close all day,"

he reported nervously. "He's too dern close fer my likin'."

Charley took a good squint himself.

He tipped back his hat and said, "Well, it's a free country, Feather Martin. A man can ride back there and eat our dust if he's a mind to. We can't stop him from doing that, now can we?"

"Ain't ya even interested in him one bit?" asked Feather, scratching his head.

Charley spit a stream of tobacco juice.

"Nope," he said simply. "Our job is to just keep them cattle movin'."

A few minutes later, with Sunday back in the lead, the herd approached and passed a small sign that stated: TEXAS—20 MILES.

Fifteen minutes after that Roscoe, Kelly, and Henry Ellis—with Buster in the back—passed the same sign as they bounced along in the wobbly old chuckwagon, trying to catch up to the others.

Roscoe had to swing over slightly to avoid the dark-clad horseman walking his mount along at a steady pace in the center of the road.

As the chuckwagon passed the lone rider, Roscoe and the others took a quick glance and saw that the sinister-looking desperado was staring—with an odd, hypnotic gaze—straight ahead, completely unaware of the chuckwagon's presence.

With the cattle bedded down for the night, most members of the outfit were gathered around the chuckwagon, which served as both the cooking area and trail headquarters.

Some of the men were back in line for seconds, while others sat around scraping their plates or picking their teeth. They were listening to some harmonica music being played by Sleepy, one of the Colorado cowboys.

A campfire burned brightly in the moonless night. Behind the chuckwagon, a lantern shed its glow over the entire cooking area.

Neil enjoyed an after-supper cup of coffee, while Lucky joined Sleepy's harmonica, singing a cowboy song. The song they were in the middle of was "The Streets of Laredo—A Cowboy's Lament."

Gerald sat nearby, listening to the soft, western ballad.

Buster was curled up beside his empty food dish, already asleep—while Henry Ellis, Charley, and Rod relaxed beside the fire, sitting on several bedrolls nearby. They were watching Feather, who stood at the edge of the camp looking off into the obscurity.

Roscoe and Kelly dished out some of the remaining grub, spooning the beans onto four tin plates.

Roscoe walked over, serving the victuals to Charley, Rod, and the boy. He held up the final plate for Feather to see.

"You gonna just stand over there gawkin' at nothin' all night, Feather?" he called out, "or are ya gonna eat somethin'?"

Feather turned around at the mention of his name.

"Huh?" he muttered, his mind engrossed in other things.

"Beans is on," Roscoe told him. "I never knowed you ta miss a meal, Feather Martin."

Feather moved over to the chuckwagon, the ringing

of his spurs following along behind. He took the plate from Roscoe, then went over and sat between Rod and Henry Ellis.

"What are you looking for out there?" asked Rod.

"That fella that's bin follerin' us," Feather told him.

Kelly, standing by the chuckwagon, cut into the conversation.

"He's really got you spooked, doesn't he, Feather?" she said . . . "that mysterious rider."

The half-pint cowboy continued looking off into the night as he ate.

"Nasty," he said shivering. "That's how he looks. Just plain nasty."

"We saw some fella out on the road today," said Roscoe. "He was wearin' a black outfit an' carryin' a couple a' real pretty, matched Colt .45s. Looked like one of them ol' tintypes my mama used ta show off on top a' the mantel in the parlor."

"That's him!" yelped Feather, perking up. "Real spooky . . . Like a ghost or somethin' . . . Even spookier."

Henry Ellis was listening with his eyes wide.

Kelly laughed.

Charley put down his plate and stood up, moving away from the others. Then he turned.

"Feather, didn't I tell you to forget about that fella," he repeated, lighting his pipe. "Times are tough enough around here without you dreaming up more difficulties."

Charley walked away, moving into the darkness toward the herd.

The others watched after their trail boss as he disappeared into the darkness.

Feather forked in another bite.

"Ol' C.A. sure has bin rank lately, hain't he?" he said with his mouth full.

"Mr. Sunday's got a lot on his mind," offered Rod. "We still have a long way to go after we cross the state line into Texas."

"Well," said Feather, wiping his mouth with his long-underwear sleeve. "It still don't give him cause ta treat us like the hired help."

"Ahhh, stuff yer mule face an' hush up," Roscoe told him. "We *are* the hired help."

Charles Abner Sunday walked slowly over to where the longhorns had been bunched up for the night and stopped. With help from the glow of the campfire and lantern behind him, he fumbled in his pocket, finding another match.

He struck the phosphorus tip with his thumbnail and relit his pipe.

The sparks from the match illuminated Charley's bedraggled face for a brief moment—his features revealing a tremendous fatigue. He appeared to be drained of any strength. He looked as if he hadn't slept in days.

His eyes raised to the sky overhead.

"Willadean?" he said softly. "Put in a good word for us with the Man Upstairs, will you?" Then, after a long moment, "I miss you, Willadean . . . I surely do."

He puffed the pipe's embers alive, drawing in a deep wisp of the smoke. Charley squinted around at his herd—smoking, thinking—standing there all alone in the moonless night.

The lone rider eased his way slowly through the longhorns, reining up at a distance, silently watching the older cowboy with the pipe who had seemed to be talking to the cattle.

He waited some time—until the old man had made

his way back to the lighted area—then he continued on his way toward the small encampment.

Minutes later, Roscoe stoked the campfire as Charley sat nearby, going over his maps.

Rod sat on his bedroll, studying a law book; Kelly wrote in her notepad while she sat beside him.

Henry Ellis was already asleep in the bed of the chuckwagon.

Buster hadn't moved from where he slept by his bowl near the fire.

"When do ya think we'll hit Texas soil?" asked Roscoe.

Charley began folding the maps.

"Tomorrow morning, I suspect," he answered.

"Sure will be nice ta get home, won't it?" said Roscoe.

Charley nodded.

"Home's more than a bit further on down the line than the border up ahead, Roscoe." He chuckled. "Texas is a big state. Or have you forgotten that?"

Feather rode up on Chigger. He was about to go on nighthawk duty. He looked down at Rod.

"You gonna relieve me at midnight like yer supposed ta, Lightfoot?" he asked. "Or am I gonna have ta keep singin' to 'em 'til the sun comes up?"

Without looking up, Rod threw him a wave.

"I'll be there," he answered, turning a page.

"Hey, all of ya," Feather called back as he rode out of camp. "Just keep yer eyes peeled fer that ghost in black, ya hear?"

Before the undersized drover was clear of the others, a voice called out from the shadows.

"Hello the camp," it bellowed.

Everyone was startled—they all got to their feet.

Even Buster woke up.

Rod checked the hunting knife in the leather scabbard on his belt while Kelly hushed Henry Ellis, who had been aroused by the traditional call for entry.

After a moment of hesitation, the callous stranger in black stepped into the glow of the campfire. He was on foot.

His frock coat fluttered in an eerie gust of wind, revealing the pearl handles of his matched .45s.

The man, as Feather had told them earlier, was a ghostly sight indeed.

"Figgered you boys might have some extra grub ta spare," the man said.

"Come again?" asked Charley, cocking his head.

He bit off a chaw of tobacco, standing and then moving in closer to the new arrival. "Maybe if we knew who it *was* going to be breaking bread with us," he continued, "we might just have something to share with you."

The stranger walked into the center of the camp, his spurs jingling an ethereal tune.

Roscoe stood ready by the chuckwagon's tailgate, an iron skillet in his hand.

Henry Ellis's jaw had dropped at the sight of the man in black—and it had stayed that way.

Buster was too overwhelmed to bark.

From the edge of camp, Feather was pointing uncontrollably.

"That's him, boss," he shouted from his saddle. "That's him! *The Phantom Rider*."

The man threw back his shoulders, casual like, resting his hands on his guns.

"Holliday's my name," he let them all know, "Plunker Holliday. Maybe you boys heard a' me?" he added.

The men shook their heads slowly—they had not heard of him, and their expressions showed it.

Holliday continued.

"Does the name 'Doc' Holliday mean anything to you yahoos?" he asked them.

Of course they had heard of the legendary gunfighter. Their nods let Plunker Holliday know that they had.

"Uh, s-sure," stuttered Roscoe. "He an' Wyatt Earp kilt some fellas up in Dodge, didn't they?"

"Naw," corrected Feather. "It wasn't Dodge, it was—"

"*Tombstone*," said Holliday, waxing poetic.

"That's it," said Feather. "Tombstone it was."

"Wyatt Earp's brother was the marshal," said Holliday.

Charley tossed aside the maps he'd been folding.

"Which way are you headed, Mr. Holliday?" he asked the man.

Holliday answered with a gallant sweep of his arm.

"Wherever the sand blows free," he crooned.

"Ahhhhh," grumbled Feather. "That's pure corn."

Charley, ignoring the little guy one more time, stepped in closer to Holliday, offering his hand.

"Well," he began as they shook. "Why don't you go get your horse, unsaddle him, and tie him up at the picket line? You'll find some water and grain over by the chuckwagon.

"Ain't much beans left, I'm afraid," he added. "But I'm sure Roscoe over there'll let you lick the pot if you're as hungry as you say you are."

By six a.m. the outfit had eaten breakfast and saddled their horses. They had started to break camp and were about to begin moving longhorns once again.

Roscoe, in the chuckwagon with Henry Ellis and Kelly, drove off after the herd. Gerald, in the horse-drawn darkroom, followed. Roscoe called back to the others, "See y'all in Texas, boys."

Buster came bounding out of the bushes where he'd been doing his business. He caught up to the chuck-wagon and leaped over the side rail into the bed like a young pup.

Charley and the cowpunchers laughed at the old dog's accomplishment as they mounted their horses.

About that time, Holliday rode up.

"We ought ta make twenty miles today, at least," he told them all.

"Is that a fact?" said Charley.

"It is," said Holliday. "If these boys a' yours can work cattle like they say they can."

Feather erupted with, "Now you look here, Pistol Pete. Who are you ta be makin' fun of anyone? You probably ain't never even seen a longhorn 'til the other day."

Holliday leaned back in his saddle, offended.

"I'll have you know," he verified, "that I worked for the Tonto Basin outfit up Verde way."

"For how long?" asked Charley.

"Oh, not too long," Holliday told him casually. "Maybe a week or so."

"That's long enough," said Charley. "You can ride drag."

He swung his mount around with a swift kick to the flank.

"Let's move 'em out!" Charley yelled to his men. "Let's get 'em on the trail!"

Feather, Rod, and the other cowboys started off toward the cattle with Holliday right behind.

"Holliday," Charley called out. "That's the wrong direction."

"Huh?" said the man in black as he turned his horse.

"*Drag* means the tail end of the herd," Charley told him bluntly. "It's up to you to keep the laggers up with the rest of the bunch."

Holliday showed absolutely no embarrassment about his small error. He just swung around easily and rode off toward the rear of the herd.

Charley watched after him and chuckled. Then he rode off himself.

The longhorns moved on through the flat country with the men pushing them hard. All the while, Kelly kept writing to meet her daily deadline.

Charley rode to the crest of a small rise and reined up. He dismounted and knelt down, taking up a handful of dirt and then letting it sift through his fingers to the ground.

Feather galloped over, sliding to a stop.

"Trouble, boss?" he asked.

Charley stood up smiling and held out some of the dirt for the little cowboy to see.

"Texas soil," he exclaimed, "if I'm reading it correctly. It won't be long now, Feather Martin."

Like Charley, Feather's mouth grew into a wide grin.

"That's what the monkey said when they cut off his tail," he joked. "Mind if I tell the others?"

"We're pushin' longhorns, not monkeys, Feather," Charlie said, chuckling. "Sure, go ahead and tell everyone of 'em."

The pint-size cowboy took off his hat and twirled it in the air.

"Yaaaa-hooooooo!" he howled as he spurred Chigger back toward the approaching herd.

The American public was enthralled. They just couldn't get enough of Kelly King's reporting on the Colorado to Texas longhorn cattle drive.

They read about it in their private homes, in their favorite bars and restaurants, in village shops, in large editions, in small-town papers, in the backseats of expensive carriages, on horseback, and even in Flora Mae's pool hall.

On the front page of the Juanita *Centennial*, there was even a full-page photograph of the outfit beside an Oklahoma-Texas border sign, with the herd grazing behind them.

Kelly's continuing saga began below the photo:

"The longhorns . . . *and* the Texas Outfit," her words began, using the special term she had coined for Charley's band of misfits, "are finally back on their own soil. Back where they belong, back in the state of Texas where the longhorn initially had its beginnings.

"Earlier today I talked with Mr. Charles Abner Sunday. I've spoken with him before as you know. He's the leader of the band of Texas old-timers responsible for getting the longhorn cattle this far. A fine group of respectable gentlemen with whom I have had the pleasure of traveling the past month, *and* whom I have also gotten to know as if they were members of my own family."

There was a smaller photo of Charley astride Dice.

Kelly's commentary continued.

"I asked Mr. Sunday if he was feeling really proud of himself."

"Proud ain't the word, Miss Kelly," he answered with

reserve. "Just makes a fella grateful he's a Texan, that's all."

"Now that you're in your home territory," I asked him, "what will you be looking forward to?"

Sunday shook his head and said, "Well, the toughest part's still ahead of us, I suspect," he told me. "Texas is a mighty big state."

"I then asked him this question: You'll be facing *much* bigger odds from now on, I'm told . . . rougher terrain?"

"Well, ma'am," Charley answered, "they did it back in the old days as a matter of everyday survival. I don't suppose we're any that much different from our ancestors, do you?"

"It appears that you're headed in the approximate direction of Amarillo," was my next question. *"Am I to assume you plan on going around the city? Amarillo is a very large and busy metropolitan area, Mr. Sunday."*

"Yes, it sure is a big one," Charley affirmed to me. "But going all the way around Amarillo would put us way behind our schedule. As long as we have the good Lord on our side, Miss Kelly," he added, "I'm sure we'll get cooperation from the city folks . . . same as we have from the country ones."

That evening Kelly let Charley know that the American public was totally enthralled with his Texas Outfit. Because of her employer, the newspaper syndicate, her series of articles were now running daily in nearly every big city and small town newspaper in the entire country—not to mention that a European newspaper syndicate had already picked up rights to the continuing story.

"The American people are reading all about your cattle drive, Charley," she said, "from those who dine in the ritziest restaurants in New York City to the ones who fight for scraps behind the sleaziest dockside joints on San Francisco Bay."

CHAPTER TWENTY-FIVE

The longhorns converged onto a main dirt artery that led toward the West Texas panhandle city of Amarillo—its turn-of-the-century, developing, metropolitan outline etched against the yellow sky in the near distance.

Coming down the roadway toward the cattle drive was a cluster of men on horseback.

Charley, riding point as usual—and on this particular day with Henry Ellis at his side on a borrowed horse, plus Buster at their feet—raised his arm so the others, directly behind him, would stop the herd.

The horsemen drew closer.

Charley squinted to see if he might recognize who they were.

"Who are they, Grampa?" asked Henry Ellis.

"Looks to me like a whole danged militia," grunted Charley, pulling on his nose.

The group of riders turned out to be eight Amarillo law enforcement officers—uniformed policemen.

As they neared the herd, they slowed considerably, coming to a complete stop directly in front of Charley, the boy, and the dog—all of whom, it appeared, were blocking the law officers' way.

The Amarillo city police chief, backed by the uniformed officers, reined in facing Charley, his eyes wide at the sight of the longhorns so close to his municipality.

The chief stared cautiously at Charley and his grandson. Henry Ellis had dismounted and now held tight to the growling Buster's collar.

"Morning, officers," said Charley, beating them to the punch.

The chief shook his head, whistling.

"Whooee," he declared. "There sure are a lot of 'em, ain't they?"

He looked at Charley.

"With all that newspaper coverage you and your boys have been gettin'," he said to Charley, "it seems like the whole danged state has turned out to see you and your 'horns,' mister. I've got folks lined up on both sides of the streets, so try an' keep 'em bunched up as best you can."

Charley scratched his nose, puzzled.

"You mean you *ain't* gonna try and stop us?" he questioned.

"Hell no, cowboy," answered the police chief. "If I did that, the mayor'd have my badge. No-sir-ee-bob" he went on. "We come out here as an official escort for you, Mr. Sunday. So many people showed up in the last day or so, we'd be the crazy ones *not* to let you fellas bring those longhorns through our city. Business is booming."

Charley nodded his thanks, then he turned to Henry Ellis.

"You ride back and tell the others, will you, son?" he asked the boy.

"You bet, Grampa," said Henry Ellis as he swung into

his saddle, wheeling his mount around and spurring away toward the milling cattle. Henry Ellis shouted to the others as Buster sprinted after him, barking his head off.

Charley stood his ground at the front of the herd, nodding every so often, smiling at the well-groomed law officers—even so, he seemed to be just a little self-conscious of his own shabby appearance.

The police chief had been right on the button. The people had indeed turned out in throngs.

Out-of-towners and locals alike lined the sidewalks.

Smiling faces were everywhere—some waving from upper-story windows, while others had climbed lamp poles for an even better view.

Newspaper photographers were all over the place, gathering images as the longhorns were herded slowly down the city's main street, following their police escort.

An equestrian unit separated the cattle from the citizenry at curbside. Children and adults waved small American and Texas flags, while a high school brass band played "The Eyes of Texas Are Upon You."

Kelly and her photographer, Gerald, were busy reporting the event on notepad and film along with several other newspaper crews—some of them from foreign countries.

Colorful banners added to the festivities. Some of the pennants read: WELCOME HOME TEXAS LONGHORNS, while others thanked THE TEXAS OUTFIT for doing such a fine job.

Charley, Rod, Feather, and Henry Ellis rode along with the cattle through the streets of Amarillo. The Colorado cowboys, along with a few local hands, kept the livestock in tow as they were paraded before the spectators in what was beginning to resemble a rollicking pageant.

Each and every member of Charley's crew waved and smiled back at the cheering crowds, while Roscoe drove along slowly in the chuckwagon with Buster yapping on the seat at his side. Having taken on several attractive local girls as passengers, the outfit's one-and-only "Cookie" was having the time of his life.

Finally, when all the cattle had moved on past the multitudes, Plunker Holliday brought up the rear—still riding drag.

Though dust covered and dog tired, the old gunfighter nonetheless managed to sit a proud saddle, occasionally pulling back the skirts of his coat to show off his matching six-shooters to those who had remained until the very end.

The crowd loved Holliday—they really did—responding with applause and cheers alike.

Near an Amarillo city park, several blocks ahead of where Holliday was displaying his prowess, was a recreational area, where the crowd had thinned out quite a bit. Charley still rode at the head of the cattle drive. Henry Ellis had fallen behind him by more than a few yards.

Charley had just entered a grassy square with the longhorn leaders on the pavement directly behind him.

By now, a good distance away from his grandfather, Henry Ellis continued to wave and smile at everyone he passed.

Two older looking boys giggled from a nearby sidewalk, making fun of Henry Ellis as he rode past them. After a moment, one of the youngsters removed a homemade slingshot from a rear pocket, set a small pebble in the pouch, then fired the undersized missile in the boy's direction.

The projectile struck the rump of Henry Ellis's horse, causing the animal to plunge and jump.

Henry Ellis grabbed for the saddle horn, holding on for dear life as the frightened beast broke away from the herd, bucking awkwardly across the street toward an open expanse of lawn.

Rod Lightfoot had been riding along several horse lengths behind. He was laid back, enjoying the parade, but closest to Henry Ellis. It was Rod who saw that the boy was in deep trouble way before anyone else did.

He spurred out after the frightened lad as fast as he could, just as Henry Ellis's horse slipped, then scrambled through a parting crowd of spectators on the far sidewalk.

The youngster let out a shriek as his horse began to run.

Rod continued to race after him in hot pursuit.

Feather, who had nearly passed the park square, immediately saw the drama that was playing out on the grass.

"Hey, boss!" he yelled over to Charley, "runaway! It's yer grandkid!"

Charley heard Feather's warning and snapped his head around.

From his position, he couldn't see a thing.

On the other side of the trees that were blocking Charley's view, Rod reined his galloping steed in beside Henry Ellis's frightened horse, reaching out, then scooping the boy from the saddle.

In moments, he had slowed both horses and stopped.

He lowered Henry Ellis to the ground.

Rod was dismounting himself when Charley and Feather rode up.

Charley swung down, taking his out-of-breath grandson in his arms.

"It's all right, son," he comforted. "Everything's all right . . . You're gonna be just fine."

Henry Ellis pulled back just enough for Charley to wipe a small tear from his cheek. The old man hugged the boy closely.

Henry Ellis looked up to Rod who was standing nearby.

"Rod saved my life," he told his grandfather, "didn't he?"

"That he did, son," assured Charley. "He sure did."

Charley stood up slowly, holding his trembling grandson in his arms.

"Maybe you better ride in the chuckwagon with your uncle Roscoe for a little while," he suggested. "At least until we get on through the city."

Henry Ellis nodded his accord.

"But not forever?" he said.

Charley shook his head, tousling the boy's hair, kissing him on the cheek.

"Not forever," he answered, smiling softly. "Only until we get through town."

When the boy tightened his hug on his grandfather, Charley had his first chance to make eye contact with Rod. He silently nodded his sincerest gratitude.

Rod accepted the gesture without a word.

CHAPTER TWENTY-SIX

As usual, Buster was sound asleep.

Roscoe was busy cleaning up after another supper of armadillo stew, beans, and sourdough bread, Rod and Kelly talked softly near the chuckwagon, and Feather was out riding nighthawk again.

Sleepy's harmonica music drifted across the still night air as Holliday practiced his fast draw, clicking off silent shots at a make-believe enemy.

He reholstered his left .45 and quickly drew the right—fanning the hammer. Suddenly the gun fired:

KA-BOOM!

Buster sat bolt upright, the hair bristling on his neck.

The log near Rod's and Kelly's feet literally exploded into a shower of splinters. They jumped back in complete disbelief.

Charley ran over, followed by an extremely concerned Roscoe.

Out with the herd, Feather rode among the uneasy longhorns, speaking low, reassuring words to the anxious animals.

Back at the camp, Holliday stood frozen, staring quizzically at the smoking Colt in his quivering hand.

Totally bewildered, he moved slowly over to Roscoe and Charley.

Charley took the gun, checking its cylinder, extracting several shells. He checked them out before handing the pistol back to Holliday.

"What in the devil are you doing packing live ones?" he asked. "Are you crazy?"

Holliday toed the dirt at his feet, fearing Charley's wrath.

"I-I reckon I forgot t-to take 'em out," he stammered.

Charley held up one of the unspent cartridges, squinting, examining it closer.

"Snake shot?" he asked the old gunfighter.

"I had me a trick-shootin' gig up in Cheyenne," he told Charley. "I shot supper plates outta the air. Snake shot makes it real easy ta hit the target . . . 'Specially when a man's gettin' on in years . . . Like me."

"Your *pistola* going off like that could have spread the herd over half this county," lectured Charley. "If you're going to pack them irons, Mister Holliday, then keep 'em holstered—*and* empty. That's an order, mister."

Holliday looked away, his lower lip quivering like a small child caught with his hand in the cookie jar.

When he finally did look up, he found himself staring at Charley. And Charley was staring right back.

Holliday quickly turned his eyes to the others. With all he had in him, he tried to smile—instead, he shrugged.

About then, Feather rode into the camp and dismounted.

"What's goin' on?" he asked. "Sounded like some gunfire poppin' off over here."

He glanced over to Holliday who was jamming his pistol back into its holster, still not daring to look anybody in the eye.

After several long moments, Holliday's eyebrows quivered and he began to speak—slow and easy.

"You folks think I'm just a silly ol' coot, don't ya?" he chortled, pushing back the skirts of his coat nervously.

He turned, taking a few steps back, then he spun around quickly on his heels to face the group again.

Holliday smiled an evil, all-knowing smile. His eyes darted from one face to another—one eye squinting awkwardly in the light of the flickering campfire, the dancing flames creating unpleasant shadows across his furrowed brow.

"I helped kill the Clantons," he told them flatly.

Holliday did not wait for a reaction. He whirled around quickly once again—a three-hundred-sixty-degree spin—pointing a finger at the entire group once more.

"I woke up that morning to a knockin' on my door," he continued. "I had me a quick shot a' red-eye . . . ta quiet my cough."

He coughed.

"It was Wyatt Earp!" he snapped. "He an' his brothers had bin havin' some trouble with some local cowboys—the Clantons an' McLowerys. They was waiting for the Earps up near Fly's photography studio close ta the O.K. Corral."

He made a slow circle, then began talking once more when he was facing the group again.

"I finished the whiskey an' said . . ." He coughed again. "Wyatt . . . so help me, I'm goin' with ya.

"I picked up my scattergun, an' Wyatt thanked me," he went on. "We was old friends from Dodge City, ya know. Oh," he waved a gloved hand, "we'd had our differences, but we was still amigos.

"It was quiet in Tombstone that mornin' as we walked down Front Street toward the corral," he told them. "We stopped the other side of the boardin' house . . . me, Wyatt, an' his brothers, Morgan and Virgil. An' there *they* was . . . Ike and Billy Clanton, the McLowerys, an' that worthless sheriff, Johnny Behan. That lousy lawman was backin' that worthless pack a' wolves. Ya see, the sheriff was out to get Wyatt, too."

Holliday stepped wide of the campfire, resting the heels of his hands on the butts of his guns.

"We faced off," he continued, bending his knees, his eyes wide. "It was a cold silence . . . us lookin' at them, an' them lookin' back at us.

"Wyatt called out ta Ike, tellin' him he was under arrest. Then Ike, he called a name back ta Wyatt.

"Billy went for his gun, and all hell broke loose! *BLAM, BLAM, BLAM!!!*" Holliday fanned the air.

"Singin' lead an' whistlin' bullets filled the desert air," he told them. "Black powder smoke," he said, "so thick a man could a' cut it with a Bowie knife swallered up the entire town.

"Finally," he concluded, "the air cleared some, an' we could see 'em all layin' there on the cold, hard ground . . . all dead . . . all of 'em layin' in pools a' bright, red, glistenin' blood. Except Ike," he said . . . "That fool coward had slipped away durin' the battle."

Roscoe raised an eyebrow.

Holliday dropped his look to the ground. The others followed his gaze.

"It was all over," he testified solemnly. "An' that's the way it happened. That's the *whole* story."

He drew in a deep breath, letting it out slowly.

"Then the crowd would applaud," he added. "An' we'd take a bow."

He grinned.

"Then the fellers on the ground would get up an' they'd bow, too."

The others were beginning to react, showing more than skepticism.

"Yes, boys," Holliday finalized, "that's the way it went, two shows a day, seven days a week . . . in the Buffalo Bill Wild West Show . . . in the year 1892."

With that, Plunker Holliday walked slowly over to his bedroll and sat down. He lay back, pulling his hat brim over his eyes. All the while the small group watched in a state of bemusement.

"Night, boys," Holliday said simply. "See ya when the birds chirp."

As the truth of the matter began to sink in, the group couldn't stop staring at the lanky pistolero.

"Ah, heck," muttered Roscoe. "He's just one a' them fancy-pants, stage-show gunfighters. Kinda tetched in the head, too, I imagine."

Charley smiled, then he lit his pipe.

"Maybe," he said with a wink, "maybe not." Then he moved off with Henry Ellis. Buster followed along behind.

Chapter Twenty-seven

1960

"I'm hungry," said Noel, interrupting her great-grandfather's story.

"Me too," said Caleb.

Evie said: "How about you two . . . Josh . . . Grampa Hank? I have some TV dinners in the freezer."

"OK by me," answered Josh.

"Yeah," said Hank. "I could use a bite. You got a roast beef and gravy?"

Evie got up and headed for the kitchen one more time.

"Was Plunker Holliday a real person, Grampa Hank," asked Josh, "or did you just make him up?"

"Oh, Holliday was real, all right," said Hank. "He was just a bit tetched, as Feather would have said. That means Holliday was slightly off his rocker . . . just a little bit crazy. But most of the time you couldn't have asked for a gentler person."

"And they let him carry real guns?" asked Caleb. "My teacher says people with mental defects shouldn't be allowed to own guns."

Josh cut in, "Your teacher also told you that no one at all should own guns."

"She has a right to her own opinion," said Caleb.

"Only if she tells you it's her own opinion in the first place," said Hank.

"Did he really work in Buffalo Bill's Wild West Show?" asked Noel.

Hank said, "The man told us he did. No one questioned him about it. You never questioned a man's word back then. You might have just got your head shot off."

"Remind me not ever to question you again, Caleb," said Josh.

Caleb answered his brother with "I'll remind you even if you're not questioning me."

Noel cut in.

"Stop it, both of you," she said. "Or I'll tell Mommy."

"The boys aren't doing anything wrong, sweetheart," said Hank. "They're just having fun with each other."

"Mommy doesn't want them fighting," said Noel. "It sounded to me like someone was starting a fight."

"Go play with your dolls," said Caleb, "and leave Josh and me out of it." He turned to his older brother. "Sorry, Josh. I didn't mean anything by that . . . honest."

Their mother entered the room.

"OK," she said. "Dinner's almost ready. Who's going to set up the TV trays?"

Both boys jumped up and went to a nearby closet, where they found five TV trays. Caleb was in charge of setting up the trays while his brother, Josh, rearranged some furniture so they would still be facing their grampa Hank while he continued telling his story.

"Back in my day," said Hank. "Dinner was what you call lunch nowadays. The evening meal was called supper, not dinner. Breakfast was still called breakfast any way you want to look at it."

After everything had been set up and everybody was in their respective chairs, Evie entered from the kitchen with a large tray containing five steaming TV dinners.

"Noel?" she asked. "Can you give me a hand with these? And make sure Grampa Hank gets the one with beef and gravy."

"Then, as soon as we're all ready to eat, Grampa Hank can continue with his story."

CHAPTER TWENTY-EIGHT

Just as dawn was breaking and the outfit was finishing up breakfast, Feather came racing into camp on Chigger shouting, "We got some horns missin' . . . Some sneaky SOBs run off with some a' our cattle durin' the night . . . an' I never seen nor heard 'em do it at all."

Charley and Rod ran up to Feather as the little cowboy dismounted.

"Who was it, Feather?" said Charley as he was nearly run over by the little man's fast movements.

Charley grabbed him by the collar of his vest and yanked, stopping him in his tracks.

"Like I said . . . I didn't see nothin' and I didn't hear nothin'," Feather went on. "I only realized they was missin' when I was takin' my end-a'-shift count just a while ago."

"You say you didn't see or hear anything?" asked Roscoe, who approached still drying one of the tin plates. "Tell us the truth, mule face. Were you sleepin' on the job?"

"Don't you go accusin' me a' sleepin' on the job, Mister Nap-All-Day Pot Banger," said Feather, flashing his anger. "If you ever had ta nighthawk fer just one time, you'd fall asleep before the sun went down."

"Just hold on, you two," interrupted Charley. "Feather says we got a bunch of longhorns missing. You two can finish your fight after we find those missing cattle, how's that?"

He turned his attention to Feather. "You got any idea of what direction they might have run off to? And how many are we talking about, exactly?"

"Well," said Feather, "I follered their tracks just so far an' I'd bet money they was headed due east. As fer how many are missin', by my count around thirty or so."

Thirty, Charley said to himself. *Damn . . . that's my ten percent.*

Then he turned so he was facing east and pondered some more. "Nothing off to our east except Palo Duro Canyon."

"How about tracks?" said Rod. "Did you happen to see any other hoofprints besides the ones made by the cattle?"

"If there was any," said Feather, "they sure wasn't wearin' horseshoes or I'd a' noticed 'em."

"Could they have bin Indians?" said Roscoe.

"Now don't you think if it was Indians I'd a' knowed it?" said Feather.

Roscoe shook his head. "'Course not. You was sleepin'. You couldn't a' seen nothin' if you was sleepin'."

"I was not sleepin'," said Feather.

"Was too," countered Roscoe.

"We're just wasting our time here," said Charley. "We'll leave Holliday and the Colorado boys in charge of the herd until we can find the missing longhorns."

"I'd like to go along with you," said Kelly. "I promise I won't be a burden."

"Me too," squealed Henry Ellis. I won't be a burden, either."

Charley started to show some displeasure. Then he caught himself and offered a suggestion of his own.

"Make up some sandwiches for Holliday and the Colorado boys, Roscoe. We'll take the chuckwagon along with us. It's better we don't suffer from empty stomachs while we're searching out there. Having no food along with us could hamper our search if we're out more'n one day. Now, for those of you who ain't saddled up yet . . . saddle up!"

Both Henry Ellis and Kelly got a little help from the men, saddling up.

Feather led them all to the place near the rear of the herd where numerous longhorn tracks split off from the rest of the herd and started heading due east.

They all dismounted and studied the ground surrounding them. It was decided that the small trace of horseshoe prints they did find were the ones previously left by Feather when he followed the longhorns' trail for a short distance that very morning before reporting the disappearance to Charley and the others back at the camp.

"All right," said Charley, "let's spread out some. There may be a maverick or two got separated from the cattle that broke off, too."

He swung into his saddle.

"Now, let's get moving," he said.

The others mounted—after that they spread out, following Charley.

* * *

A mile or two later Henry Ellis galloped over to his grandfather, reining up.

"What's on your mind, son," said Charley.

"Me an' Kelly found some more tracks over there," he said, pointing back to where Kelly was waiting.

Charley could see that Rod and Roscoe had already dismounted and were studying the ground. He spurred Dice out and rode over to the others.

By then, every member of the search party had become curious and had ridden over to where the group was reassembling. Not one of them said a thing as Charley and his grandson rode in and dismounted, joining them.

Roscoe and Feather were on their knees following Rod's finger as he pointed out the differences in the newly discovered tracks.

"Mr. Sunday," said the young Indian as Charley and the boy moved in closer. "Those're horse tracks all right . . . only they don't belong to Feather, and they certainly aren't Indian ponies . . . because they appear to be wearing shoes."

"Tell him about the other ones," said Feather.

"We did find two sets of horse tracks back aways that are unshod. At first I thought they were Indian ponies, but now I'm not so sure."

By then Charley had dismounted. He also knelt down to look at the tracks for himself.

Henry Ellis was right behind him, down in the dirt at his grampa's side.

Kelly stayed in her saddle, watching over the goings on.

"These look to me to be shod horses," said Charley. "I never reckoned that Indians . . . or anyone else, mind you . . . would think that thirty longhorn steers, out here, all by their selves, were running free . . . or just left to fend for themselves. Look," he pointed, "three of the unshod horses joined the thirty right over there, but the cattle don't change direction one bit."

Rod said, "But the two unshod horses we tracked were with the cattle the whole time. Do you think it could be white men and Indians working together?"

"Looks ta me like whoever it is are drivin' 'em to Palo Duro Canyon fer sure," said Feather. "Maybe they got a camp down in there."

"Naw," said Charley. "The JA Ranch has owned damn near all the land in and around Palo Duro Canyon for years . . . ever since Charles Goodnight and John Adair partnered up to found the JA Ranch back in '76. Over the years they've been buying up the other Palo Duro ranches to enlarge their spread. And please believe me when I say that not one Indian has set foot in that canyon since 1874. That was when the U.S. Army was ordered in to remove all the Indians that had settled there and send 'em back to their reservations in the Indian Territory. No," he went on, "if there're any cattle in Palo Duro Canyon . . . they belong to the JA Ranch."

Rod stepped in closer. "So there's already a ranch in Palo Duro Canyon, that's fine with me," he said, "but the evidence is right there in front of us . . . the tracks show us that five horsemen, two of them without shoes, are now herding thirty of our longhorns straight into Palo Duro Canyon."

"Well then," said Roscoe, "what are we all standin' here wastin' time fer? We need to be follerin' them tracks to wherever they're gonna lead us."

"Roscoe's right," said Charley, standing, then lifting Henry Ellis back into his saddle before remounting himself. "The only way to figure this out is to continue on doing what we're doing."

He reined Dice around. The horse made a small circle while the others remounted. Then they all moved away, following the cattle's hoofprints, which were still headed due east.

No more than fifteen minutes later, while they were still following the breakaway longhorns' tracks, they came across the JA Ranch. They could see the spread from where they sat horseback about a mile away.

"Y'all keep up the search," said Charley to the others. "Me and Henry Ellis'll go on over to the ranch and pay 'em a visit . . . find out if anyone's seen our missing longhorns."

Several JA cowboys were breaking in a string of mustangs when Charley and Henry Ellis rode up. Two of the men watched as a big palomino mare bucked her rider off in mere seconds.

The other cowboys who were participating in the horse-breaking exercise gave the new arrivals several looks, but nothing that Charley found offensive or worth bickering about.

As the cowboy in the corral remounted the mare with the assistance of two other men, Charley called over to another ranch hand sitting on a corral fence.

"You boys seen any longhorn cattle hereabout this morning?"

The closest cowboy shook his head, scratching an ear, then rubbing his sunburned nose.

"I ain't seen nothin' but angus," he answered. "Angus is what we breed here on the JA. I ain't seen a Texas longhorn in years, mister."

"You don't suppose Mrs. Adair is home right now, do you?" said Charley.

The man took off his hat and wiped his brow with his sleeve. He chuckled.

"Not at this ranch house, mister," he said. "This ranch you're on now is just one of the original ranches in the area that Mr. Goodnight and Mr. Adair bought up for expansion. The JA is just too big now to have but one main ranch house on it, anyways."

"Like I said earlier," Charley went on, "we're looking for some lost longhorns. Do you think anyone would mind if we kept on following their trail? I got no idea where it's gonna take us."

"That's fine by me, mister. Just let me make a telephone call to the main ranch across the canyon over in the next county. I'm pretty sure it'll be all right with Mrs. Adair. She's stayin' here on the ranch until next week. Then she'll be off to Ireland and England to check up on her overseas properties."

As Charley and Henry Ellis tried to comprehend the vastness of the woman's holdings, the man added, "Longhorns don't look nothin' like angus anyhow. So believe me when I say that nobody on the JA spread will shoot you for rustling when you find your missing cattle."

The longhorn tracks belonging to Charley's ten percent of the herd led them next to a cattle trail that took them to the canyon's bottom. On their way down they passed several small herds of angus cattle being driven out of the canyon by JA cowboys.

When asked, these JA Ranch employees answered that they had seen nothing out of the ordinary on JA property that morning. When questioned about the longhorn hoofprints that were obvious to anyone who knew cattle, the JA cowboys could only shake their heads and mutter something like, "Them's sure tracks of a bunch a' unfamiliar cattle, but we still ain't seen no longhorns down here in the canyon. Only angus."

It kept up like that—the questioning of the JA cowboys, and the headshakes they always got in return.

Shortly after noon they stopped while Roscoe rustled up something for them all to eat. It was during this meal that Henry Ellis and Buster decided to go climbing to see what they could see from the higher bluffs that surrounded them.

Henry Ellis and Buster puffed their way to the top of one of the mesas and sat for a spell, catching their breath. It was during this break that the boy looked up to take in the view and saw the missing longhorns corralled in a blind canyon off a trace of a road by the river.

Going down the mountain was much easier than the climb to the top had been. But when Henry Ellis and Buster slid down the last twenty-five feet of shale on their rear ends to get to the area where the search party was eating their midday meal, Henry Ellis still had breath enough to say, "We seen 'em, Grampa . . . The longhorns! . . . They're right over there." He pointed. "Right down that way about a quarter of a mile or so."

As far as Charley could tell, his ten percent of the longhorns were being guarded by a gang of barely grown boys.

From his position behind a small outcropping of

boulders where he had positioned himself after se-
cretly approaching the cattle with the other members
of his outfit, he could only see two of the rustlers.

He caught a glimpse of Roscoe, who had concealed
himself on the other side of the thirty head of longhorns, and he raised two fingers to let him know the
number of rustlers he had in his sights.

Roscoe pointed to his left and raised three fingers,
meaning he had spotted three more rustlers near his
position.

Charley raised his look to a higher position on the
canyon's wall where Feather had settled in behind
some saplings. The pint-size cowboy had a view of the
entire steep gully containing the cattle. From there he
could see both Charley's and Roscoe's rustlers—there
were no more. He raised five fingers and made a slash-
ing movement across his throat, meaning five was all
he could see in total.

Rod, who was about to enter the small chasm on
horseback, read Feather's message from high on the
hill, so he knew in advance what they were up against.
First he nodded to Charley and got a nod in return.
Then he threw nods to both Roscoe and Feather.

He waited a moment or two, then spurred his horse
into the rift.

Rod's horse had taken no more than five or six steps
when a squeaky, teenage voice halted his progression.

"Hold it right there, mister . . . and drop any
weapons you might be carryin'."

Before Rod could do anything, Charley moved up
behind the rustler and dropped him with a tap from
the barrel of his old pistol.

Rod watched as his trail boss moved back out of
sight, then appeared again dragging the other uncon-
scious young horse thief.

After a few more seconds, Roscoe appeared—he had disarmed the other three boys and was bringing them over at gunpoint to join up with the others.

When they were all gathered at the entrance to the small gulch where the longhorns were being held, the two boys Charley had captured were just coming out of their stupor. Charley helped the one who had accosted Rod to his feet.

"Well, well, well, now . . . it looks like we've been chasing rustlers that're still a little wet behind the ears, don't it?"

Roscoe nudged one of his captives with the barrel of his Colt.

"What are your names," asked Charley.

"I'm Jeeter Richards," said the one who seemed to be the leader. "My friend over there is Eddie Parsons. These other three are just some Amarillo street kids we've been hanging around with lately who agreed to give us a hand when we told them our plan."

Roscoe stepped in closer.

"You better have a pretty good reason fer stealin' our longhorns," said Roscoe.

The cattle thieves were all standing together by then so Charley lined them up side by side. They all looked to be no more than a few years older than Henry Ellis.

"Who wants to spill the beans?" said Charley.

The one named Jeeter stepped forward. He appeared to be more embarrassed than frightened.

"We saw you and the longhorns when you drove 'em through Amarillo. At first we were just going to have some fun. We bet each other that we could steal some of the longhorns without getting caught. And when we saw that your nighthawk was sleeping in his saddle, we run off as many as we thought we could handle."

Roscoe threw an I-told-you-so glance Feather's way.

The smaller man looked down sheepishly.

Charley continued with his questioning.

"Where did you get your horses?" he asked. "I'll bet you right now that two of 'em ain't wearing shoes."

Jeeter cleared his throat.

"Me an' Eddie have never owned a horse . . . Our parents say we're too young for a responsibility that large."

Eddie, the other boy, cut in. "We went out on our own and roped some wild mustangs . . . broke 'em all by ourselves, and now we ride 'em bareback."

"We keep 'em out at Barlow's barn . . . it's been abandoned for years. These other guys hang out there . . . that's where we first met up with 'em."

"So you just up and decided to steal our cattle?" said Charley.

"We aren't rustlers, mister," said Jeeter. "We were gonna bring 'em, back . . . Honest we were."

Ed tried to back up his friend's statement.

"That's right, sir," he said. "We were gonna hide 'em here all day, then sneak 'em back into your herd tonight . . . when everyone was asleep."

"Includin' the nighthawk," said Roscoe, glancing Feather's way.

Feather glared.

"Naw," said Jeeter. "We figured it would be a lot easier to move the cattle we took in close to the rest of your herd, then the others, sensing that these long-horns were close by, would let 'em mingle in with the rest of 'em . . . all by themselves."

About that time, Henry Ellis and Kelly rode up to see what was going on.

When Jeeter and Ed saw Henry Ellis, they both turned away.

"Hey," said Henry Ellis, after getting a quick look at

the two boys, "those are the kids that shot at me with their slingshot back in the park."

Charley immediately turned again to the ruffians. "Is that so?" he said. "And to think I was about to let you and your friends off with only a warning. But now I think we'll be taking all five of you back to Amarillo and turn you over to the proper authorities. I reckon I don't have to guess about Amarillo having a juvenile court, because I somehow feel that all of you have been there before."

Later on that same day Charley and the other searchers came out of the main double doors of the Potter County Courthouse in Amarillo, stopping at the bottom of the steps to listen to Charley who had a few words to say to his grandson.

"Lying, stealing, and injuring others and their property don't ever get a person ahead in this life, son, as you just saw in that courtroom," he said. "The last thing I ever want to do is be any part of a blemish on the record of a child. But those boys gave up being children when they committed their first crime. And as we all found out from that judge, stealing our longhorns wasn't the first time those boys have been in trouble with the law.

"Now, c'mon," he said, "let's all get mounted. We got three hundred longhorn cattle that need every one of us."

They all went to their horses, which were tied in front of the county building, and mounted up. Just before Charley turned Dice around to spur away, he yelled, "Oh, I'll be needing to have a little talk with you later, Feather Martin."

The pocket-size cowboy was caught off guard

yawning. He turned to Roscoe. "What'd the boss just say?" he wanted to know.

This time, one of the rear wheels on the old chuck-wagon had stopped turning. Roscoe, beside his open toolbox, worked on the hub, packing it with grease. Buster was sprawled under the canopy in the bed of the chuckwagon, snoozing, while Kelly and Henry Ellis watched from the front seat.

Charley rode in and reined up.

"Again?" he questioned, tipping back his hat. "What's wrong with it now?"

Roscoe stood, wiping his red face with his necker-chief to rid it of some active perspiration.

"W-well," he stammered, "I don't rightly know, C.A. . . . This time the wheel up an' stopped turnin' . . . Period. I reckon it don't look that good at the moment, but I'm doin' my best."

"We'll be setting up camp in about an hour," Charley told his friend. "I'll send Feather back to give you a hand."

"I can make it on my own, by golly," maintained Roscoe with some visible frustration. "I'll be all right . . . an' I sure don't need no help from that pint-size saddle tramp."

Charley nodded, then he turned and rode off.

Roscoe wiped his hands on the neckerchief, and then he picked up the toolbox and moved around to the driver's side, climbing up beside Kelly and the boy. He slapped the reins to the team.

There was some heavy screeching but the wagon wouldn't budge. Roscoe stepped down from the seat and knelt by the offending wheel, totally frustrated.

About then, the herd began to pass the immobilized wagon. Roscoe stood up. He once again grabbed his toolbox and circled back to give his full attention to the wheel hub one more time.

That was when Plunker Holliday galloped over. He looked down at the sweating, exasperated Roscoe bent over the reluctant wheel.

"You can always ride a longhorn," he suggested with a chuckle. "I'll help ya rope one, if yer a mind ta."

He rode off after the cattle—laughing.

Roscoe watched after him. Suddenly he had an idea. He went to the side of the wagon and pulled two coiled ropes out of the tack box. "Henry Ellis," he said, "come here."

"What are you doing, Uncle Roscoe?" asked Henry Ellis.

"Never you mind, sonny," said Roscoe. "Go on, get on down from there an' gimme a hand."

Just as Charley had predicted, within the hour the herd was grazing, and the members of the outfit had a nice campfire going, though there was still no sign of Roscoe, Kelly, Henry Ellis, Buster—and the chuck-wagon.

Charley looked off in the direction from which the herd had come. He turned to the others with some concern.

"One of you better saddle up and go back an' look for 'em before it gets too dark," he suggested.

Feather countered with, "If that ol' chicken plucker said he'd be here, then he'll be here, boss."

"Chuckwagon comin' in!" echoed a familiar voice from outside the camp just moments later.

It was Roscoe—and he sounded like he was pretty close.

Everyone turned in the direction of the voice to see the old chuckwagon as it screeched and rumbled into camp—*but* it was not moving under its usual two-horse power. Two longhorn steers had been tied to the front of the wagon in makeshift rope harnesses—they were pulling as hard as they could alongside the two horses.

The wagon's team and the longhorn steers trudged along faithfully, pulling the chuckwagon behind them. Roscoe walked beside the wagon, urging the large creatures along, using the long rope ends as reins. Henry Ellis drove the horses from the front seat, a grinning Kelly at his side.

Buster had his front paws up on the back of the front seat, helping him to stand on his two back feet. That way, he could look over Henry Ellis's shoulder at Roscoe as he maneuvered the longhorns, just to make sure all was going well.

Charley and the others watched as the two steers helped pull what was once the rickety old two-seat buckboard into the center of the campsite.

Rod and Feather moved over to help stop them.

Roscoe tied off the rope-reins as Henry Ellis, Kelly, and Buster jumped down from the wagon seat.

Charley scooped his grandson into his arms, hugging him tight.

Rod moved over beside Kelly.

"That's one heck of a four-horse unmatched team you got there, Roscoe," Charley chided.

"Not much speed, either, Grampa," said Henry Ellis, laughing, "but they sure did the job . . . *and that's a fact!*"

Charley laughed from his belly. He reached over

and tousled the boy's hair while the others chuckled. Then he looked over to Roscoe.

"No luck with the wheel, huh?" he asked.

Roscoe shook his head.

"Threads are worn so thin we're lucky we didn't lose it back a ways," he told him. "I'll pick up some new parts in the next town we come to."

"Should be a junction with a blacksmith shop about eight miles up ahead," said Charley. "There ought ta be a little general store close by, too, if I recollect correctly."

"Good," said Roscoe, "'cause we're gettin' low on supplies, too."

That night, in numerous parlors across the nation, the final paragraph of Kelly's daily syndicated newspaper account of the cattle drive was being read aloud to countless children who had also become fixated followers of the colorful characters in Kelly's continuing story.

That day's tale had taken place somewhere on the road with the cattle drive. Kelly's final remarks for that particular edition concluded with the words:

The Texas Outfit will be moving off the main byways and into some pretty desolate country for the next week or so, and I'll be without my customary means of communication. But I will keep on writing and taking photographs. We'll get it all to you as soon as it's feasible.

Meanwhile back at the cattle camp, Roscoe continued to work on the wheels and axles of the chuckwagon by lantern light while Holliday slept beside him on someone else's bedroll.

Charley, Rod, Kelly, and Henry Ellis sat around the

campfire near the dozing dog. A couple of the Colorado cowboys—one who sang and Sleepy on his harmonica—performed a soft Western ballad that flowed through the camp.

When the song was over, the rattling of a newspaper drew everyone's attention to Feather.

"Hey, boss?" he called out, "can you give me some help with this word here?"

Charley looked up. "Word?" he said. Then he saw the newspaper in Feather's hands.

He got to his feet and moved over to where the little cowboy was sitting.

Several others followed out of curiosity.

"Where'd you get that newspaper, Feather," Charley asked.

"Oh, I found it on the side of the trail today," said Feather. "Some local cowboy must've used it to wipe his—"

"Feather," Charley called out, "remember we have a lady and a child in our company."

Feather showed his embarrassment. He handed the newspaper to his boss.

"Here, you read it. It's missing the last three pages anyway."

Charley called over to Roscoe, "Got my magnifier, Roscoe?"

"I done forgot it this trip, C.A.," said Roscoe.

"Here, you can use mine," said Holliday, handing Charley a pair of wire-frame reading glasses.

Charley put them on, then started back toward his bedroll. Suddenly, he looked up with a big grin.

"Hey," he called out, "there's a story in here all about us. And it wasn't written by Kelly."

Everyone else left what they were doing and gathered around.

Charley began reading out loud:

"The cotton fields, the Alamo, the Rio Grande River, and the badlands of the Big Bend Country—these are all historical settings in Texas."

He took a breath, but before he continued reading the story he said to them:

"It's all about the history of the longhorn and how its popularity has dwindled so much over the years that hardly anyone remembers what one looks like anymore."

Charley went on with his reading. The story changed and was now talking about how Charley and his Texas Outfit bid on a few steers and ended up with all of them—and how Charley decided to drive the cattle back to their home state exactly like it was done in the past.

Charley's face took on a grim expression when he came to the next paragraph of the story. It informed the reader about a local Texas cotton combine that had promised they would not allow someone's herd of filthy cattle to cross their pristine cotton fields due to crop risk, high loss, and property damage.

Right about then Charley ran out of pages to read.

Feather jumped in. "That's gotta be where the guy tore it off so he could—"

"That's all right, Feather," said Charley. "Spare us the details. We know what we're facing."

Charley was thinking. Still sitting upright, he puffed on his pipe.

"Shucks," said Roscoe. "I reckon the Ol' Boy Upstairs wouldn't listen if it was just *me* a-talkin' to Him."

"Oh, I reckon He just might, Roscoe," said Charley with his eyebrows raised. "You and me are made of the same leather, and He sure listens to *my* prayers."

Charley turned the pipe over and shook out the embers, tapping the bowl against his palm.

"Maybe you should give it a try," he added.

He looked at the ground. Then he looked at his friends around him. It was a long pause—then:

"We're going to have to cross those cotton fields, you all know that."

Kelly stepped in beside him. "Couldn't we go around?" she asked.

"'Fraid not, Miss Kelly," said Charley. "It'd be the middle of next winter before we got the herd to Juanita if we done that."

Charley stared into the fire. Finally he said,

"We're crossing those cotton fields tomorrow, no matter what."

Roscoe scratched his ear.

"Now, how'll we do that, C.A.?" he questioned, "if them cotton combine folks won't give us permission ta cross their land?"

"We're stopped right here dead in our tracks, ain't we?" said Feather. "There ain't no other choice."

Charley kept staring into the fire, but now his jaw was set—annoyance was building inside.

"What do you want me to do?" he asked impatiently. "Spell it out for you? . . . Draw you a picture?

"Permission or not," he told them all, "we're crossing them cotton fields *tomorrow,* and no one's going to stand in our way. *No one!* And that's a fact!"

CHAPTER TWENTY-NINE

Early the following morning—on a dusty, flat, West Texas, cotton combine plantation, surrounded by acres and acres of the fluffy, white bolls with stalks sowed deep in the dark Texas soil from horizon to horizon—a cluster of hired workers milled around an official T&T Cotton Combine wagon.

Mel Porter, the cotton combine's muscular foreman, stood firmly in the bed of the large horse-drawn vehicle talking to the assemblage through an outsized megaphone.

"I just got the news from our higher-ups," he was saying, "there'll be a fifty-dollar bonus to any man who'll help me keep that herd of cattle from crossing T and T Cotton property."

The men discussed the offer among themselves, a low murmur running through the gathering.

Some called out:

"I'm with ya, Mel."

"Count me in."

"We'll stop 'em, brother."

"They won't get past us."

"All right, let's do it."

And other things similar.

"All right then," the foreman went on. "Y'all spread out across the road," he ordered. "I don't want an army of boll weevils to be able to get past you men."

Carrying pieces of wood and pipe as clubs, plus ax handles and other tools as weapons, the cotton workers moved to take up their positions blocking the road.

"Some a' you boys cover the fences," commanded Porter. "And some a' you others protect the seed bins. The rest a' you stay here and back me."

More than a few of the workers complied with the foreman's order.

Porter stepped down from the bed of the wagon and moved to the passenger side of the vehicle where Sidney Pike, the Colorado meat packer, was sitting. He leaned over, making eye contact with the foreman, smiling greedily.

"Very good, Mr. Porter," he said.

"Forget the compliments," grunted the foreman. "Just don't forget, we have a deal."

"You'll get your money," said Pike. "Just stop that herd . . . Any way you have to."

Someone yelled, "Here they come!" causing Porter to glance back up the road. Porter quickly returned his attention to Pike.

"You comin' with me?" he wanted to know.

"Not right now," answered Pike with a cowardly smirk. "It'll look better if you handle this alone."

Porter nodded, then moved over to where his men stood impatiently watching as the cattle approached in the near distance.

Charley's small crew kept the longhorns moving toward the makeshift roadblock. Charley, Rod, and Feather could see the cotton workers up ahead, blocking their path.

Roscoe pulled the old chuckwagon to a stop as Kelly and Henry Ellis squinted through the morning haze.

Buster, in the wagon's bed behind them, had his paws on the back of the front seat, also keeping an eye out.

Charley spurred his horse on, loping ahead of the herd, reining up in front of the blockade created by the irate cotton workers.

Mel Porter stepped out in front of the others, facing the old cowboy.

"You've gone as far as yer gonna go, old man," Porter warned.

Charley ignored the man's threat as he glanced around at the incensed expressions focused on his presence.

He dismounted slowly, moving over to face off with the foreman and the cotton workers.

He tipped back his hat, casually spitting some tobacco juice at Porter's feet.

"You boys have some kinda gripe with me?" he asked solemnly, pulling on his nose. "Because if you do, and it's a fight you're looking for, me and my outfit are ready for anything you might want to throw our way."

No one, including Porter, would answer.

"Look," Charley continued, "I ain't searching for trouble. I'm just trying to get my cattle home, that's all."

Porter sized up the older man.

"There's no tellin' what could happen if those cows stampeded," he told Charley. "Hell, they could wreck everything it's taken us years to accomplish here."

Charley shot back, "That's pure hogwash! They ain't gonna stampede unless *someone* stampedes 'em."

"That's what *you* say, old man," countered Porter. "But I say that cattle *and* delicate cotton fields spell nothin' *but* trouble."

"My longhorns have come over five hundred miles

without a lick of trouble, mister," said Charley, "no matter *how* you want to spell it."

"Well, you sure got trouble now, cowboy," replied Porter, drawing a small-caliber pistol from his belt.

He thumbed back the hammer, firing a shot into the air.

The cattle spooked slightly at the gun's sharp report, causing some of the longhorns to bawl uneasily.

Rod, Feather, and Roscoe moved cautiously among the restless steers, trying to quiet them.

At the rear of the herd, still in his position as drag rider, Plunker Holliday was also aware of the gunshot.

He spurred his horse around the herd, galloping easily toward the confrontation at the front of the drove.

Roscoe stood near some steers, talking gently to the animals, as Holliday thundered by.

For some reason, Roscoe instinctively knew that things would soon be under control.

At the front of the herd, Porter had the gun trained on Charley.

"*Now*," he was telling him, "I'd say you was stopped, old man."

Holliday rode up, stepping down from his stirrup while his horse was still in motion—at the same time sliding the horse to a butt-skidding stop.

He adjusted his gun belt, slowly walking over to, then standing beside, Charley. Holliday showed no fear—he was just as calm as he could be.

He touched the brim of his hat.

"Mr. Sunday," he said in a nonchalant, monotone voice.

Charley smiled softly, also touching his hat brim.

"Mr. Holliday," he acknowledged. "This here fellow, and those men of his over there, are aiming to stop us from crossing this here cotton patch. What do you think about that?"

Holliday looked at the large assembly of cotton workers, his squinting gaze finally falling on Mel Porter and the smoking revolver he held.

Ever so slowly, Holliday stepped between Charley and the foreman.

Unhurriedly, he thumbed back the skirts of his coat, revealing the mother-of-pearl handles of the Colts.

Porter looked this mysterious stranger up and down.

"Well now," he joked, "who do we have here, Wild Bill Hickok?"

Holliday's left eyebrow began to quiver—his one good eye grew wider and wider, while the other continued to squint.

"You got just ten seconds ta make up yer mind, *sonny boy*," he warned.

Porter chortled. "Make up my mind about what?"

"On whether ta use that little peashooter yer holdin'," he slowly challenged, "or ta put it where the sun don't shine."

Holliday's hands slid to the butts of his matched weapons.

Porter was no longer smiling. He didn't quite know how to take this man dressed in all black.

For the next moment or two it became a staring match.

"You don't look so tough to me, mister," said Porter, talking through gritted teeth.

Holliday continued to eye the foreman. He began to pull off his black leather gloves—one finger at a time.

He turned to Charley with a sly grin on his face, speaking loud enough for Porter to hear.

"Sort a' reminds me of the time Sam Bass pulled on

me," he recalled. "I shot 'im dead six times 'afore he hit the dirt."

He tucked the gloves into his belt.

Porter turned to Charley.

"You'd better get this cockeyed half-wit outta my way," he demanded.

"Oh?" said Charley, tilting his head. "I think Mr. Holliday knows what he's doing, all right . . . and he means what he says, you know."

He raised an eyebrow, adding, "And that's a fact!"

Porter looked over to Holliday one more time.

The old gunfighter's one walleye appeared to roll in its socket as he stared back at the foreman.

"Now," Holliday said bluntly, "I'm gonna turn my back on ya, an' then I'm gonna step off twelve paces. Mind ya," he went on, "I can hear a fly land on a cotton boll at fifty yards, so, if ya get ta feelin' froggy, just go ahead an' try me."

He spun on his heels and began marching slowly back in the direction of his horse.

He stopped after twelve strides, his back still turned away from Porter.

Holliday drew his .45s, one at a time, spinning each of the cylinders as if he were checking the bullets. After that, he twirled the heavy Colts, dropping them back into their holsters at the same time.

Only then did he turn to face the confused foreman, still holding his hands barely a horsehair's width above the hammers.

Out of the side of his mouth, he cautioned Charley.

"You best step outta the way, Mr. Sunday, I'd hate ta see you get hit by one a' *his* wild shots."

Charley didn't quite know what Holliday had up his sleeve, so he stepped back slow and easy.

Holliday, both hands at the ready, squinted even harder at Porter.

"Any time ya feel the itch, amigo," he told the man, "just let 'er rip. It's all up ta you now."

Porter's smile was long gone, erased completely from his troubled countenance. Still holding the small pistol at his side, he looked to Charley for help—then back to Holliday.

"Now you look here—" he started to say.

Holliday was really living the part. He was at center stage, enjoying every golden, dramatic moment.

"Draw, or back off," he challenged, "one or the other."

Porter coughed—he looked around at his men nervously.

"Hell," he sputtered with a hollow laugh, "we don't wanna kill nobody, do we, boys? I can't see no harm in lettin' these men and their cattle cross the cotton fields."

The workers mumbled to each other, then they began moving away.

Porter turned and started to follow them.

He only got a few yards before Holliday called out to him.

"Just where do you think you're goin', amigo?" he asked.

Porter stopped in his tracks. He tucked the pistol back into his belt, then turned to face the gunfighter once again.

"Why, nowhere," he floundered. "I—"

Holliday was still standing—legs apart—hands at the ready.

"I'd say you owe Mr. Sunday here an apology," he told the cotton boss.

Charley moved in closer to Holliday, whispering harshly into his ear.

"I asked you not to load them guns."

The old gunfighter whispered back, "They *ain't* loaded." He whispered again, "But *he* don't know that."

Charley sighed to himself.

"Go on back with the others, Holliday," he said in a very low voice, "before he gets wise to your game."

Holliday continued to stare hard at the burly foreman, then he slowly turned and walked back to his horse.

Holliday mounted with a simple swing into the saddle. He wheeled around and rode off back to the herd.

Charley crossed over to where Porter was standing. The foreman had decided he could hold his own with Charley, now that Holliday was out of the picture.

"You just cost me fifteen hundred dollars, old man." Porter swore. "Now I'm going to make your life as miserable as you just made mine."

"That'll be the day," Charley countered as he delivered a pounding left to Porter's jaw, sending the foreman staggering back, almost falling.

Charley squared himself, ready for more. Both fists were now clenched.

"This old man," he began slowly, "has plenty more where that came from . . . *if* you're feeling up to it."

He spit some tobacco juice on the ground at Porter's feet.

Porter charged at Charley like an enraged bull, and the fight was on.

The two men crashed to the ground, rolling over and over, each trying to take advantage of the other's weaknesses.

Porter pulled Charley to his feet, hitting him hard in the stomach.

The old trail boss doubled over.

But before Porter could deliver an uppercut, Charley drove his head into the foreman's midsection.

Gasping for air, the beefy Porter staggered backward.

Charley was on him in seconds, swinging a roundhouse right that sent Porter flying backward before he went down.

Rod, Feather, Kelly, Holliday, Roscoe, and Henry Ellis could see the fight from their positions near the longhorns.

I sure hope I ain't lost my touch, thought Charley while Porter was getting to his feet. *I'd hate to look like a loser in front of Henry Ellis.*

Porter took a wide swing.

Charley blocked the punch, driving his right fist straight into the big man's nose.

Blood sprayed everywhere as Porter grabbed his gushing snout with both hands.

The big foreman watched the runny red goop pour out through the cracks between his fingers. He looked over to Charley.

Charley Sunday seemed annoyed, he stood ready— battered and roughed up—but still with mucho fight left in him.

All Porter could say was, "Oh, my God, ya broke my nose."

Charley started for the man again, but Porter backed away quickly, holding up a hand up for Charley to stop.

"I've had enough," Porter cried out. "It wasn't my idea to stop you anyways. Pike!" he squawked, "it was him started all the trouble. He's the one that got the combine owners all stirred up in the first place."

Charley stopped in his tracks.

"Pike?" he questioned. "That little, piss-ant, con

artist, SOB? . . . The Colorado meat packer? . . . Here in Texas?"

Porter was pointing to his wagon.

Charley turned—then he walked slowly over to the foreman's vehicle.

When he got to the passenger side, he looked up cautiously.

And there he was, the squirming maggot—Sidney Pike—in all his manipulating glory, crouched low, almost under the seat, trying to hide as best he could.

His quivering hands were clasped together like a parish sinner asking for forgiveness.

When he realized he was being observed, he looked down slowly with a very weak smile, trying to cover his face.

Charley stepped on a spoke and reached up, dragging Pike down roughly from his perch.

"N-now you look here," Pike stammered and sputtered.

Charley paid him no mind. He drew back, ready to smack the little worm.

"I'm sorry, Mr. Sunday," Pike yelped. "You can't blame a man for trying."

"Sorry don't cut it, Mister Pike," replied Charley. "But I can sure blame a man for trying *too* hard."

He relaxed his cocked fist.

He loosened his hold on the smaller man, shoving him back against the company wagon.

Turning, he walked back to his horse, mounted, and rode off toward the herd and his outfit.

As he passed Mel Porter, the defeated man called out, "Mr. Sunday?"

Charley stopped; he reined Dice around.

The foreman moved up to him now, holding the bloodstained handkerchief to his nose.

"You know," he began slowly, "I've been punched and stomped a whole lot a' times before, but I never fought a man like you."

Charley thought a moment, then his eyes began to twinkle.

"I suspect," he said as he chuckled softly, "that's because you never fought a man who had so much to fight for."

He touched the brim of his hat.

"And that's a fact!"

ROSCOE BASKIN

by Kelly King

"I was born on a cattle drive," says Roscoe Baskin, partner to Charley Sunday, foreman of his ranch, and chief cook and bottle washer—along with me, Kelly King—on the Colorado to Texas longhorn drive. "My mother was traveling to a larger town with my daddy where they had a doctor in residence," Roscoe went on. "The little town they were from had no one to assist in birthing babies, not even someone with a midwife's knowledge. The only way to get to this other town safely was to tag along with a small cattle drive where there was men with muskets.

"This was in the 1820s, in Ohio's Scioto Valley, and they only drove cattle for short distances back then, I've been told . . . within the state and sometimes to neighboring states. I was born right there on the trail, so I've never had a real place to call my home."

I asked Roscoe how he met Charley Sunday. "Me and Charley have been together for so long I forgot just how we did meet. But I'm sure it was when we was Rangers together. The Rangers weren't that big of an outfit back then . . . so you pretty well knew everyone who was serving when you wore the badge.

"Me and Charley . . . and old Feather Martin were assigned a few cases together and we done good. Our superiors decided we made a good team so they kept us three together for a long, long time."

Says Roscoe, "I was never married, you know. I reckon I just couldn't find the right woman . . . or one who could cook to my likin'.

"I killed only four men in my time with the Rangers," he says. "Some people say it don't count if they was Indians or Mexicans or Negroes, but believe me, a person drawing down on you is still a man trying to take your life. So I say it don't matter what color he is if he's the one trying to kill you. That's why I count those four I done in as honest-to-goodness brave men. Being born a white man don't ever make a person any braver when he's chosen gunplay as his life's work. That's why those I killed were undeniably brave men in my book."

Besides myself, Roscoe let Charley's grandson, Henry Ellis, help him with the cooking and other chuckwagon chores during the longhorn drive. "I've known that little button since he was the size of a . . . little button," Roscoe says about the boy. "He's always bin a good kid . . . You know that, Kelly. Minds his manners, always willin' ta give his all . . . And he attends church on a regular basis, or so his grandfather tells me. Besides, I need him there to keep a watch on you so you don't go messin' with my daily menus."

Roscoe continues, "Now, Feather Martin and me have been best of friends on and off for a lot of years. Besides the both of us fightin' on the same side during the War Between the States, he's always been a good drinking buddy, too . . . until a few years ago, that is. When he showed me he can't be trusted to handle the stuff anymore. He ain't touched even a sip since we been on this drive, though. Maybe some of the things that were botherin' him inside don't seem so bad now that he's been sobered up for a while."

Roscoe told me that he enjoys working for Charley.

"Charley an' me 're supposed to be equal partners when it comes to the ranch, because I helped him out one time by lending him a few dollars to pay part a' his mortgage. But it never did really seem fair to me . . . me becoming half owner in his spread just for lending him a few dollars. That's why I help out around the place. Charley's still the ranch owner is how I look at it. I can only do what I can for the man who's remained my only true friend for all these years."

Were you ever a cowboy yourself, I asked him. "You mean, did I ever drive cattle like these other yokels around here . . . ? Sure I did," he said. "But when I was cowboyin' I watched all the others complaining all the time about the hours and conditions out on the trail so I decided to become a cook instead. As the cook you're up early every day and you can spend some time by yourself with no one else around. Same as when you're driving the chuckwagon . . . gives you time to think, or just day-dream. My bedroll stays inside the chuckwagon . . . only this time out I gave up my sleepin' spot in the wagon to Henry Ellis. Even though, I've never been the type who enjoys sleeping on the ground."

What are your feelings about outsiders? I asked him. People like Holliday, the Colorado cowboys, and Rod and me? "I reckon I never gave that much thought," he says. "I've always said that if a man . . . a person," he corrected himself, "could pull his . . . or her . . . own weight, then I had no complaining to do. Just as long as they don't grumble about my cookin', I'm fine with everyone I meet."

What makes you happy? I asked Roscoe. "A good stove, a comfortable bed, a hot meal, and nothing to in-terfere with my sleepin'," he answered.

CHAPTER THIRTY

Back in open country again, the cattle were progressing slowly down a long draw, low hills on each side. Roscoe, now on horseback, rode to the front of the herd, joining Charley and Henry Ellis. Buster followed at their heels.

"Uncle Roscoe," beamed the boy upon seeing him. "What happened to the chuckwagon? Did it break down again?"

Charley chuckled. He reined to a stop.

The others reined in, too.

"Look at his horse, son," said Charley. "Don't you recognize the animal?"

Henry Ellis took a harder look at the mount Roscoe was riding, then his eyes lit up.

"That's Rod's horse," he exclaimed. "You let Rod drive the chuckwagon?"

"Sure did, by golly." Roscoe laughed. "Your grand-pop an' me thought we'd let Rod an' Miss Kelly have some time alone ta get ta know each other a little better. So we sent 'em both on up ahead fer supplies. We even give 'em time off from Buster," he added, indicating the panting dog on the ground beside them, scratching at a flea.

Sunday smiled.

"Those two've been actin' like a couple of natural-born lovebirds ever since the first time they met," he explained. "Ain't that so, Roscoe?"

"They sure have, by golly," he said with a chuckle, backing Charley's story. "Ain't bin much time fer either of 'em ta get together since we left Colorado, so we thought we'd give 'em a chance."

He winked at the boy.

Henry Ellis grimaced at the thought of it all. "Uuuuuggggggghhhhh!!" was all he could manage to utter.

Roscoe and Charley laughed out loud at the boy's reaction.

The three of them rode on a little farther—then Charley said soberly, "Keep lookin' straight ahead."

"Huh?" whispered Roscoe.

Charley's eyes didn't waver.

"Don't look around," he said in the same low voice. "We got some company. Bad company, I imagine," he added.

Silhouetted against the Texas sky, on a low hill in the very near distance, was a procession of leather-clad Indians on horseback, moving parallel with the long-horns.

Roscoe casually flicked his eyes in their direction. He spoke through the side of his mouth.

"Who do ya suppose they are, C.A.?" he asked.

"Hush now," warned Charley. "Just keep on riding."

The Indians moved on past the herd.

When Henry Ellis finally had the courage to look over, all that remained were several swirls of dissipating dust.

* * *

Besides being one of many stops on a stagecoach route, Pepper's Station also included a roadside general store and a blacksmith shop out in the middle of nowhere—an oasis for the overland traveler and those who had lost their way.

Rod Lightfoot hadn't actually lost his way, he was just doing what every red-blooded American man eventually found themselves doing—*waiting* for a woman.

Rod leaned against the side of the chuckwagon, the only vehicle tied to the single hitching post that stood in front of the rest stop. He had watered the team and filled the canteens, and he was now killing time wiping dust off the horses' harnesses while Kelly finished up the shopping inside the adobe building that housed the general store.

A two-horse conveyance appeared on the horizon of the cracked, dirt-covered road that passed the insignificant establishment, growing into Pike's familiar team and carriage.

When it reached the store, the driver turned the horses so the vehicle could pull over, then it moved on toward the chuckwagon.

The sound of wheels crunching on gravel finally helped Rod to notice the carriage's approach.

The luxurious coach swung in beside Rod, coming to a stop.

Pike leaned out of the window behind the driver with a brand-new cigar between his teeth.

"Well, well, well," he smirked, squeezing out a sly smile, "if it isn't my trusted assistant, the Indian who wants to be a lawyer.

"Whether you know it or not, Lightfoot," he went on, "you're one of the best cards I've got going in my deck . . . the *only* ace in the hole I have up my sleeve right now."

He slipped a match out of a sterling silver matchbox, striking it on the side of the case, igniting the cigar's tip. He puffed several times until it glowed.

"Those longhorns are getting just a little too close to home for my comfort," he advised. "So I sure hope those old Texans trust you by now."

Rod shook his head. He was about to take a firm stand.

"I'm afraid I can't help you anymore, Mr. Pike," he confided.

"What?" answered the surprised meat packer.

"I'm sorry, sir," Rod continued, "but I've had a lot of time to think things over, and I've made up my mind. I just can't be a party to this game of yours anymore . . . *or* to anything else you might want me to do for you in the future."

Pike cocked his head, squinting down his nose.

"Game?" he said. "Do you realize what you're saying, kid? Do you realize how much money you're throwing away?"

"I don't look at it that way, Mr. Pike," said Rod.

Pike's eyes slowly began to tighten.

"Am I supposed to take this as your official resignation?" he wanted to know.

"What do you think?" said Rod.

"I think you're out of your mind," snapped Pike. "I was paying you a lot more money than most people of your kind have ever dreamed of being paid."

He looked Rod up and down disgustedly.

"But I'm sure I can find somebody else who won't turn rabbit on me," he went on, "someone who'll understand exactly what a huge bundle of *dinero* can buy."

There was a long look between the two, with Rod unable to hide his abhorrence for the little chiseler—and

Pike's expression growing more and more venomous with each moment.

Then Pike nodded to his driver and the carriage drove away, leaving a wake of spattering gravel.

Rod watched after the carriage until it was just a speck on the flat West Texas skyline.

He had done it—Rod had finally stood up to Sidney Pike.

"Rod, can you give me a hand?"

It was Kelly's voice.

Lightfoot turned around to see the attractive newswoman coming from the store. She struggled to carry several gunnysacks filled with supplies.

He went to her side and took the bags, moving over and setting them down on the ground by the chuckwagon's tailgate.

"Sorry, I guess I didn't think you were buying that much," he said.

Kelly helped him as he unpacked the groceries, finding a special place for each item in the cook's cupboard that was located beside the toolbox Roscoe stored in front of some other supplies in the wagon's rear end.

"You sure don't talk much about yourself," said Kelly as they sorted and stored the provisions.

"Naw," said Rod, shaking his head, "there's not really that much to talk about."

"Oh," Kelly went on, "I don't know about that. Charley Sunday says you've really pulled yourself up by the bootstraps, that you're actually making something of yourself . . . All on your own."

Rod chuckled as he kept on rearranging the groceries. Then he dropped the rolled tarp covering down over the entire cook's pantry and began lashing it in place, securing it with tie downs.

"More like, 'moccasin straps' to be honest," he replied with a laugh. "I aim to put myself through law school . . . if I can find a school that'll take me. I've nearly earned my tuition fees from my exhibition winnings. If that's what Mr. Sunday's talking about.

"I always had a dream that maybe I would be the one who would lead my people out of their oppression."

He chuckled to himself at the silly thought.

"You know . . ." he went on, "the Great Indian Law Counselor, defending the helpless Native American indigent against the white man's lies."

"And?" questioned Kelly.

Rod looked away, a somber expression creeping onto his countenance.

"*And*," he repeated, "real life isn't exactly like it was in my dreams."

Kelly moved around, adjusting herself so she could see his face.

"Have you really tried?" she asked softly. "Tried to help your people?"

Rod was finding that he couldn't look at her directly. He just shook his head slowly.

"No," he said in a whisper. "I haven't."

Kelly asked, "Why not?"

Rod finally managed the courage to face her.

"Because my people haven't asked me to," he said with some embarrassment.

He drew in a deep breath, letting it out slowly.

"With Indians," he explained, "a boy has to prove that he's a man, even in these modern times. He has to do something . . . something worthy in the eyes of his people, so they can trust him . . . be proud of him . . .

as a *man*. I was trying to do that something," he told her, "by doing whatever I could to get into law school, and proving I was completely serious by working for Pike's meatpacking company."

They held a look between them for a long moment, with Kelly desperately wanting to take him in her arms to let him know everything would be all right.

Suddenly there was the building rumble of galloping horses slicing the still air.

They both looked up the road to see a long line of Indians galloping toward them—the same group of Indians that rode past the longhorn herd—now converging on Pepper's Station.

Rod took Kelly by the arm. He led the confused woman to the chuckwagon's passenger side and helped her climb up. He untied the team and in seconds he was around to the driver's side and in the seat. He grabbed the reins just as the first Indian swung his horse onto the gravel, sending a shower of pebbles raining down on the chuckwagon's canvas top.

"I don't recognize this tribe," he told her. "We'd better get back to the herd quick. If these guys find out where those longhorns are . . . there could be some serious trouble."

Another Indian literally slid his horse into the gravel area, swinging off to the ground—holding his clenched fist high as he let out a ghoulish scream.

"I-EEEE-HA!"

"Hey, I agree," said Kelly. "Let's get going!"

Rod released the brake and slapped leather to the team of horses. The old chuckwagon/two-seat buckboard moved out and onto the road, just as the rest of the rowdy Indian bunch swarmed Pepper's Station, yelling and appearing to be all-around obnoxious.

As Rod whipped the chuckwagon's horses into a gallop, the last Indian rider dismounted in the space where the chuckwagon had recently been located. On the Indian's back was a sign reading, JOHN WALKING BEAR AND HIS AUTHENTIC INDIAN DANCE TROUPE.

CHAPTER THIRTY-ONE

Several miles away from the road Kelly and Rod were using as they left the store in their escape from the Indian troupe—in the low hill country to the west—the herd was still moving along slowly, both cattle and cowboys becoming increasingly aware of the churning, black clouds rolling in angrily overhead.

Every so often, lightning would flash and distant thunder would roll.

Within minutes, an inhospitable wind blew in from the north and began to gust unsympathetically. Shortly thereafter, gravel-size raindrops began to plaster everything in sight.

Feather and Lucky, one of the Colorado cowboys, rode up to Charley and Henry Ellis at the front of the herd—both men holding on to their hats for fear of losing them.

Charley and the boy had put on their yellow slickers by then. Buster was already drenched to the bone, as the rain had begun to come down in solid sheets.

"There's a sad excuse fer a box canyon 'bout a half mile back yonder," Feather yelled to Charley over the shrieking wind and driving rain. "More like a rift," he shouted. "But we can corral the herd in it. An' I seen a shack near there where we can take cover ourselves 'til this gully-washer blows over," he added.

"Just be glad we're out of that creek bed," hollered Charley. "This looks like it could be a real toad choker."

Now it was Feather and Lucky who pulled yellow slickers from their saddlebags, putting them on quickly as the rain pummeled with horrific ferocity.

Charley held up his arm for the cowboys behind him to see. He made a circling motion with his hand, signaling the men to reverse the cattle's direction.

Lightning flashed again, followed closely by a much louder clap of thunder.

The storm continued to rage.

The rain fell in blinding layers, whipped by the unrelenting wind. After the demanding three-mile drive back to where Feather had suggested they would find safe harbor, the longhorns were now milling around, clustered together in the small "box canyon"—a natural enclosure located at the base of a steep escarpment.

A hastily built, brush ramada had been constructed across the entrance to the fissure to keep the animals confined as the thunder and lightning continued its discordant symphony in the dark, gray sky overhead.

At the nearby line shack Feather had told them about earlier, the nonstop, driving rain kept beating down with concentrated fury on the structure's roof.

The figure of a horse and rider stumbled toward the small broken-down cabin through the hammering downpour, both man and beast nearly obliterated by the drenching cloudburst.

The rider dismounted near a ramshackle corral beside the line shack where he unsaddled his horse.

He slung the saddle over his shoulder, then opened the gate, turning his mount out with some other horses that stood with their rumps to the storm in a far corner of the enclosure.

The man turned, leaning into the wind as he moved hastily toward the door of the shack.

Inside, with the rain pounding the tin roof, Roscoe had a small blaze going in the ancient stone fireplace. Feather was checking out the wooden cots and storage shelves. Henry Ellis had found an old kerosene lantern, and Holliday was doing his best to get the pre-historic contraption going.

The three Colorado cowboys were drying everyone's clothing on a makeshift line they had strung in every which direction. Buster, of course, was already asleep and snoring near the hearth.

The door flew open with the howling gale as Charley entered the tiny enclosure. He dropped his saddle to the floor and closed the door behind him. As soon as it was latched securely he turned to the others.

"I stretched a couple more ropes across the opening to the canyon," he said, shaking off the rainwater. "And I piled on some extra brush for the fence. I sure hope it stays put," he added.

"Those horns'll be all right, boss," assured Feather. "Those longhorns appreciate shelter from a storm just like us humans do."

Now that Holliday had the lantern going, Henry Ellis moved over to a window. The boy just stood there, staring into the soggy gloom on the other side of the uneven glass.

Roscoe was telling Charley, "I found some makin's fer some coffee, C.A. I'll have some drinkin' ready in two shakes of a lamb's tail. How's it look out there?" he asked.

"It'll probably last until morning by the feel of it," said Charley. "I suppose we'll all have to bed down in here tonight. Any blankets?" he asked.

"A few," answered Feather, holding up several for the rest to see. "They're kinda musty, though."

Outside the shack, intermixed with the battering rain, even more lightning flashed, which illuminated the canyon's entrance. As the following thunder cracked and growled, several mysterious figures in rain-drenched slickers moved cautiously down from the rocks.

Once on flat ground, they began to pull away some of the stacks of brush Charley and his men had piled there as a temporary barrier to help keep the cattle inside the natural corral.

Once the ropes that kept the foliage in place were untied and lowered, several curious longhorns poked their heads out and began to leave the box canyon.

The mysterious figures moved in behind the cattle, hazing the remainder of the herd out into the tempest.

Behind a small boulder, with a hooded poncho covering his head and face, Sidney Pike's ever-present cigar tip glowed from behind the wall of rain that camouflaged the dishonorable deed.

A sharp blaze of lightning threw an eerie glow onto the meat packer's nefarious smile, though the sound of his evil laughter was drowned out entirely by the storm's frenzied cacophony.

* * *

Inside the cabin, the rainwater kept on rolling down the windowpane in rippling waves as Henry Ellis continued to stare out into the darkening blur.

Charley couldn't help noticing the worried expression on his grandson's face as the window-glass reflected the storm's violence over the boy's visage.

Charley stood up and went over to where Henry Ellis was standing. He put a reassuring arm around the youngster's shoulder.

"What's the matter, son?" Charley asked.

The boy answered, "I'm worried about Rod and Kelly. I sure hope they made it across that wash in time."

Charley tousled the boy's hair, patting him on the cheek.

"Don't you be overly concerned about those two, son," he told him. "They're grown-up adults. They'll know what to do 'til this thing blows over."

The once dry creek bed was alive with a fast-flowing torrent. The bubbling foam made it absolutely impossible for anything, or anybody, to get across.

The old chuckwagon/two-seat buckboard and the team were stopped on the opposite bank, across the whirl of raging water. The heavy rain battered the canvas roof with an inharmonious staccato.

A lighted lantern beneath the canvas covering enhanced the entangled silhouettes of Rod and Kelly, barely visible through a small opening that was left when the canvas had been pulled shut. They appeared to be actively engaged in the rudiments of heavy lovemaking. The disheveled duo pawed one another and kissed passionately, with *much* more electricity than the surrounding thunderstorm could ever hope to accomplish.

Back at the cabin, Holliday's snore, combined with the same from Feather and Roscoe—plus the heavy rain falling on the tin roof—had been keeping Charley Sunday awake for what seemed like hours.

He got up for a moment and put some more wood on the fire. On his way back to his bedroll he stopped to check on Henry Ellis.

It put the old man at ease to see his grandson snoozing peacefully with a slight smile on his lips. Charley bent down and kissed him on the cheek. Then he stood and walked back to his own warm place of rest.

Charley climbed in between the wool blanket and canvas sleeping roll and made himself as comfortable as he could. Lightning flashed and distant thunder rolled once more as he closed his eyes again, hoping he would fall off this time.

A shrill whinny—followed by several sharp snorts and blows.

Charley was feeling reality slip away—his mind was traveling back many years in time to 1874 when he and his friends were working together as Texas Rangers.

A cattleman who raised stock near the Rio Grande River had reported his entire herd missing. The rancher and his foreman had caught the rustlers in the act and given chase. When the cattle thieves finally urged the herd across the Rio Grande River, the rancher and his foreman had to stop their pursuit. It was then they rode to the nearest Ranger station and reported the theft to the proper authorities.

The United States Army was notified immediately and after being given directions to the place the rustlers had crossed into Mexico, they gathered up some men and equipment and took off for the river where they were to meet several Rangers who had been assigned to the case.

1874

Forty-five-year-old Charley Sunday sat motionless in the saddle, his anxious bay gelding knee deep in the Rio Grande's easy flow. Charley had positioned his horse next to a chipped and partially toppled stone marker designating the international border between the United States and Mexico. The chiseled marble had been planted there long ago on what was now all that remained of an insignificant island set in the middle of the river.

Charley glanced down at the circular star pinned to his lapel: a shiny symbol of law and order, barely visible beneath his trail-worn duster. The peso-size badge identified him as a Texas Ranger. He held the rank of captain.

With a drooping mustache and cool gray eyes, the lawman was once again feeling the passion of a deadly predator on the hunt.

He rose slowly in the stirrups while the saddle leather creaked like an old rocking chair. He carefully surveyed the Texas side of the muddy watercourse, searching for familiar sign. Removing his gold watch from a vest pocket he checked the time—the bold Roman numerals told him it was six fourteen. He drew in a deep breath. It helped ease the tightness in the pit of his stomach—a feeling that always came before unavoidable bloodshed.

The gelding's head jerked. Charley looked up. The bay snorted once again—louder this time—nostrils flared, ears perked. An uneasy hoof pawed the water's surface. Charley's keen eyes acknowledged something on the northern periphery—elongated shadows, advancing. He slowly raised a gloved hand. From just beyond the horizon of the otherwise lifeless terrain, sun-rimmed silhouettes of men on horseback appeared. One by one they followed, the dark patterns of their shadows traveling across the sandy brush country before them. They were Texas Rangers—two in number. They wore once white, now gone to gray, muslin dusters similar to Charley's. They rode several paces ahead of a small six-man detachment of United States Army Negro Infantry. Charley watched as the dust-covered men trod silently, yet boldly, across the high-water pebbles, then on down to the river's edge where they reined up. Nearly half the river's flow stood between the new arrivals and Charley. The two Rangers acknowledged the other Ranger midriver before dismounting. Without discussion, the soldiers quickly unloaded the several pack mules they had brought with them. Some men hurried to create makeshift fortifications. Others went about assembling two Gatling guns, affixing them to sturdy tripods. The rest of the men checked pistol cylinders and chambers and fed cartridges into their Winchesters. No one spoke—just the precise sounds of hushed, mechanical preparation.

Charley continued to wait—unmoving—watching silently from his position on the underwater ridge.

When the men had settled into their places behind the armaments, their leader, Ranger Sergeant Roscoe Baskin, stood up, took off his wide-brimmed sugar-loaf, and waved it—a signal to Charley that he and his men were ready.

Charley nodded back, touching the edge of his own hat's brim.

The two initial Rangers were his friends, Roscoe, the

sergeant, and Feather Martin, who continually carried the rank of private. Charley had personally requested that both men be sent to back him.

When it was time, he reined around in the direction of Mexico and spurred off the sandbar into deeper water. He drew his Winchester and Colt pistol from the saddle scabbard and the holster at his hip, then let the horse pull him out into the gentle current.

Early morning shadows darkened the rocky soil surrounding the adobe structures that made up the unkempt ranchito. Situated a little less than a mile into Mexico, the scruffy collection of crumbling adobes were concealed from prying gringo eyes by several jagged rock formations standing between the callous setting and the river to the north. Not a hacienda by any means, the small compound consisted only of those few scattered structures, several makeshift corrals, and three outbuildings.

On the far side of this meager spread of crude, decaying structures—at the crest of a slight incline—two hundred and fifty head of prime Texas cattle stood peacefully inside two of three primitive enclosures. The corrals had been constructed from dried mesquite, hacked into posts and crossbars by men with machetes. They were tied together with strips of rawhide.

Inside the third corral, a string of rangy horses, many of them still saddled. Several tired lookouts—mustachioed vaqueros—rode watch among the livestock. Their compadres slept soundly on the uneven porches of the buildings nearby. Charley figured there must be more men sprawled inside the cramped dwellings as well.

With the morning sun at his back, and keeping the

gelding in a slow but steady gate, Charley entered the encampment.

The Ranger had thrown his duster over the rump of the gelding, hoping the garment would resemble a serape with the sun behind him. He had also popped the creases out of the crown of his Stetson, flattening the curl from its brim to make it appear more like a sombrero. Charley looked like a Mexican, and now he rode like a Mexican. He was hoping he'd be completely mistaken for one of their own by the two heavy-eyed sentries. He was extra sure of himself, and of the direction in which he was riding, as he started up the incline toward the three corrals, boldly walking the gauntlet between the cracked adobe dwellings. He appraised the situation thoroughly as he passed by the sleeping bandits—all of them heavily armed men—who snored soundly beside their empty liquor bottles. He rode his horse under a wooden latticework, beneath its hanging water gourds and dangling strings of drying peppers. The gelding's hooves echoed lightly between the adobes.

Charley reached the far side of the last building, putting him quite close to the mesquite enclosures that contained the cattle. He brought the bay horse to a halt. After a moment, he casually reined the animal around completely, putting his back to the guards. Without emotion, he looked down on the entire bandit compound. Slowly removing his lariat from the saddle, he began building a solid loop. He glanced over his other shoulder. The Mexican sentries were still nodded off in their saddles. They appeared to be waist deep in a pond of shimmering, dusty hides, completely unaware of the Lobo Americano in their midst.

Turning, Charley gently threw his rope across the

top rail of the third corral, expertly dropping the loop over the large horn of the Mexican saddle on the horse nearest his position. He took a half hitch around his own saddle horn, then he spurred his horse hard. The gelding shot forward. The Mexican pony was jerked harshly sideways, toward Charley, losing its balance and going down with a frightened squeal. This sent a terrifying message to the other horses tied along the same line. Within moments, all were plunging and jumping, whinnying and snorting, snapping the rawhide tie downs that secured them.

The cattle in the other two corrals were immediately provoked; they moved around anxiously, bumping one another. Seconds later the expected chain reaction ignited. Before the two guards could sense trouble, ten to fifteen head had jumped through the makeshift barrier, flattening it to the ground in a successful attempt to get away from the panicky horses that were now escaping from the other crude holding pen.

Charley's Whitneyville Walker Colt .44 roared, blasting the nearest sentry from his saddle. The second lookout had all he could do to keep his own bucking mount from throwing him under the hooves of the runaway steers. Charley took aim again and fired, dropping the man easily.

The two sharp cracks from the Ranger's revolver had startled the cattle and horses into a full-blown stampede. Charley's plan had been for all the corrals to be destroyed on their eastern sides—and it was in that direction the frightened animals began to run.

He emptied his Whitneyville Colt into the morning air behind the fleeing beasts as he spurred out after them. He put the reins between his teeth and pulled his Winchester from its scabbard. Several of the porchside bandits who had been rudely awakened by the gunfire and the deafening roar of hooves found themselves trapped. The cattle swooped down on them before they could ready their weapons, swirling past in a quickly blooming dust cloud. Support posts crumbled and men screamed for their mothers, their lives, and for their God. The trampling of cloven hooves consumed all.

More bandits piled out of the adobes, pulling on shirts and buckling belts. They scurried for their terrified mounts, grasping blindly for reins that were no longer there.

Charley broke away swiftly, using the runaway herd for cover. He twisted himself in the saddle, took aim with his Winchester, and fired back at the bandits who had begun to give chase. He could tell that only a few of the Mexicans understood what was happening. Some had spotted him and the outline of his horse through the veil of dust. The Texas Ranger's rifle cracked repeatedly, picking them off like coyotes.

More bandits, some who had been lucky enough to capture a horse, joined the pursuit. Charley rode low, hanging on to the neck of his mount, making himself as invisible as he could in the chaos that surrounded. By then, close to half a dozen members of the cattle-rustling outfit had organized and were galloping after him—every one of them surrounded completely by the rumble of the runaway herd.

Ricocheting bullets echoed through the chalky air, cattle bawled, hooves thundered. Charley knew his comrades at river's edge could hear the near-distant sounds of gunfire. The muffled roar of the stampede would also signal the cattle's approach. The mushrooming dust on the Mexican skyline, similar to the smoke of a fast-moving prairie fire, would verify to the waiting defenders that the confrontation for which they had prepared was only moments away.

As he galloped toward the river, Charley could see Roscoe gesture to the men. He knew breaches were being checked a final time, weapons recocked. All eyes would be focused on the rising brown haze across the flowing river, which had begun to sweep down like a swarm of locusts toward the water's edge.

Charley rode his foaming mount Indian style, hanging from one side of the saddle while firing his carbine under the gelding's neck. The Ranger shot with astonishing accuracy, blasting a pursuing bandit from his saddle with every bullet fired.

In the Texas trenches, Roscoe raised a hand to get the men's attention. "Hold your fire," he roared. "Wait until they hit the Bravo." The men sunk lower behind their defenses. The soldiers readied the Gatling guns and the Rangers their Winchesters. "And be careful," Roscoe added. "Don't no one go shootin' Captain Sunday, gawdammit, or I'll personally have his rotten hide myself."

Breaking out of the rolling ball of dust, the stampeding herd hit the water, sending fans of brilliant, rainbowhued spray exploding across the river's surface. Wind-whipped sombreros and crossed bandoleros set apart the bandits who rode among the confused cattle. They found they had to turn their attention away from the Yanqui invader as they needed desperately to divert the panicked animals away from the Rio's northern bank. This task proved to be impossible before the cattle found deeper water, forcing them to swim.

On the Texas side, the Gatling guns were ready and sighted. Pistols were cocked, rifles levered. "Just the Mes'cans," cautioned Roscoe. "Kill a steer, or shoot Captain Sunday, and it'll come out of your goddamn pay."

Feather took a few steps toward his horse, then scissored one leg over the saddle putting both boots into the stirrups and his rump into the seat. With a sharp spur to both flanks, he galloped to one side of the advancing herd. He rode the horse into the river at full speed, the horse lunging through the water as it became deeper.

Once Feather was on the Mexican side, he searched for Charley in the chaos. When he spotted him, Feather kicked his mount forward and rode into the mêlée with pistol and rifle blazing.

As the leaders of the herd began to clamber up the muddy Texas bank, Roscoe yelled, "Now, damnit! Fire at will."

The incessant Texas volley raked the space directly above the horns and hides of the swimming cattle, dropping Mexican bandits left and right. Some bullets hit several of their horses, which, like the riders, were elevated above the sprawling blanket of bawling steers.

Army Gatling guns rattled, Colts and Winchesters barked, both spitting their deadly projectiles with accuracy.

Feather caught Charley's eye, then they both galloped toward a Mexican trio who had arrived late to the party. At a dead run Feather took out two of them with his Walker Colt while Charley, coming from the opposite direction, blasted the other one with his rifle.

The next volley loosed into the riverside mayhem convinced the remaining bandits to turn tail and head back for the cover of a rock pile on the Mexican side. Looking up briefly from their splashing, stumbling horses, there were scarcely seconds for their eyes to show surprise before they were gunned down without mercy by Charley's and Feather's Winchesters.

Charley and Feather met up behind a small rock configuration. They waited like two wolves on the Mexican bank for their prey to show any sign of retreat.

Charley ejected a spent shell, blowing the exposed chamber clear of smoke.

It was finally over.

Roscoe raised his hand. "Hold your fire, gentlemen," he shouted. "Cease fire!" The men did.

One of the soldiers moved to Roscoe's side and the two men waited until they were joined by Charley and Feather, who splashed their way back across the waterway on their horses to join their allies.

When the cattle finally cleared the river, the bodies of the dead bandits were allowed to float away with the other decaying detritus that was always found in the passive rush of the Rio Grande del Norte.

CHAPTER THIRTY-TWO

1899

The door to the line shack swung open abruptly, flooding the interior with blinding light. Charley's dream ended abruptly as he opened his eyes to see Feather rimmed by the early morning sun's glare, appearing as a silhouette in the splintered portal.

"They're gone!" he shouted. "The whole, gol-dern herd is missin'."

With the morning's blue sky and puffy clouds overhead, Charley scrambled out the door, brushing past the pint-size cowboy, who turned and tagged along at his side. Charley stopped abruptly—Feather almost bumped into him but caught himself in time. Charley was looking toward the mouth of the box canyon.

The ropes and piled brush had been trampled flat. The canyon was completely void of any living creature.

Roscoe and Holliday came out of the cabin, followed by the three Colorado cowboys and a yawning Henry Ellis with Buster on his heels. All of them tracked Charley's dumbfounded gaze with their squinting eyes.

"Well, don't that just take the cake?" said Roscoe, his

agitated hands on both hips. "We've lost every dang one of 'em."

Roscoe turned abruptly to Feather.

"Maybe we shoulda put out a nighthawk like we always do," he glowered.

"That's closin' the doors on an empty barn, Roscoe," interrupted Charley. "Naw," he said, "it was all *my* fault."

Charley stopped talking for a moment, continuing to ponder the dilemma, his eyes still scanning the surrounding country.

Roscoe moved to his side.

"So, what're we gonna do now, C.A.?" he wanted to know.

Charley threw him a determined look.

"What do you think, Roscoe?" countered the gritty trail boss. "We're gonna go out lookin' for 'em, that's what we're gonna do."

He turned to the others, calling out, "Let's saddle up, boys. We got another big day ahead of us."

Charley Sunday's Texas Outfit spent the morning searching for the missing longhorns. They scoured gullies, valleys, and hilltops. They searched down secluded ravines and washes, in the heavy brush, in the low hills, and even between the many treacherous rock formations that dotted the area.

Charley walked his horse, probing the expansive horizon for any sign of the cattle. The sound of approaching hoofbeats turned his attention to Roscoe and Henry Ellis who were galloping toward him.

"Heeeeee-yoooooooo!!! C.A.!" echoed Roscoe's yelling.

Roscoe and the boy reined up beside Charley. Both appeared to be pretty energized about something.

"What is it, Roscoe? Henry Ellis?" asked Charley. "Did you see the longhorns?"

They both shook their heads.

"Uh, no we didn't actually see 'em," explained Roscoe. "But"—he indicated the boy—"the grandkid here saw somethin'. Tell 'im all about it, Henry Ellis."

Charley's look went to the boy who was pointing off to a nearby low hill.

"They're mean looking," said Henry Ellis. He made a menacing face. "Probably the scariest-looking bunch of people I've ever seen."

Charley looked over to Roscoe, puzzled by his grandson's wild description. Then his attention was pulled toward the rise where Henry Ellis had pointed.

The rumble of galloping hooves could be heard. Three members of the Indian troupe, astride their painted ponies, crested the hillock, slowing their animals to a walk as they rode down the incline toward the others.

As they got closer, Charley and Roscoe could see that the riders were not only leather clad, they also wore beaded headbands and silver jewelry.

The three Indians moved up to Charley, Roscoe, and the boy, stopping in front of their snorting horses.

Roscoe was prepared for the worst, while Charley tipped back the brim of his hat and smiled.

"Morning, gents," he proclaimed.

The Indians acknowledged the greeting, nodding silently.

Their muscular leader edged his horse in a little closer, squinting at Charley.

"Did you cowboys lose something?" he asked them, the words rolling off his tongue with a slight accent.

"Why?" questioned Charley, "did you fellas find something?"

The three Indians chuckled among themselves.

"You're that Texas Outfit, aren't you?" said the leader. "The ones we've been reading all about?"

"Could be," said Charley with a subdued twinkle. "Who are you?"

"They call me Potato John," offered the leader. "I ride with an 'outfit,' too. We came across something this morning that just might belong to you fellas."

Potato John and the other two Indians turned their heads toward the low rise behind them where the faint sounds of hoofed animals could be detected.

Within moments, the lead longhorn appeared on the ridge of the slope—it was followed by another, then another. Eventually, the entire skyline was alive with the subdued frenzy of lumbering longhorn cattle heads and horns bobbing—as the entire herd, guided by seven or eight Indians, moved along toward the small assemblage gathered at the bottom of the knoll.

More Indians on horseback girdled the herd, circling slowly, shepherding the drove toward Charley and the others.

Mouths agape, Charley, Roscoe, and Henry Ellis observed the overwhelming sight, their lips finally curling into grateful smiles.

Charley looked over to Potato John.

"Well, I'll be danged," he said. "What made a bunch of fellows like you go to all that trouble?"

There was a long pause—plus a look between the Indian leader and the older cowboy—showing respect in each of their eyes for the other.

Potato John winked at Charley, and said, "Just maybe . . . we wish we were *you* guys."

He nodded, then turned to go. As he did, the other two Indians followed. The rest of the Indians turned the herd over to the cowboys and fell into line behind their leader.

The last one to join the column revealed the INDIAN DANCE TROUPE sign on his back for all to see.

Charley chuckled. He turned to Roscoe who had already begun to laugh. Then Henry Ellis joined in until everyone was laughing so hard it was difficult to remember why.

By noon, the herd was moving along peacefully once again, the cowboys hazing at their heels. A dirt cloud boiled up casually from behind the cattle, moving in alongside the dusty longhorns.

It was the chuckwagon with Rod and Kelly.

They bounced along beside the herd, waving to Feather and Roscoe. When they were able to catch up to the front of the drove, Rod slowed the team, edging in beside Henry Ellis, who was still riding point with his grandfather.

"Hey, thank God we found you," said Rod, waving to both of them. Kelly waved, too.

Charley and the boy kept their looks straight ahead.

"Did you think *we* were lost," said the stoic Charley.

Rod and Kelly began to explain—both at the same time—each with a different story.

When they realized they were overlapping each other, they began to chuckle.

"I suppose you had time to get better acquainted, wherever you were," said Charley, teasing the pair.

Rod reacted with some embarrassment while Kelly

scooted in closer to him, putting a defiant arm around his neck, cuddling the young Indian openly.

"You bet we did, Mr. Charles Abner Sunday," she swore. "And that's a fact!"

Charley and Henry Ellis exchanged quizzical looks, as if they didn't know what Kelly was talking about. Finally Charley turned to the couple, smiling.

"How'd you like to work the herd for a spell, young lady?" he asked.

Kelly appeared to be at a momentary loss for words.

"I, uh, *me*?" she questioned. "A drover?"

Then her lips curled up into a wide grin.

"When do I start?" she wanted to know.

"Henry Ellis," said Charley, "why don't you help Roscoe with the cooking tonight, let Miss Kelly have your horse for a while."

The boy smiled, nodding his agreement.

"Rod," said Charley, "you go and get your horse back from Roscoe, and then both of you can relieve Mr. Holliday until we stop for the night."

Rod and Kelly exchanged sweet nothings. Then Rod looked over to Charley.

"Relieve Holliday?" he questioned, cocking his head slightly. "But he's riding drag."

Charley chuckled.

"I always like to start newcomers off riding drag," he said. "Teaches 'em humility . . . Besides," he went on, "just think of all the privacy you two'll have back there . . . hidden inside that swirling blanket of solitude."

A half hour later, the longhorns were still on their boundless journey toward their new home, plodding along slowly as the cowboys of the Texas Outfit urged them on, clucking their tongues and slapping coiled ropes against weather-beaten chaps.

To the rear of the herd, billowing clouds of dust were constantly rising.

Kelly and Rod rode side by side on the heels of the longhorns. The dry earth boiled in humongous swirls that billowed all around them.

Suddenly, a calf darted out from the herd, heading who knows where into the sagebrush.

Kelly spurred after it, lariat in hand, building her loop as her horse galloped furiously in pursuit of the maverick.

She pulled her mount alongside the frightened maverick, throwing her rope. The loop encircled the calf's head, then tightened.

As the animal reached the end of the riata, Kelly's horse planted all four feet and the calf was tugged to a standstill.

Kelly relaxed her hold on the reins, allowing the horse to ease up on the tightness of the rope that secured the bawling calf.

Rod was already there, waiting beside the balking animal. He dismounted, removed the noose from its neck, then slapped it on the rump. As he remounted, the animal scampered off back toward the herd and its mother.

Kelly had begun to recoil her lariat as Rod moved in beside her.

"That was big-time, championship roping," he told her, grinning. "Where did a newspaper reporter ever learn to ride and rope like that?"

Kelly smiled to herself, glowing with satisfaction as she retied the rope to her saddle.

"Hey," she said, speaking in a feigned, heavy Texas accent, "I was born an' raised just a little southeast a' these here parts, pawd-ner. An' when yer name also happens ta be *King*," she added, "ya learn a whole lotta stuff like that . . . just by growin' up a *King*."

Rod perked.

"You're a part of that south Texas cattle company? . . . Ha!" He chuckled . . . "Folks say the King Ranch has expectations of becoming one of the biggest Texas cattle spreads ever."

"There're some things about my past I don't want too many people to know about," she told him directly. "My grandmother isn't much for it, but I'm making it on my own, too."

She narrowed her eyes, then smiled. "Just like you are . . . Mr. Rod Lightfoot."

CHAPTER THIRTY-THREE

1960

"I didn't know this was going to be a love story," said Caleb as he scraped some unbuttered mashed potatoes out of his metal TV dinner dish. "Love stories make me want to throw up."

"Henry Ellis thought the same as you do about that," said Hank as he tried to cut his roast beef. "He didn't want any part of it. But Rod was single . . . and Kelly was single. They were close to the same age, and they had the same interests. Well . . . sometimes when two people have the same likes and dislikes, they find a way of getting together."

"Except," said Caleb, chewing on his potatoes, "Charley was the one who got them together. Aren't I right?"

"You're right," answered Hank. "Actually, the whole outfit was hoping they'd get together from the get-go."

"So when the rest of the outfit saw that Charley was trying to set something up between them," said Evie, "I'll bet they were all happy."

"As happy as chipmunks in a peanut tree," said Hank. "Yeah," he said, "happier than chipmunks in a peanut tree."

CHAPTER THIRTY-FOUR

1899

Roscoe watched the large bean pot—used earlier that evening for cooking supper—as it soaked on the chuckwagon's tailgate with warm, soapy water inside.

Nearby, Rod was fastening a large canvas tarpaulin around two five-foot yucca staves he'd planted in the ground very close to the chuckwagon's right side.

When he had finished with that, he easily attached one end of the tarp to the side of the wagon—then he hooked it on around the two yucca staves and pulled it back to the wagon, where he tacked it to the same side again with a nail, using his knife handle as a hammer.

When he had finished the task, he called over to Kelly who sat near Charley and Henry Ellis by the campfire.

"Miss King," Rod informed her, "your royal bath is waiting."

Kelly smiled, excused herself, and stood up. Then she went over to the chuckwagon where Rod held the tarp open for her. She stepped inside.

"Oh," she remembered, turning to the others as Rod was about to refasten the tarp, "no peeking."

Rod kissed her on the cheek.

"Don't you worry, Miss Kelly," he promised, "I'll keep 'em all at least fifty feet away."

Kelly nuzzled his nose with her own, kissing him back.

"It's not them I'm concerned about," she told him. "It's you."

She kissed him again, then pulled the tarp closed.

Rod turned his back, chuckling.

While she was getting out of her dirty clothing, Charley called over, "You can clean up, too, Lightfoot, if ya want," he said. "A man can get pretty darn filthy ridin' drag."

"Naw," answered Rod. "I don't want to smell any better than the rest of you guys. Besides, there's probably a wild animal or two out there that would pick me out of the whole bunch of you if I was clean . . . because I'd have a different stink to me."

"All right, I'm ready," Kelly called out as she peeked over the top of the makeshift shower stall. She handed her dirty clothing to Roscoe. Of course, she was shielded from prying eyes by the tarpaulin Rod had erected for her.

"Ya ready, ma'am?" Roscoe asked her from the rear of the wagon where he was stashing her clothes.

"You bet, Roscoe," said Kelly. "I'm just as dirty as my clothes are and can hardly wait another minute."

Roscoe slipped on a pair of leather gloves. He picked up the pot, with its warm, soapy water, and carried it over to the tarp that screened the newswoman. He closed his eyes, looking away.

"Any time yer ready, ma'am," he told her.

"I'm as ready as I'll ever be," she said. "Go ahead."

Roscoe raised the pot, easing the water out, pouring it over Kelly's head.

"Ouch," yelped the newswoman. "That's hot."

"Sorry, ma'am," replied Roscoe, still looking away, "but it's the only spare water I got right now."

He continued to pour until the pot was empty. Then he returned to his chores at the tailgate.

"Where'd you get that bathwater, Roscoe," Kelly asked him over the top of the canvas tarp. "It feels a little greasy to me."

"Oh, that," Roscoe answered. "That was the leftover dishwater, ma'am. I can't afford ta waste the good stuff. That's only fer drinkin' water."

"I thought so," said Kelly. She had just begun to dry off. "Because I just found a pinto bean in my left ear."

HENRY ELLIS PRITCHARD

by Kelly King

"I'm ten and a half years old and I've been riding horses nearly all of my life," says Henry Ellis Pritchard, Charley Sunday's grandson. "My grampa Charley put me in a saddle way before I could walk . . . and I actually went riding with him while I was still in diapers."

You told me that you and your parents lived in Austin, I said. "We live up there in Austin now," he admits, "but me and my parents were living on Grampa's ranch in Juanita when I was born. When I was around two or three years old we moved up to Austin because of my dad's work . . . his job has something to do with Mexican imports. So I've traveled to Mexico, too.

"In Austin I go to a private school and I don't like it at all. I'd rather be down in Juanita with my grampa Charley. I've been visiting him every summer, ever since I can remember. Lately it's been every two summers. I have never gotten tired of living on his ranch or gotten tired of his friends. His best friend is Roscoe, who lives on the ranch with my grampa Charley. He's supposed to be my grampa's ranch foreman but I think my grampa is really in love with Roscoe's cooking . . . I am, too, when I'm staying there on the ranch. He makes the best strawberry flapjacks in the world. They're really special. Roscoe also does the housekeeping and clothes washing. He lets me help him out when I'm there."

I asked Henry Ellis if he feels any different about living on a West Texas ranch now that he's no longer a little boy. "When I turned ten," he answered, "my parents asked me if I'd like to change where I go on vacation in the summer. I think they think a boy my age should be interested in other things . . . you know, sports, city stuff, and history. To be honest, I hate living in the city. Even though Austin still has a lot of vacant lots and parks to play in, I prefer the wide-open spaces out here in West Texas. Besides, my grampa and his friends have taught me more about Texas history than I've ever learned in school. Some of my friends still tease me about my loving the country like I do . . . but if they were really my friends I don't think they'd want to hurt my feelings like that.

"It's hard for me to find any friends my own age in Juanita because I'm only there in the summer and school's out in the summer. There are a few kids my age I know from Grampa's church, but they all work full time on their fathers' ranches every day and they never have any time to play . . . especially with an outsider like me.

"I'm really not that close to anyone. I mean, I love my parents, and all that, but how can you be friends with your parents? My grampa Charley's different . . . maybe it's because he's really old, and I've heard when you get really old you start acting like a kid all over again. I think that's the main reason we get along so good. It's the same with Roscoe . . . and Feather . . . and all of Grampa Charley's really good friends."

What about Rod? And me? I asked. *We're not that old, and you still like us, don't you?* "You two are different," he said. "You don't tell me what to do like my teachers, and most other adults your age, think they have to do all the time. You and Rod are kind a' like Buster . . . you're quiet and don't always think you have to come up with something you think I should be doing. To tell the truth," he went on, "I kind a' like being left on my own once in a while . . . to do my own thinking . . . most days. Now I really like old Buster. I've known that dog for as long as I can remember. Grampa Charley tells me Buster's around my own age . . . maybe a little older. Him and me have always gotten along. He even saved my life once or twice. I know he's saved Grampa Charley's life before. Sometimes Grampa Charley lets Buster sleep with me. But that's only when my mom and dad aren't around. They look at dogs differently than Grampa Charley and me. To them, Buster's just a dog . . . to me and my grampa, dogs are furry people.

"Grampa Charley's also taught me to show animals the same respect I've been taught to show to people.

"I had a horse . . . he was really a pony . . . my grampa used to let me ride him when I visited him on his ranch. My mom, who is also Grampa Charley's daughter . . . she had the horse before I did, so he was really old. His name was Pinto Tom. He was a pinto, of course, a big one, about twelve and a half hands high. I could still ride him two years ago when I visited my Grampa. Pinto Tom died last winter. I grew an inch or so since I last rode him two summers ago . . . and I was looking forward to riding him again this summer, if I hadn't grown too big for him. Oh, well," he says nonchalantly, "everythings gotta die. That's what Grampa Charley says."

I watched him as he sauntered away, Buster the dog at his side, and I think to myself that this boy . . . this young man . . . really has a lot more knowlege about life than any of those other pupils who attend that private school of his in Austin . . . the one Henry Ellis hates so much to attend.

CHAPTER THIRTY-FIVE

The next morning, before sunup, when most of the outfit was gathered around the campfire's glowing embers eating breakfast and trying to warm up, Roscoe asked Henry Ellis if he would run down to the nearby creek and bring back a bucket of water for washing dishes.

The boy was more than happy to do any chore he was asked to do, especially if it was his uncle Roscoe who needed the assistance.

With the moonlight fading, Henry Ellis grabbed the bucket, whistled for Buster to follow, then disappeared into a small stand of trees, racing down a steep incline to the creek at the bottom.

Balancing himself on the smooth rocks with water flowing all around him, the ten-year-old dipped the bucket into some deeper water—then he turned and made his way back to the bank using the same stony path he had taken to get there.

Upon reaching the pebbly edge of the creek, he noticed that old Buster was acting as if he wanted to play.

The sky was beginning to grow lighter so the boy set

the bucket aside and picked up a stick. He tossed it a few yards down the creek bank beside the water's flow.

Buster was more than likely feeling younger this day than usual. He did his best, bounding after the thrown object. He fetched the stick and walked back at a good clip to where the boy was standing. He dropped the stick at Henry Ellis's feet.

The boy and the dog repeated the game several more times until Buster began to show signs of fatigue.

Noticing that the dog was looking tired, Henry Ellis said, "All right, Buster, that ought to be enough for now. Let's get back to camp."

As tired as he was, Buster picked up the stick one more time and circled Henry Ellis twice, trying to interest him in resuming the diversion.

Suddenly Buster dropped the stick, his ears perked as he stared at something in the tall grass. The dog barked, then stopped.

Henry Ellis called to him, "What's the matter, Buster, do you hear a rabbit over there?"

The boy took a few steps in Buster's direction. The dog let out another bark.

Henry Ellis continued walking toward the high grass. His intentions were to flush the rabbit out into the open.

"What's the matter, Buster? You can't be afraid of a little bunny," teased the boy.

Buster started barking anxiously even though by then it was all for nothing.

Henry Ellis had reached the tall grass. As he took his first step into the thicker ground cover he heard the snake's rattle for the first time.

There was not an instant to turn. The rattler struck, piercing the boy's right leg with both sharp fangs.

Buster was on the reptile in a split second, snatching

the creature by its neck, then shaking it until there was no life left.

The old dog dropped the snake's limp body, then turned back to Henry Ellis who was now sitting on the ground with tears rolling down both cheeks. His hands were squeezing the flesh above the rattler's wound while a stream of blood ran down his calf.

"Go get Grampa Charley, Buster," he said. "Go get Grampa . . . NOW!"

The dog appeared to understand what Henry Ellis was asking him to do. He walked over to the dead snake and picked it up in his teeth. After that he moved on up the hill as best as he could manage.

Feather was the first to see the dog stumble into camp with the lifeless body of the snake dangling from his teeth.

"Oh, my God," he said softly to himself. He yelled over to Charley, "Boss! . . . Buster just came back with a dead rattler in his mouth. There ain't no sign of yer grandson . . . and they both left together."

Charley got to his feet and ran as fast as he could to where Feather was standing. It was an awkward situation as Charley tried to pry the dog's mouth open and Roscoe approached from the chuckwagon with a six-inch butcher knife at the same time.

"Drop the snake, Buster," said Charley. "Drop it now."

Buster dropped the snake.

Charley found an old tree branch and used it to pick up the snake's body and toss it aside.

"Did I hear someone say Buster left camp with Henry Ellis?" asked Charley.

"I sent the boy fer some water," said Roscoe. "Buster followed along with 'im."

"Well, there's no sign of my grandson in this camp right now . . . and that's a fact."

Feather and Roscoe exchanged glances.

Charley shook his head in disgust.

"C'mon, Buster," he called out to the dog. "Take me to Henry Ellis . . . take me to my grandson."

He made his way through the trees and down the slope with the dog directly in front of him. Both Feather and Roscoe decided they'd better follow.

Henry Ellis hadn't moved an inch since he'd sent Buster back to the camp. He sat in the same position, only now he had his belt tightened around his leg, keeping pressure on the artery above the wound.

Buster reached him first, planting big wet licks wherever he could find an inch of exposed skin. Charley was next, almost falling as his boots hit level ground.

He saw his grandson and immediately went to the boy's side. He wiped Henry Ellis's damp forehead with his bandanna, then kissed him on the top of his head.

"You can thank Buster for helping us find you," he told the boy.

Feather and Roscoe came into view, stumbling down the slope going just a little too fast. Both of them put on their brakes sooner than they should have and their spurs got tangled, spilling them both onto the ground beside Charley and Henry Ellis.

By the time the two could get to their feet, Charley had tied his bandanna above Henry Ellis's belt as a secondary precaution. He was preparing to suck out the snake's venom.

He fished his penknife out of the front pocket of his trousers.

"Here, take this," Feather told the boy. He put a .45-Colt bullet between the boy's teeth. "Bite on it as hard as you can. Your grampa has to make a couple a' cuts on yer wounds with his pocketknife. After that, he'll get out all that poison you got in there."

"Here," said Roscoe, holding out the butcher knife to Charley, "this one's cleaner than that old thing a' yours . . . and sharper."

Charley repocketed his folding knife, then took the larger knife from Roscoe.

Henry Ellis flinched as Charley spit out his chaw of tobacco.

Charley leaned in and made the two incisions as Henry Ellis grimaced.

Charley immediately put his mouth over the snakebite and began sucking, then spitting, sucking, then spitting—over and over, until he felt he had removed what venom was left inside that hadn't already entered the boy's bloodstream.

"All right, you two," he told Roscoe and Feather, "pick him up and let's get him back to camp. My grandson needs a doctor as soon as we can find one . . . So get moving."

The sun was just rimming the distant horizon as Charley burst into the camp shouting, "Anyone know where the nearest town is? . . . I gotta find a doctor for Henry Ellis."

About that time Rod was riding his horse into camp after a long second shift as nighthawk. He heard Charley's request and saw Roscoe and Feather carrying the boy out of the trees. He spurred his mount over to where they were.

"There's a little town less than three miles that way," said Rod as he dismounted beside Charley and the boy, who was now resting on his grampa's bedroll with Charley's saddle blanket as a pillow. "I've never been there," he continued, "I just saw it on a map once."

By then, Kelly had joined them, moving in beside Henry Ellis. She comforted him as best she could.

"Someone get the boy a blanket," she called out to those who'd started to gather around. One of the Colorado cowboys brought her a wool Army issue.

She wrapped it around the child who was now beginning to show signs of fever.

Charley turned to Roscoe. "Make some space for him in the chuckwagon, will you? Then we'll head for that town."

He turned to Feather and the Colorado cowboy. "You two go harness the team. Roscoe, get up in that seat so you're ready to drive the boy."

The lazy town of Dundee, Texas, was just waking up as the chuckwagon, being driven by Roscoe, rolled down the single-sided Main Street. Feather and Holliday rode on either side of the wagon staying abreast of the team.

When asked, a lone storekeeper sweeping the boardwalk in front of his establishment pointed out the doctor's office for Roscoe.

Charley and Rod were already there. Both had dismounted and tied off their horses. They were standing in front of the doctor's office front porch waiting for Roscoe and the chuckwagon.

When they saw Roscoe, Holliday, and Feather with Kelly in the seat coming down the street in the wagon they both started yelling and waving their arms for them to stop.

Roscoe saw the two men and he turned the team. In moments the chuckwagon had pulled up in front of Charley and Rod.

By then the doctor had joined them on the porch.

He was still in his nightshirt. He fumbled with a pair of wire-rimmed glasses, slipping them on over his nose and ears.

The doctor was well over fifty, with a bushy mustache and stubble-covered cheeks. His hair was mussed from a night of hard sleep.

He held out a hand to Charley. "Dr. Ambrose Stone. I'm the doctor here in Dundee."

They shook hands.

"My grandson's in the back of that wagon, Doc," said Charley. "His name is Henry Ellis. He's ten years old, and he's been snake-bit. We can bring him inside for you if you'd like. Just show us the way."

"Put him on the table in the examination room. I'll do my washin' up and meet you in there in a minute or so," the doctor said.

The inside of the office was made up of two adjoining rooms. The larger side room, which was the examination room, was divided from the main office by some white, sterile-looking, floor-length curtains.

Henry Ellis was placed on a leather-covered table located in the center of the side room. Charley, Kelly, Roscoe, Rod, Holliday, and Feather surrounded the boy, all trying to make him as comfortable as possible.

The doctor entered through a space between the curtains, shaking the excess water from his hands. He had also donned a white apron. Under that, he still wore his nightgown and slippers.

"Everyone step back, please," he asked the group. "The first thing I have to do is remove the poison."

"If that means you're going to suck it out," said Charley, "I've already done that, Doc."

Kelly interrupted with, "We just need you to dress the wound and put him on some proper medication."

"Could you at least let me take a look at the boy's

wound?" asked the doctor as he shook a thermometer he'd taken from a nearby glass vial.

Everyone moved back even farther as the doctor squeezed in closer to Henry Ellis. He nodded for the boy to open his mouth. Henry Ellis did and the thermometer was inserted.

Next, the doctor examined the snakebite, unwrapping the towels from around the wound.

The observers remained quiet as the physician went about his business.

"Will he be all right, Doc?" asked Charley.

"He won't die of snakebite, if that's what you mean," said Doctor Stone, "but with all of you in here hovering over him like he was already gone to meet his maker, he'll more'n likely suffocate instead."

The small group of onlookers, the boy's friends who were observing, mumbled their apologies.

"Why don't you all get out of here and come back in an hour or so," the doctor said to them. "By then I should know if he'll be requiring any hospitalization or not."

Close to an hour later, the friends of Henry Ellis were still milling around on the doctor's office porch, talking about the boy's incident with the snake. No one was blaming anyone. They were all discussing Buster's heroism.

Charley stepped through the front door, hat in hand. Everyone gathered around their leader.

"The doc wants to keep him overnight for observation . . . or until his fever breaks," Charley said. "He advised me that we should all check into the local hotel or get a room at the boardinghouse for the night.

Hopefully, Henry Ellis can be released in the morning and we can all be on our way."

He turned to Feather. "Feather, you ride on back to camp and tell them other Colorado boys we're having a slight setback."

"Will do, boss," said Feather. He slapped his horse on the rump, then took off, mounting the already running Chigger pony express style.

He galloped out of town.

As the little cowboy thundered past on Chigger, Bart Pickens, the sheriff of Dundee, stepped out onto the sheriff's office porch. Pickens was pushing fifty, with an evil-looking scar running down the side of his face. He was followed by his deputy, Leroy Stubbs. Leroy was freshly shaven with remnants of soap under his chin and behind both ears. Both men scratched their heads as they watched Feather's dust fade into the distance.

The deputy pointed over in the other direction to where Charley and the others were still gathered in front of the doctor's office.

"C'mon," said the sheriff, "we best go see what's going on over at the doc's."

He stepped off the porch. His deputy followed.

"Here comes trouble," whispered Roscoe when he saw the two lawmen approaching. Charley put a hand on his friend's shoulder, moving past him. He extended his hand to the approaching sheriff.

The lawman didn't appear to want anything to do with Charley's hand, let alone to shake it. He basically ignored the old cowboy and spoke to Rod instead.

"We don't allow Indians in our town, son," he told Rod. "If any of the rest of you claim this man as a friend or relative, we don't want you here, either."

Charley had been caught without words. He just stared back and forth between Rod, the sheriff, and the door to the doctor's office.

"I don't think you folks heard the sheriff," said the deputy. "We don't allow In-juns and their kind in Dundee, Texas. It was In-juns just like him that burned our town to the ground fifteen years ago."

Charley and Roscoe started to say something but were stopped before they could speak.

"I reckon you strangers don't hear so well, either," said the sheriff. "You're not wanted here."

He turned on Rod in a flash. "And you, Indian . . . I told you we don't allow Indians in Dundee. You have violated one of our four town statutes . . . and therefore I'm putting you under arrest."

Before anyone could move, Holliday drew his guns, aiming them at the two lawmen.

"Go on, Rod. Get on outta here while you can," he said.

Both Charley and Kelly stepped in between the two lawmen and the old gunslinger. Charley pushed Holliday's wrists so the weapons were pointing down.

"Holster those right now," he told the Wild West show performer. "There's no reason for gunplay."

"There will be soon," said the sheriff, drawing his own pistol and firing at the now disarmed Holliday.

KA-BOOM!!

Charley's Walker Colt exploded at the same moment the sheriff pulled his trigger. Charley's Colt's hand-poured lead projectile blasted the sheriff's gun completely out of his hand. Charley swung the old Ranger Colt over to cover the deputy. The secondary lawman didn't have the courage to draw.

Charley turned his attention back to Holliday.

"Did he hit you, bub?" he asked.

Holliday checked his coat, trousers, and hat. He found the bullet hole in his left pant leg.

"Any closer and he would have," said Holliday.

By then Roscoe and Rod had both of the lawmen covered, as did Charley.

The gunshots had aroused some of the citizenry, who were now gathering down the street. Several of the men were dressed in business suits, others in shirts and wool trousers—even more were still in their bed-clothes. Charley made a note to himself that none of the men were armed.

The townspeople discussed something between themselves, then they all turned and began walking toward the doctor's office.

Kelly turned to Charley and said, "Looks like the town fathers don't like seeing their law enforcement officers out-gunned."

Rod moved over to her side and put his arm around her.

"It's all my fault," he said.

"No, Rod. It wasn't your fault," she answered. "These lawmen are in the wrong. They were going to arrest you for just being who you are. That's not right at all."

"You can bet your bottom dollar it ain't right," said Charley. "Now all we got to do is convince these vigilantes of the same thing."

"We are not vigilantes, sir, if that's what you're thinking," said an unfamiliar voice.

The group of townsmen had reached Charley and his outfit.

It was one of the men wearing a suit who was doing the talking.

"We're just here to thank you for freeing our town from the likes of these two," said the better dressed man. He held out his hand to Charley. "Ben Perkins," he said, still holding out a hand. "I run the general store here in Dundee."

The two men shook.

"But I'm also the mayor . . . and these four gentlemen beside me are members of our city council."

Everyone nodded their greetings.

Perkins went on: "These two . . ." he indicated the sheriff and the deputy, "and their gang . . . rode into town about four weeks ago. They killed our elected sheriff and deputy, then told us they were taking over. Everyone had to turn over their guns. We had no way to protect ourselves. They've been running this town ever since."

"Where's this gang you mentioned now?" asked Charley.

"There's only two more of them left and they're drunk as skunks over in Dundee's one and only saloon. The rest of them have killed each other off fightin' over card games and the saloon's one and only soiled dove."

"Roscoe, Holliday," said Charley, "you both go over to the saloon and get those other men. Meet me at the jail and we'll lock 'em up with these other two."

He turned back to the townspeople.

"I reckon the town belongs to you folks again," he said. "And oh, there's just one more question I'd like to ask."

Charley leaned in close to Perkins. "Was this town burned to the ground fifteen years ago by Indians?"

"Oh, no sir," said Perkins. "This town wasn't even on the map fifteen years ago."

"Grampa," came the call from the doctor's office door.

Everyone turned. Henry Ellis stood on the porch with the doctor at his side.

"I think he's ready," said the doctor. "No more fever, so I'll release him early. He can go back to your camp with you today if you'd like. Everything should be like new."

Later on that evening after everyone had returned to camp and the cattle had been moved a few more miles, Charley was sitting near the campfire going over his maps. Suddenly he sat bolt upright, holding one of the charts closer in order to see better in the flickering firelight.

"I'll be danged," he said in a whisper. He turned and called over to Roscoe.

"Hey, Roscoe, could you come over here for a minute?"

Roscoe set down some pots he was polishing and moved over to Charley.

"Sit down, will you, Roscoe?" Charley asked him.

His old friend obliged, kneeling down beside him.

"Take a look at this map, will you?" he said. "I just figured out I had it folded wrong for the last few days and now something's not quite right."

Roscoe studied the wrinkled chart.

"Looks ta me like where we're more'n just a tad off where we're 'sposed to be, don't it?"

"Roscoe," said Charley lowering his voice, "I'm not much for admitting to it when I'm wrong, but it looks to me like we've been headed in the wrong direction for the past few days."

"That long ago?" said Roscoe. "I don't think we could be off the trail by that much, C.A., but you're right about bein' off a little."

"Remember that wide, shallow river we crossed Tuesday morning?" said Charley.

Roscoe nodded.

"We thought it might be a tributary of the Devil's, but it wasn't. I'm beginning to think it was the Pecos River running half underground instead."

He pointed to the map. Roscoe's eyes followed.

"If that's true, C.A., we gotta do some back-trackin'."

Charley gave him a disgusted look. "I know that, Roscoe. Do you think I'm stupid? I just don't want the others to know it . . . 'specially my grandson."

Roscoe was catching on. His lips curled into a wide smile.

"Then we need to turn the herd around slow an' casual-like over the next couple a' days. As soon as we're headed southeast again we'll be all right," he said. "Then we'll have ta cross back over the Pecos, down lower here," he pointed to the map, "closer to the border, and start lookin' fer some familiar landmarks."

"Do you really think we can do it?" said Charley.

"Do you mean, can we fool the others?"

"I'm not worried about the others," answered Charley. "The question is: Will we be able to fool Henry Ellis?"

The sky turned overcast and held for the next couple of days, which made it much easier to hide the fact they were turning the herd one hundred and eighty degrees and heading the other way for a while. At one of their several camps along the way Charley thought he'd been found out for sure.

It started when Kelly drifted over to where Charley was bedding down that night and asked him, "Are you sure we're headed in the right direction?"

Charley froze inside. His mind whirled with thoughts: *Have I been caught up in my own lie? Does Kelly know more about geography than I've given her credit for? Does she have a compass of her own I didn't count on? Has she seen by some of my actions that something isn't quite right? Or is she just guessing?*

"What makes you think we might be off course?" he asked her.

"Oh, nothing really," said Kelly. "Henry Ellis just asked me if we were headed in the right direction after the noon meal today. I don't even know why he brought up the subject, but I thought I'd ask you anyway."

"No, we're doing just fine, young lady," he told her. "We should be home before you know it."

Rod Lightfoot

by *Kelly King*

We know him by the name he chooses to use in the white man's world, Rod Lightfoot—even though he is known to his blood family and his tribe as Man Who Walks with Cougar.

"I figured using Rod Lightfoot as my name would work better for me on law school applications and for introducing myself before I was to be interviewed.

"I was born on my tribe's reservation in Indian Territory (Oklahoma) twenty-six years ago," he begins. "When I was a child, I grew up and was educated in the traditional Indian ways by my parents until I was twelve. At that time my mother and father were urged by an Indian reform group to send me to a reservation boarding school, where I lasted only a few years. But it was enough time for me to learn to speak and read English, which I'm grateful for. I also learned about the white man's laws, and how men study to learn those laws so they might protect others who have mistakenly run afoul of the law or those who are just plain ignorant of the laws and are being taken advantage of like our people had been before the Trail of Those That Cried (The Trail of Tears).

"I was nearly fifteen years old when I escaped from

that boarding school. I stole some white man clothing from where they dry on a rope and found a hat big enough to hide my hair. Then I traveled south to Texas and went looking for work on any ranch that would have me. I was befriended by one ranch owner I had asked for a job, and he hired my services as a post hole digger—I also worked as a cowboy when his herd was ready for market. That was my first cattle drive and we moved that herd to Dodge City, Kansas.

"It was in Dodge City where I saw my first real lawyer in action. I had been arrested and was put in jail for the crime of being an Indian. The city marshal there in Dodge City took a liking to me and suggested that I hire his friend, who was a lawyer, to defend me. The lawyer's name was J.M. George, and when I told him why I had been arrested and the fact that I was broke, he offered to defend me for nothing. During my trial, Mr. George proved that there wasn't a city law against Indians being inside a saloon. And that what everyone had thought was a law was just an old rule made up by a few hypocrites who happened to own all the saloons in Dodge. I was set free, and please believe me when I say there was more than one white man who bought me a drink after the trial . . . including my lawyer."

Mr. Lightfoot continues, "J.M. George, hired me to be his personal assistant and I worked out of his office looking up previous cases in his law books for other trials that came up for him. Mr. George also allowed me to read any law book I wanted to read in his library, plus he would personally answer any questions I had about the law. It was at that time I made up my mind I really wanted to be a lawyer. Mr. George also told me just how much money I would need for tuition fees for law college. And when he realized I wasn't making enough working for him to even think about opening a savings account, he advised me to use the talents I had gained

growing up on the reservation—mainly my experience
with horses: riding bucking broncs, bulldogging, and
roping cattle. He told me I should enter cowboy exhibitions. They were becoming a popular pastime in the
Southwest and consisted of a series of different events
a cowboy could enter, like riding a bucking horse, and if
I won I would be paid money for my efforts. So I started
doing that. I found that the majority of small towns put
on these exhibitions every so often, usually on weekends
or national and local holidays. I was in San Antonio for
one of those events when I heard that U.S. Army Colonel
Leonard Wood—on orders from Assistant Secretary of
the Navy Theodore Roosevelt—was looking for expert
horsemen from all walks of life to volunteer for an Army
equestrian division he was putting together to take to
Cuba to fight in the war with Spain, which had just
begun. It was called the First United States Volunteer
Cavalry. I volunteered and I qualified hands down, and
being of Indian birth was not a problem for me this time.
Just the fact that I could ride a horse, and ride it well,
was the only thing that mattered to Colonel Wood. The
one big problem we faced when we landed in Cuba was
that our horses were not with us. They had become separated from us through someone's mistake so we immediately became infantry soldiers—something none of us
had ever been trained for. We were ordered at once to
march on a small town and were met with resistance
before we had time to realize what was happening. I had
never been close to death and destruction like that
before in my life. When it was all over we marched on.
Some of us were reunited with our horses, so when we
reached what was called San Juan Heights, what Ameri-
cans are now calling San Juan Hill, I at least felt like a
cavalry soldier again. We fought alongside the Tenth and
Twelfth Infantry Regiments—the Buffalo Soldiers. Even
though these gallant Negro soldiers did most of the
heavy fighting, the American press gave Roosevelt and

Wood's Rough Riders the most attention . . . Roosevelt had been given the rank of lieutenant colonel by then, plus he led the charge. Believe me . . . we didn't take that hill all alone. We won the battle but we lost a lot of men. I thank God every day that I was able to get through it all uninjured."

Mr. Lightfoot, paused, remembering. "After the war I went back to Dodge City, hoping to get my old job back with Mr. George. But I was told he'd married and moved his practice to Arizona. I continued entering cowboy riding events like I had been doing before the war. In Denver I met Mr. Pike through coincidence—he had just taken out an ad in the local Denver newspaper for a personal business attorney. Why I answered that ad I still don't know. Now that I look back, Pike either didn't have that many young lawyers show up to be interviewed, or they all wanted too much money. I'm sure now it was all about how much Pike was willing to pay. Anyway, when I got there and told him a little about my background and my dreams of wanting to go to law school, he hired me on the spot. I was on my first assignment for Mr. Pike when I met you."

CHAPTER THIRTY-SIX

The sign said it was the PECOS RIVER VIADUCT. Feather referred to it simply as the High Bridge. It was three hundred and twenty-one feet high, with a span of two thousand one hundred and eighty feet. There was a narrow, wooden walkway beside the railroad tracks on top, but no guardrails. It was a long fall if someone made a fatal misstep.

The engine and fifteen cars of a passenger train stood at a dead stop in the center of the towering over-pass; black smoke puffed from its stack, and steam hissed from the boiler releases.

Quite a few passengers had their heads protruding from open windows, squinting quizzically toward the front of the train where something was definitely blocking the engine's progress.

The other half of the trestle, from the engine's cow-catcher to the west end, was filled with Charley Sunday's three hundred longhorn cattle.

Outlines of cowboys on horseback rode the narrow, wooden walkway between the cattle and the edge, attempting to keep the herd from panicking. Several steers had already started to bawl. Now others were beginning to show their displeasure. Longhorn horns rattled, cowboys sang softly to the herd. So far, not one animal—or human—had spooked.

A local county sheriff and several railroad workers—including the conductor and engineer—stood between the train's engine and the cattle, facing off with Charley, Rod, Holliday, and Roscoe.

All of these men—the railroad men and the cowboys standing by their horses—were discussing their predicament while Henry Ellis, Kelly, and Buster watched from the chuckwagon, positioned near the western side of the Pecos River's gorge. Henry Ellis gawked while Kelly wrote descriptions in her notepad.

"That's sure a long bridge," said Henry Ellis.

Kelly nodded. "And high, too."

"Why do you suppose my grampa let the others herd the longhorns out onto the bridge, anyway?" asked the boy.

"I don't think he gave much thought to the possibility of a train coming from the other direction," answered Kelly.

A single rider, an older man with a white beard, dressed in shirtsleeves, faded green suspenders, and a battered top hat, rode up from behind them on a saddled mule. Without saying a word, the man urged his animal past the chuckwagon and out onto the bridge. Then he began making his way through the tangle of cattle and cowboys, heading toward the center of the span.

He would tip his hat and smile as he squeezed by the Colorado cowboys and Feather, but he never said a word. It was only by his presence that he seemed to command respect from every man he encountered.

The angry county sheriff was saying something to

Charley and Rod as the bearded man wearing the top hat rode up and reined to a stop.

"You're going with me," the sheriff was telling Charley and his men. "Those are my orders."

"But what about my cattle?" fumed Charley, "I just can't leave 'em here. Now can I?"

"They'll most likely have to be impounded, I reckon," answered the just-as-angry law officer. "Once they get across," he added.

"And how are they supposed to do that?" said Charley. "Are you blind? There's a damn train in the way."

"Just a minute," Rod cut in. He turned to the sheriff. "I'm familiar with the law, sir. In order for you to impound these cattle, you're going to need a court order."

"Come on now," countered the lawman. "I don't need one a' them things. This gentleman has willfully obstructed the flow of railroad traffic on a railroad bridge. This is railroad property. How can you argue with that? If I can't make it any clearer to you all, then you're *all* under arrest!"

Charley clenched his fists. "That'll be *after* the fight," he informed the officer. Charley squared off.

"Look, cowboy," said the sheriff, sighing, "I'm only doing my job."

Unbeknownst to the deputy, the rider in the top hat had dismounted and now stood directly behind him. He tapped the sheriff on the shoulder.

The officer turned.

"Oh," he said when he saw who it was. "Howdy, I'll be with you in just a minute."

He turned back to Charley and Rod.

"Now listen, Mr. Sunday," he continued, "I'll need for you to come with me peacefully."

As the deputy reached for Sunday's arm, the bearded

man stepped in between the two. He tipped back his top hat, extending his hand to Charley.

"Howdy, C.A.," he said warmly.

Charley's mouth grew into a wide smile. He shook the man's hand vigorously.

"Why, I'll be danged." He grinned. "Good to see you, Roy. You remember Roscoe Baskin? And Feather Martin is right over there."

He pointed.

The sheriff pulled on Charley's shoulder, turning him around.

"Hey," he asked Charley, "what do you think you're doing?"

The man with the top hat cut in.

"I was just about to ask *you* the same question yourself, youngster," he told the peace officer with sincere conviction.

"You can see what I'm doing," the sheriff told the old man. "This cowboy is blocking private railroad property with these longhorns."

He looked the bearded man up and down, inspecting his rumpled clothing and slipshod appearance.

"And what business do you have here anyway?" he continued. "This is *my* jurisdiction."

"Would you say we're standin' in the center of this railroad bridge?" the man asked the sheriff.

The lawman looked one way, then the other. "Why yes," he said. "It looks like we're dead center to me, only where we're standing is a little west of dead center."

The older man moved in as close as he could get to the deputy's face. "West of the Pecos is *my* jurisdiction, sonny boy," he shouted. "I'm Judge Roy Bean from Langtry, 'bout twenty miles that-a-way. And I don't see no cattle here . . . just a few old retired Texas Rangers tryin' ta get home, that's all."

"Now you look here," said the sheriff.

"Wrong!" argued the old judge. "*YOU* look here, boy. I'm taking over. We may be law officers in the same state, but we ain't in the same division. I'm pulling rank. Now get on over there with those railroad men and start backin' up that train. Pronto!" he commanded. "Move!"

The sheriff would have liked to continue with his objection, but thought different about it when he saw Charley shaking his head—plus, he knew the judge was right.

He shook his own head, then turned to the railroaders, saying, "C'mon, you men . . . let's get this train backed up and off this bridge. I got a cowboy here needs to get his cattle across."

When he and Judge Roy were alone, Charley chuckled to himself.

"You'll get a lot a' heat over this one, Roy," he cautioned.

"People like me," said Bean, "have *always* taken a lot a' heat, Charley . . . you know that. You just keep them horns movin', all right? An' I'll do my best to make sure the law in these parts steers clear of you an' your outfit whenever you feel like visitin'."

Chapter Thirty-seven

Another long day's drive had come to a peaceful end by the banks of the Devil's River. Some of the livestock were drinking while others grazed under some large cottonwood trees nearby.

Feather and Holliday rode up to where Sunday waited, sitting his horse, chewing tobacco—spitting an occasional stream.

Roscoe and Henry Ellis drove up in the chuckwagon, while Rod and Kelly, covered head to toe in powdery trail dust, spurred their mounts through the longhorns, joining the others.

Sunday was pointing.

"We'll make camp over there tonight," he told them all. "We'll cross the river tomorrow morning."

By late afternoon the river camp had been set up and several armadillos were roasting slowly over the campfire.

The herd grazed peacefully nearby.

On a large rock above the river, Rod—in his long

underwear bottoms—dove headfirst into the clear blue water below.

Kelly, Henry Ellis, and Buster the dog sat watching from the far bank, the boy in his citified underwear, while Kelly sported a thigh-length old work shirt that had belonged to Charley.

Henry Ellis and Buster were both wet from a previous dip. Kelly, still dry, had yet to work up the needed courage for a plunge into the lazy watercourse.

Rod's head broke the surface.

"Hey," he sputtered, "it's great! C'mon, Kelly!" he prodded. "C'mon in!"

He tried coaxing her again.

"It really isn't that cold," he added.

Kelly laughed, shaking her head humbly.

Henry Ellis suddenly sensed he was just a third party. He stood up, excusing himself.

"I think," he said, "I'll go on and see what the other guys are up to."

Kelly smiled at the youngster's wisdom, patting him on the leg as he departed. He stopped to gather his clothes, then ran off down the embankment with Buster in hot pursuit.

"C'mon, are you afraid?" yelled Rod, daring the woman to join him.

Kelly turned her attention back to Rod.

"Nooooooooooooooo," she shrieked. "It's much too cold!"

In another area of the river, a few dozen yards away, Roscoe, Holliday, two of the Colorado cowboys, and Charley sat waist deep in a shallow pool, skinny-dipping, while they relaxed and enjoyed the coming evening.

They watched curiously as Feather, the only one wearing a garment—his faded red, patched, and tattered flannels, a one-piece unit, complete with trap door in the rear—splashed himself intermittently as he whistled an old Western tune.

Roscoe chuckled to himself, turning to Holliday.

"Little nippy," he said, "don't ya think?"

"Nippy, hell," answered Holliday, "it's downright freezin'!"

Charley leaned back against a moss-covered rock, letting the water drift up to the sunburn line on his neck. He smiled softly, smoking his pipe.

"You both love it and you both know it," he chided the pair.

Feather chimed in from across the pool.

"Any time I can get close ta water without soap," he hollered, "I *DO* love it!"

Feather slapped some more water up under his armpits.

"Why don't you take off them long-handles before ya do that?" questioned Roscoe.

Feather replied, "What I wear when I'm bathin' is my own dern business, mule face. *My good* mama taught me some modesty."

He put his nose in the air as if to snub Roscoe.

"Besides," Feather went on, sniveling, pointing to Holliday, "slick over there said it was nippy, an' a man my age is entitled. Why, I could catch my death a' cold without sumpthin' on my back ta keep me warm."

"Sheeee," said Roscoe. "I got me a chisel in the chuckwagon. I'll go get it, an' we can chip off some a' that bull-ony."

"Hush!" said Holliday in a sharp whisper.

All heads turned at the seriousness of the gunfighter's

tone. He was standing belly high in the river's flow—his look professionally following a dark shadow just beneath the surface.

Everyone present got quiet immediately; they continued watching silently.

Holliday's one good eye didn't flicker a bit as the dark outline underwater moved closer to him.

Slowly he began to raise his right hand as if he were preparing to draw his gun.

Then, the hand darted swiftly beneath the waterline—quicker than the eye could see—and came up grasping a floundering rainbow trout.

Roscoe's eyes were as wide as saucers.

"Did you fellas see what *he* did?" he asked, totally astonished by the feat.

"I can almost *taste* what he did," said Feather, also bug eyed.

Charley chuckled and puffed his pipe.

Holliday held up the fish so he could see it better, checking it out with his one good eye.

He really hadn't thought he could do it. He continued to study his catch curiously.

"I'm fast," he said with a sinister leer. "I'm *really* fast."

At the other pool, Kelly was now on her feet, poised to dive. Rod urged her on.

"I'm afraid," she told him one more time.

"Ahh," said Rod, "it's all in your mind. C'mon."

With Charley's shirt buttoned tight, Kelly took her dive, arcing into the Rio Diablo's clear blue current.

Rod watched as her underwater bubble trail approached his position, then she grabbed him while she was still under the surface, causing him to double over with ticklish laughter.

"Hey! Stop that!" he yelped, followed by an embarrassed laugh. "What're you doing?"

A giggling Kelly broke the surface, flinging something to the far bank.

Rod backed away from her, covering himself beneath the waterline.

"Those were my long-john bottoms, Kelly," he howled, turning crimson. "Kelly!"

"So?" she answered, cocking her head.

She was smiling in a coquettish way as she waded over closer, her arms moving around his bare shoulders, her firm breasts pressing against his chest through Charley's clinging, wet work shirt.

It really wasn't that difficult for Rod to discontinue his resistance. He instinctively found the buttons on Charley's old shirt with his fingers—then he found Kelly's lips with his own.

Charley Sunday walked down a small path beside the river, drying his silver hair with an old dish towel.

For some reason or another he happened to glance up, and what he saw stopped him in his tracks.

It was his grandson, Henry Ellis—now fully dressed—sitting on a log with Buster snoozing at his feet. The boy appeared to be more than a little downcast.

With compassion spreading across his wizened face, Charley moved in quietly behind the boy.

"Somethin' wrong, son?" he asked softly.

Caught off guard, Henry Ellis whirled around at the sound of his grandfather's voice. A single tear glistened for a brief moment before he brushed it away.

Sunday moved in alongside the youngster, sitting down on the log beside him.

Buster opened his eyes, calmly raising his head at his master's arrival, having caught a whiff of Charley's scent. The dog stood, slowly turning his rear end toward his master.

"Want your butt scratched, do you, Buster?" Charley asked the dog.

Buster edged his rump in closer to Charley, and the sagacious old cowboy began gently scratching the easygoing dog's backside.

"This ol' dog's been doing this for as long as I can remember, Henry Ellis," Charley told the boy. "He just loves getting his butt rubbed."

All three watched the longhorns grazing on the opposite riverbank for a long time.

"It's going to be all over pretty soon," said the boy just as softly as Charley had spoken to him, "isn't it, Grampa?"

Charley nodded, continuing his tender butt rubbing.

"In a week or so, I reckon," he answered as a matter of fact.

"Then I'll have to go back to being a normal boy again, won't I?" said Henry Ellis. "That means school and all that stuff."

Charley found his pipe and pouch in a pocket. He began filling the pipe's bowl.

"Oh, I don't know," said Charley after a moment of silence. "It's all in how you look at it, I suspect. Now me and Roscoe—"

He coughed, clearing his throat.

"Now, me and Roscoe and Feather, we have to go back to being growed up," he countered with a cocked eyebrow.

Henry Ellis appeared to be puzzled.

Charley went on. "It's funny, ain't it?" he said, chuckling softly to himself. "When a man's young, he wants to be older. Then, as soon as he gets to be older, he wants to be a youngster again."

"That's not funny, Grampa," scowled the boy.

"No," answered Charley, shaking his head. "I reckon when you think on it some, it sounds downright dumb."

"Not dumb, Grampa," said Henry Ellis, "just, sort of . . . mixed up."

Charley had to chuckle again. "Life sure does get a little bit confusing at times," he said with a laugh, tousling the boy's hair. "Don't it, son?"

"It sure does, Grampa," said Henry Ellis, grinning, "it sure does."

"Well," declared Charley, settling back and lighting his pipe, "why don't you and me . . . and ol' Buster here . . . just sit back and watch the sun set . . . enjoy every minute of it while we still can."

John "Plunker" Holliday

by Kelly King

It is ironic that John Holliday—nickname Plunker—is always being teased about being named after the infamous dentist of Tombstone, Arizona, gunfight fame—because this John Holliday was born way before the Tombstone Doc. "I'm probably old enough to have been the dentist Doc's old man," says Plunker Holliday. "That's why I go by my middle name . . . so no one will get us mixed up. Oh, I know Doctor John Henry Holliday died a few years back so there's no way now to get us mixed up anymore—but I have run across a lot of folks who haven't heard that John Henry died, so they repeatedly think I'm him. Dressin' like I do also helps 'em to mix the two of us up. Whereas the dead Doc was born in Georgia, I was born in Jackson, Missouri, in Cape Girardeau County. My parents were not married when I was born but they tied the knot before my first birthday. They was both travelin' show people, my parents—Daddy was a pretty good juggler, and my mother was the target for the knife thrower. They both had an agent in Saint Louis who would book them into theaters, saloons, church picnics, and whatever else needed their talents all over the country. They were not carnival performers, mind you—they were both top professionals in their fields. When I was doing my shootin' act at the Chicago World's Fair back in '93, some

of the old-time performers I met still remembered my
folks. Anyhow, when I turned five, my parents thought I
should join them on stage with an act of my own. My
father had a little .22-caliber pistol he used to carry for
our protection. He used that revolver to teach me to
shoot at moving targets. I became an expert shooter after
my pop showed me how a cartridge filled with bird shot
was the only sure way to never miss. I did that act fer fifteen years, up until people started to question the fact
that I didn't look like a child anymore. The first time I met
up with Buffalo Bill Cody was when I approached him
with the idea of re-creating the Tombstone, Arizona,
shootout between the Clanton/McLowery families and the
Earp family, with assistance from Wyatt Earp's friend,
Doc Holliday, of course. Today, some are starting to call
it the Gunfight at the O.K. Corral, even though it never
took place in, only near, the O.K. Corral. I spent around
five years with Buffalo Bill's Wild West, until Bill Cody got
tired of the same old thing on the bill every show and
fired me for drinkin' on the job. I wandered for a spell
after that. As far as I was concerned I owned that O.K.
Corral shootout re-creation show, so I got some friends
of mine together and along with several other acts, I took
the show on the road. I wish it would've lasted longer but
Wyatt Earp himself happened to be in the audience at one
of our performances and he came backstage to warn me
that he held the copyright to the O.K. Corral gunfight,
then he handed me a cease and desist court order, unless
I wanted to deal with him on a professional level. Funny
he'd never heard about my O.K. Corral act when I was
workin' for Bill Cody—it was only after I had left Cody's
employ that Earp showed up."

Holliday says, "After that, I picked me up a few jobs as
a cowhand here and there—and I even rode down to the
Big Bend to do a little prospectin'. I spent less than a year
down there buildin' my poke, but never strikin' it rich.
Then one day a gang a' Mes'kin border bandits raided my

camp and took my bag a' nuggets an' dust. Just like that, they did, swooped in behind me while I was sleepin', knocked me silly, and then searched my belongings until they found my gold. They also warned me to get out of the Bend because they were part of a movement that had plans to take that land back from the United States.

"I traveled up through New Mexico to Colorado after that and started doin' my O.K. Corral shootout re-cre-ation show up in Central City for the miners and towns-folk. They loved it—at first. But how many times will someone pay to see the same show over and over again? Well, I paid off the men I'd hired to work in the show and that left me close ta broke again. So I worked myself from mining town to mining town doin' my shootin' act. It was in Georgetown where they demanded to look at the am-munition I was usin' ta hit those movin' targets. When they found out I had bin misrepresentin' myself by usin' bird shot I dang-near got myself hanged. I went on back ta Denver and hired on with another cattle company for a while. The boys in the bunkhouse where I slept decided they didn't like my snoring and poured a couple a' buck-ets a' water on me one night an' I sat up shootin'. Thank God those bird shot shells were still in my guns so I didn't do too much damage or kill someone. Even so, a few a' them cowboys got hit by the bird shot, so they took a vote and kicked me out a' the bunkhouse for good. They told me I'd better get myself out a' the state of Colorado just in case someone reported the incident to the law. That very same night I saddled up and headed for Kansas."

I asked Holliday where he landed next. "Somehow I must've took the wrong trail and found myself in the pan-handle of Oklahoma. That was the first time I run across you and the cattle drive. I decided to follow because I'd never seen an outfit that moved cows north ta south before . . . only south ta north. So I kept follerin' an' fol-lerin' until one night I realized I hadn't had a bite to eat in days. That was when I rode inta your camp and we all met up for the first time."

Chapter Thirty-eight

1960

"OK, everyone," said Evie, "I'm going to need some help with these TV trays. Everyone walk your own back into the kitchen so I can wash them down before we fold them up and put them away."

"But what about Grampa Hank's story?" said Noel. "I don't want to miss what's next."

"Don't you worry, sweetheart," said Hank as he stood, then picked up his own TV tray. "The story can't continue unless I'm here to tell it." He laughed.

Noel giggled. "Now why didn't I think of that myself?" she said.

"Because you're not as smart as Grampa Hank," said Caleb, ducking quickly to avoid Noel's little fist.

"Noel," came her mother's yell from the kitchen. "No fighting with your brother. Haven't we talked about that?"

Noel's look dropped to the floor. "Yes, Mommy," she said.

"Now get in here and help me with these trays," said Evie.

Right about then there was an extremely intense

burst of lightning outside—it threw eerie patterns over everything as it leaked its brightness through drawn curtains and shades.

It was followed immediately by an ear-shattering, double clap of thunder.

Noel and Caleb looked up to the ceiling just as all the lights went out.

"No way," said Caleb.

Noel said, "I'm scared."

Within moments, Evie, followed by Grampa Hank and Josh, re-entered the front room, all of them carrying candles.

"If we were watching a television show we'd all be in deep trouble," said Evie.

"But since it's my story I'm telling," said Hank, "and not no TV show, we don't need electricity for me to go on with it. So feel around," he said, "and try to find where you were sitting, and I'll continue on."

CHAPTER THIRTY-NINE

1899

The next day following the noon meal, just minutes after the last cowboy had remounted his horse and galloped off to his position in front, beside, or behind the longhorn herd, Henry Ellis, Roscoe, and Kelly were still working hard to finish washing the dinner dishes. They were drying then repacking the eating utensils into the chuckwagon's storage area near the front of the wagon's bed.

"There's not enough room in the cupboards to hold all of this stuff, Uncle Roscoe," Henry Ellis called out from under the canvas cover where he had stationed himself.

"Sure there is, button," Roscoe yelled back to him. "Just gimme a minute an' I'll climb up there and give ya a hand."

Kelly dropped what she was doing and started climbing up to the chuckwagon's bed from the other side.

"You stay where you are, Roscoe," she said. "I'll help Henry Ellis arrange the utensils."

"Ah hell," mumbled Roscoe.

"What was that?" Kelly asked from behind the canvas cover.

"Heck, awww, heck," said Roscoe, "I just don't like to let newcomers organize my storage facilities. They never do it like I want it done."

"Well, I guess you're going to have to like it this time, Mister Roscoe Baskin," she said, "because I'm no newcomer when it comes to stacking dishes. My grandmother put me in charge of the bunkhouse dining room on the ranch where I was raised when I was eight years old. So I'll bet I'm more of an expert on stacking dishes than anyone else in this outfit, if you want the truth."

"I'll take you up on that little bet," said Roscoe as Kelly and the boy started their climb down from the front of the chuckwagon.

"I'll out-stack you dish for dish if you're really serious about a contest," said Kelly. She went about dumping the dishwater and drying the large pots. Then she handed them up to Henry Ellis who had stopped halfway and he put them on the floor of the bed just under the storage cabinet.

After that, Henry Ellis settled into the chuckwagon's seat where he waited for Kelly and Roscoe to join him. By then the sounds of the cattle drive had faded into the distance. For all three of them this was the quietest it had been since the day had begun.

Kelly climbed up beside the boy, brushing a lock of hair away from his eyes.

"I just love being outside in the open country when it's peaceful and quiet like it is now," she said softly.

Henry Ellis didn't reply—he wanted them all to enjoy the moment.

"Times like this I can truly believe there's a Creator up there in heaven," said Roscoe as he buckled up some of the loose harness straps on the horses. Then he started his climb up to the driver's seat beside the others.

"Don't either of ya ever tell Charley Sunday what ya just heard me say," said Roscoe, continuing. "He thinks I don't have a relationship with the Man Upstairs . . . when I really do. It's just that C.A. finds God inside a church buildin'—and I find mine out here under the blue sky."

They all sat silently, listening to the quietness—the pure sounds of nature.

From another direction came the combined noises of a bullwhip cracking, a stage driver's yelling, the increasing clatter of four wheels turning, harnesses jingling, and horses' hooves galloping.

In moments the rugged outline of a Butterfield stagecoach being pulled by six mules could be seen on the horizon following the faint sketch of a road that appeared to curve around a stand of trees, then cross trails about seventy-five yards ahead of where the chuckwagon was. Both conveyances were moving toward a possible interception.

"There's something we'll never see again in our lifetime," said Roscoe. "Six mules pullin' the long-distance Jackass Mail. It'll all be gone by the new century when trains take over the rest of the post office delivery system . . . just like they done with the stagecoach passenger service."

"That driver is really putting' it to those poor mules," said Roscoe.

"It looks to me like they're being abused," added Kelly.

"Naw," said Roscoe. "He's only pushin' that team hard and fast like he is because someone's chasin' him. Look," he pointed.

Sure enough, Roscoe was right. No more than thirty

yards behind the coach rode a band of eight to ten Mexican bandits, hightailing it after the mail carrier while firing their guns and rifles.

"I'll be darned," said Kelly. "Here I am again without my photographer . . . just when I really could use him."

The coach continued to careen down the road, advancing closer and closer to the spot where it would cross the trail Roscoe was using for the chuckwagon.

"For God's sake, Roscoe, stop this wagon before we collide," said Kelly.

Roscoe quickly reined in the chuckwagon's team, and the made-over two-seat buckboard came to a very bumpy, grinding halt.

The stagecoach was close enough by then for all three of them to see the shotgun guard take a bullet to the shoulder, which knocked him off his perch, sending him sprawling onto the ground below.

The driver immediately jerked on the reins, slowing and then stopping the coach within a fraction of an inch from the chuckwagon's team.

The bandits circled the two conveyances, now firing into the air as a warning for no one to move. Both the stage driver and Roscoe raised their hands.

Henry Ellis and Kelly followed suit, raising their hands slowly.

The agitated horses and riders closed in around the drivers of both vehicles.

One of the Mexicans, who appeared to be the leader, nudged his horse in closer than the others. He had black curly hair under a faded black felt sombrero. His deep brown eyes sparkled in the bright afternoon sun. The rest of his face was hidden behind a bandanna mask, the same type worn by all the other riders.

One of the bandits threw a loop over the stagecoach

driver's head, shaking the rope until it settled down around his neck. Then he jerked it into a tight noose and yanked the driver out of the seat. He landed on the left wheeler's withers, startling not only that one horse, but all the others as well. He slid to the ground dead from a broken neck.

Another masked bandit grabbed for the coach's reins, then pulled the team up short before their fear started them running again.

The leader shouted some orders to the others: "Go see if the mail pouch is up there in the boot, Francisco. Pablo . . . the strongbox should be inside. Bring it to me."

"*Sí, jefé*," said the men. They went about following his orders. The one named Francisco slid from his saddle to the coach, climbing up to the driver's seat. He reached down into the boot and came up holding the mail pouch, stuffed to the brim with envelopes and small packages.

"Go ahead," said the leader. "See if there is something worth anything inside . . . if no . . . get rid of it."

Pablo, the other bandit, was already inside the coach, rummaging around.

"It is here, *jefé*," said the one named Pablo. "But it is chained and locked to a heavy ring on the floor."

"We will have to take the entire coach, then," said the leader in Spanish. "We will have to find somewhere they have blacksmith tools."

"What about the three Americanos?" said another outlaw. "The old one, the pretty woman, and the boy. We cannot just let them go?"

"Tie them up for now and we will bring them along with us," said the leader. "You never know when we may need them. Let them ride inside the stagecoach. And bring the other wagon, too . . . I have a feeling it is filled with many good things to eat."

A few miles away the longhorns were moving along at a good pace when Rod rode up to Charley, reining in beside him.

"It's been a while, Mr. Sunday," he said, "and the chuckwagon hasn't caught up to us yet. Do you think something's gone wrong?"

Charley turned to him, scratching his head. He pulled out his pocket watch and gave it a glance.

"You're right, son," said Charley. "Why don't you go get Feather . . . uh, first find Holliday and tell him to lend you one of his pistols, and make sure you load it with real bullets . . . Then you find Feather, and the both of you go back and see what's keeping Roscoe and the others."

"Will do, Mr. Sunday," said Rod. "But, why the gun?"

Charley answered, "I trust you more with Holliday's gun than I trust Holliday with it. Now get going. Find 'em and tell 'em to get a move on. There's only so much daylight to burn in one day."

Holliday showed no reluctance in lending one of his weapons to Rod when asked. He only felt bad that Charley hadn't asked him to go along with the young Indian instead of Feather.

Feather was delighted to join Rod when he was asked. There was only one thing that worried him.

"That's one of Holliday's guns you've got tucked inta your belt, ain't it?" he asked the young Indian.

Rod nodded.

"Did Charley say we should be expectin' trouble?"

"Mr. Sunday wanted me to have a loaded gun . . .

so I guess we better be on the lookout for anything suspicious."

They both spurred out, moving through the cattle, heading back the way they came.

The stagecoach led the way. The six mules were now being driven by one of the bandits. It was followed by the chuckwagon with another gang member in charge of those two horses.

Roscoe, Kelly, and Henry Ellis had all been bound and then moved inside the stagecoach where they could all ride more comfortably and where it was much easier for the holdup men to keep an eye on them.

Their feet had not been tied so it wasn't that difficult for them to maneuver the strongbox around on the floor so they could see the chains and large lock that secured it to the ring that had been welded through the floor to the coach's frame underneath.

"Someone really went to a lot of trouble to protect that money box," said Kelly.

"That's why they need to find some blacksmith tools," said Henry Ellis, "so they can open the box."

Rod and Feather had come across the intersecting tracks of the chuckwagon and the stagecoach.

"What does all that boot-scuffin', hoofprints, an' wheel marks tell ya, Indian?" asked Feather, staring at the point on the ground where the chuckwagon and the stagecoach crossed trails.

"It tells me that we have three friends in some kind of trouble," said Rod. "And if we don't find out where they are pretty soon the two of us are going to be in a lot of trouble ourselves."

Loud moaning coming from the grass caught their attention. Eyes searched the nearby countryside until Feather saw something move several yards in the distance.

Feather pointed. "Over there," he said, "it looks like he's been hurt."

The shotgun rider's wound turned out to be superficial. After Feather had bandaged him up with the man's own shirttail, he was able to sit up and tell Rod and Feather all about what had happened on the trail. As for information on Roscoe, Kelly, and Henry Ellis, he wasn't that sure about their fate.

"I saw all three of 'em when their wagon first tangled with the stagecoach," he told them. "I was already on the ground by then and my vision was blocked some by the tall grass. I must've passed out for a few minutes, too. Last I remember they was headed off in that easterly direction with the chuckwagon following the coach." He pointed. "I could see for sure that your friends weren't no longer in the chuckwagon when they all rode off," he added.

"Do you think you'll be all right if we move you over into the shade of those trees?" asked Rod.

The shotgun rider nodded. "Just leave me some water and fetch my scattergun over there and I'll do just fine," he said. "Just don't forget to come back an' get me after you find your friends."

"Don't you worry yourself, mister," said Feather. "We'll be back fer ya."

Rod and Feather hadn't ridden more than a mile following the tracks of the covered wagon and stagecoach when Feather spotted their trail dust up ahead. He reined up sharply—Rod did the same.

"There they are," said Feather, pointing.

"There sure is a lot of 'em," said Rod. "I count around eight or so. Maybe one of us should ride back to the herd and get us some more guns."

"That won't be necessary," said Feather. "Me an' Roscoe an' Charley run up against the same kinda situation back when we was Rangerin' together. Roundin' up a gang that size shouldn't be difficult for the two of us." He leaned in closer. "We'll just keep our distance 'til they look like they're about ta stop, then we'll . . ."

It was almost two more miles before the gang's leader called for the man driving the stage to pull up. He reined in the six-up mule team. The driver of the chuckwagon did the same.

The other bandits milled around. Some dismounted to have a smoke, and others chewed off a bite of jerky to relieve their hunger.

The outlaw leader rode up alongside the coach. He bent down to look inside. He had a man with him who spoke English who translated for him.

"Which one . . . of you . . . does cook-ing?" the man asked in broken English.

Inside the coach, Roscoe, Kelly, and Henry Ellis exchanged glances. Then Roscoe spoke.

"I'm the cookie," he answered. "These other two are my assistants."

After the leader spoke again in Spanish, the man translated:

"Do you think maybe you prepare something for all of us to eat?" the leader asked through the translator. "We have had nothing to eat in over two days."

"Sure I can," Roscoe said, nodding. "If ya want meat, though, you'll have ta provide it yourselves . . . but if you'll be satisfied with beans an' rice, all I'll need is my can opener."

"Frijoles and rice are good," said the leader without waiting for the man to translate. He turned and called over to one of his men. "Pepe," he said in Spanish, "we will camp here. Come over and untie the old man, then you and Pedro collect some wood for a cooking fire."

Watching from behind some rocks where they had concealed themselves when they realized the bandits were going to make this more than a meal stop, Rod and Feather were trying to figure out their next move.

"Don't 'spose there'll be time enough fer one of us ta ride back to the herd and get Charley and Holliday?" said Feather.

"That'd take too long," answered Rod. "Besides, we already have three extra people on our side right over there in that coach."

"If you're talkin' about Roscoe, Miss Kelly, and the boy," said Feather, "it looks to me like they're all being held prisoner."

Rod chuckled. "You just saw that Roscoe isn't tied up anymore when they let him out of the coach to start cooking their supper. All I have to do is get into the coach and untie Kelly and Henry Ellis. When they're all free," he said, "we can make our move."

Roscoe was still opening tin cans and emptying beans into a large cauldron when the men returned with heavy branches, sticks, and kindling and began preparing the cooking fire.

"Cookin' the rice'll be easy, but it used ta be I'd have ta boil up raw pinto beans and let 'em simmer fer quite a while," Roscoe was telling the bandit who'd been left to keep an eye on him. "But ever since they've been packin' beans in these store-bought air-tights, all I gotta do is open some tin cans, then heat 'em up over the fire. Pretty simple, ain't it?"

He got no response from the bandit, but he sensed the man was very hungry by the look in his eyes.

It was then he saw Rod on the ground on the other side of the stagecoach. He was crawling through the high grass. The young Indian stopped when he saw Roscoe had spotted him. Rod raised his hand in a gesture to Roscoe.

Roscoe threw him a slight nod and continued preparing the meal.

After a moment, Rod continued his crawl up to the stagecoach's step. When he was sure he couldn't be seen by anyone else, he began pulling himself up into a standing position.

Inside the coach Kelly and Henry Ellis sat across from one another, both of them still tied securely. The strongbox was on the floor between them, chained firmly to the ring embedded in the floor. Henry Ellis was the first to see the door handle turn. Before the boy could say anything Rod was through the door and hunched down on the floor between him and Kelly.

"Check out the window," Rod whispered to them both. "Make sure nobody saw me."

Both Kelly and the boy looked outside and saw that none of the Mexicans were near the coach at that moment.

"All clear," said Henry Ellis with a grin from ear to ear.

"How did you find us," whispered Kelly.

"First let me get you untied and out of here," said Rod.

Staying as low as he could, Rod moved in even closer to them and began loosening their bonds.

There was just time enough for Rod to flatten out on the floor when they heard the leader's voice calling over to them once again.

"If you two will be patient," said the leader, "I will have one of my men bring you some food . . . when it is ready."

Kelly scooted over to the window, covering Rod with her long skirt just before the leader spurred his horse up closer to the coach. His eyes searched the vehicle's interior.

Henry Ellis saw that Rod's boots were visible outside of Kelly's skirt so he turned in his seat to block the leader's view.

The leader's only interest was in Kelly. He leaned down from his horse, took her by the nape of the neck, then kissed her roughly before she knew what was happening. "You eat, beautiful one," he told her. "Then the both of us will find a secluded place to get to know one another better while my men rest after their meal."

"You go to hell," said Kelly, spitting in his face.

The leader pulled back, wiping his chin. He laughed—then he reined around and rode away.

Rod pushed Kelly's skirt away from his face. He looked up into the newswoman's eyes. "I'm going to kill him for that. Just so you know it."

Henry Ellis's face held a blank stare.

The sun had begun to set.

Feather had moved in closer. He was now concealed behind a large boulder a few yards from the right rear wheel of the chuckwagon—close enough to the cook fire and Roscoe to make contact.

The only problem was the bandit that had been left to guard Roscoe. He had found an old log and now sat several yards away with his rifle cocked and ready.

Feather pursed his lips, then hooted like an owl.

The outlaw paid no attention.

Roscoe recognized the birdcall as a signal from his Texas Ranger past. He caught sight of Feather through the wagon's front-wheel spokes and he nodded.

Feather winked, then pointed to the guard and mouthed some silent words—after that he made a hammering motion with his hand.

Roscoe understood what his friend wanted him to do. After a moment he turned to the guard.

"Hey, you," he called out.

The man got to his feet and walked over to where Roscoe was cooking. "I need ya to taste these beans . . . see if they're spicy enough."

Feather began his move the moment Roscoe called the man over to the fire.

When the bandit was about to taste a spoonful of the heated beans, the blued barrel of Feather's Colt knocked him out cold. He fell face-first into the steaming cauldron.

Roscoe dragged him out of the pot, rolling his body away from the fire. He picked up the rifle and pulled the man's pistol from its holster. Then he moved over closer to Feather who was licking some of the beans off the man's face using his fingers.

"How many men did you bring with you," Roscoe asked.

"It's just me an' Rod," said Feather.

Roscoe shook his head. "That might not be enough," he said. "But I bin told all it takes is one Ranger to quell a riot." He went on, "An' right now we got two ex-Rangers . . . an' a Indian."

". . . Plus one pretty tough woman and a half-growed boy who ain't scared a' nothin'," said Feather. "We oughta be able ta get somethin' done 'tween the five of us, don't ya think?"

They were joined by Rod, Kelly, and Henry Ellis. Rod had untied Kelly and the boy before he'd helped them down from the coach. All three were crouched low as they moved in beside the others.

"All right," said Feather, "here's what we're gonna do."

Fifteen minutes later, the campfire area had been cleared of any sign that might tip the bandit gang to what was about to take place.

Roscoe knelt by two large pots dishing out beans and rice to the lineup of bandits who waited for their food.

The leader sat beside the chuckwagon eating and talking with his second in command. He looked up and saw the man who had been guarding Roscoe through the crowd. He motioned for him to come over.

Rod, dressed in the guard's clothing, neck scarf, crossed-bandoliers, and wide-brim sombrero, nodded in the leader's direction. He pulled his serape up around his neck and began moving slowly through the crowded space filled with men eating.

The sun dipped behind a distant mountain, putting most of the camp in shadow.

The bandits continued eating, paying no particular attention to Rod, dressed like one of their own, as he walked slowly toward their leader and his second in command.

Feather scooted along on his belly through the high grass until he came to the picket line of tethered horses belonging to the gang.

Both teams were there. The six-up stagecoach mule team and the two horses that pulled the covered wagon had been unhitched but not unharnessed. They were tied off on this other side of camp near the conveyances they pulled.

Feather came up fast and silent behind the sentry in charge of watching the picket line, taking him out of commission with a quick hand over his mouth and the blade of a Bowie knife shoved deep between his ribs.

Not a sound was heard.

Then the little ex-Ranger began untying each horse, one by one, until they were all free. Feather batted several of the animals on their rear ends with his hat to help head them out and away from the camp.

Henry Ellis could see the entire campsite from his position inside the stagecoach.

Kelly held the rifle that once belonged to Roscoe's guard as she hunkered down in the driver's boot beneath the seat.

Roscoe, who was still dishing up beans and rice, watched Rod as he continued his slow walk through the eating bandits toward the leader.

Henry Ellis could see that Rod was nearing the leader and the second in command. He knew that what was about to happen would trigger a shootout, so he ducked back away from the window like Roscoe had told him to.

Outside, Rod was almost face to face with the leader when the man suddenly realized he was dealing with a stranger, not his own man.

That's when Henry Ellis heard Rod's shot—or was it Rod's shot? He wasn't sure. He'd felt the sound had come from an entirely different direction.

He slid back over to the window and peered out.

The leader was slumped into Rod's arms, blood pouring from a wound in his head.

With all the strength he could muster, Rod shoved the dead leader's body onto his bewildered second in command while at the same time drawing and firing Holliday's gun point blank into the co-leader's stomach.

Another shot rang out. Henry Ellis turned to see a bandit fall into the cook fire. He also saw his grampa Charley behind a tree as the old rancher fired another shot with his old Colt, killing another bandit outright.

On the far side of the small campsite Holliday was blasting away with a rifle—each bullet found its mark.

Rod dropped to one knee and fired Holliday's other gun with just as much success.

None of the bandits had yet fired back—they had been caught way off guard. First off they were confused and frightened and couldn't figure out where the bullets were coming from.

A bandit ran past Roscoe and was hit in the back of his head with the caldron of beans Roscoe threw at him. He tumbled over—out cold.

Another frightened bandit took off running for the picket line, but when he saw the horses were no longer tied there, he made a quick dash for the six-up team. A bullet from Kelly's rifle cut him down in his tracks.

As the gunshots died down, Feather led the final two bandits into the campsite with his pistol trained on them both.

When he saw Charley and Holliday, he did a double take.

"Where in tarnation did you two come from?" he said, scratching his head.

Charley took a few more steps toward the little ex-Ranger.

"After we got the herd all bedded down for the night, we were hungry enough to eat a live bobcat," said Charley. "That's when we decided you fellas must be in some kind of trouble. We backtracked and picked up your trail . . . and here we are."

Henry Ellis flew out of the coach and into his grandfather's arms.

Kelly met Rod in the center of the camp and they kissed.

Feather looked at Roscoe and Holliday.

"Now don't you two go getting any ideas," he told them.

CHAPTER FORTY

Flora Mae Huckabee, still in her bathrobe and slippers, sat across one of her poker tables facing her bartender, both of them enjoying small dishes of homemade ice cream covered in chocolate sauce and whipped cream. The bartender was reading to her from the local Juanita morning newspaper. Though it was the bartender's voice that spoke the words, the writing was pure Kelly King:

"I hate to interrupt your morning bacon and eggs with something so trivial," said Kelly's words, "but Charley Sunday's Texas Outfit is only weeks away from bringing the three hundred longhorn cattle to their new home in Juanita, Texas.

"'It's all downhill from here,' said Mr. Charles Abner Sunday, the leader of this venerable crew, when I asked him how it was going earlier this morning.

"Well, at least Mr. Sunday *thought* it would be all downhill . . . for the next week or so, that is. Until he ran across one of the greatest obstacles the cow outfit had faced since leaving Denver, Colorado, with the longhorn herd a couple of months and nearly a thousand miles ago.

"At this writing it is after the fact. I'm sitting in our chuckwagon with Mr. Sunday's grandson, ten-year-old Henry Ellis Pritchard. We are now far from the area this incident took place. I'm writing now, hoping to describe to you what we witnessed barely four hours ago.

"The herd of longhorns was at another standstill . . . actually it was a standoff. This time it was Charley Sunday's Texas Outfit! vs. the United States Army.

"A fence, that's right, an extremely well-constructed wood, steel, and barbwire fence extending across miles and miles of otherwise wide-open country. It appeared that this just might put an end to the longhorn cattle drive."

The bartender continued reading. "Only hours ago, Charles Abner Sunday, the determined, native-born Texan and leader of this brave band of elderly Texas cowpunchers, did what any other normal cattleman would do if faced with the same predicament. He pulled some wire cutters from a cowboy's saddlebags and cut the barbwire in two—every single strand— until there was enough space to move the longhorns through.

"The old cowboys were now facing—through the newly created access—what appeared to be a platoon of armed, United States Army Artillery soldiers—standing at attention with rifles bared.

"Off in the distance behind them, across those wide-open spaces, an assemblage of mounted, uniformed, U.S. Army officers and their aides rode ten abreast with a single rider—the commanding officer—astride a spirited white stallion at their lead. His chest was covered in a rainbow of ribbons and his shoulder boards indicated he was a lieutenant colonel."

The article goes on: "I sent young Henry Ellis over

to witness the approaching confrontation. To be my eyes and ears, so to speak.

"The commanding lieutenant colonel and his aides rode in and stopped in front of Charley Sunday and four members of his outfit, Roscoe Baskin, Feather Martin, Rod Lightfoot, and Plunker Holliday. With the assistance of one of his aides, the lieutenant colonel dismounted, then walked the gauntlet through his standing troops until he was close enough to the cowboys to exchange words with Sunday at eye level.

"Beneath his officious appearance, the lieutenant colonel fumed. He clenched the stump of a cigar between his gritted teeth, all the while eying the old drovers—and the longhorns grazing behind them—suspiciously.

"'*Whom*, may I ask,' he began, 'is in charge of these . . . bovines?'

"Charley nodded, holding up a finger. He stepped forward, brushing past Feather. He moved in as close to the lieutenant colonel as was possible, facing him nose to nose—the remains of the destroyed fence was the only thing left between the two.

"Charley spat a stream of tobacco juice into the dirt.

"'I reckon *I* am, sir,' he answered with an icy stare.

"The lieutenant colonel rolled the cigar butt in his teeth, seething.

"'I'm Lieutenant Colonel A.J. Beckley,' he said. 'Do you have any idea where you are, cowboy?'

"Charley cocked an eyebrow.

"'Oh, I got an inkling,' he replied.

"'You are on United States Government Property,' Beckley growled. 'That's where you are!'

"Charley spit again, squinting at the officer.

"'Call it whatever you like, mister,' he said. He swept

his arm across the vast horizon. 'But this here is *all* Texas as far as me and my boys are concerned.'"

The bartender read how the heated argument continued. "Beckley's eyes narrowed, his anger was building even more, as Charley went on.

"'And I got me some longhorns I wanna get from here'—he pointed to his side of the fence—'to over yonder.' He indicated the expansive terrain on the other side of the obstruction, beyond where the Army troops were standing in formation.

"Beckley cocked his head.

"'Don't you realize this is an artillery range . . . a hazardous area?' he barked. 'Don't you even care if it's off limits to the public? For their *OWN SAFETY*?!'

"He'd bellowed for the benefit of the troops around him, and in case Charley might really give a damn. 'We fire high-explosive ordnance out here, cowboy,' he added.

"Charley nodded casually, spitting tobacco juice once again.

"'That's what some of your men were telling us before,' he told the officer. 'But we figured we might just be up to getting 'em *all* across . . . *between* your explosions.'

"He shook his head.

"'Otherwise,' Charley said with a sigh, 'it'll sure be a heck of a long way around.'"

After smoothing the newspaper a bit, the bartender went on. "Beckley couldn't believe what he was hearing.

"'I don't think you understand the seriousness of it all,' he warned. 'The danger that's involved, Mr.—'

"'Sunday,' answered Charley. 'Charles Abner Sunday.'

"'Mr. Sunday,' said the lieutenant colonel, continuing from where he left off. 'This is a secured area. *NOBODY* is allowed to cross this range . . . not even me!'

"'How's that?' Charley asked. 'Wasn't it *you* that put up this fence in the first place?'

"Beckley was caught completely off guard by Charley's question.

"'I . . . uh,' was all the old soldier could manage.

"'Well,' Charley continued, scanning the armed opposition behind and beside the commanding officer. 'You're sure doing your best to make it difficult for me.'

"'There is absolutely *NO WAY* I can authorize your crossing this land,' snapped Beckley. 'My artillery men are scheduled to begin firing just as soon as their new targets are in place.'

"The piercing shriek of an artillery shell covered Beckley's words. The missile arced through the air behind the assembly.

"All eyes followed the airborne explosive as it started its descent—the old cowboys covered their ears to avoid the head-splitting blast."

With apprehension, Flora Mae leaned forward, urging the barkeep to continue.

"The longhorns' only reaction to the unnerving sound was to simply chew more desert fauna.

"The artillery shell hit its target and burst in the distance.

"Within moments the herd became very uneasy.

"'*Now*, you're disturbin' my herd,' Charley told the commanding officer.

"'You have to get out of here, Sunday!' roared Beckley. 'How can I get that through to you?'

"He moved in even closer, his nose almost touching Charley's nose.

"'If you refuse,' he said in a softer but even more threatening voice, 'I'll personally have every one of you trespassers arrested and thrown in jail! . . . I'll even have your cattle confiscated.'

"Charley stood his ground.

"'That'll be the day,' Charley stated firmly.

"Charley set his boots solidly in the sand. The two men just stared at one another in silence until one of Beckley's aides approached, saluting.

"'There's a priority telegraph message coming over the wire for you, sir,' he said stiffly.

"Beckley's eyes did not waiver from Charley's.

"'Excuse me, Mr. Sunday,' Beckley told Charley. 'I'll be right back.'

"Charley nodded."

The bartender said that Kelly wrote through Henry Ellis's observation now.

"Everything was put on hold: the cattle, the Army personnel, the old Texans, and even myself. We all just stood there and waited while the lieutenant colonel left to receive and review his telegram."

The bartender went on reading out loud. "A light breeze blew. All that could be heard across the vastness was the lieutenant colonel's footsteps as he marched over to a canvas-covered Signal Corp. Battery Wagon, where the telegrapher was waiting for him. With the help of another aide Beckley climbed inside.

"The cowboys waited and watched, but they could not hear a thing but the tapping of Morse code coming from the battery wagon.

"Finally Beckley climbed down from the wagon. He straightened himself, turned abruptly, and in a very smart military manner marched the gauntlet right back to Charley at the severed fence.

"Beckley studied the old trail boss once again, finally meeting him eye to eye. Removing the cigar butt from between his teeth, he drew in a deep breath and expelled it, glancing over to Henry Ellis—who was taking notes of everything going on for Kelly—then back to Charley.

"'It appears,' he began, 'that you have an admirer on the East Coast, Mr. Sunday. That telegram was from the governor of the state of New York, Theodore Roosevelt. I served alongside Colonel Roosevelt last year in Cuba,' he said. 'Roosevelt says he's been reading a lot about you and your outfit these days, and that if your longhorn drive ever gets close to this fort, I'm to show you every courtesy available. He also said he's kind of partial to longhorns.'

"Beckley turned to his aide.

"'Make contact with our artillery lines,' he ordered. 'Tell them there'll be a small delay in our schedule for today.'

"Feather let out a shrill rebel yell, flinging his hat into the air. The other cowboys' Stetsons, and quite a few campaign hats, followed."

Kelly's story, still being read out loud by Flora Mae's bartender, went on: "I wasn't quite sure what had just taken place, but when my cub reporter returned to the chuckwagon, his face held a grin as wide as the Missouri River in springtime.

"I climbed down from the wagon and joined my cowboy friends in celebration . . . and that's when I saw the lieutenant colonel clipping the remaining barbwire with Charley's wire cutters, to the 'whoops' and 'hollers' of everyone concerned.

"The cattle's crossing of the Army's artillery range took the rest of that afternoon."

The following evening—a few more miles down the trail—after the supper dishes had been washed and put away, everyone was either lying or sitting around the campfire reading, singing, or telling stories.

Feather walked over to Charley carrying two cups of steaming coffee. He knelt down beside his boss and handed him a cup.

"Well, thank you very much, Feather Martin," said Charley. "I thank you from the bottom of my heart."

Charley looked over to where Rod was sitting and talking with Kelly.

"Hey," he said to Feather, "if you and Rod are both here in camp . . . just who's riding nighthawk?"

Feather chuckled.

"Holliday, that's who," he answered. "Me an' Rod figgered that ol' sonofagun could use a good stayin'-up-all-night. He won't have no one out there ta talk to 'cept himself. He'll get tired, too . . . then maybe he'll doze off durin' his day shift an' *we* won't have ta listen to him talk about himself at all."

Charley chuckled as he took a sip of his coffee.

"Hello the camp," came the sound of a man's voice from just outside the perimeter.

"Wonder who's come a callin' this late in the evenin'?" Feather said to Charley as he slowly removed his Winchester from the scabbard attached to his saddle on the ground beside his bedroll.

"Who goes there?" he hollered back into the darkness.

"An old acquaintance of Charley Sunday's," said the voice.

This made Charley perk. He stood up and faced the shadows where the sound of the voice was coming from.

"Where do I know you from?" said Charley. "Do you have a name?"

"Come on over here in the firelight where we can

see ya," Roscoe called out. "I still got some grub left over if yer hungry."

For a moment or two the voice said nothing. Eventually they could hear a horse moving through the foliage—branches breaking and saddle leather creaking.

In moments the rider urged his mount into the campfire's glow.

Charley's right hand dropped to his boot top immediately when he recognized the man.

It was the same outlaw who had escaped from the Juanita bank robbery—John Bob Cason. Only now, along with his Colt revolver pointed directly at Charley, he had Henry Ellis in front of him straddling the saddle. His other gloved hand that held the reins was also covering the boy's mouth.

"If you hurt that boy . . ." warned Charley.

"If I hurt this boy," said Cason, "what are you going to do about it?"

"I'll kill you, that's what," answered Charley.

"Right now you ain't in no position to threaten anyone, Sunday. I got your grandkid."

"I'm sure you have a reason," said Charley. "Just what do you have in mind for him?"

"I'm headin' down to the border with him right now," said Cason. "And if you want him back . . . you'll have to follow me. That invitation is for you only, Sunday. All you other yea-hoops are to stay here."

"They won't make trouble for you, Cason," said Charley.

"I know they won't," answered the outlaw. "There's seven more guns out there in the dark coverin' every one of 'em. That'll keep 'em from following."

All eyes shifted to the darkness outside the ring of flickering light cast by the campfire. Nothing but shadows could be seen beyond that.

"Oh, my men're out there all right," said Cason. "And I've already given them their orders . . . Anyone moves after we leave this camp'll get dropped before they take their second step. Fair enough?" he added.

Everyone nodded.

"All right then," said John Bob Cason, "your grand-kid and me are leavin' for the border right now. Sunday, you can start after us just as soon as I'm clear of your camp."

Charley focused his eyes on Henry Ellis's eyes. He made contact—the boy was frightened but Charley could see Henry Ellis felt much better after his grand-father gave him some silent assurance.

Cason gave Charley one more chilling look—then he used his spurs with little jabs while he pulled back on the reins to make his horse back away into the shadows.

As soon as he knew he could no longer be seen, Cason turned his horse and rode away.

Immediately Kelly was in Charley's arms.

"You won't let him hurt Henry Ellis, will you?" she said.

Charley shook his head. "Of course not. No one's going to harm my grandson," he said. "You can count on that. No one's going to even have a chance to try."

"I'll saddle Dice for ya," said Feather.

"You can use my Walker Colt along with yer own, C.A.," said Roscoe. "It'll save ya from havin' to take time out to reload."

"Calm down, all of you," said Charley. "I already know where he's going."

The others threw him quizzical looks.

"We're nearly back in Kinney County already," he told them. "That's almost home for us."

Charley took several steps toward the place on the edge of the camp where John Bob Cason had been moments before with Henry Ellis in the saddle in front of him.

He stared into the blackness that surrounded.

He thought to himself, *There's only one place Cason could be taking Henry Ellis out in that direction . . . and I know exactly where it is.*

Feather leaned in close. "You go ahead an' foller him, boss, but what about his gang . . . the men he left out there in the dark that's got us all surrounded?"

Charley reached over and took Feather's Winchester rifle out of his hands. He cocked the weapon, then walked a big circle, pointing the rifle into the darkness every so often.

"Anyone out there go ahead and shoot me before I start firing this rifle. I'm bound to hit at least one or two of you."

There was no response from the shadows.

Every face in camp held a surprised expression.

"There isn't any gang," said Charley. "Never was."

"Then we're going with you, Mr. Sunday," said Rod.

"That's fine with me," said Charley. "But you're all going to have to follow my plan and do exactly as I tell you. First I want you three Colorado boys to stay here . . . watch the herd.

"And please don't forget to relieve Holliday at midnight," he added.

CHAPTER FORTY-ONE

John Bob Cason, with Henry Ellis in front of him in the saddle, rode as fast as he could over the open country in the moonlit night—south, toward the Rio Grande River.

Less than a mile behind came the thundering hooves of the Texas Outfit—made up of Roscoe, Feather, Kelly, and Rod. Charley Sunday was nowhere among them.

The adobe buildings stood empty and crumbling as Cason rode into the small, abandoned Texas border town. Henry Ellis was now riding behind the outlaw, holding on to the man's coat to keep from slipping off.

The sound of the bank robber's horse's hooves on the dry, chalky street echoed lightly between the decaying structures.

When Cason came upon a two-story building with a CANTINA sign over the main door he dismounted; then he led his horse, with the boy still mounted, through the narrow portal with its swinging doors still intact.

Henry Ellis found he had to duck going through the door; otherwise he would have been knocked from his perch behind the saddle.

Once inside, Cason dropped the reins and reached for the boy, picking him up and setting him down on the dust-covered tile floor.

Cason found an old candle on a poker table and struck a match to it, lighting up the room pretty well as long as the full moon's radiance was able to leak in through other openings.

The outlaw pointed to a chair nearby.

"You can sit over there, kid," the boy was told. "Here, you want some water?" Cason took his canteen from the horse's saddle and held it out for the boy.

Henry Ellis took several long gulps.

"You're going to kill my grampa, aren't you?" said Henry Ellis.

"I'm gonna' draw against your grandfather right out there in that street," said Cason, "just like he and my partner did twenty-eight years ago . . . and you can watch it all if you want to, kid."

"Twenty-eight years," said the boy. "That's a long time ago, mister. "W-why are you doing this now?"

"I needed to have your grandfather back in this particular town. Simple as that," said Cason. "I read that the cattle drive was going to be in the area so I waited and made my move."

"What are you going to do with me?" the boy asked his captor.

"I ain't gonna do nothin' to you, kid . . . it's how bad your grandfather wants you back is all that's gonna matter when he shows up."

* * *

The outfit was at least a half mile out from the deserted border town when Rod held up his hand for all to stop.

Reins tightened, bits were pulled back, and the running horses began to slow.

When they had all come to a complete halt, Rod stepped down from his saddle and found a place to sit on one of the many rocky formations that were a part of the terrain.

"Mister Sunday told us we should stop here . . . so we're stopping here," said Rod.

Kelly nudged her mount over beside him and dismounted, sitting on a flat rock beside him.

Roscoe climbed down, followed by Feather. Within moments they were all sitting in an uneven circle facing one another.

"What're we supposed to do now?" said Feather.

"You heard C.A., ya little runt," said Roscoe. "We wait here like he told us."

Charley had tied off Dice in the shadows across from the cantina minutes before Cason had arrived with Henry Ellis. He pulled his Winchester from its scabbard and waited.

Charley had known all along that he would have to beat Cason to the abandoned village if he wanted to retain the element of surprise.

From his position, Charley had watched as Cason and Henry Ellis rode into the town, then down the main street to the cantina where they entered the structure without the boy dismounting.

Now Charley used the shadows to conceal his move across the street to the cantina. He found an outside stairway at the side of the structure, minus a handrail and several steps. He climbed to the top carefully before slithering on inside the adobe structure through an open door.

Once he was in the upstairs hallway, Charley made his way past half a dozen open doors, plus some rooms with no doors at all, until he came to the narrow balcony that overlooked the drinking and gambling area below.

The ex-Ranger got down on his belly to traverse the last few feet to the edge of the upper gallery and finally stopped when he had a good view of his grandson, sitting alone in an old wooden chair, twelve feet below.

"That's right where you're supposed to be, Sunday," said the voice of John Bob Cason. The outlaw was right behind him.

"Uncock that Winchester and hand it to me, slowly, if you'd be so kind," ordered the desperado.

Charley followed the man's directions. He thumbed the hammer down carefully and held the rifle above his head where Cason could easily take charge of the weapon.

"All right," continued Cason, "get to your feet, then head over to the stairs. I want you to be able to see that I haven't harmed a hair on your grandkid's head."

A half mile out, where the members of the outfit still waited, Rod suddenly got to his feet.

"It's time," he said to the others. "They're all in the cantina by now."

As the rest of the small group got to their feet, Feather said, "How do you know it's time?"

Roscoe turned in disgust. "Because," he answered, "C.A. said once we got here to wait for fifteen minutes, and then we were to start movin' on."

Inside the cantina, Charley's hands had been tied securely behind him and he was now seated in a chair opposite Henry Ellis.

Cason stood facing them both using Charley's Winchester to hold them both at bay.

"What I really want to do, Sunday, is for the two of us to draw down on each other just like you drew down on my partner, Clay Poland, back in '72," said Cason. "I know I can beat you if your friends aren't around. And I hope you brought that cannon you always carry."

"Right down there in my boot top like always," said Charley.

Cason's eyes twinkled. "Damn," he said, "I almost forgot you carried it in your boot. How careless of me. But now that you got your hands tied, I don't think I need to worry about that anymore."

Suddenly Cason became very serious.

"Where do you want to die, Charley Sunday?" he asked.

Charley cocked his head. "I don't think I ever gave that much thought," he answered.

"I mean, do you want to have a go with me right here inside this cantina? Or do you want to meet your Maker out there in the street, like my partner did?"

Charley seemed to hem and haw. "If I had my druthers," he said, "I'd rather die in my own bed at home . . . from old age," he added.

"No more wise remarks, Sunday," said Cason, "or I'll drop you where you are."

"Could you at least wait until my grandson isn't

sitting so close to me? I'd hate to see him catch one of your off-the-mark shots by mistake."

"When I draw against a man," said Cason, "I don't have off-the-mark shots. I hit what I'm aiming for. So what will it be, Sunday?" he snapped, "inside or out?"

"In the street, of course," said Charley. He shook his head. "Are you really going to let me draw against you?"

"Right out of that boot top if you want," said Cason. He cocked the Winchester and then motioned to the door with the barrel.

"Outside," he said. "Right now."

As Charley began to get to his feet, he said, "Aren't you going to untie me? Or do you want me to draw against you like this?" He turned and wiggled his fingers at the outlaw, showing him that his hands were still tied securely behind him.

"Kid," yelled Cason to Henry Ellis, "untie his hands."

Moving slowly, Henry Ellis stood and walked over to his grandfather. He stepped in behind Charley and started working at the knots.

When the loosened bonds fell to the floor, Cason used the Winchester's barrel to point toward the door again.

"Maybe you should go out first?" said the outlaw.

"Naw, you go first," said Charley. "That's the way your partner did it."

"If I go out ahead of you, Sunday," said Cason, "I'll have to back out the door. I surely don't need you goin' for that boot gun while I'm not lookin'."

"Trust me, John Bob," said Charley, "you want to do this like it was done when I killed your partner, you're gonna have to trust me."

With that, Cason turned to face Charley and the

boy. He took Charley's Winchester and flung the rifle over the upstairs banister, where it fell useless onto the second-story floor. Then he began backing out the door to the street outside.

As his boot made a first step onto the wooden porch, the sounds of rifles and pistols cocking stopped John Bob Cason in his tracks.

"Hey, Sunday," he called back inside, "it looks like your friends didn't believe me about my gang having them all covered."

"No, sir," said Charley from inside the cantina. "They're a pretty smart bunch, my outfit. But they're not here to keep us from tangling with one another, either. They're here to keep our little gunfight fair."

"Do you expect me to believe that?" said Cason.

"Don't matter what you believe," said Charley. "Now go find yourself a place in the street. I'll come out when you're ready for me."

Cason's eyes flicked from building to building. He could see a rifle barrel protruding through a window curtain, the shadow of an armed man in an alleyway. He knew he was surrounded.

He stepped off the cantina's porch and moved cautiously to the center of the street.

"I'm set," he yelled to Charley.

Inside the cantina, Henry Ellis watched as his grampa reached down to raise his cuff; then Charley removed the Whitneyville Walker Colt from his boot. He stood up straight before tucking the big gun into his belt where he could cross-draw with ease.

"I'm ready, John Bob," he yelled. "I'm coming out."

Charley leaned over and kissed Henry Ellis on the forehead.

"You stay here," he said quietly, "this shouldn't take that long."

Charley reached out and tousled the boy's hair; he smiled and winked. Then he turned and walked toward the door.

Out on the street, John Bob Cason waited anxiously, his hand cupped over his gun, his thumb ready to cock the hammer as he drew.

When Charley stepped out onto the porch, Cason was slightly surprised to see that the ex-Ranger had moved the position of his Walker Colt.

"I'm putting a lot of faith in you, Sunday . . . that your men don't cut me down before I have the chance to kill you," said the gunman.

"This is between Cason and me," Charley called out to his friends. "Lower your guns. If he wins, don't shoot him. He'll have won fair and square. Let him go peacefully."

There was some muttering from the hiding places across the street.

"I'm serious now," said Charley. "If he wins, leave him be."

"You mean after he kidnapped your grandson and scared us all half to death we're supposed to let him go?" It was Roscoe's voice.

"That's right," said Charley. "You can call it an order if you want. But I mean it."

"All right, C.A.," said Roscoe. "We believe ya."

Roscoe stepped out of his hiding place just long enough to set his rifle against the side of the building. Then he ducked back into the alleyway.

Feather, Rod, and Kelly did the same.

When they had all been accounted for, Charley stepped out into the street.

He set himself facing Cason.

"Whenever you're ready, John Bob," he said.

There was a quick moment—then both men drew their revolvers.

BLAM! KA-BOOM!

Both weapons exploded at the same instant and the street was immediately filled with black powder smoke.

In the moments after, the smoke dispersed just enough so people could see it was John Bob Cason who lay on his side, blood gushing from a belly wound.

Charley stood silently in front of the cantina, his smoking Walker Colt still in his hand. It took him a moment or so to realize he had out-drawn the bank robber.

Rod and Kelly moved out onto the street followed by Roscoe and Feather. They all moved to Charley, hugging him and patting him on the back.

The only problem was that Cason wasn't quite dead. The outlaw–bank robber's eyes opened a crack. He could see the commotion everyone was making over Charley. He spotted his gun in the dirt beside his leg and reached for the weapon. He slowly sat up and sighted in on Charley's back.

BLAM! BLAM! BLAM!

Cason took three Winchester slugs to the upper chest, which slid him back a notch or two, until his body came to rest at the edge of the boardwalk on the opposite side of the moonlit street.

Charley looked around and so did the others. They saw the dead man lying where he had fallen.

Their attention was drawn to the cantina porch

where Henry Ellis stood. The boy held a smoking Winchester—Cason's Winchester.

"Where did you get that rifle?" asked Charley.

"It was in a scabbard tied to his saddle," said Henry Ellis, "inside where he left his horse.

"When you went outside to draw against him, I decided I'd better take the rifle and follow you . . . Just in case he really was faster than you were, Grampa."

A day later, Charley Sunday's Texas Outfit picked up Gerald and the movable darkroom just outside Del Rio.

The day after that, the longhorns were moving slowly along both sides of a recognizable farm to market road when Henry Ellis saw two men on horseback approaching from the opposite direction.

Charley, riding point between his grandson and Buster, raised his hand to stop the cattle drive.

As the approaching riders slowed and stopped in the middle of the road, Charley and Henry Ellis nudged their mounts over to greet them. Buster sat down in the center of the road, scratching vigorously at a flea.

One of the riders was the Juanita sheriff, Willingham Dubbs, who urged his horse even closer to face Charley and the boy.

When Charley recognized the familiar face, he tipped his hat.

"Well, I'll be danged," he said. "Howdy, Willingham."

The sheriff's eyes were wide at the sight of all the longhorns.

"Now, don't you be worryin' yourself silly about

them cattle," Charley said with some sarcasm. "We ain't planning on driving 'em through Juanita, if that's what you're thinking. I was hoping to cut 'em across my place over yonder, then take 'em straight on to Flora Mae's spread."

The sheriff shook his head.

"Nope . . . I'm afraid you can't do that, Charley," he told the tired old trail boss.

Charley reacted with puzzlement, mixed in with a little genuine resentment.

"Dangit, Willingham," he barked. "There you go again. We pushed this herd all the way from Denver, Colorado, and that's a fur piece. Now we just want to get home, that's all."

He spat a spurt of tobacco juice.

"We've been across railroad bridges," he continued with a scowl, "through cities a heck of a lot bigger than Juanita. Fought our way to cross cotton fields, Army artillery ranges . . . you name it. And now you're sayin' I can't cut across my own damn property?"

The sheriff chuckled, scratching his neck.

"That's *EXACTLY* what I'm sayin', Charley Sunday," replied the sheriff. "You're gonna have to come *through* town, whether you like it or not."

He broke into a large grin.

"You're a famous man now, Charley," he went on. "You and your outfit have put our little ol' Juanita on the international map. The governor of Texas and half the world are waitin' to see you and these longhorns . . . *in person!*"

Charley turned to his grandson to get the boy's reaction. Finally, both of them broke into peals of laughter before Charley turned his attention back to the sheriff with a straight face.

"We got a parade planned for you and your outfit

come mornin', Charley," the sheriff was saying. "You're *all* grand marshals . . . Guests of honor. *You* . . . and your *entire* outfit."

He lowered his eyes, glancing over to Charley on his horse.

"Do you think you can hold the longhorns here 'til tomorrow mornin'?" he asked.

Charley's firmly set jaw turned into a wide grin.

"You know I always like to obey the law, Willingham," he told the sheriff.

Charley turned in his saddle, took off his hat, and twirled it in the air over his head for the others to see.

"Circle 'em right here, boys," he yelled out, "and circle 'em tight! We're makin' our last roadside camp right here."

He looked over to his grandson, winked, then said, "And that's a fact!"

CHAPTER FORTY-TWO

1960

"And they all lived happily ever after," said Noel's voice in the pitch-black.

"Not so fast there, young lady," said Hank. "My story's not over just yet."

The lights blinked a few times, then came back on, relighting the room.

Hank could see his audience was starting to break up. Evie and Josh were almost through the kitchen door when he called out to them.

"Everyone back where they were," said Hank, "if you want to hear the end of the story."

Caleb, Josh, and Evie moved back to where they had been sitting. Noel hadn't moved. When everybody appeared to be comfortable, Noel nodded for her great-grandfather to continue.

Chapter Forty-three

1899

The longhorns had been bedded down for their last night on the trail. Harmonica music drifted from the spot near the campfire where the Colorado cowboys were resting.

Rod and Kelly stood by the news wagon saying their warm good-byes to Gerald, who was on his way into Juanita to set up for the following day's festivities.

Charley and Flora Mae were sitting on some logs across from the three Colorado cowboys. The Colorado boys would be accompanying the herd into town in the morning. From there, they would move the cattle on to Flora Mae's ranch, where they were to assist in making the longhorns comfortable in their new home.

As the news photography wagon pulled away, it passed Flora Mae's white carriage and matched team tied off near the chuckwagon, where Roscoe was washing the dinner dishes on the tailgate for the last time. Feather was nowhere to be seen, having drawn the final, first-shift, nighthawk duty.

Henry Ellis had already begun to get ready for bed in the chuckwagon. Buster was with him.

At the logs near the fire, Charley was poking the coals with a stick.

Flora Mae put a hand on his shoulder.

"Well, yer finally gettin' 'em home, big fella," she declared with a contented smile. "Yer dream's about to come true, Charles Abner Sunday."

"*WE* are getting 'em home," he told her. "*I* couldn't have done any of this without your personal support and financial assistance, Flora Mae. So I reckon I owe you something in return . . . for makin' it all possible."

"Weeee-llll," began Flora Mae, retaining her smile. "You did promise you'd take me dancin' . . . remember?"

Charley cleared his throat uncomfortably.

"Y-you mean, right here? R-right now?" he stammered. "Right here on the dirt?"

"Yer gonna have to make good on it sooner or later, hon," said the redhead. "Why not here?"

Charley couldn't help hemming and hawing.

Except, for Charley Sunday a commitment was a commitment—so he got to his feet. He slowly took the lady by the hand and led her toward the center of the camp.

They stopped before they got there.

The two of them looked into one another's eyes for a long moment of past recollections, interrupted only when Holliday walked up to them holding both of his guns.

"'Scuse me, *jefé*," he cut in, getting Charley's attention. "But would ya mind if I loaded up now? With the exception of Rod usin' one of 'em the other day, Ol' Booger an' Ben here have bin feelin' kinda lost without any brass beans in their bellies fer the past month or so."

Charley's eyes remained riveted on Flora Mae. He had seen something he had never noticed before: Flora Mae was a very attractive, warm, and loving woman.

"I reckon there'd be no harm in it now, Holliday," he told the man without looking at him. "Go ahead."

The old gunfighter moved on, smiling, spinning both guns. He holstered one; then he checked the chambers of the other. He found some cartridges in the loops of his gun belt and began loading up.

Charley nodded toward the Colorado cowboys. Sleepy's harmonica music was playing in a waltz tempo.

He smiled softly at Flora Mae.

She returned the gesture.

"Remember that one?" He winked.

"Of course I do," she reminisced. "It was OUR song."

Charley pulled on his nose. He cocked his head.

"That's funny," he pondered. "I don't recollect us ever being *that* tight."

Charley held out his arms in a dancing manner, coaxing Flora Mae to step into his embrace.

When she did, they slowly twirled out into the center of the encampment with the harmonica music continuing to play "their" song.

The handsome couple danced contentedly—almost delicately—while the others looked on, both of them completely oblivious to anything else but themselves.

Suddenly, Feather's voice, coming from outside the confines of the evening's stopover, interrupted all.

"Hello the camp!" he hollered.

The dancing broke off.

Heads turned.

Something was wrong.

The music had stopped.

Feather rode into the small clearing—his rope strung out taut behind him.

When the other end of the line eventually revealed itself—Sidney Pike could be seen securely looped in its coil.

Everyone, including the Colorado cowboys, gasped.

Feather gave the rope a sharp tug, and Pike stumbled to the campfire, huffing.

Everyone gathered around.

"Lookie here what I found skulkin' 'midst the cattle," Feather said with a wink. "Must be a new breed a' coyote by the looks a' them beady, little eyes a' his."

Roscoe moved to one side of Pike while Holliday took the other.

Feather loosened the rope and Pike slipped it off his shoulders.

Charley walked over to face the meat packer.

Feather continued, "I caught this little darlin' watchin', while some others of his kind was about ta round up the whole herd without us knowin' nothin' about it. The rest of 'em all run off when they seen me a-comin', but I still managed ta get a loop on this one."

He tried to hold back a prideful smile.

"Looks like they was fixin' ta rustle the herd right out from under our noses," added Rod.

"Is that right, Mr. Pike?" Charley asked somberly.

"Those longhorns should have been mine from the very beginning," countered the incensed meat packer.

He pointed angrily at Rod.

"If it hadn't been for that incompetent, blundering, redskin idiot . . ."

Rod stepped forward, his voice restrained.

"You better be very careful what you call me now, Mr. Pike," Rod warned him through gritted teeth. "I'm not working for you anymore, remember? And from what I've just overheard, *no one* will be working for you much longer . . . because I'm going to personally find every law in the state of Texas . . . *and* Colorado, pertaining to cattle rustling, and have the book thrown at you!"

Pike made a desperate grab for one of Holliday's guns, sliding the weapon free from its holster.

He stepped back.

Suddenly it was Pike who was holding the others at bay.

"Don't anyone move," he advised. "Now there's *no one* who can stop me from doing what I have to do."

The meat packer half turned, calling out into the darkness.

"Bull? Slim?" he shouted. "Are you boys out there?"

"We're right behind you, Mr. Pike," echoed Bull's deep voice from the shadows. "You can relax. We've got 'em all covered."

Pike smiled with relief, as Bull, Slim, and the other two men who were with them in Flora Mae's bar entered the campfire area on foot.

Slim held a Winchester rifle, Bull a pistol. The other two trained their guns on the Colorado cowboys and urged them to drop their weapons.

Slim removed Holliday's other six-shooter from its holster, setting it aside.

Feather leaned in close to Charley.

"Wherever there's a pile a' dog crap," he whispered, "you can always be sure ta find shit flies nearby."

Fortunately, Feather's remark was not heard by the rustlers.

Pike turned to his men.

"Find some rope," he ordered. "Tie them all up!"

One of the extra men moved over to the saddles that were serving as pillows beside the bedrolls. He removed the lariats and began to bind Charley and the rest of them, looping them together with the long coils.

"You won't get away with this, Pike," cautioned Charley.

"That's right," Kelly cut in. "The whole world knows about Charley Sunday's Texas Outfit! . . . *and* the Colorado longhorns."

Flora Mae added, "You won't get outta this county alive, Bucko!"

Pike turned on the two women menacingly.

"Shut up," he demanded. "Both of you!"

Flora Mae lashed out with a foot, catching Pike directly between the legs.

"Oooooofffff," was all he could manage to utter.

As Pike started to double over, Charley stepped in, attempting to grab the gun. But Pike managed to pull away abruptly.

In the confusion Holliday's gun discharged.

Charley was hit—he staggered backward, tripping over one of the saddles.

He went down—hard.

Slim and Bull readjusted their weapons, training them on the group.

Bull shouted, "Nobody move!"

Henry Ellis flew out of the chuckwagon with his shirt unbuttoned. He ran to his fallen grandfather's side. Buster was close at his heels.

Roscoe glared at Pike.

"Ya kilt C.A.," he muttered. "Kilt 'im dead."

The others were still in shock as Flora Mae moved over to where Charley lay.

"I said, nobody move!" repeated Bull, cocking his gun.

Slim also cocked his weapon, aiming it at Flora Mae.

The four itinerant cowboys-turned-cattle rustlers continued to hold them all in abeyance.

Flora Mae looked up at the rustlers, a tear forming in one eye.

"This old cowboy means a lot to me," she began.

"And so does the boy. I ain't goin' no further, gents . . . so don't you go a-worryin' yerself ta death about it."

Kelly, also defying Bull's order, moved in beside Flora Mae. The two women knelt down beside the sobbing Henry Ellis.

Buster whined, nuzzling Charley. There was absolutely no response from his master.

Kelly comforted Henry Ellis.

Tears trickled down Flora Mae's cheeks, her fingers caressing Charley's motionless face.

Charley's eyes were closed in a peaceful manner.

"You were a very brave man, Charles Abner Sunday," Flora Mae eulogized. "A very courageous and valiant human being . . . A true Texan . . . Down to the very end.

"You stood tall in yer saddle," she went on. "Taller 'an most men, an' you never got yer spurs tangled . . . least not that I ever knowed of . . . And ya died with grit . . . *Both boots full a' grit* . . ."

She smiled softly, adding, "Protectin' the folks you loved."

A final tear tracked its way down her cheek as the others looked on in complete silence. Then Flora Mae leaned in closer to Charley's peaceful visage.

"I *really* loved you, Charles Abner Sunday," she whispered. "You wonderful, old turkey, you."

She kissed his cheek softly and then collapsed, sobbing, on Charley's chest.

Kelly and Henry Ellis, with their tears also flowing, tried to comfort her.

Buster lay down flat, his chin between his paws, whining softly.

Holliday, Rod, Feather, Roscoe, and the Colorado cowboys, all with their own sentiments showing, watched

Flora Mae, Kelly, and the boy in their despair as the other two rustlers finished securing their bonds.

Buster, finally realizing something was awry, sat up straight. He emitted a menacing growl.

Pike's men turned abruptly to the frightening sound.

Slim warned, "Someone get that dog away from me or I'll shoot 'im dead!"

"Ahh, ya don't have ta do that," said Roscoe. "Buster!" he shouted, "get outta here . . . NOW!"

Buster understood Roscoe's command. He turned immediately, darting off into the underbrush.

Pike, now recovered, moved over to his henchmen.

"Slim," he began. "You stay here and help me keep an eye on these yokels.

"And Bull," he said, turning, "as soon as those two finish tying up the women and the kid, I want you all to get back out there and help the other boys round up the rest of those cows."

Bull nodded. "Yeah, boss," he answered.

Roscoe tugged at his ropes and said, "Pike! Yer a stinkin' murderer . . . and we're *all* witnesses!"

The meat packer stepped in closer to the securely tied Roscoe, and with a sly smile told him, "You'll all be *DEAD* witnesses by sunup, smart guy."

He turned back to Bull.

"Hold out about twenty of those longhorns," he cackled. "We'll be using their hooves to cover up any evidence."

The big man sneered, nodded that he understood. Then he turned to the two women, Rod, and Henry Ellis.

Suddenly, there was a loud groan from Charley.

Roscoe's head jerked around. He turned to Holliday and whispered, "Snake shot?"

The old gunsil whispered back, "Lightest load they make . . . sure ain't gonna kill nobody with it, that's fer sure."

A look of relief crossed Roscoe's face as Charley moaned once again.

Henry Ellis's eyes widened.

"Grampa!" he shrieked.

Flora Mae looked up.

"He's alive!" her voice echoed.

Charley's eyes fluttered and then opened. He attempted to sit up himself. Flora Mae and Kelly gave him some assistance.

"Of course I'm alive," Charley clarified, brushing himself off. "I must've hit my head when I fell. Knocked the wind outta myself, too."

Flora Mae and Henry Ellis threw their arms around Charley's neck, almost pulling him off balance.

Pike checked the cartridges in Holliday's gun. He turned to Bull.

"Geeze." He winced. "These aren't real bullets at all. They're just little BBs and some cardboard. Give me your gun, damnit," he ordered.

He tossed Holliday's weapon aside, taking Slim's pistol. He turned to one of his extra men.

"Go on," he commanded, "finish tying up the rest of them. And that old man, too. On the double!"

One of the men reached for Flora Mae and she resisted violently.

Rod stepped forward to protect her, but Slim knocked him down with a punch to the back of his head.

Pike fired his newly acquired gun into the dirt beside Flora Mae. The reality of the spiraling rooster tail stopped the woman cold.

"These," he reminded them all as he held up the gun, "are *real* bullets."

Charley turned to Flora Mae.

"Better do what the man says, darlin'," he urged.

The gang members finished tying Flora Mae, Kelly, and the woozy Rod and Charley.

Then they turned to the boy.

"Him too." Pike said as he nodded. "Go on. Just because he's a kid doesn't make any difference."

Henry Ellis rolled away from the men's reach, scrambling to his feet. He grabbed the pot of cold beans beside the fire, flinging them at the rustlers. Then he threw a canteen that hit one of Pike's men in the shin.

The quickness of the youngster's movements allowed him to shove his way past the surprised Bull and Slim—and he disappeared into the murky darkness that surrounded the camp.

Bull, Slim, and the others started after the ten-year-old.

"Leave him go," snarled Pike. "No time to worry about a frightened little kid now; he'll never get past the men at the road.

"Go on, Bull," he continued. "You and these other two boys go give them a hand out there with the longhorns. And tell them all to keep an eye out for the kid . . . *if* they haven't already caught him."

Bull nodded and moved off into the night. The other men followed.

At the picket line, Henry Ellis moved stealthily between the horses' legs as Buster tagged along quietly.

The campfire glowed behind them through the foliage.

The anxious youth finally managed to get to the horse he had been using. He untied the lead rope.

The boy stood silently, muzzling the animal's nose with one hand.

Signaling for the dog to follow, Henry Ellis quietly led the horse away from the camp and into the night.

KELLY KING

by Henry Ellis Pritchard

Kelly King is possibly the nicest female lady I have ever met in my entire life—except for my mother, of course. Kelly is allowing me to interview her for a sidebar in one of her series of articles about the Colorado to Texas Longhorn Cattle Drive. She has also taught me to use her typewriter, a new-fangled invention that prints letters on paper when you press a key with your finger. When Kelly types her stories on the machine's keyboard, she uses both hands and all of her fingers. When I use the typewriter I can only use one finger to press one letter at a time. Anyways, here is my first attempt at writing a newspaper interview for the paper.

Tell our readers a little bit about yourself, Kelly, where you were born and where you grew up? "I was born in the great state of Texas," she says, "on a ranch in the south-central area of the state. I grew up there all my life except for the time I spent in college in New York City. When I was twenty-one years old, I wrote a sample news story, a sample human interest story, and a sample sports column. Then I submitted them all with my work applications to every major New York newspaper. Not one hired me. But the editor of one of those newspapers took a liking to me and he suggested I travel to a smaller state and an even smaller town and then try to obtain work on a local newspaper. I chose the state of Mississippi and the little town of Ruleville on the Delta where I found employment immediately as the editor of their local newspaper's women's section. All I was ever allowed to do was write about social events. But I did get to meet a lot of influential people through my writing of that column—actually it was the wives of the influential people I got to know. And because of that, I became good friends with the mayor, the entire city council, the police chief, all the pastors of the town's three Protestant churches, the Catholic priest, the rabbi, plus most of the merchants and businessmen. One day one of the nearby levees happened to collapse. Pure luck had me right near there. I had been visiting a friend who lived on the river and when the levee broke I was able to write firsthand accounts of the catastrophe, which included the rescue efforts, the personal tragedies, the heroism, plus the individual stories of those who lost their homes and loved ones to the flood that followed. Later on my editor allowed me to write a feature story drawing on my original articles. When it was finished, he sold it to the National News Syndicate and my story was published not only nationally through syndication, but internationally as well. After that, the National News Syndicate received literally thousands of letters telling them how much they had enjoyed my story, and how they were waiting for my next syndicated feature personal account. The owner of the National News Syndicate made me an offer, which I took. I was extremely happy to join the ranks of other female journalists of my era like Nellie Bly and Winifred Bonfils. But my family back in Texas wasn't that excited about my new career. Grandmother knew that it would keep me from settling down with a husband and family, like all the girls I had grown up with had done or were doing. My grandmother, who is the matriarch of our family, at that time even forbade me from traveling back to New York where I would be starting my new job with the syndication service. That was when I broke all ties with my family and somehow was able to travel across the country all by myself to start my job with the news syndicate. Then, wouldn't you know, my fifth assignment brought me back to my home state, Texas—and though the ranch where I was born and raised is still some distance from where we are right now, I haven't let any of them know I'm here."

What was life like growing up on a ranch in Texas when you were my age? I asked her. "My grandfather passed away when I was ten years old," she told me. "Your age," she added.

When I heard that, I almost broke down crying . . . I guess that's because I'm ten right now myself and I don't know what I'd do if my grampa Charley died.

Kelly went on. "My grandmother took over running the ranch, and although it was one of the largest spreads in south-central Texas at that time, my grandmother's persistence continued to help it grow larger.

"I didn't walk to school like the other kids from our town did every day—I was driven to school and picked up afterward in a fancy carriage by one of my grandmother's hired hands who made sure I got home safely. If I wanted to play with any of my friends after school my grandmother made sure they would be picked up and brought to our ranch and then dropped off later at their own homes . . . I was only allowed to play with my friends at our house. My grandmother didn't think it was proper for a child of my social status to mingle with the local ranchers' children away from our ranch."

What made you want to write a story about the cattle drive, Kelly? "Well, it started out as an assignment from my boss in New York City. He had been told about the upcoming longhorn auction in Denver and asked me to take Gerald, my photographer, with me and write a human interest story on the auction and the people who made the highest bids on the cattle. Like you and your grandfather, we were led to believe the longhorns would be auctioned individually, not as an entire lot. So we loaded our darkroom on wheels and our horses onto a train, then, along with ourselves, we headed for Colorado, where we met up with you, your grampa, Rod, and the others. When it became clear that your grandfather had bid on the entire herd and was the highest bidder, I told Gerald that the real story was just beginning. And when you got absolutely no cooperation from anyone in Denver concerning your transportation problems, and your grandfather agreed we'd drive them to Texas, that was when I came up with the idea to make my little human interest story into a series of on the trail tales, all about the Texas Outfit and their daily struggles along the way with their herd of longhorns. You know the rest of my story, Henry Ellis. It just keeps unfolding with every mile we go."

I want to thank Kelly King for helping me with grammar, spelling, the typing, and just about everything else it takes to write a sidebar for a newspaper story.

CHAPTER FORTY-FOUR

A half hour had passed. Pike and Slim were perched on a large rock beside Flora Mae's carriage, some distance away from the Texas Outfit.

Rod and Feather had managed to find several small, sharp stones. As all of them had been tied back to back, it was easy for him to work undetected, sawing away at Roscoe's and Holliday's bonds.

Charley, Flora Mae, and Kelly had also braced themselves, back to back. They, too, worked with nimble fingers, trying to loosen each other's bindings.

Flora Mae winked, whispered to Charley, "I thought you always carried yer gun in yer boot, handsome."

"Ever try to quick-draw a gun out of a boot top when you're hog-tied?" he reminded her.

From Pike's and Slim's position, the bunch appeared to be quite immobile.

Outside the camp, Henry Ellis walked his horse slowly through the longhorns, stopping abruptly when he heard voices. He pointed at Buster, shaking his finger, silently instructing the dog to be quiet, too.

Not more than yards away, the longhorn herd was still being gathered together by Pike's men.

Bull stood nearby talking to one of the rustlers.

"Keep watchin' the road inta Juanita," he advised. "The boss don't want that kid sneakin' over there an' bringin' back the law."

The rustler nodded, moving off toward the roadside, where he parked himself next to a sign that read JUANITA, TEXAS—4 MILES.

Henry Ellis continued to observe from between the milling cattle, confused as to what to do next.

Suddenly, an idea swept his face. He silently mounted his horse, motioned for Buster to follow, then reined around and moved back through the herd, heading in the opposite direction from Juanita.

When Henry Ellis had gone far enough so not to be heard or seen, he spurred the horse. Hooves dug into dirt and the dog darted after him.

When the dawn finally came, the early morning sun cast its rays across the open Texas plain to where Pike's men had the three hundred longhorns surrounded.

There were about ten mounted men in all gathered around the herd.

Bull moved over to the rustler sitting beside the mileage marker, asking him a question. The man shook his head.

Bull moved back toward the clump of trees that concealed the Texas Outfit's last roadside camp.

Roscoe's and Holliday's hands were almost free— the ropes nearly cut through. They had been working on Feather's and Rod's knots with the sharp stones for some time.

Charley, Flora Mae, and Kelly continued to work at their restraints, which had loosened considerably. Charley was almost untied. He worked painstakingly on the sturdy rope—pulling, pulling.

Pike napped on the inside passenger's seat, his feet protruding through the window of the carriage.

Slim stood guard beside the chuckwagon.

There was a rustling from the bushes and then Bull entered the compound.

The big man called out, "Mr. Pike, we're ready. All the cattle have been rounded up."

Pike snapped awake. He climbed out of the carriage, joining Slim.

Bull moved over to them.

"The twenty head you wanted gathered up," he pointed, "are right over there . . . just like you asked."

Pike smirked.

"Good work," he told the man. "Now, where's that kid?"

"No sign of him all night," answered Bull. "He's probably still hidin' in the weeds somewhere nearby . . . too scared to show himself."

Pike drew his gun and moved over to the captives, followed by the two henchmen. He waved the barrel of the pistol at Charley and the others.

"All right," he demanded. "All of you . . . on your feet!"

The two clusters of bodies stood as best they could, but not without some difficulty.

"I'm afraid," Pike went on, "we can only untie you *after* the stampede . . . *after* you're *ALL* dead!"

"Then you really are planning on killing every one of us, aren't you?" said Charley.

Pike smirked again—shaking his head.

"Not quite, Mr. Sunday," he replied nastily. "I'm going to let your own cattle do my dirty work for me. Then, when somebody eventually finds your crushed and trampled bodies, it'll look like the longhorns stampeded right through the camp and killed everyone. *No survivors!*"

Pike cocked his head—listening.

A faint but growing rumble seemed to be echoing across the early morning air.

Other heads tilted, ears perked.

Pike turned anxiously to Bull and Slim as the rumble increased in fervor to a loud, galloping roar.

Roscoe and the others looked to Charley for reassurance.

"What is it, C.A.?" asked Roscoe.

Charley squinted through the surrounding foliage, looking off.

On the hill behind them, led by Henry Ellis galloping ahead on his horse with Buster right behind, Potato John and his Comanche Dance Troupe rode to the rescue, swooping down on the unsuspecting gang of cattle thieves.

Charley's lips curled into a very large smile. He turned to his friends.

"You ain't going to believe this," he told them with a chuckle. "It's the cavalry, come to our rescue just in time!"

Then, taking full advantage of the distraction, Charley broke free of his loosened bonds. He bent down and reached for his boot top.

Pulling his Colt free, he dove away from the others.

Pike, Bull, and Slim saw what Charley was up to and turned to respond.

The old cowman was already up on two feet, fanning the hog leg in their direction.

KA-BLAM! KA-BOOM! ZING!

One slug tore the Winchester from Pike's hand, while another smashed into the barrel of Slim's pistol, knocking the gun from his hands.

With a piercing rebel yell from Feather, the rest of the outfit broke free, piling onto the little meat packer and his thugs.

Fists flew, dust boiled—deep blue cuss words filled the air.

Out by the cattle, the rest of the rustlers, upon seeing the Indians, took off in all directions.

The Comanches split off from their formation in pursuit of the individual rustlers.

From their position in the camp, Flora Mae and Kelly could see all the action.

Charley could also view what was happening to the cattle rustlers who were caught over by the herd. He smiled gratefully, setting his gun aside before wading into the camp-side mêlée.

The Indian dancers jumped, tackled, and even bull-dogged the members of Pike's outlaw gang, doing whatever it took to force the rustlers into submission.

Several of the lawbreakers managed to escape into the foliage that separated the longhorns from the encampment, only to become a part of the humongous altercation taking place at the campsite.

Amidst all the commotion, Henry Ellis rode into camp, reining his mount into a magnificent, hoof-pawing rear.

Slim moved in behind Charley, grabbing him from behind so Bull could administer a beating.

Flying out of the bushes like a snarling, barking banshee, the growling Buster leaped eight feet through the

air, tackling Slim, taking the greasy-haired man to the
ground, allowing Charley to draw back his right and
pop Bull a good one on the jaw.

Then he reached into the fracas and grabbed Pike
by the collar.

The free-for-all continued in the camp's center as
Henry Ellis dismounted. He moved in beside Flora
Mae and Kelly, who were both rooting from the fringes.

As Charley pulled back to hit Pike, Flora Mae
hollered, "Give 'im one for me, Charley Sunday! Give
'im your sucker punch!"

And Charley did, sending the spineless little parasite
sprawling near Feather.

Free of the meat packer, Charley waded into the
larger brawl.

"C'mon, Grampa," yelled Henry Ellis, "you can show
'em!"

Kelly smiled, wrapping her arm around the boy.

With Buster barking energetically from the side-
lines, Rod decked Slim; then he jumped on top of the
slender man and continued the pounding.

The two rolled over and over. Finally Rod subdued
his quarry with a solid left hook. Slim collapsed in a
heap at his feet.

Rod went immediately to Kelly and Henry Ellis,
taking them both in his arms.

Holliday, Roscoe, and Feather had managed to loop
nooses around the rustlers' necks.

Charley, who had been knocked to the ground
nearby, recovered and stood up.

He watched in awe as Holliday tossed three ropes
over a low-hanging tree branch.

Charley stumbled over.

"Hold it!" he demanded. "There'll be no lynching."

"He shot ya cold . . . didn't he, *jefé*?" said Holliday.

"They were gonna kill *us all*," echoed Roscoe.

"Why not, boss?" added Feather. "They deserve it!"

"No!" yelled Kelly. "Stop it, you silly old men."

All heads turned in her direction.

Kelly, Rod, Flora Mae, and Henry Ellis moved over closer to the others.

Kelly continued, "If you did something stupid like that," she advised them, "you'd ruin everything."

Holliday, Roscoe, and Feather exchanged sheepish glances.

Flora Mae and Henry Ellis moved to Charley's side. He put his arms around both of them.

"You're famous men," Kelly went on. "You're the Texas Outfit. Don't you think you should start acting like civilized human beings?"

Several of the Indian dancers rode into camp, led by Potato John. He signaled Charley that everything was under control.

Charley waved, throwing them all a wide grin.

The Indians waved back.

"Adios," said the Indian leader.

"Adios yourself," answered Charley with a grateful smile.

"And, thank you . . . *again!*" he added.

"Hey," said Potato John, "for a minute there, just for a short time . . . we *WERE* you guys."

"That you were, my friend," Charley told him. "That you were."

Potato John smiled, nodded, and turned and rode away followed by the other Indians.

Charley pulled out his pocket watch, and he checked the time.

"Say," he began, "ain't there supposed to be some kind of celebration waiting for us all in Juanita?"

FLORA MAE HUCKABEE

by Kelly King

Lest we forget . . . Flora Mae Huckabee. She's Charley's partner . . . the investor . . . the backer of the Colorado to Texas Longhorn Cattle Drive. It was her money, continuing interest, and support that gave Charley Sunday the added incentive he needed to get this whole thing off the ground.

What is it about longhorn cattle that interested you in this project in the first place? I asked her. "There was never no 'project' at all," replied Miss Huckabee. "There was this story in our local newspaper all about a Colorado auction . . . and Charley and me read about it around the same time. He came ta visit me that evening, like he does every so often, ta play a game of pool in my billiard parlor and to think over what he had on his mind. That's what ol' Charley's done ever since I've knowed him when he's got somethin' in his head that needs thinkin' on. He rides inta town and comes to my place. He told me that he sure would like to have a few of them Colorado longhorns . . . an' that if he could end up with just a few, maybe he could keep his place from going into foreclosure. I told him that I had also read the article about the Colorado auction that morning, and that I also thought it would be nice to acquire some of those longhorns for my own ranch, as

well. Then we got ta talkin' about it and I finally offered
Charley ten percent of how ever many longhorns he
might end up with after the auction was over . . . if I put
up the money for him to use for the bidding. I was completely flabbergasted when he telephoned and told me
he'd ended up with the whole darned herd. Then he called
me back again later on ta tell me that no one in Denver
would ship the cattle . . . Not one of them highfalutin,
livestock-haulin' companies in Denver had the time or the
space to transport our longhorns down ta Texas. Can you
believe that? I knew that money talked, so I began to have
suspicions that there was someone that didn't want those
cattle leavin' the state of Colorado. When Charley con-
tacted me again shortly after, to tell me he decided he
could drive 'em all the way down here like they'd done
in the old days, his idea struck me as a pretty good one.
I called a meetin' of my company's board of directors and
in no time I had the extra money Charley would need for
the drive. You were there, honey," she said to me, "so you
know the rest of the story."

I wanted to get to know this fascinating woman a little
better so I began asking more questions. How long have
you known Charley Sunday? was my next question.
"'Bout as long as the Huckabees have been doin' business
in Juanita, Texas," she answered. "Let's see," she went
on . . . "I moved to Juanita with my parents just after
Daddy had struck it rich . . . that was quite a few years
back . . . sometime before the War Between the States.
Daddy had got into some trouble with the U.S. Army up
in Indian Territory . . . those yella'-bellies tried ta move in
on the states an' territories with Southern sympathies
way before the war got started. It was something to do
with gambling, if I remember correctly. They were going
to confiscate all of Daddy's holdings and leave us penni-
less unless he agreed to pay some outrageous tax fees on
our family's holdings. Daddy, always bein' one step ahead
of his enemies, converted everything he had inta cash and

we took off for Texas in the dead of night. Daddy decided to set us up in Juanita. It was a nice, peaceful little town and not that far from the Mexican border . . . That was in case Daddy felt things were getting a little too hot for him to handle.

"Charley Sunday an' me met up in the Juanita school-house. He was a few grades ahead of me in his studies, which made him a few years older. You might say I stuck my brand on him right then. We was hand holdin' within a month . . . kissin' in the cloak room in two. But sadly, it never went any further than that. We'd break it off for a while . . . then we'd get back together. Our relationship went along like that until he an' Willadean tied the knot. Charley never strayed in all the years he was with Willadean. So I kept clear of 'em both. I knew she wouldn't have approved of Charley's and my earlier relationship, so I just stayed away. Then he started comin' inta my place every so often ta play a game of pool or two. He even had a beer with me when he needed ta get things off his chest. That's when he first told me about Willadean's sickness . . . and that the doctor in Del Rio had told him she was more'n likely going to die from it. He spent a lotta evenings with me in my place a' business when Willadean was in the hospital over in Del Rio. Thirty miles was a good distance back then—between Juanita and Del Rio—before the railroad came through. Nowadays you can be in Del Rio in an hour or so, if you're lucky. Back then it was an all-day ride by horseback or buggy. When Willadean finally did pass, Charley's daughter, Betty Jean, moved out of the house and got married shortly after. When she gave birth to Henry Ellis, the new family had to move back in with Charley for a spell until the boy's father could find the kind of work goin' off ta college had prepared him for. When he finally did get a job, it turned out the company's home offices were in Austin. So that's where they went to settle. The boy hated to leave his grampa. For the first few months the family

was in Austin, I've been told, Betty Jean said Henry Ellis
wouldn't talk to her or Kent, his father. It was only after
they brought the boy back to Juanita the next summer
to be with Charley for a few months that the boy seemed
to accept his lot . . . and he eventually forgave his parents.
All that boy lives for is the summers when he gets to
spend time with Charley at the ranch in Juanita. Both
Charley and me ain't never told Henry Ellis about what's
gone on between the two of us. We're afraid that'd break
his little heart."

Tell me about your early years. "I was born and raised
on a small farm in Oklahoma Territory. As you might have
guessed by now, my daddy was either rich or poor when
I was growin' up. Oklahoma was considered Indian country back then. And I come ta find out later on that my
family was livin' there illegally throughout most of my
childhood. Daddy kept us there in Indian Territory so
he'd always have a safe place to come back to if one of
his money-makin' schemes got out a' hand. By the time I
was twelve, Daddy was spending a lot of time with us at
home because no one outside the Territory was fallin' for
his proposals anymore . . . What I meant to say is there
didn't seem to be that many speculators left in the surrounding territories and states that were willin' to invest
in some of Daddy's wilder ideas. One morning, Daddy
come ridin' up to the house shriekin' like a chicken with
its head cut off. 'Everyone pack it up,' he was yellin',
'Right now,' he added. 'We're movin ta Texas.' My mama
come runnin' out a' the house sayin' that the bacon was
about ta burn and the eggs was turnin' hard, so he'd
better come on inside an' eat some breakfast. 'We can
have breakfast when we get ta Texas,' he told us all as
he harnessed our two plow horses to an old wagon we
used ta go to town in for groceries and such. 'Don't worry
'bout packin' the furniture,' said Daddy . . . 'We'll buy all
new furniture after we find a town ta settle in.' Mama
asked him just how were we gonna do that when she had

just spent the last of our savin's on the bacon and eggs that was now about ta go to waste in the kitchen. First time I ever seen him do it, but he took my mama up in his arms and kissed her . . . then he looked her eye to eye. 'You don't gotta worry where the next dollar's comin' from anymore, Ida. I just won a tad over five hundred thousand dollars cash in a poker game.' 'The hell you say, Elmer,' she said. 'If we're all so rich now, just why in tarnation do you want to move ta Texas?' she wanted to know. 'Well,' he said, 'the three gents I won the money from believe I cheated 'em.' Mama's eyes opened wide like she'd been touched by Jesus. 'Then let's get a goin' before someone convinces 'em they're right,' she said. She turned toward the house. 'Com'on children. Can't you move your little butts faster than that? We're goin' to Texas!'

"Daddy found us a nice place to live in Juanita . . . a large house in town that had been built by the bank's previous owner. The townspeople . . . the banker's customers . . . had caught the banker with his fingers in the till but he up an' disappeared before anyone knew where he went. Daddy got the house pretty cheap, too . . . because the new banker needed hard cash right away to replenish what the old banker had stolen. The townspeople were all so happy that someone with cash money had come to town, no one ever bothered ta ask Daddy for his references." Miss Huckabee also let me know that before her mother and father were killed in a train wreck near San Antonio her daddy had helped the citizens of Juanita out by building 'em a new school. "He also remodeled the Methodist church and donated a bunch of new pews to the Baptists. Daddy left me everything in his will, mind you. At the first readin' of that document Daddy had left it all to my mama. But since she had died right alongside of him in the wreck, the money went to his oldest, living child . . . me. Oh, there were provisions for my younger brothers and sisters and that made them all happy. Most of the girls married right away . . . and the boys all went off to add to their small fortunes in one way or the other, while I stayed put in Juanita. The town didn't have no decent place to put up overnight visitors, so I built the hotel. There was also no place for the men to work off steam, so I added the poolroom and the saloon. That got the women folk riled up against me so I built 'em a place where they could gather for teas and other female-type events they might want to put on. In the end, everyone was delighted, and there were some people who even wanted to run me for mayor. That never happened . . . and I'll bet you know why." Because you're a woman, I answered. "That's right, Miss King," she said. "Just because I'm a woman my supporters lost interest and a man was elected, as usual.

"It wasn't long before Charley became one of my regular customers again at the pool hall and saloon. His foreman and good friend, Roscoe Baskin, used ta come in with him at first, but I reckon Roscoe got tired of Charley hangin' around so late at night when the two of us . . . me an' Charley . . . would keep on jawin' away until the wee hours. Now it's only Charley that comes ta visit me. That was until he had this crazy idea of bidding on these longhorns up in Colorado. Well, now it looks like his crazy idea weren't so crazy after all, now that him and his outfit are almost home. I'll bet there'll be a lot of sore losers tomorrow when the longhorns come ta town . . . meanin' those folks who bet against the success of Charley Sunday's Texas Outfit."

Chapter Forty-five

A small boy was intently watching the far end of Juanita's Main Street. After a moment, his eyes widened with exploding excitement.

"Here they come," he yelled, "longhorns comin' in!"

A fluttering, overhead banner proclaimed, WELCOME HOME, CHARLEY SUNDAY'S TEXAS OUTFIT!

The boardwalks on both sides of the street were packed with people who had turned out for the festive occasion—locals, tourists, the press—even Sheriff Dubbs and the smiling church deacons were on hand to welcome the drovers. The entire Calvary Missionary Baptist congregation, plus the choir, had shown up and could be spotted throughout the pulsating crowd.

The American Stars and Stripes and many Texas State Lone Star flags lined the street, waving in abundance.

News cameras on their wooden tripods had been set up along the route.

All of the sunburned faces were turned to observe.

The longhorn herd rounded a corner and started up the street—led by Flora Mae's all white team and fancy carriage, with its top folded back . . .

Flora Mae's bartender drove, with Buster at his side,

while Charley, Flora Mae, and Henry Ellis sat up higher on the back of the rear seat, waving to the cheering multitudes.

Directly behind them, the Juanita Chamber of Commerce Brass Band, all five of them—dressed in their best spit and polish—began to play "The Yellow Rose of Texas."

A special stand had been constructed along the parade route. It had been decked out in festive red, white, and blue bunting. The governor of the State of Texas, and many other state officials, made up the majority in that exclusive section surrounded by photographers and news reporters.

All heads were turned in the direction of the approaching herd.

The three hundred longhorns moved, quite grandly, into the small Texas town.

Charley sat tall and proud beside his smiling woman and his gleaming grandson as the longhorns followed along behind the musicians that trailed Flora Mae's carriage.

Applause and cheering arose from the crowd as the band played on.

Rod and Kelly rode side by side on horseback alongside the cattle. She waved to her photographer, Gerald, who had his camera situated on the roof of the traveling darkroom, covering the event from curbside.

"Well, I guess this is finally it," said Rod with a sadness to his words.

Kelly turned to him, reaching over, caressing his cheek—smiling.

"Yes," she answered. "I reckon it is over . . . the cattle drive. *Just* the cattle drive," she reminded him.

"It sure has been a lot of fun," said Rod, missing the whole meaning of her touch.

Kelly pulled back from him. She stared straight ahead—fuming.

"What's wrong?" he asked, confused.

"You may have been the brightest boy in your tribe," she articulated. "But when it comes to feelings, you're clueless."

"I, uh, er," were about the only words Rod could muster.

Kelly wheeled around in the saddle, facing him.

"Open your eyes, Rod Lightfoot," she told him with tears rimming both her eyes. "Can't you tell when a woman's in love with you?"

Rod reined up—so did Kelly.

"Y-you . . . *love* . . . m-me?" he stammered.

"Of course I do, you fool," she told him, weeping with happiness. "I love you so much I just quit my job with the news syndicate because I knew I wouldn't be able to stand it if we had to be apart."

Rod was in complete shock—he was literally voiceless.

"Well, don't just sit there on that old pony of yours twirling your spurs, Mr. Indian Lawyer-man." She sniffled. "Get your rear end over here and kiss me!"

Feather rode by on Chigger, spinning his lariat, tossing the loop over a pretty local gal on the boardwalk, then reeling her in for a big hug. The crowd loved every minute of it.

Henry Ellis, in the carriage, took his grandfather by the hand, pointing out his parents—Kent and Betty Jean—on the jam-packed sidewalk.

"Henry Ellis! Dad!" shouted Betty Jean over the crowd's noise.

Charley and the boy smiled and waved back.

"We just got back," she hollered again. "We read

about you in San Francisco every day, including every town we stopped in on our way back."

Henry Ellis and Charley exchanged glances, laughing.

The carriage moved on, passing the governor's stand.

The governor called out to Sunday. "Mighty fine job, C.A." He grinned, waving at the older cattleman. "Welcome back to Texas! Welcome back to the Lone Star State!"

Charley nodded, half-smiling, waving back, acknowledging the state's leader.

He turned to Flora Mae and his grandson, leaning in as close as he could get to both of them.

"Did you see that?" he whispered. "The governor of the great state of Texas even knows who I am now . . . and I didn't even vote for him. Ha!"

Flora Mae and the boy laughed, too.

Flora Mae snuggled up closer to Charley.

"Would ya mind comin' by the hotel tonight after all this fuss?" she asked.

"Well I—" Charley began. But he stopped.

He turned, looking the woman directly in the eyes.

"What do you want me to come all the way over there for?" he asked.

Flora Mae nuzzled up even closer.

"Oh," she spoke gently, "I just thought maybe you might wanna finish our dance."

Charley looked deep into Flora Mae's eyes—and she into his—for a very, very, long time.

Finally Henry Ellis let out an extremely loud "Uuuuuuuuuuuugggghhh!"

He turned to the dog and said, "Yuck, Buster, let's get out of here. We have to get away from these silly old lovebirds. They sure don't need us around."

He hopped down and climbed over into the front seat between the smiling bartender and Charley's dog.

Flora Mae and Sunday didn't miss him at all—they had reawakened a passion long buried and had been kissing the entire time.

At the rear of the parade, the old chuckwagon/two-seat buckboard, without its canvas covering, was being driven by a waving and smiling Roscoe. It moved past the crowd, surrounded by Potato John and the jovial members of his Comanche Dance Troupe performing one of their authentic Indian dances.

Plunker Holliday sat beside the cook's cupboard on the chuckwagon's tailgate, facing toward the back, twirling both of his six-shooters to the delight of the onlookers.

Behind him, on the other side of the cook's cupboard in the chuckwagon's bed, jammed together, were the roped and hog-tied members of the cattle-rustling gang—Bull, Slim, and the rest.

The old gunfighter glanced down another rope that stretched from the rear of the chuckwagon.

Sidney Pike hurried along on foot at the rope's other end—finalizing the parade—his arms and shoulders securely bound.

As the old chuckwagon jumped ahead, and the rope jerked the meat packer to attention—one could only say that Pike was literally . . . *riding drag.*

EPILOGUE

1960

A 1958 Ford station wagon pulled up in front of the Old Soldiers Home, allowing Hank's granddaughter, Evie, and his three great-grandchildren to drop off Grampa Hank. Genuine hugs and kisses were exchanged, plus a slew of appreciative "thank-yous" from Hank's family for the wonderful afternoon they had just spent together.

The apartment door opened and a hand groped for the light switch inside. Two lamps were turned on in Hank's living space. It was a simple setting—one small room: a single bed, a table, three chairs, and a small television set. In one corner a sink, small refrigerator, and a hot plate, with cupboards and shelves above and below. The door to the bath was across the room.

The front door swung open even wider and Hank entered. With the echoes of children's laughter still ringing in his ears, he moved slowly to his easy chair, steadying himself as he hobbled along. Then he flopped. He'd had a full day.

Hank's blue-veined hand reached for the television switch, and the TV was turned on. After what seemed like an hour, a black-and-white picture came on. It was a 1930s Lone Star western, starring John Wayne.

The old man smiled. As the musical score overrode, he settled back, ready to watch a movie he'd seen many times before.

On the TV screen, John Wayne was beating the bejeezus out of three bad guys.

Hank loved every minute. Then his eyes were drawn to something on the wall behind the television set.

In a framed, glass-covered wooden case surrounded by other cases displaying his wartime souvenirs, ribbons, and medals, hung a .44-caliber, antique, Colt revolver.

It was the Whitneyville Walker.

His grampa Charley had given it to him the summer before he passed away.

GREAT BOOKS,
GREAT SAVINGS!

When You Visit Our Website:
www.kensingtonbooks.com
You Can Save Money Off The Retail Price
Of Any Book You Purchase!

- **All Your Favorite Kensington Authors**
- **New Releases & Timeless Classics**
- **Overnight Shipping Available**
- **eBooks Available For Many Titles**
- **All Major Credit Cards Accepted**

Visit Us Today To Start Saving!
www.kensingtonbooks.com

All Orders Are Subject To Availability.
Shipping and Handling Charges Apply.
Offers and Prices Subject To Change Without Notice.